HEROES & HOOLIGANS IN GOOSE PIMPLE JUNCTION

by
AMY METZ

Southern
Ink
Press

Published by Southern Ink Press, an imprint of Blue Publications, 2014.
1st Edition
2nd volume in the Goose Pimple Junction mystery series.
Printed in the United States of America

Cover by John Charles Gibbs. Image © www.gibbsgallery.com

Cover design and Interior design and formatting by:

www.emtippettsbookdesigns.com

SUMMARY: Life is once again turned upside down for the residents of Goose Pimple Junction with the arrival of hooligans in the form of a philandering husband intent on getting his wife back, another murderer loose in town, a stalker intent on frightening Martha Maye, and a thief who's stealing the town blind. The new chief of police has his hands full trying to fight crime and his feelings for a woman in need of a hero.

ISBN-13: 978-0989714044
ISBN-10: 0989714047

HEROES & HOOLIGANS IN GOOSE PIMPLE JUNCTION

To Jake, Michael, and Liz: my heroes.

PROLOGUE

What you don't have in your head, you have to have in your feet.

~Southern Proverb

Ray moved like a bee-stung stallion. As soon as the jogger's footsteps passed him in his hiding place behind a large crepe myrtle bush, he pounced, jumping the man and pulling a plastic bag over his mark's head. He held it securely and tightly with his right hand and controlled the man with his left arm that wound around in front of the man in a vice grip. They struggled, but Ray held on. Mark pulled loose from Ray's left arm, and with the bag still tight over the man's face, Ray punched him with his left hand in three quick jabs. Blood exploded inside the bag, as Mark fell to the ground. But Ray held the bag firmly in his hand and went down with him. Two more jabs caused the man's head to hit the pavement like a ping-pong ball.

And then he was still.

Ray straddled him, looking down at his former friend as he twisted the bag tighter and tighter, making sure no oxygen was reaching the man's lungs.

With his adrenaline pumping, he'd hardly noticed the ninety percent humidity. Now that the heat of the moment was over, so to speak, he realized sweat emanated from every pore of his body. It was only seven o'clock in the morning, but the air blanketed him with wet stickiness. Recalling an episode of *World's Stupidest Criminals* where they nailed the killer over DNA from his sweat, Ray decided he'd better rid the man of his clothes. He lifted his nose and breathed deeply. There was a smell a rain in the air, and he figured the impending storm would wash away any other evidence on the naked body.

Wiping his face with the side of his arm, he tried to catch his breath. He'd waited for Mark for over an hour. Not his real name, but Ray's secret nickname for his friend ever since "Mark" had nicknamed him "Ray." Smiling bitterly to himself, he remembered the man once telling him that aliens must have zapped him with a stupidity ray.

"Heck, they turned you into a stupidity ray," Mark had said. That comment had turned his friend into a mark.

Now Ray stared at his former friend's body thinking, "Stupid's better 'n dead."

ONE

Marry in haste, repent in leisure.

~Southern Proverb

L enny drove to his neighborhood bar with the windows wide open and Johnny Cash blaring on the radio, but he was oblivious to both. He was thinking about the phone conversation he'd just had with his ten-year-old daughter Carrie. It made him crazy the way her mother's family called her "Butterbean." *What kind of a name was that for a child?* But today he was crazy for a whole new reason. Jealousy and anger tore through him faster than small-town gossip. His daughter had spilled everything, and just when he thought he'd finally gotten a break, she said, "Mama kinda had a boyfriend but not anymore." And: "Mama was kidnapped, but she's back now."

He pulled into the parking lot of the bar thinking, *Boyfriend? We literally aren't even divorced yet and she had a boyfriend?* He pounded his fist against the steering wheel. He knew she'd been cheating on him. And now she'd done it right in front of their daughter. No doubt about it, he was going to have to do something about this Martha Maye situation.

Pulling into a primo spot at the front door, he looked up at the old rusty sign that had been over the entrance for years: TEETOTALERS AIN'T WELCOME HERE. He winced at the loud screech announcing his car door opening, followed by the same screech when he slammed it shut. He glanced around the parking lot and saw the same cars that were there every night. His feet crunched on the gravel as he walked, and he remembered waking up three months earlier and slowly realizing his wife and daughter weren't there.

The familiar bacon and coffee smells were gone. Cartoons weren't blaring on the TV. His wife's clothes were missing, along with his daughter's, her teddy bear, and her dolls. The bookshelves were dotted with bare spots where Martha Maye's favorite knickknacks and paddywhacks had been. And then he saw the note on the kitchen table that said she was divorcing him and that he shouldn't try to find them. The realization that she'd left him in the middle of the night and taken their daughter seared through him like a red-hot poker.

Pretty stealthy for a woman who could literally be outwitted by a jar of marshmallow fluff. If she thinks she can literally run out on me and then humiliate me by going out with some scumbag before we're even divorced, she has another think coming. I'll show her. I'll put on the charm and win her back.

Country music blasted as he opened the door, turned his head, and spit in disgust. *She literally can't be let her out by herself. Just look where it got her: kidnapped and almost killed.*

His daughter had told him they'd been staying at his mother-in-law's house. He should have figured. He'd always known Louetta to be a meddlesome old biddy. *She lied to me when I called looking for my wife and daughter. She aided and abetted a woman leaving her husband. She allowed nefarious suitors to court my wife. Both of them must have literally stopped to think and forgotten how to start again.*

And then there was his no-account, good-for-nothing brother who, upon learning of the impending divorce, wanted to know if Lenny would mind if he dated Martha Maye. *Boy, I'm gonna slap you so hard, when you quit rolling your clothes'll literally be outta style. My baby brother and my wife. Yeah. Over my dead body. How could he even ask such a thing?* Both of them were *nothing but a bunch of backstabbing traitors.*

He hitched up his jeans under his overflowing beer belly, swaggered into the bar, and ordered a Colt 45. The jukebox was playing, "I Want a Beer as Cold as My Ex-Wife's Heart," and he thought that was pretty darn perfect for his life at the moment.

Looking around the room, he spotted a hot blonde giving him the eye. He sucked in his gut—a move that didn't yield the desired result—and looked back, waggling his eyebrows suggestively. She brazenly smiled back at him.

How dare Martha Maye leave me? I can literally get any woman I want. And two on Saturday.

A football star in high school, homecoming king, and voted best looking his senior year, Lenny was used to women coming onto him, not leaving him. He put the bottle to his lips and downed half of it.

That woman was literally lucky to have me. Sure, I've put on a little weight, but only in the gut. I practically have to fight women off with a stick. Looking around the room again, he saw female eyes on him from several tables in the room. *Yessirree, sir, I still got it.*

Lenny started to lift his bottle to his mouth again but halted midway when two men sat down heavily on barstools on either side of him; they looked capable of eating their young. Both men were muscular and tough. One was as tall as a telephone pole. One was as short as a gnat's tail. The taller man had black eyes under bushy eyebrows, and the other man wore aviator sunglasses on a flat, wide nose. He pushed the glasses to the top of his head to give Lenny his best glare.

"We've been looking all over Hell and half of Georgia for you, boy." Eyebrows scooted his stool in close, crowding Lenny.

"Shoot." Lenny's hand automatically moved to his ankle holster, checking for his knife. "That don't surprise me none. You literally couldn't find oil with a dipstick."

"Solly says he's had about enough of you," Eyebrows said.

"Yeah," Mr. Gnat joined in, "he's had about enough of you."

Lenny snorted. "You can tell Solly to blow it out his butt," Lenny said boldly, more boldly than he felt. He shelled a peanut, popped it in his mouth, and threw the shell into Mr. Gnat's face.

"Solly says not to let you off the hook this time."

"Yeah, not to let you off the hook." Mr. Gnat's left eye twitched.

"What's with Mr. Echo over here?" Lenny pointed his thumb at the short man.

The telephone pole ignored him and said, "Solly says you've screwed him over for the last time."

"Yeah, the last time."

"I didn't screw him over the first time." Lenny drained his bottle. He felt like his mouth was full of cotton. "Solly wouldn't tell the truth to save his life from dying." Lenny tried to stand up, but the men had him penned in.

"You can't talk about Solly that way."

"Yeah, not that way," Mr. Gnat echoed.

Eyebrows looked behind Lenny to his friend. "This boy has the mental agility of a soap dish, Joey."

"Yeah, a soap dish."

Lenny leaned in real close to Joey, who said, "Whatta you think you're doing?"

"Just wondered if I got close enough if I could literally hear the ocean."

"Boy, what you need is an education," Eyebrows said.

"Yeah, an edj-ee-cation." Gnat strung the word out.

The men grabbed Lenny's arms, lifting him off his stool. The song on the jukebox had ended, and Lenny heard the crunch of peanut shells as the men propelled him toward the door.

"Boys, y'all best not be messing with me," Lenny snapped, trying to break free.

"That's mighty big talk for a punk like you." They stepped aside as someone came through the door, and then they threw Lenny through it. He landed on the ground but sprang right back to his feet, his dukes up, ready to fight.

Eyebrows was fast. He knocked Lenny to the ground again with a left hook. Joey followed up with two kicks to the ribs.

Lenny pulled himself into a ball, both to protect himself from further harm and to have better access to his ankle holster. But Joey saw the knife and kicked it away as Lenny drew it from his pants leg.

The men both grabbed Lenny by an arm again, pulling him upright, and Eyebrows punched him in the gut, causing him to double over. They double-teamed him and left him on the ground bloody and beaten, as cars whizzed past on the road in front of the bar.

Right before Lenny passed out, he thought: *Tomorrow I'll pack up and head for Goose Pimple Junction to reclaim what's rightfully mine. I'll literally be a devoted husband and father and get my family back. I ain't gonna let that woman leave me. Nobody leaves Lenny Applewhite.*

TWO

A mule can be tame at one end and wild at the other.

~Southern Proverb

L ate-afternoon sun filtered into the room as Martha Maye kicked off her pink flip-flops and sank into the couch, emitting an exhausted sigh. She looked around her new living room in silent contentment, even though it was full of unpacked boxes. Sure, it was a rental house, but she felt like it belonged to her—her and Butterbean.

She'd left most of her things months ago when she and her daughter had fled her husband and their home in the middle of the night. After Lenny threatened to kill her if she left him, she knew what she had to do. The tragedy of her great-grandmother's murder years earlier had taught her to never underestimate a jealous man.

And finally, things were looking up. She had landed a teaching job, rented a house, and furnished it with garage sale and flea market finds. The mistake of taking up with the wrong man was starting to be a faint memory. A slight breeze caused the drapes to billow. Laying her head against the couch, she listened to the soft giggles of Butterbean and her friend playing outside.

The front door opened into the living room, and Martha Maye watched as Johnny Butterfield came in carrying another box. He stood six foot five, had a thick neck, sculpted shoulders and arms, and he reminded her of Paul Bunyan. His heart was every bit as big as his body. Martha Maye couldn't help it—she was smitten, but she'd learned her lesson about jumping in too fast with a man, and besides, she was technically still married.

"This is the last of it, Martha Maye," the new police chief said, putting the box down. He joined her on the couch, his bulk taking up more than one cushion. Martha Maye turned toward him, tucking her feet underneath her, looking at the muscles straining the sleeves of his Goose Pimple Junction Police Department T-shirt.

"I can't thank you enough for all your help." She reached for the beer she'd gotten out for Johnny and handed it to him. "But here's a start."

"Aw shucks, Martha Maye, my pleasure. I know you're excited to be on your own again. Your mama's house was getting a might crowded, huh?"

"I'll say. There wasn't enough room to swing a cat. But she likes it that way. Mama's happiest when she's busy, and she always did like a full house and taking care of people."

Her eyes went to the service revolver on his hip. He noticed and asked, "Does the gun bother you? I usually wear it, even when I'm not on duty."

"Well actually, I'm scared to death of guns." She hugged a throw pillow. "Always have been. Maybe it's on account of my family history. Too many murders, all by gunfire."

"And at the filling station? Before you got free?"

She was quiet a moment and then said softly, "I can still hear the sound of bullets hitting the Co'Cola machine in the office where Tess and I were holed up."

"You must have been scared out of your mind."

"You know, that Jim Bob wasn't a career criminal, but he had a gun, and I can still remember the stark-white fear of that day."

"You think about that day often?" His voice was soft and sympathetic.

"A little. Not much." Her face brightened. "I try to only think about the good stuff. You know, like you kicking in the door and standing there in your state police uniform and . . ." Her voice trailed off into a giggle, remembering how she flew into his arms once they'd broken free of the building.

"That sure was a way to meet, huh?" He stretched his long legs out in front of him, lacing his fingers behind his head.

She nodded. "That was *some* way to meet."

He shook his head slowly and exhaled theatrically. "It's a tough job rescuing beautiful women, but it was all in a day's work." His smile filled his face, lighting up his dark brown eyes.

Martha Maye wondered if Johnny was as interested in her as she was in him. Their eyes locked and held until the moment was broken by the sound of the wall clock chiming five times.

"So, Martha Maye . . . tell me some things."

"Like what, Johnny?"

"Oh, I don't know. I'd just like to get to know you better. What's your favorite food?"

She tapped her lips with a finger. "Hmm. Probably fried chicken. Yours?"

"A big juicy steak." He tore off some of the label on the bottle of beer. "Movie?"

"I don't know if I could narrow it down to one. I love movies."

"So do I!"

"Maybe …" She rubbed her bottom lip with her thumb and forefinger as she thought. "Maybe *Driving Miss Daisy.*"

"That was a good one. I liked *The Green Mile.*" His thumb rubbed at the leftover label residue.

"Ooh, yeah, that *was* a good movie."

"Okay, what about TV?"

"I don't watch much, but I do love *Justified.*"

He sat up, excited, and leaned toward her. "Me too, Martha Maye. Sounds like we have a lot in common."

They were silent again, and Martha Maye stood and walked to the window to check on her daughter and to put an end to the awkward moment.

"I'm so glad Butterbean has a new friend." She pulled the drape aside and looked out into the yard.

Johnny cleared his throat. "It was a lucky stroke when this house opened up right next door to Honey and her daughter."

He joined Martha Maye at the window, standing so close behind her she could smell his aftershave. *That man always smells so good.*

"I think the Lord's watching out for us." Martha Maye pretended not to notice how close he was to her. "The way I met Honey at school and us having so much in common, the luck of this house being available . . . when she told me about it, I jumped at the chance. It'll be real nice having her for a neighbor. And the Bumgarners on the other side of us are good people, too."

"What do they do for a living?" Johnny placed a tentative hand on her waist.

Inside, every nerve ending was on high alert, but outwardly, she tried to show no reaction. "Hector's retired and Estherlene has always been a homemaker."

"And what about Honey? What does she teach up at the school?"

"She's the phys ed teacher." She craned her neck to the right. "And speak of the devil." Martha Maye abruptly moved away from the window.

Honey Winchester knocked three times and opened the screen door, calling out, "Yoo-hoo! Anybody home?"

"Come right on in, Honey. Have you met Police Chief Johnny Butterfield?"

"Well, hidee-do, Chief," Honey crooned. "Martha Maye said you were as big as Paul Bunyan but yowza, Paul ain't got nothing on you, darlin'." She sidled up to him and held out her hand. "I'd fight tigers with a switch in the dark for you."

"Pleasure to meet you, ma'am." Johnny blushed. He tried to get his hand back, but Honey now had it between both of hers and showed no signs of letting go.

"Now what's a big honking man like you doing blushing?" Honey teased. She got closer to him and whispered, "You come on over to my house sometime and I'll give you something to blush about." She took one hand away from his and squeezed his enormous bicep. "Ooh. Now that's what I'm talking about," she murmured. "Big muscles." She looked down at the hand she still held. "Big hands." Her eyes met his. "Big eyes . . ." Her voice got husky. "Got anything else — ?"

Martha Maye cleared her throat and interrupted before Honey could say what she thought she was going to say. "The girls sure are having fun out there."

"Hmm . . . what?" Honey finally took her eyes off Johnny and let go of his hand.

"The girls. Outside. Fun." Martha Maye wasn't used to such forward women, and she didn't appreciate the tremendous amount of *friendliness* her new neighbor was showing Johnny. Honey's particular brand of friendly was different than most people's. It seemed like she never met a man she didn't like.

"Oh yeah, they're having fun. Maddy Mack is so happy to have a friend right next door now. Say, whatchy'all up to in here all by your lonesome? Y'all haven't been smooching and mooning, have you? You know, Johnny, Martha Maye isn't quite a free woman just yet." Honey batted her eyelashes at him. "But I'm free as a bird."

"Free and easy," Martha Maye muttered, plopping onto an overstuffed chair.

"What's that, sugar?" Honey asked, running her fingers through her short strawberry-blond hair.

"I said, maybe we could play Parcheesi." She rubbed her nose, an habitual nervous gesture.

"Oh sugar, I like to play games"—she paused to give Johnny a coy look—"but I prefer the more . . . physical ones." She fluffed her spiky hair and let her hand fall slowly to her chest.

Martha Maye didn't think Honey would go beyond innuendo, so she called her bluff. "Such as?" she said sweetly.

"Oh, you know, I like football, basketball, anything *physical*." She looked right at Johnny, who shoved his hands in his pockets and looked down at his shoes. "Say! Maybe we could play that game—whatsit called, Foursome?"

Martha Maye rolled her eyes and said, "You mean Four Square?"

"Oh, of course, Four Square. Maybe we could play that with the kids some time."

"Yeah, uh, that might be fun." Johnny hitched a thumb over his shoulder. "Listen, ladies, I'm gonna have to shove off. Got to go check in at the station." With the look of a cornered animal, he began backing toward the door.

"Don't be a stranger, Chief," Honey called in her Southern twang.

Martha Maye walked to the door with him. He stepped out onto the porch, then turned, and their eyes met. She hoped he was finally going to ask her out, but he simply squeezed her hand and said, "Let me know if you need any help getting set up in there."

"I will, Johnny, thank you for your help."

She turned to go back inside but looked over her shoulder and saw Johnny looking back at her.

"Anything else?" she said hopefully.

He looked at her for a long moment. Her heart sped up.

He adjusted the ball cap on his head. "Nah, I reckon not." A shy grin appeared on his face. "See you later, sweet tater."

Flustered, she went back inside to find Honey making herself at home on the couch. The screen door slapped shut loudly behind her.

"He sure seems nice," Honey said in a singsong way. "And cute as a bug's ear." She crossed her long, tanned legs gracefully. Honey had the perfect body. She was not only a PE teacher, she was also a personal trainer, and she looked it. She had a tiny waist, toned, shapely legs, and a man-made chest that left men unable to remember her eye color. Her short, spiky hair made her look slightly tomboyish, but she was all woman.

"He's very nice," Martha Maye said, sitting down across from Honey.

"Is he taken?" Honey asked.

"He's not married or seeing anyone, if that's what you mean," Martha Maye said, trying to keep impatience out of her voice.

"Are you two …" — Honey waggled her finger in the air as she stretched out the word "two" for a few seconds — "an item?"

"No. You know we're not." Martha Maye tucked her feet under her.

"I don't know. He seemed kind of sweet on you, Mart." Honey reached for the bottle and took a swig of Blue Moon beer Johnny had left behind.

Martha Maye looked earnestly at her friend. "You think? I feel like there's something between us, but he won't ask me out."

"So you two are just friends." She finished the bottle off in one astonishing gulp.

"Just friends," Martha Maye sighed, making the word sound like "free-unds."

"Well, if you don't mind—" Honey was cut off by the ringing phone.

"Saved by the bell," Martha Maye muttered under her breath.

"What's that, sugar?"

"I said, that's my cell." Martha Maye smiled sweetly. But as soon as the person calling said one word, her smile disappeared.

"How did you get this number?" she hissed, surging to her feet.

"Never you mind about that, darlin', I'm just calling to make sure you're all right. I heard you were almost killed." Lenny's voice boomed over the line, his words full of emotion.

"Where'd you hear that?" she asked in a flat tone.

"Aw baby, don't be like that. I love you, of course I'm gonna worry about you when I hear you were kidnapped, for Pete's sake. I'm just glad you're okay. You *are* okay, aren't you, baby?"

"I'm just fine." Martha clamped her eyes shut, willing the tears to go away. "And I'm not your baby."

"Listen, sweet pea, I'm not mad. I know you did what you had to do. Both of us have had time to cool off and think about things, and honey, literally, the only thing I think about is you. Let me come talk to you. We can work out our problems. I know we can. I'm a changed man. Losing you was literally the worst thing ever happened to me, and I swear on a stack of Bibles I've changed. You were right to leave, but I miss you something awful, you and Carrie. I can't stand being without y'all—"

"Lenny!" Martha Maye interrupted his pleading. He was quickly giving her a headache. "That's enough. I'm happy now. I'm teaching up at Butterbean's school, and we're settling into a new life. Leave me be."

"What about Carrie? You can't just go off and expect me not to see our little girl anymore. I got my rights." Lenny started crying. "I just miss y'all so much, Marty. Please let me come see y'all. Pleeeeaaaassse."

"I'll think about it, Len," Martha Maye said softly. "I'll think about it.

Don't call me. I'll call you." And with that, she punched End on her phone.

"Sugar, are you all right?" Honey asked, coming up beside her. "You look sorta pale. More than usual."

"Yeah, yeah, I'm just fine." Martha Maye ignored the slight insult. "I'd rather not talk about it right now, okay?"

"'Course it's okay," Honey soothed, rubbing Martha Maye's back. "Listen, why don't we take the girls and go get some ice cream? That would take your mind off things, wouldn't it? I scream, you scream, we all scream for ice cream."

"Yeah, well, I scream when I look at my scale." Martha Maye let out a big sigh. "That sounds nice, Honey, but you've helped me lose weight, now don't go putting it back on me. No ice cream for me."

"Oh sugar, you're back in fine form, you look like a million bucks. Your pear shape is more like an hourglass now, but you gotta show it off by wearing clothes that fit."

Martha Maye looked down at her baggy T-shirt and loose-fitting jeans. She didn't think she looked too bad. *But I suppose I don't look too appealing, either. I'd be embarrassed to go to Wal-Mart dressed this way. No wonder Johnny wouldn't ask me out.* Twenty pounds had come off, but she hated to buy new clothes before the final ten were gone, and they were sticking like glue.

She took a deep breath and let it out, sounding forlorn. "I still have ten more ugly pounds to lose."

"And you will. You keep working with me, and pretty soon you'll have men lining up at your door. Now let's sit down and work up a plan." Honey tugged on Martha Maye's arm, pulling her toward the couch. "We'll plan our work and work our plan, and in no time we'll find you a man."

Martha smiled stiffly, thinking she'd already found one, if only he'd ask her out.

Lenny clicked the phone off. *She hung up on me,* he thought with spite. *Lenny, my man, what you need is a plan,* he told himself, getting a pencil and a piece of paper. He sat down and began to write.

Step 1: Go to Goose Pimple Junction and get a job.
Step 2: Go see Martha Maye and Carrie. Beg forgiveness.
Step 3: Visit Louetta. Get on her good side.

Step 4: Get on the good side of the law in the junction.
Step 5: Woo Martha Maye.
Step 6: Play the devoted family man.
Step 7: Move in and reclaim rightful place as head of the household.
Step 8: Make Martha Maye pay for what she did.

THREE

There is much that cannot be understood by the poor soul who thinks words are the same as thoughts.

~Southern Proverb

Lenny slicked back his dark brown hair and pushed his fake Ray-Bans up to rest on top of his head. He pulled at his shirt slightly in an attempt to lessen the strain his beer belly put on the middle buttons. It didn't work.

He flexed his neck like a fighter going into the ring and walked into Goose Pimple Junction's Car Country Auto Sales, confident and ready to schmooze. He was on a mission: to win back his wife and child. Step one was getting a job in their new town, and that was exactly what he intended to do.

Not the kind of man to be put off, and used to getting what he wanted, he wasn't going to wait any longer for Martha Maye to *let* him come for a visit. *Just watch her try to avoid me now,* he thought with a smirk.

Lenny's cheap brown ankle boots clacked on the floor, making him seem more important than he was. He strode up to the used-car salesman, Darryl Daigle—"Big Darryl D"–as the sign said out front. He was as tall as a redwood and weighed more than Lenny cared to guess. *They don't call him "Big" Darryl D for nothing,* Lenny thought. He stuck out his hand.

Big Darryl shook his hand with a vise-like grip. "What can I put you in today, my good man?"

"You can put me in that there office." Lenny pointed toward one of the small cubicle offices belonging to the salesmen.

"Zat right?" Darryl D sized him up. Lenny could tell he was ready to give him a hard time and send him on his way. But Darryl was putty in his hands, and thirty minutes later, Lenny had been hired. Darryl said he was impressed with Lenny's confidence, was sure that his good looks would be a hit among the ladies, and thought his outgoing personality would win over the men.

"My intuition tells me you are whatcha call a natural used-car salesman," Big Darryl D said.

Lenny assured him he was.

"So that's pretty much it," Big Darryl D finally said after showing him around. "Our little corner of the world." He nudged Lenny in the stomach with his elbow. "Oh, and you can help yourself to any of the cars on the lot. Sign them out over there; the keys are on the pegboard above the sign-out sheet. Just make sure you log a car out each night you take one home and keep them neat and clean. I don't care what you do in them, just keep them clean." Darryl D winked at Lenny. "Welcome to Car Country," he said, pumping Lenny's hand.

"Glad to be here." Lenny flashed a smile full of teeth and added, "More'n you know."

"I LIKE your new clothes, Martha Maye, but I think it's time we get you a whole new wardrobe." Honey gripped Martha Maye's arm lightly as they walked down the sidewalk under the canopy of decades-old trees with leaves just starting to turn colors. "You need to show off that new figure of yours, and it's time to get fall clothes anyway. Half of your things hang off you like a scarecrow. Let's go shopping!"

Martha Maye was taking Butterbean, Honey, and her daughter, Maddy Mack, to her mother's house for dinner. The two ladies lagged behind the little girls, who skipped merrily down the uneven sidewalk, which had buckled with the huge tree roots.

"I can't really afford much right now." Martha Maye waved to Paprika Honeywell. "Butterbean needs new school clothes, and I have the rent, utilities, and food. I'm a single mom now, you know."

"And you're gonna set aside some money for yourself, too, sugar. You gotta."

Martha Maye wanted to get Honey off a subject that had been coming up all too often lately, so she said, "Listen, when we get to Mama's, just talk to Aunt Imy like normal, but don't be surprised if some crazy talk comes out of her mouth."

"Crazy talk? Like what?" Honey dodged an anthill on a crack in the sidewalk.

"Since she had the stroke, she comes out with commercial slogans every now and then. Sometimes it's funny, but try not to laugh. I don't know what goes on in her head, but she doesn't realize she's said anything weird. She's got that Altenheimer's disease, too."

"You mean Alzheimer's?" Honey hooked her arm with Martha Maye's.

"Yeah, that's it. So just try to act normal around her."

"Alrighty dighty. I won't laugh. Do the doctors think the commercial lingo will go away?"

"They don't know. But even if it does, she'll still have Alten . . . Altzey…"

"Alzheimer's."

"Yeah, that."

"And who else did you say is living with your mama?"

"That's kind of a long story," Martha Maye said. "Mama took Charlotte Price in about two months ago. She's Henry Clay's daughter."

"*The* Henry Clay? Your mama took his daughter in?"

"Yeah. Charlotte's mama ran off a while ago, and her daddy's . . . uh, he's a little too busy for parenthood right now." They both chuckled. "She didn't have anyone to turn to. Mama is good people, but I think she figures she's been given a sort of gift with Charlotte coming to live with her. It's almost like she has another daughter. And Lord knows, that girl needed a mama."

"No wonder you wanted a place of your own. Charlotte and your aunt living with your mama—whew! That's a full house. I expect you were a might crowded."

They walked for a bit, commenting on the flower gardens they passed, the beautiful hundred-year-old houses, the smell of someone grilling steak, and the cooler nights they were having now that October had arrived.

As they approached Louetta's house, Honey said, "Good job changing the subject, but don't think you can get me off the topic of new clothes forever, missy."

Martha Maye made a face as she followed the girls up Lou's front walk.

They reached the door, knocked once, and went in. Louetta came running to greet them wearing lime-green pants and a hot-pink blouse. Her brassy red hair was in the usual bouffant style, and her makeup was applied perfectly, if not a little heavy. It clashed slightly with the bold cabbage rose wallpaper behind her. At nearly eighty, Louetta was definitely still alive and kicking. She was a stout, hefty woman and a whirlwind of perpetual energy.

"My babies! Come on in, y'all," Lou gushed, hugging them all. "I hope you brought your appetites," she said, ushering them into the kitchen that wafted of heavenly smells of fried chicken and hot yeast rolls. Lids jiggled on boiling pots on the stove, chicken fried in an old cast-iron skillet, and dirty dishes filled the sink.

"Hi, Aunt Imy, hireyew?" Martha Maye leaned down to hug the frail old lady in the chair. She had on a blue flowered housecoat, stockings that were rolled down to her ankles, and loosely tied white Keds tennis shoes. The side of her left shoe was cut at the big toe to ease the pressure on her bunion. Her short brown hair was set in tight curls, making it look kind of like she had a Brillo pad for hair. She couldn't have weighed more than ninety-eight pounds wet.

"I'd walk a mile for a Camel." Aunt Ima Jean sat sideways with her legs spread out, like a man would sit, with her knobby knees protruding through the housecoat that hung over them, maintaining her modesty.

"Who wouldn't?" Honey said with a big smile.

"Aunt Ima Jean, this is Honey Winchester and her daughter Madison Mackenzie. Folks call her Maddy Mack."

"I'm very pleased to meet you," Honey said, reaching out to shake hands.

"Ow!" Ima Jean pulled her hand from Honey's.

"Honey's a personal trainer and a PE teacher," Martha Maye interjected. "She doesn't know her own strength." She patted her aunt on the shoulder, while Ima Jean rubbed her hand dramatically.

"What's doing up at Robert E. Lee Elementary?" Louetta asked.

"We're humming right along," Martha Maye said. "I've got some rowdy ones and some sweet ones, too."

"Oh, in first grade every one of them's sweet," Honey said. "Try teaching all the grades. Then you get a taste of rowdy. How many love notes do you get a day, Martha Maye?"

"Hmm. About two or three. Some of my little boys are smitten, or so they think."

"Just wait until you give them their first report card. That'll bring their little heads down to earth," Lou said.

"Where's Charlotte?" Butterbean asked.

"She's out with Pickle, as usual. They'll be here in a little while, I expect he won't pass up pie."

An hour later, after finishing a dinner of fried chicken, mashed potatoes and gravy, green beans, sliced tomatoes, and hot rolls, the doorbell rang.

Butterbean ran to answer it and came bouncing back with a huge bouquet of roses.

"Ooh law, Buttabean, who are those for?" Lou asked.

"They're for Mama," she said, handing the bouquet to her mother and opening the card that came with it.

"Oh my stars, who are they from, Butterbean?" Martha Maye tried to grab the card from her daughter.

Butterbean, looking confused, read: "It says, 'From your secret admirer.'"

Honey squealed and clapped her hands. "You have a secret admirer? How exciting! I'll bet it's Wally, the fifth-grade teacher up at school. No, maybe it's Henry Clay . No, I've got it! Maybe it's Johhhnnnny," she said, drawing out the name.

"But why would they be delivered to Mama's house?" Martha Maye's forehead was scrunched in a wrinkle.

"Maybe whoever it is thinks you still live here," Honey suggested. "After all, y'all moved out not long ago."

"Who delivered them, Bean?" Martha Maye asked, turning over the envelope, blank except for her name.

"I dunno." Butterbean shrugged.

"Well, ain't that something." Louetta reached for the flowers. "A secret admirer. Here." Her chair squeaked as she stood up. "Let me have them so's I can put them in water." She started for the kitchen, calling over her shoulder, "Buttabean, you and Maddy Mack clear the dishes. I'll bring out dessert."

"Can me and Maddy Mack go outside and play? We don't want dessert."

"*Me* and Maddy Mack?" Martha Maye said disapprovingly. "*Can?*"

Butterbean rolled her eyes and said, "Maddy Mack and I. *May* Maddy Mack and I go outside to play before it gets too dark?"

"You don't want dessert?" Lou shrieked from the doorway, her ample bosom and the bouquet of flowers preceding her into the room. "Are you sure you didn't pick her out of a punkin patch, Mart? There ain't never been nobody in our family who didn't want dessert."

"Can we eat it later, Granny?" Butterbean hopped up and down in front of her grandmother, her hands in a prayer position.

"Oh, gwon outta here." Lou tried to suppress her smile and affectionately swatted at her granddaughter's bottom. "It'll still be here when you get back, but clear the table first, now."

"So who do you think the flowers are from, Mart?" Lou said a few minutes later, as she served pieces of caramel apple pie.

"I have no earthly idea." Martha Maye stared at the flowers as if in a trance.

"Martha Maye, be happy." Honey put her hand on Martha Maye's arm. "Flowers are a good thing. I told you you'd be attracting men left and right."

"Who's attracting men left and right?" Charlotte asked, coming into the room with her boyfriend, Pickle. They were a mismatched pair if ever there was one. Charlotte was a short fifteen-year-old beauty with long honey-blond hair and big blue eyes. Pickle, only a year older, looked like a tall stick figure with oversized arms and legs. His hair was so blond it was almost white, with a cowlick at the top of his head that made a tuft of hair stick up. He had big brown eyes and freckles across his nose. Charlotte looked like the cheerleader type, and Pickle looked like Ichabod Crane.

"Oh, there's the little darlins now. Sit down and have some pie," Lou said.

"Nothin' says lovin' like somethin' from the oven," Ima Jean piped up. The expression on her face was almost always serious.

"Ain't that the truth," Honey said.

"Have y'all met Honey? She's Mart's neighbor and fellow teacher," Lou said. "Honey, this is Charlotte Price and Peekal Culpepper. Charlotte lives with us, and Peekal purt near does too, on account he's here so much to see Charlotte." She winked at him.

Pickle blushed as he took the piece of pie Lou offered.

"You sure did wear the right shirt to this house, Pickle." Honey was looking at his T-shirt. It said, EVERYONE HAS TO BELIEVE IN SOMETHING. I BELIEVE I'LL HAVE ANOTHER PIECE OF PIE.

"Wull, I had help," Pickle said, grinning. "Charlotte told me Mizz Louetta was baking pie."

"Aw, you're cuter'n a box full a puppies," Honey crooned, but Pickle was too busy gulping pie to notice her.

"He's my stock boy up at the bookstore, too. I'll bet I see him more 'n you do, Charlotte." Lou pinched Pickle's cheek. "But don't worry, he's too young for me. I won't steal him from ya."

"'Cause your heart belongs to Jack," Ima Jean said.

"Oh, hush up that crazy talk," Louetta protested. "The man's fifty-two years old. I'd have to be T minus dumb and counting to be interested in someone that young, and besides, he belongs to Tess. They're a match made in heaven if I ever saw one. I swan, the two of them are so cute together. If only all of us could be that happy."

"Mr. Jack and Ms. Tess are out front with Butterbean." Charlotte took a dainty bite of pie.

"He's outside? I sure would like to meet him," Honey said, wide-eyed.

"He's taken, Honey," Martha Maye said quickly.

"Oh really? Maybe he's your secret admirer? Is that what you mean? You got something going with Mr. Jack?" Honey teased.

"Oh no, Honey, Jack couldn't be the secret admirer. Hello! Aren't you listening? We done told you fifty eleven times he's taken by Tess. Matta fact, he's mighty taken *with* Tess." Lou giggled.

"Tess was also kidnapped when I was," Martha Maye whispered to Honey. "And Jack was one of our rescuers." Louder, for everyone to hear, she said, "Jack's a best-selling author. He's lived here for about five years now. And Tess is from up north. Jack translates our Southern speak for Tess, although sometimes even he gets stumped."

"Have Mizz Tess and Mr. Jack set a date for getting hitched?" Pickle asked, his mouth full of pie.

"I don't think they have yet," Lou answered.

"What's this about a secret admirer?" Charlotte asked.

"Somebody sent Martha Maye these here flowers. Card said they were from a secret admirer," Honey explained.

Charlotte gulped. "Who do you suppose they're from, Martha Maye?"

"Don't rightly know. I don't have the foggiest idea."

"Don't worry, Martha Maye, we'll figure it out. And once we get you into some new clothes to show off that new body, he'll come a-knocking for sure." Honey put her arm around Martha Maye's shoulder.

"Gentlemen prefer Hanes," Ima Jean said.

FOUR

If you have to eat dirt, eat clean dirt.

~Southern Proverb

enny pulled the black Caddy to the side of the road, six houses down from Lou's. He could see his daughter playing in the yard with some others. *And who might that be,* he wondered, eyeing the blond bombshell. *Hmm, she looks awful friendly with that dude out there. I could give him a run for his money, though. She takes one look at the Lenmeister, and he'll literally be toast.*

In his mind, he was becoming intimate with the angel in the yard when suddenly Lou's front door opened and people started spilling out of the house. He recognized his mother-in-law right away and squinted hard at the old prune who held onto Lou. He thought she looked vaguely familiar. Someone he'd met at the wedding maybe. Then he saw a spiky-haired blonde who he most definitely did not know, but whom he thought he should. She looked spunky. His eyes were roaming slowly over her body when another person walked out and stood next to the old prune. *Yowza, who do we have here?*

It was when she waved to the old ladies and started walking in the other direction down the sidewalk that his eyes nearly bugged out of their sockets. He'd know that walk anywhere. That couldn't be Marty. Could it? He couldn't believe his eyes. When she turned to wave good-bye to Lou and he saw that smile, he was certain. Then Butterbean reached up to hold her hand as they began walking, and he said out loud, "Well, I'll be darned." His wife had changed quite a bit in the three months since he'd last laid eyes on her. Yessiree, a separation had done her some good.

He was too far away to tell much about her new figure, but he could tell she'd dropped some serious weight. Maybe she'd be worth getting back after all.

He was just about to put the car in gear and follow along at a safe distance when a city police car pulled up behind him. He watched in his rearview mirror as a huge man got out. He walked up to Lenny's door and said, "Sir, we got a report of loitering. State your business, please."

Lenny said, "Oh thank goodness, Officer—"

"Chief. I'm Police Chief Johnny Butterfield."

"Right. The thing is, *Chief*, I'm lost. I just stopped to look at a map, but I literally feel like a monkey trying to do math. Maybe you could help me. I'm looking for Big Darryl D's Car Country." *Or at least I was two hours ago.*

"Sure. It's up the road a piece." The chief raised his arm and pointed his finger. "You go on up to the stop sign and take a left. At the next stop sign, take a right. Go straight down Main Street, and when you reach the Get 'N Go, turn right. It'll be down about a block or so. You can't miss it."

"Thank you kindly. I 'preshade that. I didn't mean any harm, *Chief*. I'm just enjoying this purty street. I'll certainly be moving along now." He'd kicked up his Southern accent a notch or two.

Johnny clasped his hands on the window ledge and leaned down to study the man's face. "What did you say your business is in Goose Pimple Junction, sir?"

"I'm a new resident, Chief. I'll be making this fine town my new home."

"Oh really?" Johnny looked skeptical. He stood up, crossed his arms over his chest, and stared down at Lenny through his aviator sunglasses.

"Yessir. Gonna get me a job over at Big Darryl D's, and I'm looking for a nice little house to call my own."

"On this street?"

"This is a right lovely street," Lenny said, looking around.

Johnny stretched his neck, looking past Lenny into the car, where there was no map in sight. "Thought you were looking at a map."

"Oh, I *was*." Lenny searched for an answer.

Johnny cocked one eyebrow.

"On my phone. I was using that Google Map thingy on my phone," Lenny hedged. "Then I was sitting here listening to the quiet, imagining living on a nice street like this one. I can literally picture myself out under one of these trees waxing up my car."

"Well, you'll need to move on now, sir."

"Yessir, I didn't mean to cause any trouble. I'll be on my way now."

"All right then." Johnny ducked his head to look Lenny in the eye and tapped the door with his hand. "You have a real good night, sir." He tipped his hat and walked back to his car.

It pained Lenny to have to suck up to the chief that way, but he reckoned it was fortuitous he'd run into him. Step four—or was it step five? It didn't matter. One of the steps of his plan was to get on the good side of the law. He figured he had the man eating out of the palm of his hand now.

Now for step two, he thought. *Go see my wife and child.*

"Butterbean! Don't get so far ahead!" Martha Maye called to her daughter bright and early the next morning. She was walking as fast as she could, but toting her book satchel to school slowed her down. Besides, it was a beautiful fall morning and she wanted to be able to enjoy her walk to school.

"Morning, Mizz Whitaker." She waved to a woman who was getting her newspaper, then hurried on after her daughter, who waited for her at a stop sign.

"Butterbean, you have to slow down. I can't walk that fast."

"But I can't ride that slow," Butterbean whined.

"Hey now. Mind your manners. Don't sass me."

The crossing guard motioned for them to walk, and they started off again. "Morning, Mizz Hinkle, hireyew today?"

The crossing guard flashed her usual hundred-watt smile. "I'm ugly as sin, but I got a pure heart."

"Oh, you." Martha Maye patted her on the arm as she passed, then she whirled around when a shrill whistle sounded right behind her. She jumped in surprise and turned to see the fifth-grade teacher, Mr. Tierney, barreling toward them on his skateboard.

"Mr. Tierney, you slow it right down, now." Mrs. Hinkle pointed a bent finger sternly at the man. "You're nothing but a public menace on that thing. We've got pedestrians and bike riders all over the place. You can't come barreling through the intersection like that. You're liable to kill somebody dead."

"Is there any other way?" Martha Maye leaned in to mutter. The guard ignored her. Her eyes were on the man on the skateboard.

"Okay, okay, I'm slowing down. Sheesh, Mizz Hinkle, you're wound tighter than a Gibson guitar. You gotta lighten up, sugar."

"I'll sugar you—"

She started toward the teacher, but Martha Maye held her back. "Let him go, hon, he doesn't mean any harm."

"But that's just it. He don't have to mean harm to plow someone down flat as a pancake. He comes through here every day on that dadblamed skateboard. He's not eleven years old anymore, you know. Grown man acting the fool—"

"I know, I know," Martha Maye interrupted, patting her shoulder. "But I think he's being more careful than you give him credit for. Fact, I think he barrels through here just to get your goat."

"Grown man, riding a skateboard to work every day. Never seen anything like it in all my born days."

"You have a real good day, Miss Hinkle. Don't let him rile you up." Martha Maye headed across the street and was proud to see Butterbean waiting for her.

They were within eyesight of the school now, so Martha Maye said, "You can go on, sweetie. Lock up your bike, and I'll see you after school. 'Kay?"

"'Kay, Mama. Bye!"

Martha Maye checked in at the office, got her mail out of the little box marked *Room 118*, and walked toward her classroom, speaking to students and other teachers along the way. She stepped into her first-grade classroom, cut on the lights, and headed for her desk at the far end of the room. From her book bag she removed the spelling tests she'd graded the previous evening, put them on her desk, and headed to the chalkboard to put up the day's sentences for the children to copy. She took one look at the chalkboard, put her hands on her hips, and laughed.

Someone had drawn a huge heart with *I Love You* written in the center. She couldn't tell by the handwriting who had written it, but if it was the student she suspected, she wondered how he'd reached that high to draw such a huge heart.

Feeling bad for having to erase it, she did anyway, so she could post the day's assignments.

She looked at her watch when she was finished, realized it was time for the kids to come to class, and walked out into the hall to greet them.

"Slow down, Eric. Dannon," she called down the hall. Two little boys slowed down but walked as fast as they could without running, continuing to race each other to the door of the classroom. She stepped into the doorway to block their path.

"And how are you two doing this morning?" She dropped her arms, palms out, causing the boys to bump her hands and stop in front of her.

"Good," both boys said in unison, clearly itching to be the first one in the door.

"I've never seen anybody in more of a hurry to go to class than you two." She pushed them gently back into the hallway so she could look down at their faces. She held out one hand. "Do you boys have your homework assignments?"

The boys reached into their backpack and pulled out a sheet of paper. She glanced down; seeing the usual heart next to Eric's name, she smiled to herself.

"Do either of you know anything about a message on my chalkboard?" She put her hands down on their bellies once again to stop them from brushing by her. Both boys shrugged and looked at each other. Eric mumbled, "Huh?"

She scrutinized their faces and let them go.

Throughout the day, she received two *I love you* notes and a *You're pretty* note from three boys in her class. She studied each child carefully but didn't come to any conclusions about who might have put the heart on the chalkboard.

After seeing the children out the front door of the school at three o'clock, she returned to her classroom to find Butterbean up on a chair, erasing the blackboard, as was her habit.

"Hey, Bean, how was your day, darlin'?" She kissed her daughter on the cheek as she walked past her to her desk.

"It was good. Ms. Winston gave us—"

Behind her, Martha Maye heard Butterbean gasp and then squeal. She whirled around to see Lenny standing at the classroom door.

"Daddy!" Butterbean jumped off the chair and ran to him.

"Carrie!" Lenny caught his daughter in a big hug.

"Lenny," Martha Maye said softly but unenthusiastically.

FIVE

A pig knows enough arithmetic to take the shortest cut through a thicket.

~Southern Proverb

Lenny took his wife and daughter to Slick and Junebug's Diner for an afternoon snack. After Martha Maye ordered water and Lenny ordered French fries and vanilla milkshakes for himself and his daughter, he got up and walked over to the jukebox. He put two quarters in, and the words to "I Fell in a Pile of You and Got Love All Over Me" came streaming out.

Martha Maye had tried her best to be polite in front of Butterbean, but she knew that's why Lenny had planned this reunion in front of their daughter, and she was seething on the inside. She told Butterbean to wash her hands, and once their daughter was gone, Martha Maye lit into him.

"I thought I made myself clear on the phone, Lenny. I distinctly remember saying don't call me, I'll call you. I don't know how I could have been any plainer than that."

"I know, baby, but I couldn't wait any longer. I was literally going plum nuts not being able to see you and Carrie."

"No, you always were nuts," she hissed, looking up and switching to a smile, as Junebug delivered their order to the table.

"Two white cows, one order of frog sticks, and a glass of city juice for the lady. Can I getch'all anything else?" She eyed Lenny suspiciously.

"Thanks, Junebug, that'll do it." Martha Maye took a sip from the glass of water.

"How's your mama and them?" Junebug propped her hands on her hips and looked at Martha Maye.

"Mama and Aunt Ima Jean are doing all right, Junebug. Thanks for asking."

"You got a new beau?" She motioned with her head at Lenny.

Lenny's eyes squinted ever so slightly, but he managed a big smile and said, "Naw, she's got an old husband."

"Do tell. I thought your mama said you's divorced, Martha Maye."

"Not quite," Martha Maye said through her teeth.

"Name's Lenny." He stuck out his hand. "And I'm here to win back my wife's love." Junebug gave him a hard stare, ignoring his outstretched hand. He took his hand back and continued.

"I literally must have been dumber'n four o'clock noon to let this woman go."

"I'd second that." Junebug's face showed no sign of buying his charm.

"But I am going to rectify the situation," Lenny drawled, flashing his best phony smile. Junebug's glare didn't soften.

"See that you do, son. Martha Maye is one of our own, and I'll jerk a knot in your head if you mess with her."

"Yes, ma'am. I do not want no knot on this here head." He tapped the top of his head with his index finger.

Junebug harrumphed and left the table, tousling Butterbean's hair as they passed each other.

"Can Daddy stay with us, Mama?" Butterbean slid back into the booth next to her daddy.

"No, Bean, he cannot stay with us."

"Aw, why not?" she whined. "I want it to be like it used to be—all of us living together. Please, please, please, Mama?"

"Eat your fries while they're hot." Martha Maye pushed a bottle of ketchup toward her daughter.

"So you're not living with your mama anymore?" Lenny asked.

Martha Maye narrowed her eyes. "How'd you know we were living with Mama?"

"I told him," Butterbean piped up. She saw her mother's disapproving look and lowered her head. "Sorry. I forgot I wasn't supposed to."

"Aw, Marty, it pains me to hear you felt you had to tell our daughter to keep your whereabouts from me. But I'm here to show you I'm a changed man. We can be a family again, just like Carrie wants. You won't have to work no more."

Martha Maye glared at him, and he quickly changed his tune, holding his palms up to quiet her down. "Unless you want to, of course. It's entirely up to you."

"Nice of you to allow me to choose how I want to live my life." She rooted in her purse and then abruptly got up and walked to the jukebox. She slid two quarters in and punched the button for "I'd Rather Pass a Kidney Stone Than Another Night with You."

Lenny's mouth was a thin line. "I deserved that," he said, nodding, when she sat back down at the table. "I was wrong to act the way I did before, but you'll see, I'll literally devote the rest of my life making it up to you and Carrie."

"I'm not moving back, Len. Butterbean and I have a new life here in Goose Pimple Junction."

"I ain't asking you to move back."

"Then how're you gonna make it up to us?"

"*I'm* moving *here*, baby. I quit my job and already got a new one here in town."

"A job? In Goose Pimple Junction?" Martha Maye shrieked so loudly the other customers looked over at their table. She lowered her voice to a hiss and leaned across the table. "What do you mean?"

"Just what I said. I am gainfully employed." He grinned like a possum, raising his chin proudly and puffing out his chest.

"Where, Daddy, where?" Butterbean asked, unable to keep her bottom still in the seat. She tugged at his shirtsleeve.

"Over at Car Country Auto Sales. You're looking at their newest salesman."

"Just because your cat had her kittens in the oven doesn't make them muffins." Martha Maye stared at her glass of water as she ran her finger down it, wiping the condensation off. She couldn't look at Lenny.

"What's that mean, Mama?"

"Means your mama don't think I can hold down a job as a car salesman. But I'll show her. You'll both be proud of me."

"Where you staying?"

"Got me a room at the Stay A Spell Hotel. Of course if you want me to move in with y'all ..."

"I didn't say that. I thought we'd already covered that subject."

"YOU'RE LOOKING awful good, sugar plum," Lenny whispered later, patting her backside as they left the diner. "How about I come over after Carrie goes to sleep tonight? I'll show you just how much I've missed you."

Martha Maye wavered. He did seem intent on trying to be a good husband. Why was she being so cold to him? Maybe it took the shock of her walking out to make him want to change. He'd come all the way to Goose Pimple Junction to find them, he'd gotten a job, and he was so complimentary of her new figure. Not to mention Bean wanting to be with her daddy. She felt his finger caress her cheek, and she saw the pleading look in his dark brown eyes. She let out a deep sigh.

"All right. You can come over." She cocked her eyebrows at him. "But just to talk."

"Whatever you want, baby," he said, patting her hip and leering at her.

AFTER CLEANING up the dinner dishes, and while Butterbean did homework, Martha Maye slipped next door to talk to Honey. Armed with sweet tea, they headed to the front porch to sit and talk. The humidity and heat of summer were no more, and the temperature was mild in the early October evening air.

"What's up, sugar? You look like something's on your mind."

Martha Maye plopped down hard on the wicker chair. "It's my husband. He says he wants me back."

"Humph. Wanting and hoping don't get you any toys on Christmas morning." Honey tucked her legs up under her on the seat.

"He says he's moved to Goose Pimple and gotten a job over at Big Darryl D's. He says he's a changed man."

"And what do you think?"

"I think that man knows how to be slick as snot on a doorknob, but he did truly come across as a changed man. I used to think there wasn't a skirt he wouldn't chase, but he swears he's only got eyes for me now. And when I think about his temper, I don't see any sign of it anymore, either."

"What do you mean, his temper?" Honey's eyebrows rose nearly to her hairline.

"Oh, my stars, he used to have a horrible temper. My preacher told me to keep my car keys by the back door in case I needed to make a fast getaway."

Honey slapped the arm of the chair. "You're lying like a rug!"

"I wish I were." Martha Maye shook her head.

"Did he ever hit you?"

"No, but I always expected him to. One time we'd had a fight—over what I can't remember." She shook her head, looking down, picturing it in her mind. "I told him I was taking Bean and leaving. He walked to the dresser and swept his arm along the entire top, throwing everything onto the floor. He said I'd leave him over my dead body. I was terrified."

Honey looked confused. "You'd leave him over *your* dead body?"

"Yeah, sometimes his brain waves fall a little short of the beach, but not this time. He wanted it to sound like a threat, so he said *my* dead body."

"Jimminy Christmas." Honey stared at Martha Maye, shaking her head slowly. She pulled her legs up against her chest and wrapped her arms around them, her chin resting on her knees. "So what are you going to do? You don't believe him now, do you?"

"I don't have any reason not to. He *did* get a job, and he *did* come here looking for us. Those are two steps in the right direction."

"Do you know for a fact he got a job?"

"Well, no ..."

Honey moved closer to Martha Maye. "You be careful, Mart. I don't know if you should trust him just yet."

"It's not like I have to beat men off with a stick, and he says he wants to win me back. That's the best offer I've had." Wryly, she added, "Other than from a murderous kidnapper."

"Don't you sell yourself short, Mart. There will be plenty men interested in you if you give them half a chance. You already got yourself a secret admirer. Don't settle just to settle."

"But Honey, he's Butterbean's father. Maybe my leaving shook him up. He might have changed."

"Might? Mites don't fly this time of year."

Martha Maye rolled her eyes and Honey continued, "Just do this for me, Mart, go slow and don't make any rash decisions. 'Kay?" Honey had been rubbing Martha Maye's arm, and she gave it a little squeeze when Martha Maye agreed to go slow and to call her if she felt the least little bit threatened.

As MARTHA Maye crossed the lawn back to her house, Johnny pulled into her driveway.

"Hey, stranger," Johnny called, getting out of the car. I haven't seen you in a while. Where you been keeping yourself?"

"Just working, Chief." Martha Maye stopped next to his car, putting her fingers in her back pockets, thumbs hanging out.

They stood smiling and looking at each other for a long moment. Martha Maye felt like a lot, yet nothing, was said in the look that passed between them.

Johnny broke the silence first, talking in a rush. "Lookit, Martha Maye, I know your divorce isn't final yet, but I heard Dude's Steakhouse has great steak and great fried chicken, too. I was wondering if we could go up there sometime."

Martha Maye didn't reply right away. She looked down at her feet scuffing in the gravel, squealing to herself on the inside.

In the momentary silence, they heard Dispatcher Teenie White over the air: "Officer Beanblossom, Mizz Odette over on Hidden Ridge Road is reporting a raccoon wandering around her backyard. She's afraid it's afflicted with rabies and is gonna get her dog Whitey. Can you run over there and take care of it?"

Hank's voice came over the speaker: "Sure thing, Teenie. I'm less than a minute away from Hidden Ridge."

Johnny added, "Together. You 'n me."

Martha Maye thought about the talk she'd just had with Honey. She wished she could feel excitement for Lenny like she felt when she saw Johnny. She didn't feel anything for Lenny except for indifference and maybe a little fear.

As she tried to decide what to do, the silence stretched out, so Johnny said, "Doesn't have to be dinner. Maybe lunch, or coffee, or ice cream —"

"That sounds real nice, Johnny," she blurted, looking up at him. "I'd love to go to Dude's with you."

"Really?" Johnny's voice came out a lot higher than intended. He cleared his throat, and in a tone too low he said, "Really?" Clearing his throat again, his normal voice came out of a mouth that held a shy smile. "If I'd known it was gonna be that easy, I'd have asked a long time before now."

She laughed, still absentmindedly kicking at the dirt on the driveway.

"All you had to do was ask," she said, smiling sweetly. Then her face clouded. "But Johnny, I need to tell you something."

"I knew that was too easy." He slapped the top of his car.

Butterbean ran out the front door and screeched to a stop next to her mother. "Hi, Chief Butterfield."

"Hi yourself. How's school?"

"Just fine." She turned to her mother. "I finished my homework. Can I go over to Maddy Mack's for a bit?"

Martha Maye looked at her watch. "Just a short bit. It's almost time for a bath."

"I took one of them yesterday." Butterbean tried to maintain a serious face but her smile broke through.

Martha Maye swatted her daughter's bottom. "Yeah, unfortunately, dirt found its way onto your body again."

Butterbean headed for her friend's house, saying over her shoulder, "Can I stay an hour?"

"Half an hour and not a minute more," Martha Maye called. She turned to Johnny and shook her head.

"You're doing something right with her, Mart." Johnny leaned back against the side of his cruiser. "Now, you had something to tell me?"

She nodded. "I *do* want to have dinner with you, but I just want you to know that some things have changed since I saw you last." She saw Johnny swallow hard. "My husband—soon to be ex-husband—is in town."

"What for?" His eyebrows dipped to a V.

"Wellll, he says he wants me back."

"What do you say?" Johnny asked softly.

"I say he's delusional. Lenny says he's changed, but I don't know if that's possible. Since the divorce isn't final, and he *is* in town, maybe you and I should just start off slow, like with coffee or something. I don't want people to talk. Mama always said a reputation is the best thing a girl has."

He made an attempt to smile at Martha Maye. "Do you still love him?" The vulnerable look in Johnny's eyes contrasted with his big, manly appearance.

"I don't know." She sighed. "No. I don't think so."

"Maybe I should let you figure that out before you break my heart," Johnny said, as if it were already too late.

"Johnny, that's the sweetest thing anybody's ever said to me." Martha Maye put her hand over her heart.

"Well, I've got more." He smiled that shy smile, cocking his head to one side.

"And I'd love to hear them," she said coyly, her eyes daring him to continue.

Teenie White came back over the air: "Officer Beanblossom, Rita Flares over on Hidden Ridge Road is reporting a possible peeping Tom. Says someone's out there by her bedroom window. Since you're in the area, will you check it out?"

Johnny shook his head and looked up at the heavens.

"What's wrong, Johnny?"

"Wait for it." He chuckled.

The next voice was Hank Beanblossom's. "Uh, Teenie, that would be me. I'm out here looking for that raccoon. The Flareses and the Raineses are next-door neighbors. Remember?"

"I do now. I'll tell her the strange man in her yard is just you."

Johnny chuckled and rubbed the back of his neck. Then he and Martha Maye both began to laugh, and the serious moment melted away.

SIX

Trying to understand some folks is like guessing at the direction of a rathole underground.

~Southern Proverb

enny sat seething in his car down the street from Martha Maye's small Arts & Crafts bungalow, as he watched the police chief flirt with his wife. He didn't like their body language. The way she giggled and tilted her head up at him. The way he looked at her. Lenny could hardly believe what he was seeing.

First: she left him. Second: she made him look like a fool. And now third: she was flirting with another man in broad daylight.

The police chief? That GI Joe? Seriously? That sure shoots step four — or is it step five? No matter, there goes my plan to get into the good graces of the law. I ain't playing nice with a man who's making a fool out of me.

He started the car and drove to Humdinger's, a bar on the outskirts of town. He was nursing a bourbon and Coke when a tall, very tan, bleached-blond thirty-something woman in a miniskirt and tube top climbed onto the stool next to him.

She leaned over and whispered in his ear, "Poof." Then she straightened to order a whiskey sour and light a cigarette.

"'Scuse me?" Lenny leered at the woman.

"Here I am. What are your other two wishes?"

He looked at her for a long moment, taking in her purple tube top, which was insufficient for keeping her bust confined, and her red miniskirt, which was indeed mini. His eyes followed her legs down to her spiky, red four-inch heels, then reversed direction, going all the way to the tip of her brown roots, which led to brittle, bottle-blond big hair, coiffed and sprayed into place. He finally settled back on her bloodshot eyes, heavily lined in black eyeliner with goopy clusters of mascara coating the lashes.

"Now, what's a nice girl like you doing in a place like this?" He flashed his lady-killer smile at her.

"Looking for love in all the wrong places, sugar." The woman gulped her drink and wiped her mouth with the back of her hand.

"Say, Genie, why'nt you and me go outside and see if we can discuss my other two wishes."

He hopped off his stool, and she led him by the hand to a blue minivan with a DO NOT DISTURB bumper sticker on its dented, slightly rusty back end.

"Genie, I think this could be the start of a beautiful something or other." He quickly scanned the parking lot before pulling the van door closed.

Thirty minutes later, Lenny pulled into the parking lot of the Piggly Wiggly. He bought a bunch of carnations, a box of Russell Stover candy, and some breath spray, then drove back to Martha Maye's house. He sprayed some breath freshener in his mouth, combed his hair straight back with his fingers, and headed for the front door, whistling "You Are My Sunshine." Genie had put an extra spring in his step.

Martha Maye opened the door with a wary smile. He looked her up and down, taking in her fitted jeans and red blouse before handing her the flowers and box of chocolates. "Candy is dandy, but liquor is quicker. Offer me a drink, baby."

She held the door open for him, and he managed to brush up against her as he came in the house.

"Lenny, thank you for the chocolates and flowers. That was awful nice of you. I'll pass on the candy right now, though."

He stood looking from the box to Martha Maye.

"Oh. Would you like some?" She unwrapped the cellophane from the box and held it out to him.

"Don't mind if I do." He proceeded to pinch three of the chocolates until he found the flavor he wanted. He saw her watching him and felt flattered.

"I noticed you ate the vanilla cream—my favorite." She put the lid back on the box and set it on the hall table before walking to the kitchen.

"Heck, it's my favorite, too," he said petulantly.

"Would you like a beer?" she asked over her shoulder.

"Does Dolly Parton sleep on her back?"

Reaching the refrigerator, she turned briefly to roll her eyes at him, then reached inside, took the cap off a bottle of white ale, and handed it to him. "Don't be crude. And here I thought maybe you'd changed."

"Oohwee, you done got all fancy on me, girl. Rolling Rock White Ale? You must be sitting in high cotton. Y'ain't got no Colt 45? You know that's my favorite."

"I wasn't exactly expecting you to stop by when I went to the store a few days ago." She led him to the den.

"'Zactly who *were* you 'spectin when you bought it?"

She sat in a chair opposite Lenny, who sat on the sofa, and ignored his question.

"Whatchew doing all the way over there, sugar plum?" he complained. He put his feet up on the coffee table and patted the seat beside him, looking at her with puppy dog eyes.

"Lenny, what do you want? And get your feet off my table."

"You, baby, I just wanna be with you."

"Yeah? Well, I'm done being a maid and a cook. I haven't missed waiting on you hand and foot, and I haven't missed your indifference, your condescension, or your temper. I've had a taste of freedom, and let me tell you, Leonard *Skynyrd*, it tastes mighty good."

"Well, haven't you become little Miss Spunky?" He laughed. "I like it. You're sexy as Hell, Marty." He scooted closer to her. "I know I done you wrong before, I know I was a jackass, but here I am on my knees." He actually got on his knees and knelt before her, clasping her hands in his. "I'm literally begging your forgiveness and asking for another chance."

She shook her hands loose. "Oh, Leonard, get up. You're making a fool of yourself."

"I'm a fool for you, baby," he drawled, conjuring tears in his eyes.

"Tell me about your plans. How are you gonna make it up to me and Butterbean?"

He laid it on thick. "I plan to be the best car salesman Goose Pimple Junction has ever seen. I'll sell car after car after car, and pretty soon I'll own that place. Once I've made a little money, I'll buy you a house for the three of us to live happily ever after in." He paused and then added with a wink, "Maybe we can even make it the four of us."

She stared at him. "Who are you and what have you done with the hooligan I left just three months ago?"

"Hey! Watch your mouth, baby. Let's just say I've seen the error of my ways. I'll even start going to church with y'all every Sunday, and afterward we can go to Applebee's over in Washington County." He looked at her for a moment and then said, "Just what is a malcontent, anyway?"

She ignored him. "You'd start going to church with us?"

"I said I would." He made every promise he could think of and none he planned to keep. He could tell she was wavering and decided not to push his luck.

"I've given you a lot to think about. Even though I'd like nothing more than to put my hands all over that hot new bod of yours, I'm going to show you what a changed man I am. I'm going to leave before I lose control of myself."

With that, he got up, kissed her on the cheek, and started to leave. At the door, he turned around. "I'll show you, baby. Just give me a chance. Sure as the vine twines 'round the stump, you are my darlin' sugar lump."

Walking to his car with a smirk on his face, he thought, *Check step five off the list. Or was it step six? I really need to find that list.*

MARTHA MAYE sat in the chair in which Lenny had left her and wiped the sloppy kiss from her cheek. She wanted to believe him, for Butterbean's sake, but she wasn't sure.

And then there was Johnny to consider. There had been something between them since the moment she flew into his arms after the kidnapping. Maybe it was just that he'd helped save her, and he'd been the first person to make her feel safe again. She could still picture him standing there in his state trooper uniform, looking large and in charge. She thought it was more than just hero worship, though. She felt happy when she was with him. She found herself thinking about him during the day. He was sweet, brave, and thoughtful. He made her feel special. They had intelligent conversations, he listened to her when she talked, and he didn't make her feel dumb. Why couldn't it be that way with Lenny?

Because Johnny made her feel like a woman—like a desirable woman. "You make me feel like a natural wo-man," she sang softly to herself, hugging a throw pillow and picturing Johnny's smile.

No, Lenny isn't going to make me change my mind so fast. He's going to have to prove himself, if he can. And by gosh, I am going to have coffee with Johnny. And maybe even dinner.

AT A Blue Million Books, the bookstore Louetta owned, she and Tess were going through their closing rituals for the day. Lou counted the cash register, while Tess straightened up the tables.

"Lou, did I see Caledonia in here earlier?"

Lou put her finger in the air to indicate she needed another minute. When she finished counting, she looked up and said, "Yeppie. She and Peanut were in just to bring Peekal some supper. She says she doesn't see much of him anymore, what with him over to my house all the time with Charlotte."

"That's sweet." Tess picked up a brown leather book. "I like this journal with the marigold on the front."

"I do too, Tessie. I'm gonna order more."

"I think that's just about it for tonight." Tess walked toward the back room.

"Is Jackson coming to get you to—" Lou stopped speaking when the bell over the door jingled. Tess saw a tall, good-looking man with a beer belly, slick-backed dark hair, and pork chop sideburns reminiscent of Elvis Presley walk in.

Where's your white sparkly jumpsuit? Tess thought.

"Evening, ladies," Elvis said.

"I'm sorry, we're closed for the night—"

Lou interrupted Tess. "We're closed forever to the likes of you, boy." She squinted at him, so narrow they were almost closed.

"Aw, Lou, you ain't got no call to treat me that way. I *am* your granddaughter's father, after all. And I'm a changed man —and I mean to prove it to all y'all."

"Lenny, a steaming pile of poop may stop steaming, but it's always gonna be a pile a poop. Don't you try to sweet-talk me, boy. I'm so old I owe Jesus a nickel, and I know a thing or two." Lou had her hands on her hips, radiating disgust. A natural pink flushed underneath the red rouge on her cheeks.

"I want you to know I feel just awful about the way I treated Martha Maye, Louetta. I got a wake-up call when she left me, and I'ma prove to y'all that I'm worthy of her taking me back. I got a job rightcheer in town, and if you'll just give me a chance, you'll see."

Lou glared at him and said, "That don't butter no biscuits."

"Huh?" Lenny scratched his head.

"I can say I'm Minnie Pearl, but that don't make it so."

"Who?"

Louetta glared at him, while Tess gawked.

"Louetta, if I'da knowed better, I'da done better. Now I know better.

All's I ask is that you keep an open mind and urge Martha Maye to do the same. I know how much stock she takes in your counsel."

"You want me to tell my daughter to give you another chance, even when every fiber of my being is screaming, 'Do not give that heathen one iota of anything'?"

"Even then." He nodded vigorously. "I'll prove to you both I'm not the same man who drove Marty away. I freely admit it was all my fault before, and I aim to make it up to her."

Lou eyed him for a long moment. Tess stood by silently, unsure of what to do. Her eyes went from Lenny to Louetta.

"Whatchew think, Tessie?"

"I . . . I . . ." Tess was saved by the bell over the door when Jack walked in. He looked at all three of them, arched an eyebrow, and closed the door.

"Everything all right in here?" he asked, looking from person to person and walking over to Tess. He kissed her on the cheek.

"Tess, Jack, this here's my son-in Martha Maye's ..." Lou stammered and finally settled on, "Buttabean's father, Leonard Applewhite."

"Call me Lenny." He strode forward in three broad steps, holding his hand out for Jack to shake. He shook Tess's hand too, reluctantly and limply, as they all exchanged pleasantries.

"Well." He looked around nervously. "I won't be keeping y'all any more. I just wanted to stop in and say hey." He moved to Lou, leaned in, bobbed awkwardly from one side to the other, and finally gave her a quick kiss on the cheek. "Abyssinia." He turned, strode quickly to the door, and then he was gone.

"Abyssinia?" Tess was puzzled, and as always, she looked to Jack for a translation.

"I'll be seein' ya," Southerner Jack translated for Northerner Tess.

"Whatchy'all think?" Lou walked to the door and locked it with a flourish.

"He reminds me of Eddie Haskell," Tess said.

"My thoughts exactly," Lou said. "And if you lie down with dogs, you'll get up with fleas."

OUTSIDE ON the sidewalk, Lenny confidently strode to his car, saying under his breath, "Commence step three. I may not have won over the old bat yet, but it's a start. Purty soon I'll have them all literally eating outta the palm of my hand, licking my boots, and kissing my butt."

Thinking about what Lou said about biscuits, he twirled his key ring on his finger and thought, *Biscuits belong in the oven, but buns belong in the bed.*

SEVEN

You can hide the fire, but what'll you do with the smoke?

~Southern Proverb

On Saturday morning, when Martha Maye opened her front door, a bright red present with a big white bow sat in the middle of the doormat. She picked it up and read the tag.

To Martha Maye,
I'm obsessed with you!
From your secret admirer.

"Oh, for heaven's sake."

She opened the package and turned the pretty oval-shaped perfume bottle in her hands. Calvin Klein's Obsession.

Feeling her stomach plummet, she scanned the street but saw no one. "That's weird," she said out loud. "But then, so's talking to yourself." She tried to shake off the creepy feeling of someone watching her.

"Did you say something, Mizz Martha Maye?" Charlotte, who was babysitting, emerged from the kitchen with Butterbean following. They were both holding Barbie dolls.

"What's that, Mama?" Butterbean pointed to the box.

"Here, sweet pea. Will you put this on my dresser for me? I'ma be late if I don't get going."

"Can Barbie have some?" Butterbean asked.

"Sure, honey."

"Where'd it come from?" Charlotte asked, pointing the perfume bottle and spraying Butterbean's Barbie.

"Oh, somebody dropped it off. Probably one of my students. Y'all have fun, now. I'll see you later." Her eyes swept the street as she walked to her car, but she didn't see anything suspicious.

Ten minutes later, when Martha Maye walked into A Blue Million Books, Pickle was up on a ladder dusting and replacing books on the highest shelves. He wore cargo shorts, green Chuck Taylor sneakers, and a green T-shirt that said, AS A MATTER OF FACT I WAS RAISED IN A BARN.

"Hi, Pickle, hireyew?"

"I'm right as rain and twice as shiny." Pickle came down from the top of the ladder smiling his goofy smile.

"Mama said Aunt Ima Jean isn't doing well today. She asked me to fill in for her, at least for a while."

"Hey, that's mighty nice a you considering it's a Saturday. Don't teachers always sleep in on Saturday?"

"Not with a ten-year-old in the house." Martha Maye walked toward the office.

"Hey, Mizz Martha Maye, you know that pot of flowers that was out front next to the door?"

She turned back toward him. "The marigolds?"

"Yeah. When I came in today, it wasn't there. Mizz Tess said she didn't know what happened to it. Did Mizz Lou take it home?"

"I don't know why she would have, but I'll ask her."

"Okay. It's just that it's my job to water it, is all." He pointed to the back of the store. "Mizz Tess is in the back room."

"Thank you, sugar." She walked a few steps, then backtracked to the front window, turned the CLOSED sign to OPEN, and went to find Tess, who was, indeed, in the back room and had just taken a big bite of pineapple muffin.

"Hu, Marfa Mu." Tess's mouth was full of muffin.

She swallowed and tried again, hand covering her mouth. "Hey, Martha Maye." Offering a muffin, she added, "Sorry. I shouldn't be eating this, let alone stuffing my mouth full." She put the plate on the desk. "Your mother said you were filling in for her today. Did you bring Butterbean?"

Martha Maye puckered her lips, scrunching them sideways on her face. She sat down hard in a chair. "No, she's with Charlotte until her daddy picks her up. They're going to spend the day together."

She peeled back the muffin paper a little bit and took a small bite. "Oh my gosh, Tessie. Why'd you give me this? I'm trying to keep the pounds off, and here I go eating this. Oh, but my golly gosh, your pineapple muffins are delicious." Her eyes rolled back in her head as she savored the taste.

"Thanks. I know what you mean. I bake these for other people, and then I end up eating them." Tess studied Martha Maye. "You look like something's bothering you. Are you worried about Butterbean being with her daddy?"

Martha Maye put the half-eaten muffin on the desk and screwed up her face. "Are pork chops greasy?"

"You don't think he'll mistreat Butterbean, do you?"

"I don't reckon so. He's been a decent enough daddy. It's the husbanding department he sucked at."

"Was he ever violent with you?"

Martha Maye thought for a minute. "Not really violent, but I always thought he was on the edge."

"What do you mean, *on the edge*?" Tess tossed a final bite of muffin into her mouth.

Martha Maye picked at her muffin, putting another small bite in her mouth. She was trying to decide what, and how much, to say. Tess waited patiently.

Finally, Martha Maye said softly, "Well, there was one time when we were arguing. I don't exactly remember what it was about, but we were both fussing. He came over to me and put his hands on both my arms." She got up and put her hands on Tess's upper arms, just below her shoulders. "Right about here. He squeezed so hard, and I was so afraid . . . I started crying and begging him to let me go." Martha Maye shook Tess slightly, demonstrating what Lenny had done. Her brow wrinkled as she talked.

She dropped her hands and walked back to her chair. She continued, almost in a whisper, picking at her muffin. "He slapped me across the face. Said I was hysterical."

"Oh, Martha Maye. You must have been terrified." Tess moved to her friend's side.

"I was. And if I wasn't hysterical before he hit me, I sure as shooting was afterward. I broke loose and locked myself in the bathroom." While she'd been talking, she'd absentmindedly broken off little pieces from the muffin. She stared down blankly at what used to be the muffin but was now just a pile of crumbs. Lost in thought, she poked her finger around in the mess.

"Butterbean heard the commotion and came into the bedroom just as I slammed and locked the bathroom door. I don't know if she'd overheard all of what we said, but she saw Lenny banging on the door and yelling at me to come out. I could hear her screaming and crying, but Lenny was so full of rage he didn't appear to notice or care. Then I heard a loud bang and a crash, and I was more terrified for Bean than I was for myself." Martha Maye took a deep breath and let it out.

"I opened the door just as Lenny swept past Bean, who was screaming at the top of her lungs by then. I grabbed her up in my arms and locked us both in the bathroom. Both of us were wailing away, crying and slinging snot. A few minutes later, I heard him start the car and drive away. When I came out of the bathroom, I saw he'd thrown a lamp across the room."

As if coming out of a trance, when she finished recounting the fight with Lenny, she looked up, giving Tess a weak smile.

"Stuff like that." She crinkled her nose.

Tess had been quietly listening to the story with one hand on her friend's arm, but once Martha Maye finished, she wrapped her up in a hug. "Oh, sweetie, how horrible. Why didn't you leave him then?"

"I guess I was afraid. I talked to my minister about it. Not all of what I just told you, but enough. He prayed with me, told me where some shelters were, told me to always keep my keys by the door in case I needed to leave in a hurry."

Tess shook her head. "I'm not sure that was the best advice he could have given you."

"I don't think he ever would have counseled me to leave my husband, but he tried to make sure I was safe. Reverend James offered to talk to Lenny, but I never told him. If I had, he would have been livid."

"He would have been mad you talked to your minister?"

"Mad I told the minister about him."

"And so you stayed." Tess rubbed her back in slow circles.

"Until this past summer. Until I couldn't take it anymore."

A FEW hours later, Martha Maye looked out the store's big picture window and saw Lenny and Butterbean cross the street, heading for the bookstore. She hurried to the back room, telling Tess as she passed her, "Don't tell him I'm here."

"Tell who?" Tess was confused. Then Lenny stepped through the door. "Oh," she said under her breath.

He wore a New York Mets baseball cap, which he neglected to take off when he came inside. Tess smiled and greeted Butterbean. She looked coldly at Lenny. "Can I help you?"

"You're Tess, right?"

She nodded.

"I never forget a beautiful woman," Lenny said, pronouncing it *woe-man* as he always did.

She crossed her arms and glared at him. Pickle appeared out of nowhere and stood next to her.

"Who're you?" Lenny asked bluntly.

"Pickle Culpepper. Who're you?" Tess looked at him with amusement, and he added, "Sir."

"I'm Lenny. We were just looking for my *wife*."

"We want to take her to lunch," Butterbean piped up, bouncing on the balls of her feet.

"Oh. You just missed her. She left to go, uh, to go. . . " Tess looked at Pickle for help.

"She went to Lou's for lunch," Pickle blurted out.

"Oh, that's right. She went to Lou's." Tess nodded, thinking that was a smart choice because Lenny probably wouldn't want to see Lou. She gave Pickle an appreciative look, then turned to Lenny. "We'll tell her you stopped in."

After Lenny and Butterbean left, Pickle said, "He looks like a nice enough fella. Why'd Mizz Martha Maye want to hide from him?"

"People are like corn cobs, Pickle."

"I like butter-pops." He rocked from his toes to his heels.

"Yes, well, picture them still in their husks."

"Okay …"

"You never can tell which ones might be bad on the inside."

MARTHA MAYE wasn't able to hide from Lenny for the entire day. When she left the store later that afternoon, she saw him and Butterbean waiting for her on a bench in the shade. Butterbean ran up to her and handed her a small bunch of orange and yellow flowers. "These are from Daddy. I was just holding them for you. They're, they're called Chrysanthemumums."

"Chrysan-the-mums," Martha Maye enunciated. "And they're lovely. Thank you."

"Come on, Martha Maye." Lenny took her elbow. "Come check out the ride I have today. It's a 1987 Mercedes 420 SEL."

He led her over to a long silver Mercedes and opened the door for her.

"Where'd you get this, Len?" Martha Maye ran her hand over the leather interior as she got into the car.

"Big Darryl D says I can take my pick any time, and I picked this one today. Tomorrow it'll be something different. Maybe a 1998 Lexus."

Before Martha Maye knew what was happening, Lenny had backed out of the parking space and was headed out of town on a country road. He took them for an hour-long ride, and they stopped for dinner at Dough Boy, a pizza place Butterbean picked out. The sun was setting when he pulled into their driveway. Lenny had been on good behavior, and their outing had been pleasant.

"Thank you, Lenny. That was lovely."

Butterbean yawned. "Can Daddy come in and tuck me in bed?"

Butterbean's big dark brown eyes were persuasive, and her mother gave in.

On the way into the house, Martha Maye saw her next-door neighbor Estherlene Bumgarner on her front lawn. She told Lenny and Butterbean she'd be in after she spoke to her neighbor.

"Put the flowers in some water for me, Bean."

"Okay, Mama."

"Evening, Estherlene." Martha Maye walked up to her neighbor, who was watering some marigolds. The first thing one noticed about the older woman was her big hair. "Your flowers sure are pretty, and you're looking awful pretty tonight, too." Martha Maye was being a little kind. A petite woman with a slender figure, Estherlene looked to be in her sixties although she was in fact seventy-four. Despite her sizable ears and the ravages of time, she was still somewhat attractive for a woman of that age, even though she overcompensated with too much makeup and hairspray.

"Hidee and thank yew, Martha Maye. Hireyew?"

"Oh, I'm all right, I s'pose."

"That don't sound very convincing. Who's that you got with you over there in that highfalutin car?"

"Oh, that's my husband. My ex-husband. My husband." Martha Maye winced a little, crossing and uncrossing her arms several times as she talked. She didn't know how to categorize Lenny.

"So, which one?"

"Which one what?"

"Is he your husband or your ex-husband?" Estherlene used her wrist, since her hands were wet, to scratch her nose.

"Oh. To tell you the truth, I don't really know, Estherlene. I guess he's my husband since we're still legally married, but we're separated, so he feels like an ex."

"Zat right? I seen him driving by here a bunch, but he wasn't in that there car. Matter fact, I seen him in a bunch a different cars."

"You have? Heavens to Betsy. I wonder why. He works at Car Country, and his boss lets him drive any car that's available. That one's just the car of the day. Have you really seen him driving past the house?"

"Sure. I sit in the chair by that window and watch my stories." She pointed with the hose to the bay window on the front of her house, spraying the glass. "I see purty near everything happens on the street. Wouldn't forget a face like his. He's a hunk, Martha Maye. You sure you wanna give him up?"

"Oh, he's a hunk of . . . something all right," Martha Maye huffed. "And it ain't a hunk a hunk a burning love," she said under her breath.

"It wouldn't hurt him to stop by the gym every once in a while and work off some of that beer belly, but he could read me a bedtime story any day of the week."

"Estherlene! You're a married woman!"

"Married, yeah, but not dead. I can still window-shop."

"Believe you me, window-shop is about all you want to do with Lenny."

"Oh, honey, he's a man. I tell you, if they got tires and testicles, they's gonna be trouble. Count on it. But you gotta put up with the bad in order to have the good."

"What if all you do is put up with the bad?" Martha Maye asked, looking up at the light in the dormer window — Butterbean's room.

"Oh. Well, in that case, sugar, dump him like a hot tater. Let him be some other woman's problem."

"That's what I'm thinking. Night, Estherlene."

When Martha Maye went into the house, she found that Lenny had made himself at home. He had a beer in his hand and sat with his feet on the coffee table watching *The World's Dumbest Criminals* on TV.

"Big idiot," Martha Maye muttered.

"What's that, darlin'?"

"I said, that's appropriate," she hedged.

"Come over here and sit by me, precious." He patted the seat cushion next to him. Reluctantly, she did so, sitting sideways with one leg under her.

"Lenny, have you been driving by my house checking up on me?"

Lenny's face froze for a minute. He started to take his feet off the table, then sat back again, trying to act confused. He took a swig of beer.

"Checking up on you?" he finally said, a little too high-pitched.

"Uh-huh. Have you? Don't lie to me, Len. I already know the answer."

"Well then, Mart, why'd you ask?" She gave him a look, and he said, "It's not what it sounds like."

"I'm listening."

"I'm just worried about you and Carrie, and sometimes I drive by to make sure everything's copacedrin." He sat back, pleased with himself for spouting off such a big word. Martha Maye rolled her eyes.

"You mean copacetic?"

His face dropped. "Whatever. The point is, I'm just trying to watch out for y'all. You should be happy to have somebody care for you like I do."

Martha Maye sat for a few minutes, watching the show with him but not seeing or hearing it. When she thought she'd spontaneously combust if she sat there one more second, she got up and headed for the stairs.

"Where you going, doll?"

"To tell Bean goodnight," she said over her shoulder.

She hated reality TV, and she resented Lenny making himself at home when she'd only invited him in to tuck in their daughter. And she resented him checking up on her.

But as she climbed the stairs, she began to feel bad about her attitude. *Why am I being such a witch*, she thought. *He's been nothing but nice to me since he got to town. So what if he wants to watch a stupid TV show.*

Butterbean was on her bed playing with her dolls when Martha Maye walked into her room. She scurried to get under the covers.

"I thought you were sleepy." Martha Maye stood next to the bed, hands on her hips, looking down at her daughter.

"Well, not really. I just wanted Daddy to come in. We had a real fun day. I like being with him, Mama. Do you?"

Martha Maye reached under the covers, took Barbie out of Butterbean's hands, and then put her in the basket by the bed. She lay down on her side next to Butterbean, so they could look each other in the eye.

"Do you, Mama? Do you like Daddy?"

EIGHT

Satan loads his cannons with big watermelons.

~Southern Proverb

L enny walked into the Magnolia Bar, known to the locals as the Mag Bar, strutting his stuff. He'd started frequenting it because it wasn't as seedy as Humdinger's, the bar just outside of town, and it wasn't as upscale as the Silly Goose, which was located on the town square. He thought Humdinger's had too many ladies of the evening, and the Silly Goose had too many uppity women. He felt ladies of the evening were beneath him. As for the uppity women, he always had to make the first move, and none of them seemed to like his pickup lines, for some strange reason. The Mag Bar was just right for Lenny, and he had become a regular in the few weeks he'd lived in Goose Pimple Junction.

He walked past the bar, shouting his order to the bartender on his way to the jukebox. "The usual, Cash. My mouth is dry enough to spin cotton."

Cash was bald as a billiard ball and big as a bear. He'd boxed in the past, which had left him with a wide nose that made his narrow eyes more noticeable. A couple or ten broken noses will do that to a face. He wasn't exactly a champ, but at the Mag Bar, he was in his element. Cash served as owner, bartender, and bouncer at the Mag Bar, although he hardly ever had to put on his bouncer hat. For one, the bar was rarely that kind of place, and for another, people took one look at Cash and tended to toe the line.

Lenny sat in his usual seat at the bar as "She's Actin' Single, I'm Drinkin' Doubles" wafted from the jukebox. Cash set a bottle of Colt 45 in front of him.

"You're a little late tonight."

"Been over to the wife's place," Lenny said out of the side of his mouth. "But keep that on the down low, okay? I wouldn't want it to interfere with my love life." The two men guffawed.

"Aw, you dog, Lenny. I don't know how you do it, man. You got a different girl every night. And what's this about a wife?"

"Yeah, she's crazy about me." He took a pull from his beer. "But I need my space, you know? I told her we need to separate a while and see what's what. But she keeps whining for me to come over." His voice changed to imitate a woman's. "'Lenny, come see me, Lenny, spend time with me.' Shewee, that woman wears me out."

Cash snorted. "You must got something left. You pick up enough women over here." He wiped a glass dry, set it down, and reached for another wet glass.

"It's always been that way, Cash. Women are drawn to me like flies to honey."

"Yeah, well, it seems like some men are, too. Two of them have been in here looking for you the past few nights."

Lenny had put the bottle up to his lips, but he pulled it away without drinking and set it on the bar. "What did you tell them?"

"They didn't look like the friendly type, so I told them I didn't know you, hadn't seen you, couldn't help them."

"They hang around long?"

"Oh, an hour or so each time. Saw them talking to some others. What's working in your favor is that not many folks know you. I haven't seen the dudes around in a day or so."

"Thanks, Cash. I owe you one."

"One? Shoot, you owe me two or three." Cash took the glasses he'd dried between his fingers and turned to put them away.

Lenny looked over his shoulder to check out the pickings for the night before sauntering to the jukebox again. He punched "I'll Marry You Tomorrow, But Let's Honeymoon Tonight" and walked to a table of four women.

"Ladies! Each of you dolls pick a number between one and twenty. The one closest to the number up here"—he tapped his temple—"wins a dance with the Lenmeister."

All four women said in unison, "Zero."

One of them smiled sweetly and said, "But thank you kindly."

Walking back to his seat at the bar, Lenny's eyes followed one of the waitresses as she weaved in between tables. She looked like Daisy Duke with her low-rider denim cutoff minishorts and her red blouse tied at her stomach. His eyes traveled up her body but pulled over to park when, from the toned, tanned skin between shirt and shorts, the glint of a diamond stud piercing caught his eye.

"Need a Maker's Mark, Cash," the waitress said, leaning on the bar.

Cash looked on the shelf behind the bar. "All out up here, Darlene. Go in the back and get me a bottle, would you?"

She sauntered away, and as Lenny leered at her tramp stamp, Cash shook his head and said, "She has two speeds. Slow and stop."

"I bet I could rev her engine". He looked around the room again. "Kinda slim pickins tonight."

"You've missed some, coming in so late," Cash said, nodding to someone who'd just come through the door.

Lenny looked at his watch. "It ain't that late. S'only eleven o'clock."

"Just sit tight. Knowing you, somebody'll be along."

"I don't know. I got a mind to roll on over to Humdinger's."

Darlene came back with a bottle of Maker's Mark, breaking the red seal as she walked. Handing it to Cash she said, "I thought we just got a case of this stuff in."

"Did."

"Then how come there are four bottles missing already? I didn't think we went through the stuff that fast."

"Don't." Cash looked at her blankly. "That is mighty strange."

Lenny was on his fourth beer when somebody took the barstool next to him. He looked over and saw a woman who looked to be in her sixties, but who was fairly well preserved. She was dressed a little young for her age in tight jeans that accentuated considerable thighs, and a green shirt that looked painted on, highlighting a few rolls of fat around her middle. She wasn't fat, just aged. He thought she looked familiar, but he couldn't place her.

"Buy me a drink, sailor?"

"I ain't no sailor, but why not." Lenny lifted a finger to Cash, who came toward them. "Gin and tonic." Cash nodded.

"You're not from around here, are ya?" She batted her eyelashes at him. The wrinkles around her eyes, set on a leathery face, ruined the effect for him.

"Naw. I'm new in town." Finished with her, he looked around the bar again.

"I could show you around if you'd like." She wiggled in her chair.

"It ain't that big a place." His eyes continued to scan the bar.

"I bet I could show you a thing or two."

A woman in her mid-thirties with blond hair cut Farrah Fawcett style and jeans that fit her *exceptionally* well sat down on the other side of Lenny. She wore black boots with four-inch heels, and a bright red silky blouse with the top three buttons unbuttoned. She smiled shyly at Lenny and asked Cash for a strawberry daiquiri.

"Hey, hey, hey," Lenny said, turning on the stool so his knees brushed her thigh.

"Hireyew?" she said, her eyes checking out the ring finger on his left hand.

A vast file of pickup lines ran through Lenny's mind. "I hope you know CPR, 'cause, baby, you take my breath away."

She giggled and brushed her hair off her shoulder with a flick of her wrist.

"Allow me." His attention now totally on the younger woman, he peeled off some dollar bills and handed them to Cash.

The older woman sighed and got up. She ran her hand across Lenny's back as she walked away, saying, "See you around, sailor."

He bought Farrah two more daiquiris while he chatted her up. Thirty minutes later, he said she was in no shape to drive, and he insisted on taking her home.

OFFICER HANK Beanblossom walked into the chief's office Monday morning and plopped a bag of greasy donuts onto his desk.

"We got an issue, Chief."

"Oh yeah? A donut crisis? Is Jefferson hitting the sauce again and burning the donuts?"

Hank shot him a look. "No. Bernadette says this morning the phone's been ringing off the hook with reports of pumpkins being snatched off front porches."

"Pumpkins?"

"Yeah, you know, big round orange things with a stem? They're especially prominent in October. Some make pies out of them, some make muffins, or you can turn them into jack-o-"

"I know what a punkin is, goldernit," Johnny interrupted. "But why would anyone be stealing them?"

"I got no earthly idea. It takes all kinds, you know?"

"Are they smushed out on the roads?"

"Nope. They're just gone. Poof." Hank made a hand motion as if he were a magician making something disappear out of thin air.

"Okay. Call up the *Gazette*. Tell them to print a warning for people to bring in their pumpkins at night. Tell them to ask folks to be on the lookout for a pumpkin-stealing perp. Y'all warn folks when you're patrolling, and keep your eyes out for a pile of pumpkins stashed somewhere."

"Gee, Chief, it's not like a felony has been committed."

"No, but these things can get folks fired up. Let's try to nip it in the bud."

Hank reached in the sack for a donut. "Goose Pimple Junction: a hotbed of crime."

The men were laughing when Bernadette showed up in the doorway, arms crossed in front of her, a stern look on her face. "Two things." She held up two fingers in front of her. "A couple of bozos were in here asking about one" — she looked at a piece of paper in her hand — "Leonard Applewhite."

Johnny was biting into a powdered sugar donut but gasped slightly at the mention of Lenny's name. He breathed in powdered sugar and began choking and coughing.

"Chief, you all right?" Hank got up, looking like he intended to thump the chief on his back.

"Don't you dare." He held up a hand. "I'm fine," he croaked, through powdered sugar-covered lips. He looked at Bernadette. "What did they want with him?" He coughed twice more.

Bernadette motioned for Johnny to wipe his lips. "They just wanted to know if we had a resident by the name of Leonard or Lenny Applewhite, or if there were any arrest reports on someone answering to that name. I told them the only Applewhite I know in town is Martha Maye. And Butterbean, of course. So technically, that would make t—"

Johnny slapped his hand on his desk. "You don't give out information on our residents to total strangers," he bellowed. "Who were these clowns? Did they show some ID?"

Bernadette's face lost all color. "Shucks, Chief. I'm sorry." She looked like she was going to cry. "They flashed a badge, but I didn't look at it carefully. I just assumed —"

Johnny got up and went to Bernadette, taking her by the elbow and leading her to the chair in front of his desk.

"All right, Bernadette. I'm sorry I raised my voice. Start from the beginning. How long ago were they here? What did they look like? What did they say?"

"Geez Louise, Chief. What are you getting all exercised for?"

Johnny perched on the edge of his desk in front of her and rubbed his hand over his face. "I'm not worked up. Just tell me the whole thing from the beginning."

"Well, two men came in, they's dressed real nice, but they reminded me of Mutt and Jeff—you know, one real tall and the other one . . . not. They said they were detectives from"—she took a tissue from the box on Johnny's desk—"I can't remember where from, but they showed me a shiny badge, and the tall one said he liked my hair." She looked up at Johnny, who folded his arms across his chest and stared at her.

In a small voice, she said, "They seemed real nice."

Hank said, "That's about as useful as a prefabricated post hole."

"I see that now. But at the time. . ." She stopped to wipe her nose.

"Go ahead, Bernadette."

"Well, let's see. They said something like, 'We're here to inquire about one Leonard Applewhite, also goes by the name of Lenny. Do you know of this person?' I said no I did not. I said we have a Martha Maye Applewhite and a Butterbean Applewhite, but no Lenny Applewhite." She fidgeted with the tissue in her hands. "And that was about it."

"They didn't ask where Martha Maye lived?" Johnny wanted to know. The look on her face was answer enough.

"I . . . I . . ."

"Good heavenly days, Bernadette, you told them where Martha Maye lives?"

"No, I may have had a temporary stupidity attack, but it wasn't fatal." She looked down at her lap, and her voice softened. "I may have told them she taught up at the school."

Johnny let out a deep breath and ran his hand through his hair. He stomped around the desk and dropped into his chair.

"Have we learned a lesson today, Bernadette?"

"Yessir," she said timidly, pulling at the tissue still in her hands.

"Next time someone you don't know comes in asking questions, you direct them to an officer or to me."

"Yessir."

"What else? You said there were two things."

"Skeeter was just over to the diner. He says Slick told him a box of 'nanas is gone. Says he ain't never had a box of food stolen in all his born days." She stood up, shaking her head. "Pumpkins and 'nanas. This town is going to Hell in a hand basket." She left the office muttering, "Hell in a hand basket, Hell in a hand basket …"

"What in the Sam Hill is going on? Who's asking about Lenny, and what kind of bandit steals pumpkins and 'nanas?"

"A hungry one?" Hank shrugged his right shoulder.

Johnny dropped his chin and looked under raised eyebrows at Hank. "What're you doing standing around, Officer? Get out there and catch us a thief, and I want every officer on duty looking for these two mystery men."

THE BOX was sitting on Martha Maye's back step. She nearly stepped on it when she went out to take a bag of trash to the garbage can. This one was a white box with a huge red bow and had a tag on it that simply said, MARTHA MAYE.

It was late on a Saturday night, and Butterbean had been in bed for hours. A shiver passed through Martha Maye when she picked up the box, and it wasn't due to the cool October night air.

She sat at her kitchen table and opened it, curious what the secret admirer had left for her. Inside layers of lilac tissue paper, she found a teeny tiny lacy red negligee. When she picked it up, she noticed a note in the bottom of the box. Still holding the red lingerie in her left hand, she opened the note.

I dream of you in this, was all it said.

NINE

Many good cotton stalks get chopped up by associating with weeds.

~Southern Proverb

Jumping up from the chair, Martha Maye dropped the nightgown and the note as if they were two snakes.

Is this Lenny? No, it couldn't be. But if it's not Lenny, then who? Johnny? Absolutely not. Especially not this one. Johnny wouldn't do that. Should I call him? And say what? "I found a nightgown on my porch." That would sound real classy.

Feeling unsettled and worried, she tiptoed upstairs to check on Butterbean, knowing she was safe in bed, but needing the reassurance. She pulled the covers over her daughter's shoulder and looked down at her innocent sleeping face. *How could Lenny have fathered such an angel?*

She walked quietly out of the room, back downstairs, and called Honey, needing to talk to somebody.

Martha Maye explained to her friend about the newest present. Honey was well aware of the others.

"He appears to be ratcheting up the stakes, doesn't he?" Honey said after listening to her friend.

"What do you mean?"

"Before, it was kind of harmless stuff, right? A heart on the bulletin board, some flowers, a bottle of perfume. Now he gets into a personal area with intimate clothing. I think this person is crazier 'n a Bessie bug. Why don't you bring Butterbean over, and y'all stay the night over here?"

"No, I can't do that. I just wish I knew who was behind all this. It's starting to concern, not to mention irritate, me."

"At least let me come over and sit and talk for a bit. Help you calm down. Maddy Mack's asleep, but we can sit on the porch if you want. That way we'll see her if she should come downstairs."

"Okay, that'd be nice. Thanks, Honey." While she waited for Honey, Martha Maye went around her small house closing all the drapes and checking the locks on windows and doors. She hugged her arms to herself, determined not to cry.

JACK AND Tess sat on the couch in Tess's den. She was snuggled into him, with her head resting on his shoulder, his arm around her. A fire burned in the fireplace, and Jack's dog Ezmeralda sat across their laps—her rear end on Tess's lap and her head propped on Jack's leg.

"Jack, is something wrong? You've been kind of quiet tonight." Ezzie raised her head to see if there was any mention of food.

"Well . . ." He patted Ezzie's head, and she relaxed, propping her snout on her front paws, content to have Jack stroke her head and down her back. "Yeah, there is something on my mind," he said. "I know something about someone, but I don't know what to do about it."

"Hmm, I'm pretty sure you could be a little bit more vague." Tess patted Ezzie's rump.

"It's just that I've never been one to pry into someone else's business, but in this case, I know something maybe a friend should know."

"Then what's the problem?"

"It might also hurt the friend. And she might shoot the messenger."

Tess sat up straight and looked at him. "She. Do you mean me, Jack?"

"No, no, no. I'm sorry." He squeezed her with one arm. "No. The *she* is Martha Maye."

"What is it?" She maneuvered so that she faced him, displacing Ezzie's rump.

"You and she have gotten to be pretty close since the kidnapping."

"Well, going through something like that together does tend to forge a bond."

"Do you know if she's back together with Lenny?"

"I know she has her doubts. Evidently he's been putting on the full-court press. Why?"

"I saw him last night." He brushed her hair off her neck.

"You saw him? Where? With who?"

"Shouldn't that be with whom?"

Tess slapped the couch next to Ezzie, which made her jump. "Sorry, Ez. Jackson, quit stalling and tell me what you saw!"

"Okay, okay, don't get violent on me, woman!" He rubbed Ezzie's ears. "I was at the Mag Bar last night with Hank, and we saw Lenny there."

"Go on or I'll have to hurt you."

"You couldn't hurt a fly."

She raised one eyebrow at him.

"How *do* you do that?"

"Jackson!" Her tone was threatening.

"Okay, okay. I'll tell you. He wasn't alone, Tess."

"What do you mean he wasn't alone? You mean he had a date?"

"He didn't when he went in, but he sure did when he went out."

"He picked up a woman at the Mag Bar?" Tess screeched, standing up and displacing Ezzie altogether.

"I'm not sure if he was the picker. He might have been the pickee. But either way, yes, he left with a woman. And I don't think they left to go play cards."

"Just what do you think they left to do?" Tess said, half-serious.

"The way he was hanging all over her, I'd say there was a fair amount of hanky-panky going on."

Tess looked at him for a moment, trying not to smile. "Oh. You mean they were going dancing, only . . . naked?" Tess said, hands on her hips.

"Yep. In amorous congress." Jack got up and moved toward Tess, leaving Ezzie on the couch, watching them.

Tess backed up.

"Doing the four-legged frolic?" she said, smiling and moving so the couch was between her and Jack. She knew that look in his eye.

"Dippity doo da," Jack said, accentuating "da" and moving to his left. Tess moved to her left.

"Playing doctor?" Tess said, screeching and reversing direction when Jack faked left and went right, and almost faked Tess out.

"Parking the Plymouth in the garage of love," Jack crooned, continuing around the couch.

"Doing the bedroom rodeo."

Ezzie barked twice and jumped to the floor, joining Jack in the chase.

"Having a party for two," Jack said.

"Shaking the sheets." She held up her hands. "Okay, stop!"

"Lady, do you know how beautiful you are?" Tess let him catch her, and they fell onto the couch, with Ezzie nudging their arms with her cold, wet nose.

"Jack, I feel guilty."

"Yeah, I know. We're not married —"

"Oh, you." She playfully slapped his back. "I mean I feel guilty that we're making light of the situation, and this is Martha Maye's life we're laughing about."

"We're not making fun of Martha Maye's life; we're having fun with each other. There's a difference," Jack said, kissing her neck.

"Why are men such pigs?" Tess asked.

"Hey!" Jack raised his head, acting offended.

"Except for you. I lucked out with you, my handsome man." She pulled him back toward her.

"We both lucked out," Jack said, silencing Tess with another kiss.

When they stopped for air, Tess asked, "We have to tell Martha Maye, don't we?"

"Yeah, babe. I think we do. And you know the news will go over like a pregnant pole vaulter."

"Goose Pimple Junction Police, how may I help you?" Christine "Teenie" White, the nighttime police dispatcher, said into the phone on the first call of her shift, late Monday afternoon.

"Chief Butterfield, please," Martha Maye said urgently.

"Who may I say is calling?" Teenie held the phone to her pudgy face. At five foot two and one hundred-eighty pounds, she was anything but teenie. The older woman's permed and set hair was thoroughly sprayed into place and hardly looked the slightest bit different from day to day.

"Dolly Parton," Martha Maye said impatiently. "Teenie, you know who this is."

"I'm just following proper police procedure, Dolly. You don't have to get snippy."

"Teenie, I'm a little stressed at the moment. Can I please speak to him? Like NOW?"

"One moment, please." She spoke into the intercom. "Dolly Parton on line one."

A few seconds later, Johnny came on the phone. "Dolly, I stand corrected," he said with a smile in his voice. "You said you'd call me, but I didn't believe you."

Martha Maye spoke a mile a minute. "Johnny, I didn't want to bother you with this, but Saturday night somebody left a package at my doorstep, and today I think somebody's been in my house." She finally took a breath.

He sat straight up. "I'm putting you back on with Teenie. You stay on the line with her until I get there. I'm on my way. Be there in a jiffy." Johnny punched a button on the phone, dropped the handset, and ran out of his office.

TEN

A sharp axe is better than big muscle.

~Southern Proverb

Johnny was true to his word. He arrived at Martha Maye's house three minutes and twenty-four seconds after he hung up the phone. Martha Maye was waiting outside for him.

"You okay?" Johnny rushed up the walk, his face full of concern.

"I'm okay." She nodded. "Just really scared."

"What happened?"

She sensed he wanted to reach for her. And she wanted him to pull her into his arms and comfort her. But he didn't. He was, after all, there in an official capacity. And she really hadn't yet given him the green light to be anything but official. At that moment, she sorely wished she were divorced. She led him inside.

"I came home from school and found this on my kitchen table." She handed him a homemade CD. "I was so scared, I grabbed my phone and hightailed it outside to call you, thanking my lucky stars that I sent Butterbean over to Mama's after school."

Johnny looked at the CD in his hand. "What's on it?"

"C'mere and hear for yourself." She put the CD into a player, and the song "If I Had Shot You When I Wanted To, I'd Be Out by Now" came on.

"What the—"

"That's not all." She hit Skip and then pressed Play. Johnny looked at her questioningly. Her eyes went to the CD player, not able to hold his gaze. She held up one finger. "Just wait."

A new song came on: "My Head Hurts, My Feet Stink, and I Don't

Love You."

"Mart, are you kidding me?"

She slowly shook her head. "I wish I were. Hold on, that isn't all, either." She pushed Skip again, and when she hit Play, a third song came on: "You're a Hangnail on My Heart, and I'm Gonna Cut You Off."

"Great day in the morning, Martha Maye. This was on your kitchen table?" Johnny's voice was an octave or two higher than normal.

"Yes sir," Martha Maye sank into a chair and put her face in her hands. "All wrapped up in a pretty package."

"Who would do that?"

"Don't you think I would have been forthcoming with that information if I had it?" Martha Maye's tone came out harsher than she meant. Her head snapped up, and she saw that Johnny looked hurt, so she added, "How about I get us some sweet tea?"

Johnny called the station while Martha Maye poured sweet tea over ice in two glasses. She cut a lemon and put the wedges in a small bowl shaped and hand-painted like a lemon, and she put some Mississippi mud bars on a plate. She couldn't help stealing glances at him through the doorway.

The man sure is handsome in a uniform. Heck, he looks good in anything. Matter fact, I'll bet he'd look real good in nothing, too. Martha Maye was so surprised she was having such impure thoughts, she jerked her hand up to her mouth, knocking the lemons out of the bowl, spilling the yellow wedges all over the table and sending the scent of lemon through the air.

Johnny came into the kitchen. "One of my officers will be bringing some things over. What in the world happened?" He bent to help her pick up the lemons.

"I must be all butterfingers today." She washed the lemons and put them back in the bowl.

While they sat at the kitchen table and waited, Martha Maye admitted to him about the gifts.

He listened intently without interrupting her until she finished. "You've got yourself a stalker."

"I know." She slumped back against the chair. "I'm scared, Johnny."

"Why'nt you tell me about this stuff before now?" Hurt, puzzlement, agitation, and concern played across his face.

She shrugged. "At first I thought it was just harmless, maybe one of my students. Then, to tell you the truth . . . oh Lordy, this is embarrassing." She put her head in her hands.

"Tell me, Mart." Johnny reached over and touched her arm.

"See, at first I thought maybe the gifts were from you, Johnny. I don't mean to be presumptuous, and maybe I just hoped they were from you," she said, finding the palms of her hands intensely interesting.

"Mart, number one, I like your presumptions." He leaned forward with his elbows on his legs, dipping his head down so he could look at her face. "And number two, I wish I'd thought of it—except for the last two *gifts*, and number three," his voice softened, and he reached for her hand, "I'm awful glad you hoped they were from me."

His hand engulfed hers, and they stared at each other for a long moment. Johnny opened his mouth and then closed it when they heard Hank knock on the door and let himself in.

"Yoo-hoo, anybody home?"

"In here," Johnny called, clearing his throat and standing up.

"Chief, I brought those things you asked for," the officer said, coming into the kitchen. He held a black box by its handle in one hand and a sizable toolbox in the other.

"Thank you, Bean. I want you to dust for prints. There wasn't any sign of a break-in, so dust all the doorknobs, do the countertop—oh Hell, you know what to do, just go do it. This is a B&E, no doubt about it, but she doesn't think anything was taken. In fact, it was a backward B&E."

Hank's brow furrowed, and he looked quizzically at the chief.

"The perp left something instead of taking something," Johnny explained.

Hank looked confused but just said, "Yes sir, Chief."

Johnny took the toolbox and turned to Martha Maye.

"Mart, I'm going to install some dead bolts."

"Excuse me?" Martha Maye stared at him.

"You need dead bolts on your doors. I'm putting them in right now."

Martha Maye's brow furrowed. "Sure." She nodded. "Okay." Another nod. "Thank you." She stood and watched him install an extra lock in the front door as if he were her hero, then she followed him to the kitchen and watched him go to work on the back door. Johnny looked up at her at one point and saw her watching him.

"What?" he asked.

"Thank you, Johnny. Just . . . thank you." Martha Maye paused, and then her head jerked up and she added, "Is it okay if I call you Johnny when you're on duty?"

Honey interrupted Johnny's answer when she suddenly rushed into the room. "What in the Hell's bells is going on over here? Why are there two police cruisers here?"

"My secret admirer left me another gift. This time it was inside my house."

"Oh my gosh!" The last word came out as two syllables: gow-ush. She hugged Martha Maye, and then held her at arm's length. "Sweetie, are you all right?"

"I am now."

Honey looked at Johnny working on the lock. "You moonlighting, Chief?"

"All in the line of duty, ma'am."

"Ma'am. Pshaw." She gave him a mild scolding look, but he was intent on his work and didn't see it. "I'm only thirty-five. You call me ma'am again, and you'll have to arrest me for assaulting a police officer."

"Honey, he's just a polite gentleman," Martha Maye cut in, before things got out of hand. She could see Honey's feathers were ruffled even as she joked.

"I just can't believe all this is happening to you, Mart. How do you think he got in?"

"Don't know. There isn't any sign of a break-in. Nothing's broken or torn up."

"But she didn't have the best of locks on her doors, either," Johnny said, his eyes on the screwdriver in his hand. "One putty knife's all a person would need to get through those old locks."

Honey sat at the table and picked up a thick chocolate brownie with nuts and marshmallows, topped with an inch of chocolate icing. "Ooh, Mart, you know I love your Mississippi mud bars."

Officer Beanblossom appeared in the kitchen doorway. "I think I got everything except for in here. Hidee, Ms. Winchester," he said, seeing her at the table.

"Well, hidee yourself, big boy." She exhaled a grunt through her nose. "'Ms. Winchester.' 'Ma'am.' Y'all are enough to break a girl's heart."

"Honey, they're on duty. They're just being professional. Don't take it personally."

She studied her fingernails and mumbled, "I'm a person. I take everything personally." Honey crossed her longs legs, sat back, and looked up at Hank through her eyelashes. "In that case, do you want to frisk me, Officer Beanblossom?"

Hank blushed, as Johnny said, "Negative. But he would like to take your prints." He stared pointedly at Hank.

"Oh. Yeah. Right." Hank was flustered. He set the box down with a loud clang and fumbled with the latch. "I should get both of y'all's prints for exclusionary purposes."

Hank moved to the table and sat down next to Honey. She slowly licked the sticky chocolate residue off her fingers while she held Hank's eyes. Red flushed across his face again and he looked away nervously. "I . . . I think Butterbean's will be evident 'cause they're so small," he stammered, getting the materials ready.

"Are you gonna fingerprint all my friends and family?" Martha Maye asked. "There must be a lot of people's fingerprints in here."

"Y'all will need to wash your hands before he fingerprints you." Johnny stood up and tried the dead bolt he'd just installed. "Well, whatta you know. It works." He handed Martha Maye a key. "You'll have two different keys for your locks until you can get a locksmith over here to change them and give you one key for all of them."

Hank began putting the materials back in the black box. "We're all set, Chief. I'll take all this back to the house and see if we get any hits."

"Why are you taking them home?" Martha Maye asked.

"Not home. The house. The station house."

Honey excused herself and walked the officer out, wiping a lemon on her fingers to remove the ink. Putting the tools away, Johnny turned to Martha Maye and said, "You know, Mart, we never did have that coffee."

"No, sir. No we didn't, Chief."

"Oh, stop with the 'Chief' talk."

She laughed softly, handing him the tools.

"It's past quitting time for me," he said, returning to his point. "How about we go now?"

"It's pretty near dinnertime now, Johnny, and I'm supposed to go pick up Butterbean from Mama's."

"Maybe she could stay at Lou's a little longer, and we could stretch coffee into some supper. If it's all right with you," Johnny added quickly.

"Well, I s'pose they won't mind if Bean stays a while longer. Let me call and see."

Ima Jean answered the phone. "Leggo my Eggo."

"Aunt Imy, you're using the phone, not the toaster," Martha Maye said gently.

"Who's that behind those Foster Grants?" Ima Jean shot back and Martha Maye suppressed a laugh. "It's me, Aunt Imy, Martha Maye. Hireyew?"

"Somebody stole my waffles."

"And your marbles," Martha Maye whispered under her breath. Louder she said, "Waffles? I'm, sorry, Imy. Say, is Mama there?"

Lou came on the line. "What's up, darlin'?"

"Aunt Imy sounds in rare form."

"Oh, just another day in the nuthouse." Lou whispered, "She thinks someone stole our waffles outta the freezer. I tried telling her Pickle prolly just ate them, but she's all agitated about it." Lou changed to her normal voice and said, "What's going on, hon?"

"Mama, can Butterbean eat with y'all and stay just a while longer?"

"Of course she can. You all right?"

"I'm fine, Mama. I'm just going to get a bite to eat with Johnny."

"It's about damn time," Lou shouted. Martha Maye's eyes shot to Johnny, wondering if he'd heard her mother. Judging by his grin, he'd heard.

She turned her back to him, closing her eyes and pinching the bridge of her nose. "Okay, Mama. I'll be over to get her in about an hour or two. Make sure she does her homework."

She wanted to end the call before her mother could embarrass her any further, but Lou's voice boomed out of the receiver: "Take your time. Don't you come for Bean for at least two hours. Not a minute before. I mean it!"

THEY DROVE to the diner in Johnny's car. Walking in the front door, they saw two old men were at the counter as usual.

"So she says to me, she says, 'The row's crooked.' And I says back, 'You can plant more in a crooked row, woman. Don't you know that?'"

"Women," the other man said, shaking his head.

"Hidee, Clive. Earl." Johnny raised his hand in a greeting to the two old men, permanent fixtures on the diner's front stools.

"How do, Chief, Martha Maye." Clive turned on his stool to speak to Johnny. "Say, Chief, did you catch that hardened criminal?"

Confusion showed on Johnny's face.

"The one stealing all the punkins in town? It's like the Grinch switched holidays."

"We're still on the hunt. You hear anything, you let me know, okay?"

"Sure thing, Chief. I'll tell you what—whoever it is doesn't have all the dots on his dice."

"I'd say that's an accurate assessment." Johnny gently pushed on the small of Martha Maye's back, urging her to lead them to a table.

"I seen it all," Clive said, turning back around.

"Seen it all, done it all, can't remember most of it," Earl said.

As Johnny and Martha Maye made their way to a booth in the back, he said, "You think Earl's interested in a woman? We could introduce him to your aunt." Martha Maye poked him in the ribs, shaking her head and stifling a laugh.

Martha Maye felt like everyone's eyes in the crowded diner were on them as they sat down.

"I don't know if this was such a good idea, Johnny. I feel as conspicuous as the Emperor in his new clothes."

"Mart, there isn't anything wrong with two friends having dinner together."

"You know that, and I know that, but does everybody else know that?" Her eyes self-consciously swept the room. Several people were sneaking glances at them.

"I don't give two hoots and a holler what everybody else thinks. What you think is all's important to me." Johnny looked at her with an intensity that made her heart pound in her chest and her mouth go dry. Before she could respond, Junebug appeared at the table.

"Hirey'all tonight?"

"We're hanging in there like loose teeth, Junebug, hireyew?" Johnny answered.

"I'm having a good hair day, and that's about all I can ask for." Junebug took the pencil out from behind her ear. "What can I gitchy'all?"

After they ordered, Junebug started to head for the kitchen when she suddenly reversed course and came back to the table. "Almost forgot to tell you the latest, Chief. We're missing a peck of apples. Add it to the list, 'kay?"

"Okay, Junebug." Johnny sighed, taking out a notebook from his pocket and making a note in it. "Will do. Where'd they disappear from?"

"Out back. Deliveryman stacked up some boxes by the back door. By the time we hauled everything in, and I checked it all off, we was short. I called him right up, and he swore he delivered it. I believe him. We ain't never had any problem with him before. He's as honest as a summer day is long." Junebug headed toward the kitchen, and Martha Maye looked at Johnny questioningly.

"Official police bidness," he said, with another one of his big grins lighting up his face. "I'd rather talk about you. You said you don't know who this clown could be who keeps sending you stuff, but do you have even the tiniest inkling? Somewhere to start?"

"No, Johnny, I don't. I mean, the obvious suspect is Lenny."

"Your husband."

"For the moment." Martha Maye gave him a weak smile. "I prefer to think of him as my future ex-husband."

"So, Lenny's the obvious suspect, but—there is a 'but,' isn't there?"

"But it's not his style. Lenny wants credit for everything he does if it's good, which isn't often, and that's another reason why I don't think it's him. Number one, he's never once in his life given me poems, lingerie, or perfume. And number two, he wouldn't send a gift anonymously. If he sent me something, he'd want the whole town to know it. That would be the only reason he'd do it—for the brownie points."

Junebug brought two glasses of sweet tea and a basket of corn muffins. "Rest'll be out in a jiffy."

Johnny took a drink. "Anybody at school you can think of?"

Martha Maye looked at the poodle skirt in the picture over Johnny's shoulder. She thought for several moments, then shook her head. "Nobody I can think of."

"It appears he's getting more personal, and by coming into your house, more dangerous with each new gift. Promise me you'll keep your doors and windows locked at all times."

"Yes sir."

"And you'll drive to school instead of walking." Johnny gave his stern police chief look.

"Yes sir."

"And if you see anything or anyone even the tee-ninceyest bit suspicious, you'll call me right away."

"Yes sir." Martha Maye couldn't stifle a grin. "Even the tee-ninceyest bit."

They looked at each other for a long moment, until Johnny said, "So ..."

"So . . . " echoed Martha Maye.

"Last time we talked, your husband was in town and wanted you back."

"That's what he said."

"And how's he doing with that proposition? If I may be so bold to ask."

"Johnny, I'd rather jump barefoot off a six-foot stepladder into a five-gallon bucket full of porcupines than get back with him."

"Good to know." Johnny's smile was wide, and his eyes were earnest, shining bright with possibility.

ELEVEN

Always drink pure water. Many get drunk from breaking this rule.

~Southern Proverb

L enny cruised by Martha Maye's house, not seeing any sign of life on the street except for the nosy old biddy neighbor sitting in the La-Z-Boy in her front window. Luckily, he'd picked a car with tinted windows this time. "Look all you want, old woman. You'll never know who's in this here car," Lenny said out loud.

He stopped at the four-way stop sign, turned right on Main, and drove toward the center of town, almost wrecking the car when he saw Martha Maye and the police chief come out of the diner.

That brazen hussy.

He whipped into a parking space across the street and watched in his rearview mirror as the chief helped Martha Maye into his car. When they drove away, Lenny put the gold Suburban into reverse, backed out, shifted into drive, and followed them.

Lenny watched Johnny pull into Lou's driveway. He drove past the house, did a U-turn, and parked several houses down, watching as the two drove into the house. His mind reeled as he waited. Martha Maye was out of control. He had to do something. *She's a married woman and going out on a date in broad daylight with another man. She's colder than a mother-in-law's tongue to me, and then she goes and flirts with the police chief in front of God and everybody.*

Lenny stewed about his wife until he saw her, their daughter, and the police chief come out of the house and get into the car. He followed them to Martha Maye's house and watched from the corner of the street perpendicular to Martha Maye's as she and Butterbean got out of the car. He turned off the engine and rolled the windows down, watching as she walked around to the chief's window instead of following their daughter inside the house.

She best not be kissing him good-bye in broad daylight. Act like you got some raising, woman. He could see her laugh at something the idiot cop said, her body language in full flirt mode. She shuffled her feet in the grit of the driveway, her hips swaying, while she talked and smiled into the car at Johnny. It was enough of a spectacle to turn Lenny's stomach.

Intently watching his estranged wife, a sudden "Boo!" from the passenger side startled him. He turned to see a woman's smiling face in the open window. She reached in and unlocked the door.

"You—"

"Hidee, sugar," she said. "Imagine finding you here."

"Don't I know you?" Lenny studied the woman's face, sure he'd seen her somewhere before.

"You don't mind if I join you, do you?" She didn't wait for an answer. She slid in next to him.

"Uh, well, actually, I kinda got a headache."

"In that case," she paused, with a mischievous look in her eyes, "I could kiss it and make it all better."

Lenny stared at her, dumbfounded. "Come again?"

"You know Martha Maye isn't coming back to you. Maybe I can help some of the hurt go away." Her fingers walked over the console and up his arm like a spider.

"Woman, you are batshit crazy." Lenny looked out the window at Martha Maye, who was still flirting with Johnny. "What are you doing here?"

"Whatta you mean what am I doing here? I live here. Don't you remember me? Allow me to introduce myself." She scooted closer to him.

"Is this some kind of a trick? Are you some kind of a Trojan Horse or something?"

"Oh, come on, Lenny. We're both consenting adults—"

"I am most certainly not consenting to anything with you, lady."

"Look at Martha Maye over there flirting with the chief of police, big as all daylights." She turned and craned her neck to see around the car's window frame, continuing to talk while she watched Martha Maye. "That should prove to you your wife is through with you. And why would you want her back, the way she treats you? Let me make up for that tonight."

Again he stared hard at her. "Huh?"

"I like you, Lenny. You're not afraid to go after what you want. I find that extremely sexy." She leaned over, letting Lenny get a good look down her shirt. "Are you actually going to say no to somebody like me?" she whispered.

"*Somebody* like you, I might not say no to. *You* you, yes, I most certainly am," Lenny said. He moved back as far against his car door as possible, feeling like a cornered animal. "I know what you're up to. You get me into a compromising position, and then you go running to Martha Maye saying I was unfaithful on her. Well, slam, bam, no thank you, ma'am."

She looked hurt. "I would do no such thing. Martha Maye is my friend, and I wouldn't want to hurt her. Besides, she's already made her mind up about you." She ran her hand through his hair and continued, "Come on, handsome. You and me. Let's have ourselves a between-the-sheets rodeo."

Lenny was pleased to finally see Johnny's reverse lights. He took the woman's hand in between his index finger and his thumb, holding it like it was germ infested. He removed it from his hair, dropping it in her lap.

"Lookit, this was a real nice offer, but my heart literally belongs to Martha Maye, and you will not tempt or trick me away from getting her back. Now, if you will kindly vacate my vehicle, I'll be on my way."

She let out a disgusted sigh. "Suit yourself, darlin'. You change your mind, you know where I live. But don't put all your eggs in her basket. She ain't coming back."

Lenny rolled up his windows and drove past Martha Maye's house, where he caught a glimpse of her through a window. He slowed, contemplating going inside, but instead sped off in the direction of the Magnolia Bar. He really needed a beer.

It was almost completely dark when he turned into the Mag Bar's gravel lot. He parked his car and hummed the song "If I Can't Be Number One in Your Life, Then Number Two on You" while he walked across the parking lot. He heard the crunch of gravel behind him and turned around just as a punch hit his kidneys. He let out a loud "oomph," and another blow landed on his lower jaw.

"Remember us?" Eyebrows said, shaking the pain out of his hand.

Lenny moaned, but a fist landed in his midsection, knocking the air out of him.

"You thought you could run from Solly? Solly gives you a loan outta the goodness of his heart, and you skip out on him?" Eyebrows stood over Lenny. "Ha," he said as he kicked him in the ribs.

"Ha!" Joey echoed.

"Listen, listen, listen, dude, I can make a payment. I been gainfully employed," Lenny rasped.

"Yeah, *dude*, we're gonna take your payment. But first we're gonna take a chunk outta your hide."

"A chunk," Joey said.

They were between cars, but Lenny could hear voices as people came out of the bar. He opened his mouth to yell, but Eyebrows stepped on his stomach, and he couldn't breathe, let alone speak.

The couple passed, got into their car, and drove away. Eyebrows, finally lifting his foot off of Lenny, turned to Joey and said, "Scalpel, please, nurse."

"Scalpel," Joey said, handing him a Louisville Slugger.

Lenny began begging. "Wait, wait! I'm trying to tell y'all, I can literally give y'all two thousand right now. You d —"

"Give it," the man grunted.

Lenny dug in his pocket and came up with a wad of bills.

Eyebrows quickly counted the cash. "That's just a drop in the bucket, Len. Sol said to give you a message you wouldn't soon forget." He softly tapped the bat against his leg. "So here it is: You run again, and you're a dead man. You skip a payment again, and I'ma break both your legs."

"Both your legs." Joey stepped forward and nodded once to emphasize the threat.

"And here's some punctuation on that there statement."

As Eyebrows brought the bat up over his head, some people came out of the bar. Lenny made his move. He rolled under the car and began screaming his head off. Eyebrows swore and said, "We're not done with you, Applewhite," then they beat feet to get away from the onlookers.

THE NEXT day, Johnny pulled in front of the school right at dismissal time. He parked, put on his GPJPD baseball cap, and walked through the crowd of kids and parents outside, speaking to everyone he could. But instead of the usual "Howdy, Chief," today he was met with "Chief, did you catch that good-for-nothin' so-and-so who's taking our punkins?" and "Chief, someone picked all the apples off my apple tree. Whatchew gonna do about that?" And so on.

Johnny saw Martha Maye hand over her last student to his parent and turn to go inside. He quickly followed, excusing himself as he squeezed past people.

"Martha Maye!" he called down the hall, hurrying inside. She was halfway down the long hallway but turned when she heard his voice.

"Johnny! What are you doing here?"

"I was in the neighborhood. Thought I'd drop by and see if you and Butterbean needed a ride home."

"Johnny." She crossed her arms. "You promised you wouldn't worry about me."

"And you promised you wouldn't walk to school, but I don't see your car in the parking lot." She had a guilty look on her face, and he smiled as he pointed his finger at her. "Busted."

"You're not gonna arrest me, are you, Chief?"

They laughed, but Johnny raised his eyebrows and waited for an answer.

"Oh, all right. Come on back to my room with me and let me get my stuff. But hey, aren't you on duty? You don't have time to be taking women home for no good reason." She looked over at him and narrowed her eyes. "Or is this kinda like helping an old lady across the street? Is it your good deed for the day?" She led him into her room, then immediately stopped her babbling and froze.

The row of windows that lined the back wall of her classroom caught her eye. The bottom pane of each one had a newly spray-painted heart. Something had smashed into the middle of each heart, causing cracks to emanate from the point of impact.

Johnny drew his service revolver from its holster and stormed through the room, looking into every nook and cranny.

Martha Maye lifted her arms and then dropped them. "Johnny, for heaven's sake."

TWELVE

When your heart speaks, take good notes.

~Southern Proverb

Johnny strode with purpose toward the door leading directly outside and barreled through it with Martha Maye at his heels, but the schoolyard was empty. He scanned the houses that backed up to the school to see if anyone was outside, anyone who might have seen someone vandalizing the classroom windows. He saw no one. He put his gun back in its holster, and they both walked back into the classroom in silence.

"Were you going to actually shoot a vandal? He was probably only armed with a can of spray paint."

"Just a cop-ly reflex, as Jesse Stone would say. Can't help it. Besides, he could very well have been carrying." He smiled sheepishly. "I'm assuming the windows didn't look like that when you left the room. Ten to one it's Lenny's work, and the way I'm feeling toward him right now, it wouldn't take much for me to shoot first and ask questions later."

"I don't believe that for a minute. You wouldn't hurt a fly on purpose."

"Maybe not a fly, but certainly a roach."

"You really think Lenny did this?"

"Don't you?"

She thought for a minute while she moved around the room straightening desks. "I really don't think so. But I could be wrong. It just doesn't seem his style. If he has something to say, he says it. Like I told you, if he gives a gift, I've never known him to do it anonymously. Now the last little present that was left in my kitchen. . ." She blushed thinking about the skimpy lingerie someone had left on her kitchen table, " . . . that could be him, but I think if he were going to insult me or try to scare me, he'd do it in person." She went to her desk and shuffled papers, putting things in her tote bag to take home. "It's like he feeds off the reaction. If I'm pleased, then he feels like a hero. If I'm mad, then he revels in the fact that he can punch my buttons. I just don't see this as Lenny."

"Then who's doing this crap?" Johnny brought a handful of crayons that had been left on a table to Martha Maye.

"Thanks, Johnny." She took the crayons and put them in the orphaned crayon basket. "If I knew, I'd tell you, believe you me."

She sat down in her desk chair and saw an apple on her desk. It had a bite out of it, and a small note underneath.

I'd like to take a bite out of you.

Martha Maye pointed at it as if it were a snake, and Johnny examined it and carefully put it inside his notebook.

"Evidence," he said. "You got a paper bag anywhere? I'll take that apple, too. Send them both to a lab."

She carefully pulled a lunch bag from her desk and dropped the apple inside by the stem, while he looked around for a chair he could sit in. The only chairs in the room were for little people. She sensed his dilemma.

"Here, Johnny, you take my seat. I'm happy to say I can fit into these little seats just fine now."

"Thank you. If I managed to somehow get my butt into one of those, I don't think I'd get out of it without a surgical procedure. Assuming I didn't break it into toothpicks first."

Butterbean came into the classroom just then, and while she gaped at the broken windows, Martha Maye gave the bag with the apple to Johnny.

"Who did this, Mama?"

"That's what I'd like to know. I should call the office and tell them what's going on, or maybe I'll speak to them on the way out. They'll have to get someone to fix the windows."

"Is that why the chief's here?" Butterbean walked up to Johnny, studying the sack. "What's that?"

"Just a snack, nosy Rosey." Martha Maye turned her daughter toward the blackboard, kissing the top of her head. "Now get going on your chore."

"Can I have a snack?" Butterbean asked, turning to start her daily chore.

"After while."

Butterbean started on her job of erasing the blackboard and washing it with a wet rag.

Martha Maye turned to Johnny. "Since you're here, could I ask a favor?"

"Anything."

"Can you help me hang these paper witches the students made? You're tall and can reach up high better than Butterbean or me. I can hand them to you, and it'll get done in a jiffy."

While Butterbean worked on the chalkboard, Johnny and Martha Maye hung the construction paper witches on strings from the ceiling lights. When they were done, they stood back and looked at all of the colorful witches on broomsticks. They looked like they were flying around the room.

"I love it! Doesn't it look wonderful?" Martha Maye said gleefully. "Thank you, Johnny. That took just a fraction of the time it would have taken Butterbean and me to do it. Handing me the artwork while I hop on and off of chairs isn't her idea of a fun afternoon."

"I'm happy as all get out to help, Mart."

She cleared her throat and looked around the room. "All right then, I'm ready to go if y'all are. I just need to stop in the office and report the windows."

They walked to the front of the school, and Martha Maye turned for the office, while Butterbean and Johnny went outside to wait.

When Martha Maye came out of the building a few minutes later, she saw Johnny and Butterbean on the sidewalk talking to someone. It took her about two seconds to realize who it was. She hadn't laid eyes on him since the day of the kidnapping. An older man, he was short and fat, and looked kind of like a bulldog.

"Mr. Price. Hello. I didn't expect to see you here," she said haltingly to John Ed, the former police chief. "Are you back in town for good?" she asked, trying to be tactful, and trying to hide the anxiety she felt.

"Yep. Never really left. I just moved out to the country. I try to keep to myself. Folks around here don't cotton to me much."

Martha Maye made a sympathetic sound, and she *was* empathetic to his plight, but a part of her felt he deserved the treatment he was getting, and then she felt guilty for thinking that.

"'Course I can't say I blame them," John Ed continued. "I let everybody down by trying to protect my boy. I was derelecting my duty, I know that, although it does seem like some people would have a Christian attitude and forgiveness in their heart."

"That's all water under the bridge now, Mr. Price. Folks will come around. Just give them some time."

He looked at the ground for a moment and then up at Martha Maye.

"How's my granddaughter?"

"Charlotte's real fine, Mr. Price. She's getting along real nice."

"Yeah," Butterbean piped up. "She plays with me sometimes. I like her living with Granny."

"Do you . . . do you think she'd see me?" he asked, the hurt evident on his face.

"I think she'd like that. You're still kin, no matter what. Why don't you give her a call? Ask her to meet you at the diner or something? It's probably best not to go to Mama's house, at least for a while."

"Yeah. Yeah, maybe I will call Charlotte. Doubt we'll go to the diner. I'm not much welcome there, either. But I understand about your mama and them."

"Well . . ." Martha Maye hemmed.

"I won't keep y'all. I'm just out for a quick stroll. Y'all behave." He waved and shuffled on down the sidewalk.

Johnny drove them home and insisted on going inside to check things out before he left. When he'd made sure the house was safe, he walked outside and Martha Maye followed, wondering if they were ever going to go on a real date.

As they walked to his car he said, "Um, I don't suppose, uh, would you. . ."

Martha Maye cocked her head and looked up into his eyes. "Would you like to have dinner with me sometime?" She didn't realize she'd been holding her breath.

"I'd like that, Johnny," she squeaked out. "When did you have in mind?"

Johnny let out a relieved sigh, which made her smile on the inside, knowing he'd been holding his breath, too. "I'm on duty this weekend. How about next Saturday night?" he said, putting his hat on and grinning like a fool.

"Sounds great, but ..." she paused a moment, feeling embarrassed about what she was going to say. "Why don't I meet you there? I'm not exactly a free woman yet, and I don't want people to talk."

"Sure. I understand." Johnny nodded his head. He opened the car door, turned, and looked at her. "How about we meet at the restaurant in the Buttermilk Hill Inn? You know, that country inn about thirty miles out of town? Is that too far for you to go? I just thought maybe we wouldn't run into too many people we know, is all."

"That would be lovely. Seven o'clock?"

He got into the car. "See you then."

He put the car in reverse and backed out of the driveway. His wide smile pleased Martha Maye. She hoped she hadn't sounded too needy when she accepted his invitation practically before he got it out of his mouth. Then a thought struck her.

What in the world am I gonna wear?

"SHE IS literally clueless," Lenny said to himself. He sat in his usual surveillance spot just around the corner from his wife's house. "But then again, maybe she doesn't see me because she only has eyes for *Johnny*," he said "Johnny" with a high-pitched love-struck voice and then blew a loud, wet raspberry.

His cell phone rang, and he answered it. "Yes, Big Darryl. I'm just filling the car up. I'll be right back to the store."

He hung up and muttered, "Don't get your tighty-whities in a wad." Starting the car, he continued talking to himself. "I need to get outta here anyway before that crazy witch spots me again. That woman scares me. She must be outta her ever-loving mind." He drove slowly past Martha Maye's house. *But I'll be back, Martha Maye, darlin', count on it, just as sure as God made them little green apples.*

Lenny drove off toward Big Darryl D's Car Country singing off-key, "'Cause God didn't make little green apples, and it don't somethin' in somethin' somethin' in the summertime."

THIRTEEN

It's easy to get off a bucking mule.

~Southern Proverb

L enny cupped his hand around his mouth and called to his daughter, "You're literally slower than molasses running uphill in January." She stood in the field looking for the perfect pumpkin. "You don't have to get the biggest one out here, you know."

Martha Maye, Butterbean, and Lenny were at the Spurlock Farm U-pick pumpkin patch just outside Goose Pimple Junction. It was a perfect fall Sunday afternoon. The sun was high in the blue sky, with the temperature in the seventies. The trees were brilliant with yellow, red, and orange leaves that fluttered to the ground with a light breeze. Pumpkins dotted the field for acres. Butterbean was examining every one in the patch — and some of them twice.

"What's wrong with the first seven you picked out? You got a whole row here that look fine to me," Lenny grumped, pointing to the row of pumpkins lined up beside each other on a dirt path running alongside the pumpkin patch.

"Oh, now don't get riled up over nothing. She likes to narrow it down, you know that. We go through this every year," Martha Maye told him. "When she sees one she likes, she adds it to the lineup. Then, when she's ready, she'll stand back, look at them all, and make her decision." Martha Maye broke away from Lenny and joined Butterbean in the search for the perfect pumpkin.

Butterbean eventually had fifteen pumpkins lined up, and she picked the biggest, fattest, heaviest one of them all. Lenny picked it up, and they rode the hay wagon back from the fields, paid for Butterbean's twenty-two-pound choice, and Martha Maye's sixteen-pounder, and took them to the car. Then they headed to the petting zoo. Lenny exhibited more patience with his daughter there, going from pen to pen, talking to and petting the animals with her. He made up little stories to tell her as they visited the pigs, goats, and rabbits, and Martha Maye could see Butterbean was having fun. She wished she could say the same for herself. She couldn't get Johnny out of her mind, and she couldn't help but notice that even though Lenny was being sweet with Butterbean, he was checking out every woman in the vicinity.

"Can we go up to the restaurant and eat fried chicken, Daddy?"

"I reckon so." Lenny reached for his daughter's hand.

"And mashed taters with gravy and hot rolls?"

"You know it." He held his daughter's hand and put his arm around Martha Maye. They walked past the lake, squinting from the sunlight reflecting off the surface of the water. *What a perfect day*, Martha Maye thought. *Or would be if . . .* she sighed out loud. She wished she could keep her mind off Johnny.

IT WAS dark when Lenny pulled into the driveway. The three of them were drained after an afternoon and evening at the pumpkin farm.

Martha Maye kissed the top of her daughter's head. "Butterbean, it's a school night. Go in and get ready for bed, while your daddy and I unload the car."

"Okay, Mama."

After Lenny and Martha Maye unloaded pumpkins, gourds, and apples, she stood outside, propped her hands at the back of her waist, and lifted her nose into the air, breathing in the woodburning scents from someone's fireplace.

Lenny turned to her. "We had a nice day, Marty. It was nice being a family again." He walked up and wrapped his arms around her. She let him, until she felt his hands going south, then she pulled away.

"I'd better go see about Butterbean."

Lenny followed her inside.

"Baby, you're killing me. Why you always pull away like that? It's been too long. Come on, baby," Lenny pleaded, trying to pull her to him again, but she broke free.

"Lenny, it's been a nice day. Don't spoil it. I'm going to kiss Butterbean goodnight." He followed her upstairs and into Butterbean's room. Their daughter's face was shiny clean, her long brown hair brushed smooth, her pink nightgown the pinkest of pink.

"Is Daddy spending the night?" she asked, bouncing on her knees on the bed.

"No, honey. Daddy's going back to his hotel."

"I could spend the night," Lenny piped up. Martha Maye glared at him.

"Can he, Mama? Can he?"

"Not tonight," Martha Maye said firmly.

"Then can he read to me before he goes?"

"I suppose." She kissed her daughter goodnight and added, "Just a quick one."

Martha Maye went downstairs and out to the backyard for some air. She picked a handful of flowers from the waning garden, then took them inside. As she filled a vase with water at the kitchen sink, Lenny came up from behind and wrapped his arms around her. She jumped, splashing water over the countertop. "Lenny!"

"Ah, c'mon, darlin', let me get to know the new you." He propped his hands on either side of her on the counter, pinning her in. Pressing up against her, he attempted to kiss her neck as she squirmed.

"Getting that child to bed was literally like trying to nail Jell-O to a tree, but Carrie finally fell asleep. Now it's me and you time."

"It's you and me," Martha Maye snapped, trying to get out of his grasp, but he held her in place. "And no thank you."

"Okay, Miss Schoolteacher. Let's *you and me* go upstairs. I've literally been undressing you in my mind all day, sugar. Now let me do it for real." He had her pinned so tight she could hardly move.

"Yeah, me and every other woman you saw." She dropped her head and tried to duck underneath his arm. He wrapped both of his arms around her waist, keeping her from moving.

Hands grasping the edge of the sink, and in a deadly calm voice, Martha Maye said, "Lenny. Let. Me. Go."

"Aw, you don't mean that, precious. C'mon. Show Lenny some lovin'." He moved a hand down a little until it reached the hem of her shirt. She felt his hand on her bare stomach. As it began to travel upward and his other arm held her still, she tried again to squirm free.

"Lenny, I'm not kidding. Let me go, dabnamit."

"Not until you let me go, if you know what I mean," he said into her ear, his hand exploring under her shirt, his groin mashing into her backside.

She stomped on his foot, and he yelped but tightened his arm around her. With his other hand, he grabbed a handful of her hair, pulling her head back so he had a firmer hold on her. It hurt like fire to move even a fraction of an inch.

"Stop playing hard to get, baby," he said with his lips against her ear. "You know you want me." Keeping a firm grip on the handful of hair, he steered her around to face the kitchen doorway. And then he froze.

FOURTEEN

There's not much difference between a hornet and a yellow jacket if they're in your clothes.

~Southern Proverb

H oney stood in the kitchen doorway pointing a 12-gauge shotgun at Lenny. She chambered a round, making the *chink-chink* sound reverberate in the quiet kitchen.

"Leave her be."

Lenny recovered from his initial surprise and snorted out a laugh. "You won't shoot me," he sneered. "You'll hit Martha Maye." He held her as a shield in front of him, a handful of hair still in his grip, his other arm clamped around her middle.

"Seriously? You would seriously use me as a shield? I love how you're trying so hard to be a *changed* man, Leonard. I swan, you're sorrier 'n a two-dollar watch."

"Don't test me, buster. I took top honors in the ladies skeet shooting division at the 2012 Tennessee skeet-shooting meet.

"I tell you what, all y'all done lost your minds," Lenny said. "I—"

"Mama?" The little voice came from behind Honey. Butterbean stood in the doorway with a terrified expression on her face.

Lenny let Martha Maye go, pushing her roughly aside. "Screw it. She's as cold as a frosted frog anyway. It's okay, Carrie. Go back to bed." He turned and walked out the back door, slamming it after him. The door immediately opened, and he stuck his head back into the room, addressing Honey: "Lady, you shouldn't hunt anything smarter 'n you. Try hunting worms." And he slammed the door again.

Martha Maye's knees were about to give out, so she collapsed into a kitchen chair, and Honey and Butterbean ran to her. "You're okay, sweetie," Honey cooed, patting her back.

"Are ya, Mama?" Butterbean wrapped her arms around her mother and dug her face into her neck. "Are you okay? What was Daddy doing?"

Martha Maye returned Butterbean's embrace. "Yes, punkin, I'm okay. Sometimes your daddy just has a temper, and that's why . . . that's why I can't be married to him anymore. Understand?"

Butterbean pulled back, tears brimming in her eyes. She looked at her mother and nodded. "I understand," she said softly.

Martha Maye smoothed her daughter's hair and cupped her cheeks with both hands. "Everything's just fine now, darlin'. You gwon up, and I'll be right there to tuck you in." Butterbean nodded and reluctantly climbed the stairs.

Honey put the shotgun on the table and sat down next to her friend.

"How?" Martha Maye turned to Honey. "How did you know?"

Honey nodded her head toward the window over the kitchen sink. "I saw you through the window, silly. How many times have you and I waved to each other from there? I saw what was going on and came right over."

"Thank you." She shook her head. "I don't know what I would have done if you hadn't been here."

Honey put her arm around Martha Maye. "That's what friends are for, sweetie."

THE NEXT afternoon, Martha Maye dropped Butterbean off at Lou's house and met Tess at the diner for pie and sweet tea.

"I feel like I've been chewed up and spit out," Martha Maye told Tess.

"Why? What's wrong, Martha Maye?"

Junebug arrived at the table, set down two glasses of sweet tea, and squeezed into the booth next to Martha Maye, leaning into her. "She actually came in with a shotgun?"

"Who came in with a shotgun?" Tess looked from Martha Maye to Junebug.

"Shewee, news travels fast around here," Martha Maye said.

"Apparently not fast enough. What are you all talking about?"

"Honey," Junebug answered Tess. "She rescued our girl from unwanted advances from that low-down, good-for-nothing, dirty-cur dog."

"Yeah, she really did," Martha Maye said in answer to Junebug's original question. "She was like Little Orphan Annie—"

"You mean Annie Oakley?" Tess asked.

"Is that who I mean?" Martha Maye squinted.

Tess nodded.

"Y'all, she stood there in the doorway with the gun aimed right at him, and just as cool as a cucumber, she cocked it, or whatever you do to shotguns"—she waved her hands in the air—"and it made that *chink-chink* sound. Man alive, I bet Lenny left so fast on account he had to go change his shorts."

"It's a crying shame Butterbean had to see her father like that, but it's probably just as well that she sees who he truly is," Junebug said.

"Butterbean was in the room?" Tess asked, horrified.

"The commotion woke her up. She didn't see him pawing all over me, but she saw enough. I don't reckon she'll be asking for him to spend the night any time too soon."

"Did you report him to the police?" Tess asked.

"Naw. I just wanted to forget about it, and I don't want the whole town knowing my dirty laundry."

Junebug stood up and said, "Well, I won't let it go no farther than this table. I'ma get y'all some pie. Pie makes everything better, don't you know. Y'all stay put."

"This makes what I have to tell you a little easier," Tess said after Junebug went for pie.

"What's that?"

"It's one of those things where you need to know, but it won't be pleasant to hear."

"About Lenny?" Martha Maye asked, looking over the top of her glass as she sipped her tea.

"'Fraid so. Jack saw him leave the Mag Bar the other night with another woman. He said they didn't exactly look like strangers."

Martha Maye took a deep breath and let it out, ruffling her bangs. "You know, I don't believe you could tell me anything about that man that would surprise me anymore."

"I'm so sorry." Tess touched her friend's hand.

"Don't be. It's just another nail in his coffin, far's I'm concerned. I'm gonna tell my lawyer to get on that divorce PDQ."

"PDQ?"

"Purty dern quick."

"CHIEF!"

The call came from across the street, and Chief Butterfield saw Ernestine waving madly, hands over her head, in front of her store, Ernestine & Hazel's Sundries.

Not likely I wouldn't have heard her. Her voice would peel paint. He waited for a green Ford Explorer to pass, then crossed the street and walked over to her.

"What can I do for you, ma'am?" He tipped his hat as he reached her.

Glaring at Johnny, she stood under the store's awning out of the sun, with her hands on her hips. "I want to report more missing items from my store."

"Alrighty then, calm down, now. Tell me what's missing." He took out his notebook and pen.

"My inventory's short on candy, and some men's T-shirts and . . . unmentionables," she said, looking at his notebook instead of him.

"Unmentionables?" he repeated. "You sell, uh, *those* things in there?"

"Chief, we sell a little bit of everything in there. That's why it's called *sundries*. And nowadays we sell a little less, because somebody keeps coming in and walking off with my merchandise. I'd like to know what you plan to do about it." She crossed her arms. He looked closely at her ears, checking for signs of smoke.

"Ernestine, I appreciate your position, and I assure you we're doing everything we can to apprehend the culprit."

Bright yellow gingko leaves fluttered at their feet with a gust of wind.

"And what might that be?" Ernestine shivered a bit and pulled her green cardigan closed.

"We're doing the best we can with what we got, which isn't a whole lot." He quickly qualified his statement. "Not the what we're doing part, but the what we got part. Nobody can tell us anything other than what's missing. None of y'all sees anyone or anything until it's gone."

She looked at him funny. "How can you see something that ain't there?"

"You know what I mean, ma'am. There aren't any clues except missing items."

"So in other words, you ain't doing diddly squat?" Her eyes narrowed and mouth puckered. She was rail-thin and had a nose like a beak.

"No, ma'am, that's not what I said. By the way, I've been meaning to ask you: I can't seem to find any Ernestine Baker in the database. Is that your legal name?"

"No, Chief, it isn't. I thought everybody knew I only took on the name 'Ernestine' when I bought the store. People kept asking where Ernestine was, so I finally gave in and said 'rightcheer.'" She eyed him suspiciously. "Why? You been checking me out?"

"Just routine stuff. I told you we're busy trying to find the bandit."

"You should spend more time on criminals and less on law-abiding store owners like myself."

"Just what is your real name, ma'am?"

"Just as I thought," she said huffily. "You ain't doing diddly squat." She turned and stalked to the door of her store, then stopped, turned, and said simply, "Mona."

"Mona?"

"My name. It's Mona." She slammed the door behind her, leaving Johnny standing alone on the sidewalk outside her store.

Johnny walked a few feet to the store next door and stuck his head into Rhubarb's to say hi to Pickle's mother, Caledonia, who he'd seen through the window-shopping for fruit. Backing out the door, he felt a hand on his bicep.

"Chief Johnny Butterfield, as I live and breathe," the woman attached to the hand said.

He turned to see who it was and tipped his hat. "Ms. Winchester," he said politely but formally.

"Aw, you can call me Honey," she said. "And you can call me anytime," she cooed, standing a little too close. "I love a man of authority."

"Yes, ma'am." Johnny started walking, and Honey took his arm and walked with him. He attempted to put some distance between them, but Honey held on tightly.

"Say, Chief, are you going to the Oktoberfest?" She batted her eyelashes at him, and he adjusted his GPJPD cap over his eyes.

"Yes, ma'am, I reckon I am." He looked around to see who might be seeing Honey hanging on to him. He knew how fast small-town gossip spread.

With one hand still hooked in his arm, she ran her other hand up and down it, squeezing his muscle. "Maybe we could go together, big guy."

He cleared his throat. "No, ma'am, I reckon we can't."

Honey looked taken aback for a moment but quickly recovered. "You don't find me attractive, Chief?" She dropped one hand to her side.

"I didn't say that."

She raised an eyebrow. "But?"

"But I'm kinda interested in someone else," he said, smiling down politely at her.

"You don't seriously think you're in love with Martha Maye, do you? She's still a married woman, you know."

"I don't recall saying who I'm interested in, nor that it's any of your business." Stopping in front of the hardware store, he looked down at her and added, "No offense, ma'am."

"Usually when someone says 'no offense,' it's offensive. And must you keep calling me ma'am?" She stomped her foot like a petulant three-year-old. "It makes me feel so old."

"Yes, ma . . . Ms. Winchester."

She frowned. "So what are you gonna do, pine for Martha Maye until she's free and clear of Lenny? That could be months. In the meantime, you and I could have us a peck of fun. If I were any more single, I'd be a fraction."

"Thank you kindly for the offer, ma'am." She gave him a hard look. "Honey. But I respectfully decline. Now if you'll excuse me, I need to run into the hardware store." He tipped his hat, said, "You have a real nice day," and began to walk away.

She yelled after him, "I love it when you call me Honey."

Johnny walked into the hardware store, making a note to himself to talk to Martha Maye about Honey. Lost in thought, he nearly walked right into a familiar-looking man.

"Huh," the man muttered, blocking the aisle, "look who it is—Mr. Gutterfield."

"That's *Chief Butterfield,* thank you very much." He looked carefully at the man. "Don't I know you from somewhere?" He thought the man possessed too much undeserved self-confidence. He had an air of cockiness and belligerence. Johnny looked down at him, taking in the flabby biceps underneath his T-shirt. Johnny was wider, taller, and more fit, with at least fifty pounds and five inches on him, yet the man's stance mirrored a challenge.

"I know your name, but you don't know mine, do ya? Well, *Johnny,* it's best we're properly introduced, since I just might be your worst nightmare."

FIFTEEN

When tempted to fight fire with fire, remember that the Fire Department usually uses water.

~Southern Proverb

"And why would that be?" Johnny asked, propping his hands on his hips and stepping back slightly.

"I don't take kindly to folks messing with what's mine, that's why." The bully took a step toward Johnny, back into his personal space.

"Look, it's been real nice dancing with you, but my dance card's full, so why don't you tell me what I've done to put that bee in your pretty little bonnet."

"I'll tell you who I'm *not, Chief Butterball.*" Johnny stayed silent but raised one eyebrow. "I'm not Martha Maye's *ex*-husband."

Johnny nodded. It was all clear now. "Lenny Applewhite," he said, standing his ground. He thought Lenny was mighty stupid to stand so close to him, because it allowed him to tower over the man. A vision of a bug being squished under a shoe came to his mind. He crossed his arms and glared down at the man.

"Darn tootin' I'm Lenny Applewhite. And I'm literally here to say" — he jabbed his finger into Johnny's chest with each word—"stay outta my way, *Chief.*"

"Well, Mr. Applewhite, let me tell you a thing or two. I don't cotton to you pretending to bump into me accidentally, and furthermore, if you so much as touch a fingertip to me one more time, I'll arrest you for assaulting a police officer and cart you off to jail."

"Oh yeah? Well, maybe I'll claim police brutality. It'll literally be your word against mine, *Chief* Mutterfield."

Johnny shook his head, looking around at all of the customers who were pretending to be shopping. "Somehow I think the truth would come out." He tried to step around Lenny and walk away.

Lenny blocked his path again, his big belly touching Johnny's belt buckle.

"Boy, you got your stupid head on today?" Johnny glared at him.

"You don't scare me, Mr. Big Man, but maybe I scare you, huh? Does Martha Maye know about you and Honey Winchester? Maybe I'll go fill her in."

Give me strength, Lord. Johnny said, "My mama always told me to never argue with an idiot. Excuse me." He brushed past Lenny, intent on ending the discussion.

Lenny said loudly, "So tell me, are you sleeping with my wife in addition to dining with her, *Chief Buttercup?*"

Johnny stopped and turned around slowly, narrowed eyes burrowing into Lenny's. He looked at the man with a stare capable of burning paper and said with controlled anger, "Martha Maye is a lady and you will regard her as such."

"Oh really? Here's a tip for you, Mr. Nutterfield. You can't tell me what I can and can't say. This here's a free country, and she's my wife, and I can talk about her however I want."

Johnny's voice remained quiet, but his tone was menacing. "Then there will come a time when I am not on duty and will take great pleasure in teaching you some manners."

"Ooh, I'm real scared." Lenny shook his hands in the air in mock fear. "Did y'all hear that?" Lenny spoke loudly, looking all around the store for witnesses. "The police chief here just threatened me."

"No, *Mr.* Applewhite. You've mistaken a threat for a promise." He moved closer to Lenny, pointed his finger two inches in front of his face, and said firmly, "Do. Not. Tempt me."

"Shoot, Mr. Big Man thinks he's Mr. Tough Man," Lenny said, looking around the store again to see who might be watching. There were five people in the store and all were concentrating very hard on various items in their hands, pretending not to listen in on the conversation.

"I could literally take you any day of the week, and twice on Sunday," Lenny boasted.

"You might just get your chance to find out about that. In the meantime, if you don't turn yourself around and march your scrawny little butt outta this store in about five seconds, I'm gonna call the station and have them send a car for your personal transportation to an all-expense-paid visit to Hotel Lockup. It would be my pleasure to look at that smirk through bars." Johnny held up a finger and began counting. "One."

Lenny began backing up but continued to talk so anyone in the store could hear. "Can y'all believe this? The man's screwing my wife and he's pissed at *me*."

"Three." Johnny held up three fingers.

"Ha!" Lenny pointed at Johnny. "You can't even count."

Johnny held out four fingers on his hand.

"All right, I'm going, but you can't hide behind that badge forever. Like you said, sooner or later, you're gonna be off duty ..."

"Five," Johnny reached for the phone hooked to his belt. But he didn't need to use it. Lenny turned and stalked from the store, the bells on the door clanging wildly as he pulled it open and then slammed it shut.

IT WAS a bright, crisp fall afternoon when Martha Maye took the kids out for recess. A lone figure drew her eye to the edge of the schoolyard. Lenny stood on the other side of the chain link fence, leaning against it with his arms spread wide above his head, his fingers grasping the chain links and his face up against them, watching her. She tried to ignore him, but his presence was unnerving. She ended recess early.

That afternoon when she walked her students out the front door at dismissal time, he was leaning against a tree across the street, arms folded, watching her. She hurried inside and called Johnny.

"*Now* will you take out a restraining order on him?" Johnny asked.

"What good will that do? He doesn't get close to me, and wouldn't a restraining order only require him to stay five hundred yards away? He already does that."

"Did you and Butterbean walk to school today?"

"Yes. I mean, Butterbean rode her bike ..."

"I'm coming to pick y'all up. Do not leave until I get there."

"Yes sir," she said to dead air.

LENNY WAS gone by the time Johnny got to the school. Questions abounded from Butterbean as to why Chief Butterfield was taking them home again.

Since their house was only a few blocks away, Martha Maye allowed her daughter to ride her bike home, but Johnny and she followed closely behind in the police car.

"I don't know what to do, Johnny." She rolled her window down and felt the breeze on her face. "He's following me, he shows up here and there watching me, and I keep getting strange presents. Now I'm thinking they've got to be from him."

Johnny's eyes continuously swept the area around them as he drove.

"I'm serious about you taking out a restraining order on him. If nothing else, it will send him a message that you're serious about him staying away from you."

"I don't know," she said, watching Butterbean peddle faster over a tree root protruding from the sidewalk. "I don't want to make him madder. I keep thinking if I ignore him, he'll eventually go away."

"I don't think his seatback is in the full, upright, and locked position. It's doubtful subtle is going to work with him."

The leaves—some golden yellow, some orange, and some red— danced in the air before slowly and gracefully falling to the ground. There were pumpkins on most of the front porches, and some of the yards had cornstalks or ghosts or witches for decoration.

Martha Maye sighed. "This is my favorite time of year, and Lenny's ruining it for me."

Butterbean turned into their driveway, and Johnny followed, parking beside a huge maple tree, the leaves of which had turned brilliant yellow.

Martha Maye got out with her book bag, as Johnny reached into the back seat for Butterbean's backpack.

"Would you like to come in for milk and cookies?" Martha Maye asked him.

"Does the Pope wear a funny dress?" he said, following her to the side door.

"Does he?" Butterbean piped up, catching up to them.

"Chief Butterfield is being facetious."

"What's setious?"

"FA. Fa-ce-tious," Martha Maye enunciated. "It means don't take him literally. He's being humorous."

"Aw, come on, who would say no to your mama's cookies?"

Martha Maye handed Butterbean a cookie and told her to go see if Maddy Mack could play. "And get the mail for me before you go next door, okay?"

"Okay, Mama." Butterbean skipped out of the kitchen.

"She's a keeper, Mart."

"Thank you, Johnny. I don't know what I'd do without her."

Johnny removed his hat and checked his watch.

"Can you sit for a minute?" She put some oatmeal raisin cookies on a plate. When she turned around to set them on the table, Johnny sat slightly bent at the waist, forearms on his thighs, fingering his hat between his knees, deep in thought.

"I don't want to stay too long and give Lenny any more ammunition, but I need to tell you about a run-in I just had in the hardware store before someone else does."

"Ammunition?"

"Yeah." He let out a long breath. "Lenny tried to pick a fight with me in Doc's hardware store. I kind of lost my temper and told him I'd be off duty one day and teach him some manners."

She put her hand over her mouth to cover a smile. "I would've liked to have seen that. I imagine he didn't take too kindly to it."

"Negative. He did not." Johnny shook his head and picked up a cookie. "He got all loud and started yelling about me threatening him. So I obliged him and gave him a threat. I said I'd put him in the pokey if he didn't walk away."

Martha Maye began to laugh. "You did? Oh, I wish I'd seen his face. I'll bet it was all puckered up like he'd been sucking on a lemon."

"Mart, something's not right with that boy. He concerns me." He slowly turned the cookie in his hands. "He's threatening me in public, essentially stalking you, and possibly sending you anonymous gifts. What's he going to do next?"

Quiet for a bit, she took in his words. He ate a cookie, and she sipped her tea. The kitchen was quiet. Too quiet. Only the sound of a ticking clock could be heard.

Johnny cleared his throat. "And Martha Maye, there's something else he said." She looked up at him. "He told everyone who would listen that you and I are sleeping together."

Martha Maye got up and moved to the sink to pour more tea even though her glass was almost full. Her hands shook in anger. How dare Lenny act like that after the way he'd treated her? "And that's why you threatened him?" Martha Maye said softly, turning toward him.

"I won't tolerate him talking about you that way." He stood up and rubbed the back of his neck, a move that made his bicep bulge. Martha Maye noticed it. He wasn't a body builder type, but the man did have muscles. Her gaze traveled from his arms to his eyes.

"Doesn't seem fair, him accusing us of" — she waved her hand in the air — "of *that*, when we haven't even kissed." Martha Maye's nerves were raw. She looked at Johnny's lips, and her gaze moved slowly back to his eyes. Butterflies floated around in her stomach, and her mouth went dry.

"No, no it doesn't," he said, coming closer to her and holding her gaze. His six-foot-five frame towered over her five-foot-six body. They stood so close they were almost touching. Martha Maye made the first move by touching his arm, and their eyes locked.

He bent his head and put his lips softly to hers. She wound her hands around his neck and squeezed into him, returning the kiss. He brought his hands up and cupped her face, deepening the kiss. A soft hum came from her throat, and she matched his enthusiasm. He pulled away and looked questioningly into her eyes, his thumbs caressing her cheeks. Then his lips found hers again. They held the kiss, a kiss that was three months in the making, a kiss she'd wanted since the moment she ran into his arms at the end of her kidnapping ordeal.

At the sound of running feet, they jumped away from each other, as Butterbean and Maddy Mack came racing into the kitchen. Martha Maye's hand went up to her mouth.

Butterbean hesitated, looking from her mother to Johnny, and then said, "Mama, can Maddy Mack have a cookie, and can we watch some TV for a while?"

"Sure." Martha Maye rubbed her index finger and thumb against her mouth. "If you say 'may.'"

"Um, I'd best get back to work before they put an APB out on me." Johnny started for the door, and Martha Maye followed.

"We're still on for Saturday night aren't we?" he said, opening the front door.

"Yes." She grinned from ear to ear. As Johnny headed to his car, her eyes followed. Her mind on Johnny, only for a second did she register a BMW with tinted windows slowly driving past.

SIXTEEN

The distance to the next milepost depends on the mud in the road.

~Southern Proverb

On Saturday night, Martha Maye pulled her Toyota Camry into the parking lot of the restaurant at the Buttermilk Hill Inn, a country inn about thirty miles outside of Goose Pimple Junction, where Johnny and she had arranged to meet. She'd taken great care in dressing and left Butterbean with Honey and Maddy Mack. Tess had talked her into buying a dress she would have never picked out on her own. She hadn't worn anything this revealing in her entire life, and she felt very self-conscious, which only added to the butterflies in her stomach.

She walked into the inn's cozy dining room, and the maître d' led her to the corner table by the window, where Johnny waited. She wondered if he was as nervous as she felt. Probably not, she decided. That would be impossible. She flexed her damp palms, pasted on a smile, and tried to walk with confidence, but she felt awkward.

Johnny stood to hold the chair for her, and she saw him swallow. "Wow. You look absolutely amazing, Martha Maye."

"Thank you, Johnny," she said, putting her hand to her chest, where she'd pinned the plunging neckline so that it wasn't quite so plunging. She still felt like it showed off more than it should. "Thank you for understanding about meeting me here, as opposed to somewhere in town. I don't want folks talking."

"No problem. I understand. I'm just happy you agreed to go out with me. I'd have met you at the Piggly Wiggly three counties over for a Spam sandwich if that's what you wanted." He hurried to add, "Not that this is a date, exactly. We're just two friends getting together for a meal. Nothing wrong with that."

She smiled shyly and looked out the window at the lake at dusk. It was mid-October but still warm out, although not stifling hot as in the summer. Ducks sat in the grass and floated on the lake, making the outdoor lights dance on the ripples. She forced her eyes back to Johnny, who watched her.

She bit her lip and searched for something to say. "This is a beautiful restaurant, don't you think?" *That sounded lame.*

"It sure is," he replied. "I hear tell Robert E. Lee himself stayed at the inn once."

She nodded, looking around the room. The lights were low, and a candle inside a glass hurricane sat at the center of each table. Copious bunches of white gladiolas sprang from huge glass vases in various spots around the brick-walled dining room. The ambiance of the restaurant combined with Johnny's reassuring presence calmed her nerves. *If only I could think of something to talk about.*

"How's work, Johnny?"

He groaned. "Oh, don't ask."

"Oh? You're not sorry you took the job, are you?"

"Naw, I like the job. And the town." He leaned in toward her with a shy smile and added, "And the people."

She smiled but couldn't hold his gaze.

"But we got us a mess going on."

"What kind of mess?" She crossed her hands on the table and leaned toward him.

"A petty thief wreaking havoc all over town kind of mess. I think just about every business has been hit at least once, but nobody ever sees anything or anyone suspicious. It's the durndest thing."

"Mama mentioned some items from the store had disappeared."

"Yeah, boy," Johnny said. "I've checked with every store in town, and just about everyone has had at least a few items go missing within the last month or so." He paused while a busboy set glasses of water on the table. When he left, Johnny took the lemon wedge off the rim of the glass and plopped it into the water, then continued.

"I'm thinking it must be a kid, because nothing big's ever taken, just incidentals like candy, apples, underthings, battrees." Martha Maye smiled at him and he said, "What?"

"My daddy used to say batteries like that."

He flushed but continued. "Yep. Most of the time, nobody even realizes right away that anything is gone. At first, some of the stores said no, nothing was missing, then they got to looking and called me back with a whole list, and by then the trail's ice cold. It could be anybody." He took a sip of water.

"Don't any of the shops have video cameras?"

"Only the Piggly Wiggly. Goose Pimple Junction's stuck in time as far as theft prevention goes."

"I guess noboby's ever really needed it before."

"I reckon not. Then of course, there's the great pumpkin caper. He didn't get y'all's, did he?"

"No, we were spared, but I did hear some of my students talking about that." The waitress stopped at their table to take their drink order. When she left the table, Martha Maye said, "You do like being police chief though, don'tcha?"

"I like it just fine. This petty theft stuff is aggravating, but it's a whole lot more interesting than writing speeding tickets all day like I did as a statie. Of course, chances are I won't get to do any high-speed chases, but the people are a whole lot friendlier." He looked at her and added, "And prettier."

Martha Maye straightened the silverware at her place setting, mumbling, "Thank you." Alarmed, she looked up quickly, adding, "Oh, there I go again, assuming—"

"Your assumption is correct, pretty lady," Johnny interrupted, nodding.

"Well, thank you again," she said, her eyes still not able to meet his.

"So, you haven't had any more incidents, have you? With Lenny, or with gifts?"

"No, thank goodness. It's been a few days since y'all's run-in. Maybe he finally got the point and left town, although it does seem like he would have said good-bye to Butterbean."

When the waitress brought their drinks—a frozen margarita for her and a Sam Adams pale ale for him—Martha Maye took a sip and looked up at the entrance to the dining room. She almost spewed the drink into the air. She coughed and sputtered and wiped her lips with a napkin. Johnny turned to see what had upset her. Lenny was crossing the room to their table.

"Well, well, well, what do we have here?" Lenny asked loudly, causing everyone in the room to stop talking and stare.

"Lenny, what are you doing here?" Martha Maye croaked, her face red with embarrassment.

Lenny glared at his wife. "What in tarnation are you doing out with another man? You are still a married *wo-man*, you know."

"Are you following me, Len?"

"So what if I am? You're still my lawfully wedded wife." He looked her up and down and added, "Although you look like a two-bit hussy. You two gonna hustle on up to a room when you're finished here?" Lenny somehow managed to sneer and leer at the same time.

Johnny stood up, like a redwood over a sapling. "You got no call to follow this woman or call her names. She and I are just having a bite to eat as friends. That's all. We even came in separate cars. Call her a despicable name like that again, and you'll be sipping your dinner through a straw for the foreseeable future."

"I don't give a diddly squat if you came on separate donkeys. That's my wife you're on a date with, *Chief Butterbrain*. And when she dresses like that, she *asks* to be called a hussy. A brazen hussy."

The maître d' had rushed to the table and tried to get a word in. Everyone ignored him.

"Lenny, number one, it's not a date," Martha Maye talked slowly and tried to keep her voice low. She glanced around the room and saw that other diners were openly staring at them.

"Number two, you and I are separated. Number three, I can have dinner with a friend if I want. And number four, I can dress however I want." She tugged on the V of her neckline.

"And five, you apologize to this lovely lady for calling her that shameful name and insinuating something that isn't true," Johnny added.

The maître d' stood by awkwardly. Finally he said more forcefully, "Sir, may I get you a chair?"

"NO. He will *not* be staying," Martha Maye said quickly.

"Perhaps a table then?"

Lenny looked from Johnny, who stood with his fists flexing at his sides, to Martha Maye, who looked into her water glass, to the maître d', who nervously shifted from one foot to the other.

Finally, Lenny grinned slyly and said, "Yeah. Yeah, sure. You can show me to a table." He walked off with a smirk and veered away from the maître d', finding a table himself across the room where he could sit and stare straight at Martha Maye.

"That boy is wound up like a cheap alarm clock," Johnny said, glancing at Lenny across the room. His face registered sudden recognition, and he snapped his fingers. "I know where I've seen him before. I couldn't place him in the hardware store, but now I remember. He was sitting in a parked car down the street from your mother's house a while ago. I can't rightly recall when it—"

"He was parked on my mother's street?" Martha Maye interrupted, looking stunned. "Why would he be parked on my mother's street?"

"He told me he was new in town and had stopped to look at a map."

"And I'm Crystal Gale, on my way to the Grand Ole Opry. Looks like he's been following me for a while now. Estherlene said she'd seen him drive past the house a bunch of times. And to think I almost bought his I've-learned-my-lesson-I'm-a-changed-man routine."

"Listen, it's a beautiful night, you look beautiful, and I don't want you to worry one pea-picking second about him. Can we try to forget about Lenny?"

"Kind of hard to do with him staring a hole in my face."

The waitress came to take their order, and after she'd walked away, they tried to steer the topic toward more pleasant subjects. Martha Maye and Johnny slogged their way through dinner, the conversation stilted. She could feel Lenny's eyes on her, and every time she looked up, he was staring right at her with his arms crossed and a hard expression on his face.

She vaguely heard Johnny ask how Butterbean liked her new school.

"She likes it just fine. She's making ..." Martha Maye's fork made a loud clang as she dropped it on her plate. "Isn't there something you can do?"

"You don't have a restraining order out on him, plus we're not in my jurisdiction, so I don't rightly know what I can do other than have a man-to-man talk with him, which I'm guessing won't go over real well, not to mention the scene it'll cause. I'm sure if I ask him to step outside, he'll take it as a challenge, but I have a reputation as a peaceful law officer to uphold and I'll be danged if I'm gonna ruin it on the likes of him."

They were quiet for a moment, each one thinking as they stared out at the lights reflecting off the lake.

"But I'm not taking your feelings lightly, either, and I *do* want to protect you, and I *don't* want this clown thinking he can act like this, so here's what we're gonna do."

Johnny took out his cell phone, and Martha Maye listened, breaking into a wide smile, as he formulated a plan with whoever was on the receiving end of the call. He signaled for the waitress, and whispered something to her as he paid the bill. "And here's something extra for your trouble." He gave the waitress a wad of bills.

"Okay." He rubbed his hands together with excitement in his eyes. "Teenie's gonna pass the word on to Hank and Skeeter. Give them a few minutes to get into place, and we're good to go."

"I love your plan." She grinned at him. "Johnny, tell me something while we have a few minutes to kill."

"What's that?"

"How in the world did Teenie get that nickname? I mean, I'm not trying to be mean, but, you know—"

"I asked her that once. She said she was born premature. She jokes that she was the runt of the litter. With her name being Christ-eeene, and with her size as a baby, they just started calling her Teenie, and it stuck."

"Is she married?"

"Naw. Beano says there was a rumor about her and John Ed last year, but now that he's gone, I guess she's on the prowl."

"Maybe, maybe not. He's still around, as we discovered outside of school the other day. But him and Teenie? Together as a couple?" Martha Maye's face screwed up in disgust.

"Why not? They're about the same age."

"I guess. You think she'd have anything to do with him after what he did?"

"Depends on how strong her feelings were for him to begin with." Johnny looked at his watch. "Let's wait just a little bit longer."

A few minutes later, Martha Maye and Johnny got up to leave without looking at Lenny. She looked through the round window of the door to the kitchen as she passed it and saw step one of Johnny's plan ready and waiting.

LENNY THREW some bills on his table and got up to follow Martha Maye and Johnny. As he reached the swinging door leading to the kitchen, the waitress came out with a broad tray, upon which sat a full pitcher of sweet tea and a big bowl of chicken gravy. The tray slammed into Lenny, who shrieked as he stepped back, shaking gravy and tea from his hands. Thick gravy fell off his shirt in globs, and tea dripped off his soaking-wet shirt and pants.

"Oops," the waitress said, her hand over her mouth trying to hide a smile.

The mishap didn't delay Lenny for long, but it was long enough for Martha Maye and Johnny to get into their cars. After directing a few choice words at the waitress, Lenny ran out the door after them. He glared as

Johnny smiled widely at him, waved, and drove off behind Martha Maye's car.

Lenny ran to his Ford Bronco, started it up, and raced after them. She'd just humiliated him again, and he was going to have to do something about it.

"You don't know whose weeds you's peeing in, Chief Butterfly," Lenny shouted to his windshield, through which he could see the back of Johnny's car up ahead, in front of two other cars.

Frustrated by the no-passing zone, Lenny tailgated the car in front of him and laid on the horn, but the driver didn't speed up. Lenny pounded the steering wheel, cussed, and honked, but oncoming traffic kept him from passing the car for several miles. And once he passed one, he still had to get past another. He finally swerved around the second car and floored the accelerator. He was closing the distance between Johnny's car and his own, but just as he entered Goose Pimple Junction's limits, he heard a siren and saw red and blue lights in his rearview mirror.

He slammed his palm against the steering wheel and yelled, "Son of a bitch," at the disappearing taillights of Johnny's car.

SEVENTEEN

You can't hurry up good times by waiting for them.

~Southern Proverb

"He *what?*" Lou and Tess said in unison. They, along with Aunt Imy, were in Lou's living room, working a jigsaw puzzle and listening to Martha Maye tell them about her date with Johnny.

"Yeppie. Lenny followed me, then he sat across the restaurant, drinking and staring a hole at my head, but I tell you, I would have loved to have seen his face when he was standing there dripping with chicken gravy and sweet tea. I called the waitress later that night to say thank you, and she said he was fit to be tied."

Ima Jean took a tissue that was tucked into the waistband of her skirt and dabbed at her nose. "Roll that beautiful bean footage."

Martha Maye nodded and added with a big smile, "The waitress said she felt guilty for taking Johnny's tip. She said seeing Lenny standing there dripping was payment enough. She had an up close and personal understanding of the saying 'madder 'n a wet hen in a tote sack.'"

"Ooh, law, that *is* something I'd like to see footage of." Lou pinched the middle of her bright-orange blouse and fanned her body with it a few times.

"I know, but I think he was even madder when Hank Beanblossom pulled him over."

"He pulled Lenny over?" Tess clapped her hands together in delight.

"Yep, gave him a speeding ticket." Martha Maye smacked her thigh. "He said Lenny was as mad as a mule chewing on bumblebees."

Louetta placed another puzzle piece and said sarcastically, "Now tell me that was a random event."

"Nope, it wasn't. Johnny set it up before we left the restaurant. It was a thing of beauty, if you ask me."

"Don't hate me because I'm beautiful," Aunt Ima Jean said.

Martha Maye leaned in and tried a puzzle piece, but it didn't fit. "Oh, we won't, Aunt Imy, but I'm not thinking too kindly of Lenny Applewhite right now."

"So, Martha Maye." Tess leaned toward her friend and asked hesitantly, "You and Johnny shook Lenny. And *then* what happened?"

"Yeah"—Lou leaned forward—"that's what I wanna know. Get to the good stuff."

"Nothing happened." Martha Maye slumped back in her chair. "Johnny followed me home to make sure I got there safely, but Butterbean was at Honey's, and she saw us drive up and ran out to meet us. Johnny politely said goodnight and went on his way."

"Dang. Not even a goodnight kiss?" Tess complained.

"Well, I *am* still a lawfully wedded *wo-man*," Martha Maye said, imitating Lenny.

"Huh, maybe an *awfully* wedded woman," Tess said.

"I'm sorry, sugar." Lou patted her daughter's hand. "I knew that man was up to no good when I saw him come into the shop the other night, and Tessie did, too. We didn't buy his act for a second."

"Amen." Tess nodded.

"He tried his Mr. Wonderful act on me, but I've been around for a few presidents. He didn't fool me, not one bit. A pig's still a pig even if he's wearing lipstick."

JACK STEPPED out the front door on his way next door to get Tess, but he stopped in his tracks when he saw a dark, hooded figure lurking next to a tree across the street. It looked to Jack like the person was looking through Lou's big bay window, where the women were sitting and talking in the living room. He watched with considerable concern as the person climbed up into the big maple tree he'd been standing under. Jack guessed he wanted a better vantage point from higher up.

Jack took his cell phone from his pocket and dialed the police station. Ever since the trouble of the past summer, he'd had the police department on speed dial.

Teenie White was on dispatch, and he told her to send a car to his house, lights and siren off.

"What's up, Jackson?" she asked.

"Not sure. Somebody's lurking around across the street, and I just saw him climb a tree. I don't think he went up there after a cat. It doesn't smell right. Just send somebody to check it out, okay? And tell them to kind of ease up the street. I don't want to spook whoever it is."

"Will do."

Jack hung up and stayed put. He didn't think Black Hood was aware of him, but he wasn't sure. It took only two minutes for Officer Beanblossom's car to round the corner. He pulled up in front of Jack's house, and Jack walked across the lawn to meet him. As he did, he heard leaves rustling and then saw Black Hood jump down and take off, cutting through the backyard of the house across the street.

"He's bolting!" he called to Hank, pointing. They both took off.

"Halt! It's the law!" Hank hollered as he ran. The figure didn't stop. Black Hood cleared the Rollins' back fence and Hank followed in hot pursuit. The officer had youth and training on his side; Jack had more trouble climbing the fence. Just as Jack cleared it, he heard what sounded like a huge splash. The Rollins' backyard was dark, but Jack knew his neighbors had an inground pool. *Uh-oh. I hope that was Black Hood and not Hank.*

He hurried in the direction of the splash and couldn't help but chuckle when he saw who had fallen in. Walking to the edge of the pool, he offered his hand to Hank, helping the officer climb out.

"Didn't know it was there, huh?" Jack's mouth twitched as he tried not to laugh in front of the embarrassed officer.

Hank stood there soaking wet and dripping, trying to catch his breath. Breathing hard, with his hands on his hips and his head bent toward the ground, he looked up at Jack through wet bangs. "Don't suppose we could keep this just between you and me."

"I doubt it." Jack finally gave in to laughter. He clapped the officer on the back, spraying water, then took his hand away, shaking it off.

"Aw, c'mon, Jack," Hank whined as they walked back toward Jack's house.

"Okay, partner, how about we strike a deal. I won't say anything about your dip in the pool if you won't say anything about this whoever-it-was to the girls."

"The girls?" Hank said, his shoes squeaking and squishing as they walked.

"Yeah, *any* of the girls—Lou, Tess, Martha Maye . . ."

"How's come?" Hank asked.

"Because there's no use alarming them. Tess and Martha Maye have been through enough in the last six months. Let's just keep a lid on this, at least for a while."

"I'll have to make a report. Your call's on the dispatch records."

"Will that report include your impromptu swim?" Jack asked.

"Well . . . " Hank stalled.

"Then I don't think you need to report you actually saw or chased anyone. Just report that I was mistaken. Case closed."

"I've never falsified a report before, Jack."

"And I've never been able to keep a juicy piece of gossip to myself, either." Jack's raised eyebrows implied, "Get my drift?"

"I'll need to run this past the chief. I couldn't in good conscience lie on a report."

"You're right, but you know the minute you file a report, word will get back to the ladies. Let's just do our best to keep a lid on this."

"Fudgesicles," Hank said.

"Fudgesicles melt," Jack said, handing the officer a handkerchief.

Monday morning, when Johnny walked through the back door of the police station and past the break room, Officers Beanblossom and Duke filed in on either side of him.

"Eeee doggies, that was fun on Saturday night," Skeeter Duke said as they walked. "We were on him like cheese on grits soon as he crossed into the county. And let me tell you, that Mr. Lenny Applewhite is meaner'n a skilletful of rattlesnakes. We near about had to run him in."

"I sure do 'preshade you boys handling that little matter," Johnny said.

"When we ticketed him for speeding, he accused us of ambushing him," Hank said. "You better watch your back, Chief. He said he knew you'd set him up, and he said he was gonna put a knot on your head big enough to hitch a trailer to."

"Ha!" Johnny chuckled. "He's welcome to try."

"That's what I said. I told him assaulting a police officer is a felony. Told him to go ahead and try it." Johnny's head swiveled toward Skeeter, who quickly amended, "Go ahead and try it because you'd lay him out flatter than a fritter, and I'd throw his butt in jail." Johnny nodded in approval.

"We did like you said and followed him after we gave him a citation," Skeeter said. "He finally went on home, and —"

"And I sat in the cruiser outside the hotel until about four a.m.," Hank interrupted.

When they walked into the reception area, they stopped and stared. Bernadette, at the desk, said in a overly bright tone, "Chief, there's someone here to see you."

Lenny jumped up from a metal chair, making it clang against the wall. "I want to report police harassment."

The officers protectively clustered in front of Johnny, but he pushed through them, opened the little gate for Lenny, and said, "Why don't you and me talk back in my office." It was not a request or a suggestion.

Lenny walked through the gate.

"Follow me." Johnny turned and said, "Officers, y'all may join us if you're so inclined."

"Aw, no. Y'all is just gonna gang up on me. I want a lawyer."

Johnny let out a loud sigh and turned to Lenny. "You aren't under arrest. *You* came to see *me*. Now, do you want to see me or not?"

Lenny's eyes showed doubt as they went from Hank to Skeeter and back to Johnny. He squared his shoulders and tried to stand up as tall as he could. He finally said, "Do."

They all filed into the police chief's office.

Johnny sat behind his desk and gestured for Lenny to take the seat in front of it. Hank and Skeeter stood in the doorway. Johnny tried to keep his face neutral. "Now, what's this about harassment?"

"That's right. Your men followed me around all night Saturday. They can't do that. It's a free country. I didn't do nothing wrong."

Johnny turned to his men and said, "That true, Officers?"

Simultaneously, the men said, "Negative."

"Oh, of course they're gonna deny it!" Lenny twisted in his seat, looking from the officers to Johnny.

"Sir, we stopped you for a speeding violation and smelled alcohol on your person. You didn't blow over the legal limit, but in the interest of protecting our citizens, we thought it best to keep a watchful eye on you, lest you decided to imbibe some more."

"That is total and pure, genuine bull-oney. One hunnerd percent grade A." He pointed his finger at Johnny, who stared down at him. "Let me tell you, Mr. Policeman. You keep your officers away from me, and you stay away from my wife."

Johnny leaned on his forearms across the desk. "Is that what this is really about, Mr. Applewhite?"

"It's about y'all literally traipsing all over my civil rights, *Chief Butternut,* but while I'm here, I'm giving you fair warning—again—to stay away from what's mine."

"As you stated, this is a free country. If the lady in question wants to see me, she certainly has that prerogative." He stood and leaned over his desk. "Just for the record, are you threatening a police officer?"

"Lookit, you Paul Bunyan wannabe." Lenny jumped up and matched Johnny's stance across the desk. Skeeter and Hank stepped forward, ready to pounce. "This ain't no police matter. This is between me and you. Man-o and man-o. And you better look left, 'cause you ain't right. I'm determined to keep you from sullying the good name of my wife and leading her down the dirt road into the mud."

Johnny stared at him, trying not to laugh. He leaned in until their faces were just inches away. In a controlled, low voice, Johnny said, "You ought to be ashamed of yourself. Your mouth runs like a boarding house toilet. I am nothing more than a friend to Martha Maye, and I'll not have you insinuating otherwise. Now, you take your insults and your threats and get out of my police house, and while you're at it, you leave Martha Maye alone."

"Who are you to be telling me to stay away from my wife?"

"Listen, Mr. Applewhite, if you have a police matter, I'm happy to discuss it with you, and if you want to discuss non-police matters, you call me at home, but I'm telling you, the lady does not want you around her, so you better watch yourself."

"Or what?" Lenny taunted.

"Or I'll be all over you like stink on a skunk."

"Oh yeah?"

"Literally," Johnny said.

Lenny turned to go but stopped at the door. Skeeter and Hank moved aside to let him through. He pointed at Johnny and yelled so everyone in the station could hear. "Did y'all hear that? That's the second time he's threatened me."

He pointed two fingers at his eyes, pointed them at Johnny, and then back at his eyes, before he swung around and brushed past the officers. The three officers shared a look, shaking their heads.

"That boy is a dog of his own trot," Hank said.

Bernadette appeared at the chief's door. "Elvis has left the building."

"And?" Johnny said.

"How do you know there's an 'and'?"

"Because I know that look. Go on, this is already starting out to be a stellar day. Lay it on me."

"Roddey McClansky called. Says one of his chickens is missing. Says no way it ran off by itself."

Johnny sat down, his chair squeaking, and sighed. "Okay, Bernie. Thank you."

Bernadette walked back to her desk, and Skeeter said, "What are you thinking, Chief?"

"You cannot get the water to clear up until you get the pigs out of the creek."

"Huh?" both men said.

"What's that supposed to mean?" Hank asked.

"Means we're gonna catch us a thief. Get everybody in the squad room for a meeting at five o'clock."

"FIFTEEN MINUTES could save you fifteen percent or more on car insurance," Aunt Ima Jean said as she let Martha Maye and Butterbean into Lou's house.

"Good to know, Aunt Imy. Hireyew doing?"

"Sometimes you feel like a nut "—she clucked her tongue twice—"sometimes you don't."

"I know exactly what you mean," Martha Maye said, patting her aunt on the back. "Where's Mama?"

"Ancient Chinese Secret."

Butterbean's face showed confusion until Lou bustled through the door in a bright-red dress with big white polka dots, wiping her hands on a dishtowel.

Martha Maye looked at her mother and her aunt and thought the sisters couldn't be more different. Lou was a big woman whose body type matched her personality. She wore bright makeup and loud clothes and had a bouffant hairstyle and disposition. Her appearance and temperament were larger than life.

Ima Jean was petite and almost always wore a housecoat. Her appearance belied her personality. Her plain clothes, Brillo pad hairdo, and makeup-free face made for a surprise when she opened her mouth and proved her complete craziness. Both women were good people—as good as they came.

Butterbean's face lit up. "Hi, Granny!"

"Aw, my babies! Whatchy'all doing?"

"We dropped our school stuff at home and came out for a walk. It's too beautiful to stay inside." Martha Maye kissed her mother's cheek.

"Come on back, you two. I've got some double fudge brownies in the cookie jar. We'll take them out on the patio."

"Aunt Ima Jean, did Pickle ever admit to eating all your waffles?"

"No, he did not," Lou answered for her sister. "And he didn't take the Raisin Bran, either." Lou gave Ima Jean a pointed look. This had clearly become a sore subject between the two.

"I'm sure we ate them all," Lou said, "and Raisin Bran don't just get up and walk outta the house. You can't blame Peekal for everything. I think you've just forgotten how much you ate, Imy."

"I can't believe I ate the whole thing," Ima Jean said, mimicking the old Alka Seltzer commercial.

"I know, but that must be what happened."

"'Cept it isn't. I didn't eat all those waffles. I'm sure of it."

Martha Maye left her mother and aunt bickering and went to see who was knocking on the front door. "Hidee," she said to a tall man in a bad suit standing on the doorstep.

"I'm looking for a Martha Maye Applewhite," the man said, glancing at the envelope in his hand. "I was told I could find her here."

"By whom?"

"Excuse me?"

"Who told you that you could find me here?"

"You're Ms. Applewhite?"

She nodded.

"A neighbor of yours said you'd be here. My job is to deliver this to you. Have a good day." He pushed the envelope into her hands.

Martha Maye looked from the smarmy man walking away to the envelope she now held. The return address read *Louis P. Howe, attorney at law.*

"Who was that, Mart?" Lou came up behind her. She peered out the front door and then nodded at the envelope. "What in the world is that?"

"A deliveryman of some sort. He gave me this." She held up the envelope, then turned it over and ripped it open. As they walked back to the kitchen, she began reading it, stopped dead in her tracks, and gasped.

"What is it?" Lou looked over her shoulder.

"Um, Butterbean, would you go see if Mr. Jack would like you to walk Ezmeralda for him?"

"I don't wanna right now, Mama. I wanna eat this brownie."

"In that case, take some over to Mr. Jack. Don't argue, now. Go."

"Let me wrap some up for you to take next door," Lou said quickly. The kitchen stayed quiet as she hurried to get the brownies ready, and Martha Maye continued to silently read the document she'd just received. When Lou finished, she handed the goodies to Butterbean, who reluctantly left, saying, "I know y'all just want to get rid of me."

"Only for a few minutes, Bean. You come back in just a bit."

Once she'd left, Lou said, "Darlin', what on earth is in those papers?"

Martha Maye looked up, a heartsick expression on her face.

"Lenny's suing me for full custody of Bean."

EIGHTEEN

Liquor talks mighty loud when it gets loose from the jug.

~Southern Proverb

"J unebug Calloway on line one, Chief," Bernadette yelled into the intercom. She spoke so loudly, Johnny–in his officecould hear her voice booming from her desk as well as from the intercom.

He picked up the phone and punched the button. "Good morning, Junebug. Is everything all right?"

"No, everything is most certainly not all right."

"What happened?" Johnny asked, rubbing his forehead.

"Somebody's run off with two of Slick's pies this morning. He had them setting out on the windasills to cool off. They weren't there for more than ten minutes, and now they ain't there a'tall."

"When I find the culprit, I'll string him up by his toes."

Silence stretched out over the phone. Then, "This ain't a laughing matter, Chief."

Johnny cleared his throat. "I'm sorry. You're right. You know how much I love Slick's pies, so I do consider this a capital crime."

"You still making fun?" she asked, in a tone that reminded him of his mother's.

"No, ma'am. Tell me, did you see anyone or anything? Footprints? A car? Anything?"

"Nope. Just a totally barren windasill."

"What kind of pie?"

"What's that got to do with anything? A pie's a pie, same as a duck's a duck, ain't it?"

"I'm just trying to gather all the pertinent information. I'm also wondering how one person could run off with two pies. Were they meringue? Fruit? What kind were they?"

Junebug put her hand over the phone, and Johnny could hear her muffled voice talking to Slick. She came back on the phone and said, "One was a Virtue and the other was Eve with a lid on."

"Come again?"

"Oh, for heaven's sake. Don't you know nothing?"

"Guess not."

"One was a cherry pie, and the other was an apple pie. Now what you got to say about that, Columbo?"

"Hey, I'm better looking than Columbo," Johnny protested.

"You still making light of this situation?" she said, again in her mad mama voice.

"No, ma'am. I guess what that tells us is that it could be two people, but he—or she—coulda stacked them pies, seeing as they both had crust lids, correct?"

"Correct."

Johnny sighed. "All I can tell you is we're doing the best we can with what we've got, but this bandit is slicker 'n butter on a marble. I'll write out a report, and we'll beef up patrol over there." He paused. "I really am sorry."

"I know you are. Don't let it eat you up. No pun intended. Just outsmart the booger, okay?"

"I'll do my level best, Junebug. Count on it."

He hung up and called, "Beanblossom!"

Hank showed up at the door, coffee cup in one hand, a donut in the other. "Yessir?"

"Put your breakfast of champions down and go on over to the diner. Look around, see what you find. Somebody stole some pies. See if you see anybody walking around with a cherry pie mustache."

"You got it, Chief."

Bernadette called out again, "Line one, Chief. Tess Tremaine."

"Why don't I have a good feeling about this?" Johnny muttered to himself. He punched a button on the phone. "Tess? Everything all right?"

"No. All of my babies are gone."

"Babies? What do you mean? Your grown son lives in Birmingham. You —"

"My flowers. My hydrangeas, mums, marigolds, and asters. Thank goodness it's fall and the garden is winding down, but what was there is gone. Every one of my blooms is *gone*."

The sadness in Tess's voice nearly broke Johnny's heart. *What is going on in this town?*

"Gone? Like stomped on and plum ruined?" He looked at Hank, who still stood in the office doorway.

"No. Gone, like every blossom and bloom has been cut off. Not a one left. The plants are still here, but the flowers? They're . . . not."

"Flowers and pie. Some hooligan's having himself a party."

"Or herself," Hank volunteered, gesturing with the donut.

"Whoever it is, they're having one mighty nice blowout for themselves this morning," Johnny said into the phone, looking at Hank. "Don't worry, Tess. We'll catch him. He-she-is gonna slip up real soon. Don't you worry."

Tess's disembodied voice said, "Pie? Whatever are you talking about, Chief?"

"Now he's calling me and leaving these horrible messages on my voicemail all the time," Martha Maye said to Jack and Tess later that day. The three had just settled into a booth at Slick and Junebug's Diner.

"What does he say?" Tess asked. She slid her hand into Jack's, and he squeezed it.

"He says things like I'm not fit to be a mother and he's gonna get custody of Butterbean and move far away from here. He calls me names, or he'll call when I get home from the grocery store and ask if I'm gonna serve Johnny the pork chops I bought."

"Now that's just creepy. He's following you around?"

"Like my shadow, and then he calls and says stuff to make sure I know he's been watching me. Things like, 'What book did you get at the library?' Or after I've been helping Mama out at the store he'll say, 'Glad you're working two jobs. That'll just help me prove you're an unfit mother who doesn't have time for her youngin.'" Martha Maye had tears in her eyes, and she dabbed them gently with her napkin. "He's horrible. I just don't know what to do." She took a big gulp of sweet tea, trying to keep the tears at bay.

"Have you told Johnny about this?" Tess asked.

Martha Maye shook her head, took another drink, and placed the glass on the wet ring it had made on the place mat. "No, but he did tell me that Lenny went to the station house and threatened him. I think he's out of control."

"First of all, Martha Maye, Lenny is not going to get full custody of Butterbean," Jack said. "I don't care how stupid judges can be sometimes — and as a former lawyer, I can testify there are some truly stupid judges out there. No judge would be stupid enough to give that man full custody. You have too many witnesses to testify to what kind of" — Jack searched for the right word — "*man* he is."

"It's the not knowing that's killing me. Anticipation is always worse than reality."

"I know, I know," Jack said soothingly. "When's the hearing?"

"Mid-November. What's the second of all?" Martha Maye asked Jack.

"Oh yeah. Second of all, I'm going to shadow you for a while. I think it will make you feel more confident and safe."

"Jack, I can't ask you to do that."

"You didn't ask. I offered." He thought of the hooded lurker and silently vowed to stick close to her.

"Thank you, Jackson."

"And third of all, I think you should take out that restraining order like Johnny has suggested."

"I guess so. I'll go over and do that this afternoon."

Junebug appeared at the table with a reassuring smile and a tray full of food. She put a bowl of beef stew in front of each of them.

"Here we go. This'll fix those long faces right up. Bossy in a bowl for three. I'll be right back with some corn muffins and some axle grease."

Martha Maye looked at Jack and Tess, and a sad expression crossed her face.

Tess said, "Everything's going to be all right, Martha Maye."

"Oh, I expect so." She stared at her stew, stirring it absentmindedly. "I just want what y'all have."

"And we want that for you, cutie," Jack said. "This is all going to get settled, and you're going to come out better than you ever dreamed. Speaking of dream, did you have a good date with Johnny?"

"You mean Tess didn't tell you?"

"Tell me what?"

Martha Maye told Jack about Lenny showing up at the inn and about Johnny's plan.

"He called me and told me Lenny was fit to be tied," she said.

"I just bet he was," Jack said, laughing.

Junebug returned with corn muffins and butter and placed them on the table. "There you go. Eat up. We have chocolate pie today that some people would trade their youngins for. I'll save y'all a piece."

"You're the best, Junie."

"Don't you know it," she said over her shoulder. "If Tess ever dumps you, you know where to come!"

"Sorry, Junebug, it'll never happen," Tess said.

Jack winked at Tess. She turned back to Martha Maye.

"So what else did Johnny say about Lenny's visit?"

"Oh, he threw a bunch of false accusations and veiled threats around, but Johnny told him what's what and sent him on his way."

"Good for Johnny. He's a good man, Martha Maye," Jack said.

She nodded and saw Tess suddenly stiffen, the color draining from her face as she looked out onto the sidewalk.

"What's the matter, Tess?" Martha Maye asked, looking out to the street.

"I, I thought I saw someone," she said, nervously taking a drink of tea. She took a corn muffin and butter and became engrossed in painting the bread with butter. Jack and Martha Maye exchanged confused looks.

"Tess." Jack touched her arm. "Who did you see?"

Her eyes darted outside again, and then to Martha Maye, across the table. "I thought I saw John Ed. I haven't seen him since right after the kidnapping." She shivered. "It just brought that day back for a minute, that's all. It probably wasn't even him."

"It *was* him," Martha Maye said heavily.

Jack put his arm around Tess.

"I saw him on the street the other day," Martha Maye continued. "Said he's trying to keep a low profile because folks haven't quite forgiven him yet."

"Yet?" Tess said. "Will they ever?"

"I think in time they will," Martha Maye said. "The Lord says forgive and ye shall be forgiven."

"Luke 6:37," Tess said. "I'm just still so mad at him. I kept telling him someone was after me, and all he did was accuse me of having a—"

"Hissy fit with a tail on it, I believe it was," Jack interjected. "John Ed's biggest crime was stupidity."

Martha Maye pushed her empty bowl away from her. "What John Ed did was wrong, but the real criminal is behind bars, and that's where he'll stay for a good long time. I still can't believe I was so gullible not to see through that man's lies."

"You weren't the only one he fooled, Martha Maye," Tess offered.

Junebug appeared at the table. "Y'all ready for some pie?"

"Now there's a real criminal right there," Martha Maye teased. "Pushing calories on innocent, unsuspecting, calorie-fearing people."

"Speak for yourself, honey. I want pie!" Jack said.

"Speaking of honey, here comes Honey Winchester and the girls," Martha Maye said.

Honey came in with four little girls, including Maddy Mack and Butterbean. Martha Maye started to wave, but her fifth-grade daughter gave her a pleading look that said, *don't embarrass me,* and she put her hand down.

Honey got the girls settled at a table and came over to Martha Maye's booth. "Hey, y'all. Mind if I join the adult table?"

"Not at all, Honey." Martha Maye slid over to make room. "Have you met my friends Jackson Wright and Tess Tremaine?"

"I don't believe I've had the pleasure," Honey said, all eyes for Jack, ignoring Tess completely. "You mean *the* Jackson Wright? The best-selling author?" Honey squealed. "I have all your books! Say, you don't suppose I could bring them over one night and have you sign them for me, do you?"

"Oh. Uh, well," Jack stammered.

"Honey's only been in town a couple of months," Martha Maye told Jack and Tess. Then she directed her attention to Honey. "Honey, down girl, Tess and Jack are engaged."

Honey's eyes fell to the rock on Tess's hand, and her smile fell briefly, but she quickly recovered. "Bless your heart. When's the date?"

"We haven't set it for sure," Tess said.

"Girl, you better snap this one up right quick, before someone steals him away," Honey drawled.

"It'll never happen. I found my dream girl." Jack's arm was still around Tess, and he squeezed her into him.

"Isn't that just enough to make you sick?" Honey said.

"I think it's sweet. I'm so glad y'all found each other," Martha Maye said.

"We are, too." Jack beamed at Tess. She beamed back. Martha Maye watched them enviously. Honey looked at them begrudgingly.

Junebug delivered three pieces of pie, but Martha Maye gave hers to Honey. Between bites she said, "So who's going to the Oktoberfest on Saturday?"

"Just about everybody in town, I expect," Jack said around a mouthful of pie. "It's one of the biggest days in town, other than the Fourth of July and Apple Day."

"Martha Maye, how about you and I take the girls together?" Honey said. "Or do you have a date?"

"No dates in my foreseeable future," Martha Maye answered miserably. "At least not until after mid-November."

"What's mid-November?" Honey asked.

"It's my court date. Lenny's suing me for full custody."

Honey gasped. "No! When did that happen?"

"Just yesterday."

Jack patted her hand and said, "But we all know he'll never win. He's just doing it out of spite."

"Well, of course he'll never win. How dare he even try? You're a fantastic mother." Honey slapped the table. "Oh! The nerve of that man! Maybe my trusty little shotgun and I should pay him a courtesy visit."

"Martha Maye told us about what happened that night," Tess said.

Honey laughed and nudged Martha Maye. "I won't soon forget the look on his face when he saw that shotgun pointed at him. He was so surprised, you could have knocked his eyes off with a stick."

"I wish I could have seen his face," Martha Maye said. "But I'll never forget how fast he ran out of my house. He tried to act tough, but oohwee, he was scared to death."

"He had good reason to be scared," Honey said. "I wasn't playing."

Just as they all were laughing about Lenny, the object of their mirth walked into the diner.

"Well, bless him, here he comes." Honey nodded toward the door.

Lenny glanced around the room, his eyes narrowed, and headed for their table.

NINETEEN

Never argue with a fool; onlookers may not be able to tell the difference.

~Southern Proverb

"Lenny, what are you doing here?" Martha Maye asked when he stopped at their booth. Her tone didn't hide the fact that she was less than happy to see him.

"It's a free country, ain't it? I came in to eat. Imagine my surprise to find my wife out on the town without our daughter. Again. This sure won't look good to the judge." He crossed his arms, a smug look on his face.

Jack started to say something, but Martha Maye put her hand on his arm. She said, "Bless your heart. If you weren't so busy flapping your gums, you'd see our daughter over at that table." She pointed to the four little girls. Lenny saw his daughter and his face reddened.

Jack stood up. He was about the same height as Lenny, and not as big, but somehow he made Lenny look small. Jack took his elbow, and as he walked him toward the door, he said in a low voice, "I have three speeds, buddy. On, off, and don't push your luck. You'd best be on your way now."

"And what if I don't wanna be on my way? Is that lunatic gonna pull her weapon again?" Lenny tried to shake his arm free.

"I'll see that you do *wanna*."

They'd reached the door, and all eyes in the diner were on the two men. Lenny jerked his arm away from Jack's grasp. "You don't scare me, Jack Sprat. I could literally fix your dial to the permanent *off* position."

"Last chance, Lenny. A gallant retreat is better than a bad stand."

"I'm going," he said, glaring at Jack. "But not because you want me to.

I want to." He turned around and yelled to Martha Maye, "You best enjoy your last few weeks with our daughter, *wo-man*. Purty soon she's gonna be all mine." He flung the door open and stalked off down the street.

CHIEF BUTTERFIELD and a beefy African American woman joined the group of officers assembled around the table in the break room. Coffee cups and Hostess cupcake wrappers littered the table and good-natured laughter filled the air.

"All right, everybody, listen up. I want to introduce a new hire, Officer Velveeta Witherspoon."

Everyone's eyes went to Velveeta, and she fanned her hand out in a wave.

"She's joining the Goose Pimple Junction PD as of thirty minutes ago. She comes from over in Memphis and has done some training in investigative work. I think she'll be a valuable addition to our force. So with that said, Velveeta, why don't you tell everybody a little about yourself."

Velveeta was a big woman, who stood five feet ten, with long, thick arms and beefy legs. If she lost twenty pounds, she might be considered top-heavy, but standing in front of the other officers she looked substantial, more than capable of taking care of herself and definitely capable of taking down a suspect.

"Hey, y'all. I'm real glad to be here. Okay, let's see. About me. I have one son, Roscoe, and one daughter, Cinnamon. He's six and she's eight, both cuter 'n a bug's butt." She paused while everyone laughed politely. "They got their daddy's looks." She curled her fat lips into a comedic grimace.

"My husband Roscoe senior, God rest his soul, left this world two years and five months ago. Me and the kids have been through Hell in gasoline pants." She shook her head, shifted from one foot to another, crossed her meaty arms, and continued.

"Now I'm just trying to be a good mama and a good cop. I was on the Memphis PD for ten years but decided I wanted to get the youngins out of the big city and into a town where I can raise them right. I guess that's about it." She sat down, flashing a big white smile made brighter by her dark brown skin and huge, almost bulging brown eyes.

Johnny stood. "I want y'all to make sure you introduce yourselves and make Velveeta feel welcome." The old refrigerator in the corner began to hum, and Johnny raised his voice over the noise. "She comes highly recommended. We're glad to have you, Officer Witherspoon." They exchanged nods.

Johnny looked at the six officers sitting around the beat-up rectangular wooden table and then pulled out a list from the papers in front of him.

"All right, moving on. As we previously discussed, I want Duke and Riley tailing Lenny Applewhite 24-7. Duke, you'll take days; Riley, nights. One goes off, the other goes on. I don't care if you have to sit outside his hotel all night. Stay with him." The officers nodded.

"Northington, I want you and Woodson walking the town square. Northington is on days, and Woodson, you're on nights. Keep an eye on the alley, and also the town green, where they're starting to set up for the Oktoberfest. There'll be lots of stuff our man—"

"Or woman," Velveeta interjected. "Don't be sexist."

"Or woman," Johnny nodded, "could decide to walk away with over there, so stay alert. If you see trouble, call for backup before moving in."

"Yessir, Chief."

"Witherspoon and Beanblossom, I want you in the cruiser. Beanblossom, days; Witherspoon, nights. I want a solid police presence in this town. Got it?"

"Yessir."

"And on the night of the Oktoberfest, Bernadette's filling in for Teenie, but *everyone* else is on duty. Stay on the move, with your eyes open. With all the folks up at the town square all night, there will be plenty of opportunity for mischief there *and* in quiet neighborhoods. Keep alert. Any questions?"

Pete Riley raised his hand. "Yeah, why are we sitting on Applewhite so hard?"

"One"—Johnny held up a finger—"I like him for all the theft around town. I think he's sneaky, and weird, and might just steal the town blind out of meanness. Two"—he held up two fingers—"all of these thefts started around the same time Mr. Applewhite came to town. I don't like coincidences. And three"—he held up three fingers—"he's harassing one of our citizens, and I want it stopped. Any other questions?"

"There's just the seven of us, plus you, Chief," Officer Victor Northington pointed out. "We could use some more manpower. How about we utilize the EMTs?"

"Yeah," Officer Northington jumped in, "Nosmo King drives around all day or sits in the ambulance, so how about we get him to keep his eyes open, too?"

"Good idea. I'll give the fire chief a call. If we put everyone on full alert, maybe we'll get lucky and catch this guy."

"Or girl," Velveeta said.

"Or girl," Johnny amended. "All right, everybody clear on the plan?"

Everyone nodded or mumbled in the affirmative.

"Then let's go catch us a thief. Giddyup and get along."

BIG DARRYL D picked up a set of keys to a 2005 Lexus, turned off the lights in the office and showroom, and walked outside, ready to go home for the day. He punched the key fob and heard the *chirp-chirp* of the locks unlocking. After opening the driver's side door, he threw his coat across to the passenger seat and got in with a groan because of the ache in his knees and back.

Darryl started to put the key in the ignition but stopped. His head swiveled to the right, and he froze. Something was wrong. He wasn't sure what, but something. He sniffed the air, strained to listen, and looked around. Then he turned his whole body around to the backseat and got the fright of his life. Somebody was lying down back there.

"Aaaaaaa!" Darryl screamed and jumped, bumping his head on the car ceiling. "What the--"

"Big Darryl, Big Darryl, it's just me, just me."

The figure in the backseat sat up, hands raised in an *I surrender* gesture. Darryl glared at Lenny before turning around in his seat and slumping in relief.

Darryl looked in the rear view mirror and addressed his employee. "Lenny Applewhite, you scared the living daylights out of me. What in tarnation are you doing back there? Are you sleeping in the cars? Are you homeless? How long have you been doing this? Man alive, you gave me a fright."

"Which answer do you want first?"

"You choose." Darryl's tone made it clear he was not a happy man.

Lenny rubbed the back of his neck. "I'm sleeping. Or trying to. No, I'm not homeless. Uh, what were your other questions?"

"How long have you been doing this?"

"Just tonight. I promise."

"Boy, you got money problems?"

"Naw. I got people problems."

"Come again?"

"I got a couple of people looking for me, and I'd rather not be found. So I decided to crash here for the night."

"A jealous husband?"

"No."

"Drug dealers?"

"Hell, no."

"Gambling problems?"

"Maybe." He looked past Darryl at an approaching car and dove onto the backseat again. "Darryl, just drive. I'll literally owe you big, but can you just drive?"

A dark Chevy Suburban lurked at the entrance to the car lot. Darryl started the Lexus and put it in drive. As he approached the Suburban, he lowered his window and leaned out to holler to its occupants.

"We're closed for the night, folks, but y'all come back in the morning and I'll fix you right up."

Both men in the SUV looked Darryl over and scanned the car lot without saying a word. He sat, breathing hard and watching and waiting. Finally the vehicle slowly began to move, and Darryl watched until the taillights disappeared. Lenny spoke up from the backseat.

"Are they gone?"

"For now."

"Are you gonna turn me in?"

"No, I'm taking you home—my home—but you got to get your crap together, boy. This could be bad for bidness."

Darryl sighed as he pulled out of the lot. "I thought I was hiring you. I didn't plan on taking you to raise."

TWENTY

You should dress for every occasion; there's no sense in resembling a washwoman.

~Southern Proverb

The third Saturday in October, the day of Goose Pimple Junction's forty-ninth annual Oktoberfest, was a picture-perfect day. At six o'clock in the evening, the sun was just starting its descent, bringing hints of a slight chill to the warm day. The trees were full of golden, red, and orange leaves. Every once in a while, a gust of wind sent them flying through the air like confetti.

Kids darted around the tables and booths of food and crafts for sale. The scents of spicy bratwurst, grease, and beer wafted over the cool grass while a group of girls talked and giggled, glancing covertly at a group of letter jackets and ball hats who were not so covertly looking back. Feedback from an amp brought all eyes toward the musicians preparing to play, as spectators gravitated toward festival activities. Along the pathway, some old men sat on a bench under the huge oaks and maples of the town green, smiling, nodding, and swapping tall tales.

Costumes were optional but favored at the festival. Most people in town wanted a chance to win the best costume prize—the use of a 1993 Mazda Miata for a year, courtesy of Big Darryl D's Car Country.

Martha Maye and Butterbean's feet crunched leaves as they walked down the color-laden sidewalk. Butterbean had to walk sideways at times to squeeze the cumbersome yellow horizontal cardboard cutout she was sandwiched into through the crowd. In the middle of the cutout, she had thin strips of red, orange, and green tissue paper sticking out from her brown turtleneck.

Honey and Maddy Mack were waiting at the edge of the town green. "Aw, look at you!" Honey said. "You look good enough to eat."

"I'm a taco!" Butterbean said, spreading her arms out wide.

"And you're the best gosh darn taco I've ever seen."

Maddy Mack was dressed as the Energizer Bunny, and Butterbean reached up to touch the big pink ears attached to the top of her pink hoodie. She wore pink sweatpants, pink thong sandals, a bass drum strapped to her chest, and sunglasses.

Maddy Mack began moving in a circle, beating the drum. "What about me? How do I look?" she yelled over the drumming.

"Maddy Mack, you look like the real thing!" Butterbean said, clapping.

Martha Maye, in a white floor-length dress, with rows and rows of frilly layers draped over a hoop skirt, looked like Scarlett O'Hara.

Her hands rested on top of the wide skirt. "I don't know how women wore these things." She took in Honey's costume and said, "I do declare, Elvira, you look stunning! And more comfortable than I am."

Honey's blond hair was covered with a black wig—bouffant at the top, cascading into long straight tresses. Her full-length black dress plunged at the overflowing bustline, nearly exposing her entire chest. With a slit in the skirt all the way up her right thigh, the dress hugged her hips and thin waist. There wasn't much of Honey's hourglass figure left to the imagination. Six-inch black heels at the end of long, shapely legs finished the look.

"You put the *va* in *va va va voom*." Martha Maye hugged her friend's shoulders.

Quoting Elvira, Honey said, "If they ever ask about me, tell them I was more than just a great set of boobs. I was also an incredible pair of legs." She parted her long skirt, flashing her entire leg, as well as a huge smile.

"Honey, you're too much." She looked around the town square. "Oh look! There's Tess and Jack! Aren't they adorable?" Martha Maye waved to the couple.

"They're just two pumpkins," Honey said disdainfully.

"Not just any old pumpkins," Martha Maye said. "He's a *Jack*-o'-lantern, and she's a *Jill*-o'-lantern. Get it?"

"No, I don't. Her name's not Jill." Honey frowned.

"Oh, you. C'mon, let's go watch the parade with them."

As a pack of dachshunds and their owners walked down the middle of Main Street, Jack was explaining to Tess about the parade.

"For some reason nobody seems to know, Goose Pimple Junction has had an above average number of dachshunds for years. So a while back, somebody got the bright idea to have a wiener dog race and parade," Jack explained.

"Just so long as they don't mingle the parade with the bratwurst grilling," Tess said. Then she noticed Martha Maye. "Aw, look at you! Don't you make a beautiful Southern belle!"

"I'm not just any ol' Southern belle, I'm Scarlett." Martha Maye smiled and swept her skirt side to side in a half-circle to show it off, bumping some people, who turned to stare.

"And I'm a taco." Butterbean jumped up and down.

"I see you are." Tess reached out to fluff the cheese and lettuce—the green and orange tissue paper.

"You're making me hungry for Mexican food," Jack told Butterbean.

"And *you*, little lady, you look good enough to beat the band," he said to Maddy Mack.

"Badum ching," Tess said.

"Well hellooooo," Honey said. "I feel like a pork chop at a bar mitzvah over here."

"We were saving the best for last, Elvira. Don't you poor-mouth yourself," Tess said consolingly. "You look mahvalous, darling," she said.

"Mama! Look at Ms. Schottenstein's Oscar." Butterbean pointed to a dachshund in the parade dressed as a taco. "She stole my idea."

There was also a dachshund dressed as a hot dog, one as a dinosaur, one as a cheerleader. Two dogs being walked by the same owner were dressed like ketchup and mustard bottles. Behind them was one dressed as a skunk, another as a banana split.

"They have just about everything here," Tess said, laughing at a dog dressed as Elvis.

"Oh, this is serious business," Jack said. "Some of the owners will start planning next year's costume tomorrow."

"How long you lived here, Tess?" Honey asked.

"About five months," Tess said. "I guess that makes me the newbie in town."

As the last of the dogs passed and the crowd lining the sidewalks started to disperse, Gus Crowley, the owner of the town's gas station, came by. "Bet I can whoop your butt at horseshoes, Jack."

"I'll take that bet and add a game of cornhole to the wager, too," Jack boasted. "Come on, y'all, be my good luck charms, and come watch me kick Crowley's behind."

They strolled through the town green taking everything in. There were pumpkins everywhere—short ones, tall ones, fat ones, skinny ones, big ones up on rocks. Most had been turned into jack-o'-lanterns, some had not.

Tables set up on the town green were loaded with food—barbecue, turtle soup, pork chop sandwiches, potato salad, green beans, corn pudding, zucchini bread, pumpkin bread, apple cobbler, and ice cream. Smoke billowed from a grill, sending the smell of bratwursts into the air, along with that of the fried apple pies bubbling in deep fryers, and apple butter simmering in big cast-iron kettles. It was nothing short of a feast, just as the decorations of pumpkins, cornstalks, and colorful leaves were a feast for the eyes.

By seven o'clock, the festivities were in full swing. Butterbean kept bumping into people with her taco shell costume every time she turned around. She and Maddy Mack wanted to enter the pumpkin carving contest and visit the face-painting table, so they begged off watching the cornhole and horseshoe contests, and Jack and Tess went on without them.

After they carved a tall pumpkin into a scary jack-o'-lantern and a big fat pumpkin into a silly jack-o'-lantern for the contest, the girls had bright orange pumpkins painted on their cheeks.

Next, Maddy Mack and Butterbean wanted to ride in the hay wagon. As they walked toward the tractor, they found Louetta, dressed as a nurse, and Ima Jean, dressed as a doctor.

"Aunt Imy! Look at you!" Martha Maye held out her arms. "And Mama—y'all look great!"

"I'm not a doctor, but I play one on TV," Ima Jean said.

"Want to take a hayride?" Butterbean asked them.

"Well sure, hon, that sounds like fun." Lou grabbed her granddaughter's hand.

"Martha Maye, y'all go on ahead. I'll catch up to you," Honey said, disappearing into the crowd. "I have to see a man about a horse." She waggled her eyebrows.

Lou leaned into Martha Maye. "She maybe has to see a man, but I'd bet a day's pay it ain't about no horse."

With Lou and Ima Jean in tow, the girls and Martha Maye again headed toward the hay wagon, but this time Lenny stopped them. "Carrie Lou!" Lenny, a few meters away, yelled. "Come say hello to your daddy."

She turned to look at him and nearly knocked over Mrs. Schottenstein's four-year-old daughter.

Like a baseball catcher, Lenny squatted, his arms outstretched for a hug.

Butterbean looked up at her mother, unsure of what to do. Martha Maye reassured her. "Go ahead, Bean. I'll be right here." She kissed the top of her daughter's head.

Butterbean nervously looked from her mother to her father to Lou, to Ima Jean, and back to her father. Then she slowly walked toward Lenny, scuffing her feet in the grass with her head down, like she was heading to the gallows.

"How about a nice Hawaiian Punch?" Ima Jean yelled at Lenny, her fist held high in the air.

"Shhh now, none of that, Imy." Lou patted her arm, pulling her hand down. "Come on, Bean doesn't need an audience. I can't stand to watch anyhow." The two moved on.

As Martha Maye stood by, arms crossed defiantly and eyes shooting daggers at Lenny, Johnny appeared at her side. "She'll be all right. I've got my people all around here. He tries anything funny and he'll get nabbed before he can say 'kerfuffle.'"

Martha Maye smiled up at him. "What the heck is a kerfuffle?"

He looked down at her with a serious expression. "A commotion or a fuss."

"Hey, Clutterfield, I thought I told you to leave my wife alone!" Lenny hustled past his daughter and stopped a few feet away from Johnny and Martha Maye.

"And I told you to stay away from this woman, Mr. Applewhite." Johnny stabbed his finger in the air at Lenny.

"I don't have to stay away from her. I'm married to her."

"Oh, I beg to differ, sir." Johnny clenched and unclenched his fists at his side. "As you well know, she took a restraining order out on you the other day. I just happen to have a copy of it, in case you lost the first one." Johnny took an envelope from his pocket and handed it to Lenny. "Do you need help reading it?"

"You, you—oh, never mind." Lenny fisted his hands, throwing them at his side in exasperation and turning away.

"No, no, no. You've opened this can, let's eat it all," Johnny said, stepping in front of him.

"She's literally still a married wo-man." Lenny pointed from Martha Maye to Johnny. "Your fraternacizing with her will not look good when the judge decides custody."

Butterbean and Maddy Mack huddled together, looking shocked and scared. Everyone around them had stopped talking and turned to listen to the heated exchange. Lou and Ima Jean had backtracked and returned to the scene when they heard the raised voices. Lou tried to get her granddaughter to come with her, but Butterbean stood stock-still.

"Lenny, the word is frater*nizing*, and our relationship is purely platonic. You should know Martha Maye is too much of a lady to do anything untoward like you're suggesting. Too bad I can't say the same about you."

"What's that supposed to mean?" Lenny clenched his jaw.

"For one, it means you have a reputation around town as a womanizer."

"Humph" was all Lenny could muster.

"And it means we will have no shortage of people to testify to said womanization."

To Johnny, Martha Maye mouthed, "Womanization?"

Johnny swiped his hand over his mouth as if out of frustration, but Martha Maye saw a hint of a smile before his hand covered his mouth. He looked at Lenny and continued. "And three, if you have anything to do with the mayhem that's been going on around here, I'm going to find out about it and nail your butt to the tree. We'll see how the judge likes you then, you *hooligan*." He said the word with distaste.

"I'ma get you for this, mister," Lenny hissed, his eyes narrowed, his chin jutted out.

"Not if I get you first." Johnny stood his ground with his legs apart and his arms folded in front of him.

"We will continue this conversation at another time," Lenny yelled over his shoulder, stomping away.

"How about when you're not loaded up on loudmouth soup," Johnny hollered after him.

"I ain't drunk." Lenny turned back around to protest.

"You should finish your sentence," Johnny said to Lenny, who glared at him.

"Huh?"

"You mean you ain't drunk– yet. But you're well on your way."

"This ain't over," Lenny said, his face scrunched up in anger. "Remember, I'm watching you." He motioned with two fingers from Johnny to himself as he'd done in Johnny's office, then looked at his daughter. "Carrie, I'll see you later, darling."

Johnny muttered, "In a pig's eye. Pun intended." He looked around and waved his hand. "Sorry for the interruption, folks."

Martha Maye went to hug her daughter and Johnny followed.

"Now, miss, and missy, would you care to accompany me on a hayride?" Johnny offered both arms, and they each took one, with Maddy

Mack linking arms with Butterbean and Lou and Ima Jean following.

"Johnny, I wish you hadn't done that," Martha Maye whispered, clearly embarrassed by all of the eyes on her.

"I'm sorry, Martha Maye." He put his hand against her back. "The man just makes my blood boil, and he doesn't have the right to talk to you, let alone try to tell you who you can and can't talk to." He smiled as he watched Lenny stomp toward the beer wagon. "I'm just trying to set parameters and uphold the law. Sorry if I got carried away."

"Don't try to teach a pig to sing. It wastes your time and it annoys the pig. That's my motto." She looked up at him, trying to smile.

"Good advice, Martha Maye." Johnny helped the girls and the ladies climb up on the hay wagon, then he climbed on and squeezed in next to Martha Maye, sitting so close their thighs touched. Butterbean had to sit in front of her mother on the wagon floor since her taco costume was so wide. Hay stuck to her brown tights.

Dusk had turned to evening, and the little white lights strung in the trees on the town square year-round glimmered. Jack-o'-lanterns glowed, and with the twinkling lights, glowing pumpkins, the hazy beauty of dusk, and the feel of Johnny's leg against hers, Martha Maye felt her annoyance at the confrontation lift.

She looked at the crowd as the wagon circled the town green. She saw Mayor Buck dressed as Colonel Sanders. There were three people dressed as Elvis, and someone dressed as a gorilla chased someone in a banana costume.

"Look at Mark Twain and Minnie Pearl," she said, pointing out Pickle and Charlotte.

"I thought Pickle would be a pickle," Maddy Mack said as the wagon rolled and bumped along, jostling the passengers.

Ima Jean broke out in song. "Hold the pickle, hold the lettuce, special orders don't upset us, all we ask is that you let us serve you your way."

"Now I'm hungry for a Whopper," Lou muttered.

Fifteen minutes later, the hay wagon came to a stop, and as people disembarked brushing the hay from their behinds, the group decided to head for the food tables.

After they ate, Martha Maye and Johnny went to watch the bratwurst-eating contest while the rest of the group listened to the Bluegrass band and Butterbean and Maddy Mack danced. When Martha Maye and Johnny rejoined them, they enlisted everyone to go to the wife-carrying contest.

"It will begin directly. Jack and Tess entered, even though they aren't married yet," Martha Maye explained.

"Oh, I wanna watch!"

"Me, too."

"How was the bratwurst-eating contest?" Lou asked her daughter.

"It's too bad all y'all missed it. It was great."

"Who won?"

"Slick, but Tommy Thompson filed an inquiry. Said Slick cooked the bratwurst, so it was rigged. Just 'cause Slick made 'em, doesn't mean he cheated does it?"

"Oh, look!" Butterbean jumped up and down. "Here come the first contestants." She took a hard look and then tugged on Lou's arm. "What's that sand pit for?"

"Most wife-carrying contests have a water obstacle, but it's too chilly to run through water, so they're substituting a sand pit obstacle. They have to run through it," Louetta explained, combing her hands through her granddaughter's hair.

"Oh my gosh!" Maddy Mack screeched.

"What? What?" Lou and Ima Jean said together.

Everybody looked to where Maddy Mack pointed. They saw Honey being carried to the starting line fireman-style by the chief of the fire department, Pete Lallouette.

"What's she doing with Lolly?" Butterbean wondered out loud.

"Looks like she did have to talk to a man," Lou observed. "About *being* a horse."

Everyone looked blankly at Lou.

"She's riding Lolly like a horse—get it?"

"Ohhh," came the collective response.

The race was run two couples at a time. They watched while Lolly ran, carrying Honey fireman style, through the first obstacle—the balloon course. The men had to step on and break ten balloons before they could advance to the next task. Then they had to wade through the sand pit, maneuver over a log hurdle, and finally navigate a rock garden that contained every size of rock from pebbles to bowling-ball-sized stones, all while holding their "wife."

Lolly and Honey competed against Molly Ann and Stanley, a married couple who looked to be in their late thirties. Even though Honey and Lolly just met and hadn't worked out a rhythm, they were more fit and beat the other couple by several seconds.

"Look, here come Jack and Tess. Good golly, how'd she get in that position?"

They watched Jack and Tess approach the starting line next to a couple who looked to be quite a bit older. Tess's front was against Jack's back. Her arms were wrapped around his waist, and he held onto her legs, which were around his neck.

"I know why she chose that technique," Honey said, joining them. She rearranged the long black wig on her head. She was out of costume now, but said she'd decided to keep the wig on because her real hair was hot, sweaty, and mashed to her head.

"Why?" Lou asked.

"So she could get up close and personal to Jack's butt. Shoot. I shoulda thought of that."

"There's always next year," Lou said.

The older couple had trouble from the start; the wife fell off halfway through the rock garden.

Honey, eating popcorn and watching the race as if she were at a movie theatre, leaned toward Lou. "She never shoulda used the piggyback technique. That's the worst one."

Jack and Tess received congratulations from the group, and they watched Pickle's mother and father race another couple. Then they called for all participants to line up for the last heat: the race—the wife-carrying sprint.

"C'mon, Jack, let's go," Tess said, pulling on his arm.

"Good Lord, woman. You're gonna kill me before we even have a chance to get married." But Jack acquiesced, smiling, despite his protests.

After the sprint—which Lolly and Honey won—Jack and Tess rejoined the group. Everyone sat at a picnic table eating apple hand pies until they were ready to pop.

Johnny's phone went off, and he answered it with, "Chief Butterfield." He put one finger in his ear, turned away from the group slightly, and listened for several beats. "Affirmative. Call for backup. Whoever's closest to the diner."

Johnny turned to Martha Maye. "Duty calls. There's been a theft at the diner. I gotta go."

"You're not going over there by yourself, are you?" Martha Maye grabbed his arm.

"No, I asked for an assist. Don't worry. I'll be back in two shakes of a rat's tail." He waved and disappeared into the crowd.

Louetta put her arm around her daughter. "Now, don't you worry the least little bit, sugar britches. Johnny knows what he's doing."

Martha Maye had had enough. There was too much stress: Lenny, her secret admirer, Aunt Imy's mental state, Johnny's occupation. She felt like the world was caving in on her. She needed a few minutes alone.

"Mama, can you watch the girls for a bit? I just need to run home right quick and use the little girl's room."

Lou rubbed her daughter's back and said, "Sure, sure, darlin'. You gwon. We'll be fine. Take your time, but honey, why don't you go to my house? It's closer."

Martha Maye walked to her mother's house thinking about Lenny. He worried her. She wondered what he would do next. It was completely dark now, except for the occasional pools of light coming from the street lamps. As the sounds of the Oktoberfest faded behind her, she heard a dog barking and the hoot of an owl. She'd never felt nervous to be out by herself in Goose Pimple Junction, but she had a bad feeling tonight. Maybe her apprehension was just a result of the confrontation with Lenny. She hugged her arms to her chest and hurried on.

TWENTY-ONE

A blind mule ain't afraid of darkness.

~Southern Proverb

Martha Maye walked into the house and headed straight to the half bath on the first floor. As soon as she closed the door, she knew she had a problem.

Oh, for Pete's sake. She lifted her heavy dress a few inches and then let it drop.

What would Scarlett do? She lifted it again. *What* did *Scarlett do?*

She hadn't thought about how she was going to go to the bathroom wearing a hoop skirt under frilly layers. The bone hoops in the slip prevented her from lifting it and the dress high enough, and even if she could manage to raise the slip, she had many layers of petticoat underneath. What would she do with them? She needed someone to lift it up and place the skirt over the back of the tank. She didn't think she could do that by herself. And how was she going to get her underwear off?

"Oh, Mammy, where are you when I need you?"

She tried to reach under the frilly layers of the dress, the hoop slip, and the petticoat. After stumbling around the small bathroom a few times like she was on a rocky ship in rough water, she managed to get her underwear down.

Staring at the toilet for a bit, she lifted all of the layers as high as she could. Facing the toilet, she walked forward and tried to straddle it, sitting on it backward. As she got halfway down, the skirt came up in her face, and she knew her hair and makeup would be ruined if she sat all the way down. She stood.

Priorities.

There was only one thing to do. She'd have to take off the dress and hoop slip, pee, and then put everything back on. *Or maybe I should go home and change clothes altogether.*

WHEN VELVEETA Witherspoon's cruiser turned onto Marigold Lane, her headlights swept over Skeeter Duke standing on a front lawn, waving his arms over his head. He ran toward her car as she approached the house. She rolled to a stop, lowered the passenger side window, and called out to him.

"Hey, Duke, whatcha—"

"Velveeta!" He pointed to a dark spot in the yard. "I think there's a dead body in Martha Maye's front yard. Call it in."

Velveeta didn't waste any time. "Dispatch, this is unit six. Got a 10-54 at 115 Marigold Lane. Over." The adrenaline was pumping, and she was itching to get out of the car and take a look at the body.

Bernadette responded right away, but hesitantly. "Uh, we don't use numbers, Officer. What's a 10-54?"

"It's a possible dead body," Velveeta said impatiently.

"Possible? Is it or isn't it?"

Velveeta turned toward Skeeter, who now stood over the lump on the lawn. She hollered, "Do we have confirmation of a fatality?"

"Affirmative. Got no pulse. Technically speaking, he's deader 'n a doornail."

"We've got a body. Repeat, dead body. Call the chief, and then call the coroner's office."

"What's going on? Who's dead? Isn't that Martha Maye's house?" Bernadette's voice had reached a high pitch.

"We haven't identified the deceased yet. Call the chief, okay? Over."

She ran to Skeeter and the body on the lawn, a man positioned face up. Pulling the flashlight off her belt, she passed its beam over the still form, stopping on the face.

"Holy cannoli." Skeeter bent at the waist, leaning over the corpse to get a better look.

One arm lay straight out to the side, the other was parallel to the body. The man's legs were crossed at the ankles. His eyes were open and his mouth was slightly ajar.

"Is this the way you found him?"

"Uh, no." Skeeter scratched his head. "I found him facedown. Figured we needed to turn him over so's we could see his face."

"No! Don't go touching nothing else. You'll contaminate the scene. Is there an apparent cause of death?"

Skeeter stood up straight. "Don't rightly know. I saw it, you came. Not much time to look. Besides, dead bodies make me nervous."

"How many have you run across in your career anyway?"

"Uh, including my meemaw?"

"I mean in the line of work, fool. Not in a funeral parlor."

"Well then, this would be the second."

She moved the flashlight beam down the body, stopping at the man's open jeans zipper. "For crying out catfish—"

Another cruiser, lights flashing and siren wailing, came to a screeching halt at the curb in front of Martha Maye's house. Johnny sprang out of the car and rushed to the officers, looking frantic.

"Martha Maye? Where's Martha Maye?"

Lou looked at her watch. "Law child, where's your mama? She's been gone so long I'm beginning to wonder if she fell in."

Butterbean giggled. She had taken her taco shell off and now looked like a little pixie. "Where's Aunt Imy?"

"She's over to the pumpkin seed spitting contest. I told her we'd meet her here." Louetta led her granddaughter by the hand and the group followed.

"I think they've held all the contests except for two," Tess said. "Let's head over to the polka and chicken dance contests."

"We can't miss the chicken dance contest. Charlotte and Peekal are gonna be in it," Lou said.

Tess gave Jack a meaningful look. "No way," he said. "Uh-uh. I am not entering any more contests tonight. You very nearly killed me as it is." His cell phone rang, and he answered it with a finger over his ear so he could hear better.

As Jack talked into the phone, Louetta looked around. "Anybody seen Martha Maye?"

"No," Tess said. "Not for a while." Then she looked over Lou's shoulder and pointed. "Oh! Here she comes now. Looks like she decided to leave the hoop slip at home."

"That dress is just as pretty without it."

The band broke into "Monster Mash," and they watched the polka contestants gather. Jack held up a finger to Tess, signaling that he'd be just a minute. He smiled at Martha Maye before turning and walking away from the crowd to continue his phone conversation.

TWENTY-TWO

Someone who pets a live catfish isn't crowded with brains.

~Southern Proverb

"Calm down, Chief, calm down." Skeeter grabbed Johnny by the shoulders. "It's not Martha Maye. It's Lenny." Johnny let out a huge rush of air and realized he'd been holding his breath for far too long. He bent over, bracing his hands just above his knees, trying to bring his breathing back to normal.

"Bernadette . . . said 115 Marigold . . . Martha Maye's house—I thought . . ." His voice wavered, and he walked away from the two officers to collect himself. Skeeter came up behind him and clapped him on the shoulder. "Get it together, man. It's not Martha Maye."

Johnny nodded, swiped his hand over his face, took a deep breath, and started barking out orders.

"I want lights set up so we can see what we're dealing with. Velveeta, call in and request an investigator, and get your crime scene kit. Skeeter, tape it off—the whole lawn. Hell, the whole block. I want all the neighbors questioned. Anyone seen Martha Maye?"

"Far's I know, she's still in the town square," Skeeter said.

Johnny got out his cell phone and called Jack, who picked up on the third ring. He could hear "Monster Mash" playing in the background.

"Hey Johnny, where'd you disappear to—"

"Jack, we got us a situation. Have you seen Martha Maye?"

"No, actually we were just—wait a minute." After a few seconds and some muffled talking, Jack came back on the line. "Here she comes now. Want to talk to her?"

"No. Listen up, I want you to get where you can talk privately. Right quick."

Johnny could hear movement and breathing for a few moments and then, "Okay. What's wrong?"

"Lenny Applewhite is dead."

"Come again?"

"He's no longer eligible for the census."

"Johnny, I know what dead means. I just didn't know if I heard you right. What happened?"

"Don't know, other than he's lying in Martha Maye's front yard, and his condition is non-conducive to life. Here's what I need you to do: Get Lou and have her take Butterbean to her house before word gets out. As soon as they're gone, tell Tess and Martha Maye what's going on, then bring them over here. And do not–and I repeat do not–let this get out. I shouldn't be calling you, but I know I can trust you, and I need your help. I want Martha Maye to be somewhat prepared for what's over here, but I don't want Butterbean finding out about this at the Oktoberfest. Tell Lou to let Butterbean spend the night at her house. Tell her you'll explain later."

"Sure. Sure thing, Johnny."

"Hurry up, okay?"

"OKAY," JACK said to the air, because Johnny had already hung up.

Jack went quickly to Lou. He leaned over and whispered in her ear: "I'll explain later, but right now I need you to take Butterbean home, get her in bed pronto, no questions asked. I promise we'll explain as soon as we can. I'm taking Tess and Martha Maye with me."

Her forehead took on more wrinkles as it creased in confusion. She tilted her head, and he said, "Soon. I promise. Now get going, all right?"

She studied his face and swallowed hard. "All right." She returned to the group with a smile pasted on her face. "Alrighty, let's take this party back to my house." Jack heard some mild protesting from Butterbean, as he told Martha Maye and Tess to come with him. They looked questioningly at him, and he led them away from everyone to tell them the news.

"Why's Mama and them leaving so soon? What's going on?"

"Martha Maye, something's happened." Jack put his hand on her arm. "Something awful."

"What? Is it Johnny?" she asked anxiously, looking around.

"No, Johnny's fine." He gently pushed her shoulders back so she faced him. "But he's working a murder scene."

Martha Maye searched around them as if she had an irrational need to ensure her mother, daughter, and aunt were all right, even though she'd just seen them. She turned back to Jack. "Murder? Who—"

"It's Lenny."

"It's L . . . L . . . L . . ." Her mouth tried to form words, but nothing came out.

Tess found her voice. "It's Lenny? He's –"

"Metabolically challenged," Jack finished for her.

"Jack, this is hardly a time for jokes." Tess put her arm around Martha Maye, who stood with her hand over her mouth, staring blankly into the night, too stunned to form thoughts or words.

"I don't mean to be disrespectful. It just seems gentler than saying he's . . . dead. Martha Maye, do you think you can walk? Johnny wants us over there."

She nodded, and he took her right arm, while Tess took the left. They steered her toward Marigold Lane.

"Where is he?" Martha Maye asked as they worked their way through the crowd.

"Martha Maye." He stopped and looked down at her for a long moment before saying, "I'm afraid he's in your front yard."

Twenty minutes later, Martha Maye had hurriedly changed into jeans and a T-shirt and sat sideways in Johnny's cruiser, her legs dangling out of the car and a dazed expression on her face.

Johnny crouched in front of her, his hands wrapped around her forearms. "It's gonna be all right, Martha Maye. We'll get this figured out."

She nodded at him, her face white, eyes wide. She rubbed her forehead and swallowed hard. He was worried about her. She hadn't said more than four words since she arrived on the scene.

He stood up and saw Jeb Hefflefinger, the investigator from the coroner's office, standing by the body. Johnny motioned to Tess to come over. "Be right back, Martha Maye. You be all right with Tess for just a minute?" She nodded, and he walked over to the investigator, who was peeling off his gloves.

"Whatcha got, Jeb?"

"At first glance, nothing, Chief. Not much fixed lividity. No blanching, and certainly no rigor yet. STD says he can't be more than a few hours dead."

"He had a . . . disease?"

"No. Technical term."

"Oh?"

"Stab in the dark."

Johnny bit the inside of his mouth, trying not to smile. He didn't want anyone seeing him smiling over Lenny's dead body.

"To tell you the truth, Chief, at first I didn't see a cause of death, but I felt around the body and finally found this." Jeb had turned the body onto its stomach. He moved the hoodie away from Lenny's skin and pointed his flashlight at a slit on the back of the neck.

"This is it, Chief. A fatal knife wound. Just one puncture, far's I can see. Must've hit an artery, and he went right down. I'll bet when we get him back to the office and look at his hoodie, we'll find this slice lines up with the knife wound to his neck." Jeb pointed the flashlight beam at the edge of Lenny's gray hoodie where a cut was visible. Then he lifted the hoodie and T-shirt underneath and shined the light on Lenny's back. "There's a little lividity, but like I said, no blanching evident, so I don't think he can be more than a few hours gone."

"Can't be more than two hours," Johnny said, as Hank and Skeeter walked up with Estherlene Bumgarner. The officers stared at him, and he added, "I just saw the man about two hours ago. He was alive and kicking then. Almost literally."

Johnny turned to Estherlene. "Evening, ma'am. Can you tell us what you saw tonight?"

Estherlene pulled her fluffy pink robe tight against the cool night air. "Shoot fire, I could just kick myself for missing all the commotion. I've been soaking in the tub, reading my new book all night. It's a goodun, too, and I purt near stayed in the water until I was a prune." She leaned toward Johnny conspiratorially and said, "And a woman my age doesn't need any more help looking like a prune, let me tell you, but this book—it's called *Gulf Boulevard*—I just couldn't put it down –"

"Okay, Estherlene, it's okay." Johnny raised his hands to stop her blabbering. "Think hard. You sure you didn't see anything? Hear anything?" She shook her head, biting a hangnail. "What about Hector?"

"Law, no. That man's been dead to the world since eight thirty. Fact is, he's still sleeping, even through all this excitement. The man can't hear a thing over his snoring—"

"Okay." The chief nodded. "Okay, Estherlene, thank you. That'll be all for now. You let us know if you remember anything at all. Thank you."

Velveeta walked up. "Chief, pardon me if I'm overstepping, but you need to let us handle this. You're too personally involved." He stared at her, then swept his gaze to Hank, motioning with his eyes for him to lead Estherlene out of earshot.

Once they'd walked off, Velveeta continued. "We'll report to you, of course, but I think it's best for you and the department if you're not involved in the investigation. Let me question Martha Maye."

"What for?" he asked testily.

"You know what for. Family members are always the first suspects. Do her a favor and let me clear her, okay?" Velveeta spoke kindly but firmly.

"All right." Johnny raised his hands as if to surrender. "Talk to her now."

Johnny watched Velveeta approach his cruiser and speak to Martha Maye. He studied the crowd forming and conferred with Hank until Jeb tapped him on the shoulder.

"Uh, Chief?" Jeb said.

"Yeah?"

"One more thing. Uh, you can't see it now, because I turned him over. But, uh, I'm not real sure why, but when I first examined him, his fly was open, and"—he rubbed the back of his neck and motioned at his own zipper—"his ding-a-ling was sticking out." Johnny's eyebrows shot up, but just then Velveeta returned, looking somber. Jeb backed away.

"Chief, she's got about twenty, thirty minutes where she says she was alone tonight. Says she walked to Lou's house to use the bathroom because it was closer. Said it took her a while because the dress she wore had a hoop slip. Did you ever try to pee with one of those things on?"

Johnny blushed and said no, he hadn't.

"Well, me neither, but I don't see how she managed it. I really don't. I reckon she had to take the whole thing-"

"Velveeta!" Johnny snapped. "What's your point?"

"My point is, she doesn't have an alibi for about twenty minutes. Maybe thirty. And everybody and their brother knew there was animosity between her and the deceased. I'm new in town, and even I knew. I'm just saying."

"What exactly are you saying?" Johnny's voice grew impatient.

"It's just"—she kicked at the gravel—"I think we got to be careful and go by the book. We need to take her in for questioning tonight. We don't want anyone saying you played favorites."

Johnny was quiet a minute, his eyes scanning the area. "All right. By the book. But *I'm* taking her in."

"You think that's wise, Chief?" Skeeter asked.

"I'm taking her in." Johnny's tone and glare suggested it was not open for discussion.

Word had gotten out about the dead body on Marigold Lane, and a crowd had formed. Hank Beanblossom was trying to ward people off with both arms outstretched.

"Y'all gwon back to the party. Nothing to see here, folks. Gwon back. Nothing to see."

Johnny went to his car and quietly explained to Martha Maye why she had to go to the station with him. He helped get her legs into the car and asked Jack and Tess to follow so they could take Martha Maye home once she was through with questioning.

On the way to the police station, she said, "Johnny, you know I didn't have anything to do with this, right?"

He looked in the rearview mirror, caught her eye, and said, "Of course."

"He was mean enough to bite himself, and I couldn't wait to divorce him, and I thought he was a no-good, lying, dirty cur dog, but I'd never kill him. You know that, right?"

"Yes I do, sweet pea. As much as I know my own name. Don't you worry. We'll follow procedure and get you free and clear of this. Don't you worry. I just don't understand how this could have happened. I had my cops on him like a dingleberry."

"Why on earth would they do that?"

"I was worried about you."

THEY ARRIVED at the station, and Johnny escorted Martha Maye into his office.

She sat in the chair in front of his desk, and he leaned down to her. "Can I get you anything?"

"Yeah." She nodded. "Outta here."

Johnny could see the worry in her eyes behind the face she made to lighten the mood. He grasped her hand and squeezed. "Just sit tight. You'll be outta here in no time."

"Why don't you do one of them tests on my hands? You know, to see if there's any blood whatchacallit."

"Residue?"

She nodded.

"There wasn't much blood at the scene. I don't think there would have been any on the killer's hands. It appears the knife went in and came out clean, stopping the heart from pumping any blood outta the body. I don't think a luminol kit would do any good, unless he—or she—wiped the knife on his or her hands."

From the doorway, Jack said, "And somebody could claim you were wearing gloves anyway."

"Jack, you shouldn't be back here. You're not supposed to interfere with police business."

"Chief, a little-known fact about me—"

Johnny raised his eyebrows.

"I have a law degree. Let's just say I'm here as her counsel." Jack came into the office and sat next to Martha Maye, resting his hand on hers.

"You're skating on thin ice, man. Everybody knows you haven't practiced law in years. Is your license even current?"

"No, and you're correct, I haven't practiced for years, but I can be of counsel until a lawyer is hired."

"A lawyer! I'm going to need a *lawyer*? I can't afford that. Oh Lord." Tears formed in her eyes.

Jack patted her hand. "Just a precaution."

Just then Velveeta rushed in, followed by Skeeter. "We found the murder weapon!" She was so excited she was nearly breathless. "I'll see if we can get some prints off it." She held up a long knife encased in a plastic evidence bag.

Johnny studied the bag but said to Velveeta, "Good work. Where was it?"

"In the bushes. The killer must have tossed it. I don't know if he"— her eyes went to Martha Maye—"or she"-she looked back at Johnny-"dropped it accidentally or on purpose, but we got it."

"Terrific. Martha Maye's prints are on file from the home invasion a few weeks ago. We can compare the two."

"Sure thing, Chief." She turned and hurried off.

"Skeeter, we need to have a talk about your surveillance skills."

Skeeter looked sheepish. "I know. I lost him in the crowd, so I went cruising to see if I could find him. I drove by Martha Maye's house, real slow like, and I saw this big dark blob on the grass. I'm real sorry, Chief."

"Like I said, a word—later."

Skeeter left looking sheepish, and Johnny returned his attention to Martha Maye's face, which was stark white.

"You all right, darlin'?"

"Johnny, I think that's one of my kitchen knives."

"Oh, law."

"Of course my prints will be on it." Martha Maye said.

"Unless someone wiped it clean. But we'll see if there are any others."

"Jack, I thought you were gonna stick to Martha Maye like glue tonight. Why didn't you go with her when she left the party?"

Jack shot Martha Maye a look of reprimand for going off without him, and then he gave Johnny a put-out look. "I didn't know she'd left. I thought she was with her mama and them, plus a hundred other people. I thought she'd be fine."

She looked down at her shaking hands and held them in the air. "Look at me. I'm as nervous as a fat girl in a cactus garden."

Johnny came around the desk and knelt in front of her, taking her hands in his. "You hush now. There is nothing to be nervous about. You didn't do anything. We'll prove that here shortly, and then we'll get on to finding the real killer."

"I can't believe this is happening. What am I gonna tell Butterbean?"

"Tell her he kicked the oxygen habit," Jack said.

"Jack!" Johnny glared at him.

"Sorry. Just trying to lighten the moment."

"Let's worry about telling Butterbean tomorrow, Scarlett. Tonight, we gotta get you sprung from here."

TWENTY-THREE

A good farmer stays acquainted with daybreak.

~Southern Proverb

"Velveeta, it looks like you're going to get to use your skills a little sooner than we thought," Johnny said from his desk after Jack took Martha Maye home. Velveeta had checked the knife for fingerprints and found it had been wiped clean. She questioned Martha Maye some more, and finally, reluctantly, let her go home. Now she leaned on the doorway to Johnny's office looking energized and almost gleeful, despite the late hour.

"I'm ready, Chief. I shouldn't be excited over a homicide, but I'm itching to get started on this."

"Okay. I'll let you lead the investigation. Report to me, and keep me apprised of any progress. Other than that, you decide how to proceed. I'm here if you need me." He shuffled some papers and reached for his desk light. He was ready to go home.

"Thanks, Chief." She flashed him her big toothy smile, behind full, pink lips. She cleared her throat and stood up straight. "Uh, Chief." He looked up at her, his eyebrows raised. "Mind if I start with you?"

He chuckled and sat back, lacing his hands behind his head and propping his feet on the desk. "Might as well. Ask away."

"Okay." She rushed to the chair in front of his desk and took a pencil from her hair, which she'd pulled back into a ponytail. She perched a notebook on her lap. "I may be new here, but I've heard a few things, you know."

"And what have you heard?" He wasn't sure if he should be amused or annoyed.

"I've heard you and Martha Maye might be an item." She let the statement hang in the air for a long moment. "True or false?"

He took a deep breath and let it out through his nose. "I won't deny an attraction to Martha Maye. We've been friends since summertime, but we've been out on an actual date only once. We tried to be discreet. We're friends and we've been on one date, if you can call it that. Nothing more." He shifted in his seat.

"And what was your relationship with the deceased?"

"Humph." He swiped his hand over his face. "I didn't have any relationship with the deceased. I only spoke to him a few times." He picked up a paper clip and uncoiled it.

"Were you jealous of him?"

He laughed through his nose. "For the record, no, I was not jealous of Lenny Applewhite."

"Where were you between the hours of seven and nine o'clock tonight?" She pretended to write in her notebook, avoiding eye contact.

"Oh come on, Velveeta. Seriously? You want an alibi?"

"You want me to do less than my job? If I'm not thorough with everyone, I might as well not do this."

He felt properly chastised. "I'm sorry. You're right." He scratched his jaw and let out a sigh.

"Were you with somebody? Somebody who can vouch for you?"

He thought about the question, cocking his head and squinting with one eye until it looked almost frozen in a wink. Then his face relaxed and he said, "Honestly, there were probably several minutes when I was all alone. But maybe someone saw me in the cruiser. I was with Martha Maye and them until I got a call from Bernadette about a theft at the diner around eight. Check the logs for the exact time. I answered that call, talked to Slick and Junebug and Ernestine–that woman can't keep her nose out of anyone's business. After that, I patrolled a little, checked in with the other officers. I was just getting ready to head back to the Oktoberfest when I heard the call about Marigold Lane."

"How much time can you not account for? Just a guesstimate." Her pencil stood poised over the notebook.

"Oh, I don't know." Johnny shrugged. "Maybe fifteen, twenty minutes?"

"You answered the call to Marigold Lane awful quick. How'd you manage that?"

"I was nearby, of course. I just said I was heading back to the

Oktoberfest. When I heard Martha Maye's address, I couldn't get there fast enough."

"Okay, Chief." She put the pencil back behind her ear and closed the notebook. She stood up and said in mock seriousness, "Stay in town in case I have any further questions."

He laughed. "Yep. I was right about you. You're gonna fit in just fine around here."

SUNDAY MORNING, Velveeta walked into the diner during the late-morning lull, plopped her notebook on the counter, and sat on the stool next to Clive, who was sitting next to Earl.

"I'm Officer Velveeta Witherspoon. Mind if I ask y'all a few questions?"

"Us?" Earl looked from Velveeta to Clive. "Let me cut to the chase. I can tell you. Clive did it."

"Did what?" she asked, her eyebrows knitted together.

"Whatever it is you wanna talk to us about." Earl leaned over Clive to talk.

"Officer, don't mind him." Clive hitched his chin at Earl. "He's dumber 'n a barrel of spit."

"Hey." Earl sat his coffee cup in the saucer, making it clang. "I ain't no slow leak, and you ain't got no call to poor-mouth me."

"And you ain't got no call to besmirch my good name."

"She don't wanna hear you flap your gums, old man."

A hand slammed down on the counter. "Boys!" Junebug stood behind the counter directly in front of them. "Behave yourselves or I'll snatch the taste right outta your mouths."

"Aw, Junie—"

"Don't 'aw Junie' me. Hush up now, and let the officer do her job." She smiled at Velveeta. "What can I getcha, hon?"

"I'm dry as dirt. I'd love a Co'Cola, please."

Junebug nodded. "One Atlanta special. Coming right up." She pointed to Clive and Earl. "Your orders will be out in a jiffy." Her finger waggled from one man to the other. "Unless you keep acting the fools." She turned on her heel and walked away.

"Why you wanna talk to us?" Clive said, sitting up taller on the stool.

"Because I've heard y'all know just about everything that goes on in Goose Pimple Junction. So tell me, what do y'all know today?"

"Well, I know you could throw old Clive here in the river and skim ugly for two days."

"Oh, don't listen to him. He's about as useful as a poop-flavored lollipop," Clive said.

"I thought I done told you boys to pipe down," Junebug said harshly, walking back with Velveeta's Coke.

"Boys, you want me to run you in for disturbing the peace?" Velveeta smiled, obviously not as upset with the men as Junebug.

"Officer, what can we do for you today?" Earl flashed a toothless grin and moved to the stool on the other side of Velveeta. She now had Clive to her left and Earl to her right.

Mumbling something about old fools, Junebug walked away to wipe off some tables, and Velveeta got to work.

"Did Lenny Applewhite come in here much?" Not knowing to whom she should address the question, she took a big gulp of her soda and looked straight ahead, waiting to see who would answer first.

"Couple times, I reckon," Clive said.

"'Course, last time he was escorted right out of here. Now that was a sight to see." Earl slapped his leg in delight.

"What do you mean he was escorted out of here?"

"I remember it like it was yesterday," Earl said.

"It pretty much *was* yesterday, you numbskull. Or a few days at the most," Clive said.

Earl glared at Clive, glanced over his shoulder at Junebug, and continued. "See, Lenny come in all high and mighty like, accusing Martha Maye of being a bad mama, on account of her being here without her daughter."

Clive jumped in. "Yeah, it was great. She told him to look to his right, and he turned and there was Butterbean with a bunch of other little girls."

Earl picked back up. "But that didn't stop Lenny none. He kept on, picking at poor old Martha Maye, and finally Jackson had enough. He took him by the elbow and walked his butt to the door."

"Yeah, and remember what Jack said?" Clive leaned forward, looking past Velveeta to his friend.

"Sure I remember. If you'll pipe down, I'll tell it," Earl said, leaning forward to look back.

"Naw, let me tell it," Clive argued. "He said—"

Earl talked over Clive. "He said he had 'three speeds: on, off, and don't push your luck.' It was great. And then Lenny said he'd fix Jack's speed to a permanent off position."

Clive leaned in to Velveeta. "Looks like Lenny's speed is the one fixed now, huh?"

"So there were threats between the two men," Velveeta said, standing up so she could look at both men. She was getting dizzy looking from her left to her right as the men talked over each other. "Do you remember who else was in here at that time?"

"Lady, I can't hardly remember to change my shorts every morning. You think I can remember something like that?"

Earl said, "I thought you smelled kind of funny."

Velveeta jumped in before they could start a fight again. "Do you think Jack could have killed the deceased?"

Both men guffawed. "Jack?" Earl screeched. "No way, no how. He writes about killers, but he ain't one."

"Uh-uh, no way," Clive agreed.

"He writes about killers?" Velveeta's voice rose a few octaves.

"Shoot fire, man," Clive said to Earl. "You're digging Jack in deeper and deeper, making him sound real bad, but he ain't, officer lady. Jackson could never kill anyone."

"He could just write about someone killing someone," she clarified.

"Well, yeah. He does that every day. He has eleven published nov—"

"Doggonit, Earl! Would you put a sock in it?"

Velveeta took a final sip of her Coke, laid three dollars on the counter, waved to Junebug, and turned to go. She said, "Thanks, boys. You've been real helpful."

"We have not!" Earl called to her back.

"Earl, I done told you to tick a lock. You got—you got—whatchacallit"— he motioned in the air, searching for the word—"diarrhea of the mouth. That's what you got."

"Oh yeah?" Earl got up and moved to the stool Velveeta had vacated. "Well, you're uglier 'n a bucket full of armpits."

"You always have to go there, don'tcha? You're so stupid you always have to go with the ugly jokes."

The men continued to argue as Velveeta shook her head, left the diner, and walked down the sidewalk, writing in her notebook.

Jackson Wright—alibi? Motive?

TWENTY-FOUR

When God sends us on hard paths, he provides strong shoes.

~Southern Proverb

On Monday, Martha Maye and Lou walked out of the church, with Martha Maye feeling like all her air had just been let out. "Whew! I didn't know there was so much to do in order to properly funeralize someone."

Louetta put her arm around her daughter's shoulder and squeezed as they walked back to the bookstore. "I don't think anyone would blame you if you threw him in a pine box and dropped a handful of mums over top."

They'd been to the funeral home to make arrangements, to the florist to order flowers for the casket, and to the church to speak to the pastor about the eulogy.

"Thanks for going with me, Mama."

"You're awful sweet to do all this, Mart, considering how Lenny had been behaving toward you in his last days."

"There's no one else to do it, Mama. His brother's coming for the funeral, but he won't be here in time to plan anything. Besides, the man was Butterbean's daddy. That has to count for something."

"Is Butterbean coming to the store after school?" Louetta's thick accent made "school" sound like "skule."

"Yes. Bless her heart. I offered to let her stay home and take a personal day like I did, but she said she was up to going to school. It probably was best for her. I'm sure it took her mind off her daddy."

"How's she taking the news?" Lou threaded her arm through her daughter's.

"Aw, right now she's as lost as last year's Easter egg, but I think she'll be all right in time." Martha Maye glanced at her watch. "My goodness, it's about time for the kids to get let out, isn't it? We better hoof it over to the bookstore."

Tess looked up hopefully when Lou and Martha Maye came in, but her face fell when she saw who it was.

"Don't look so disappointed. Were you expecting someone else?" Martha Maye asked, brushing the hair from her face with her fingers and dropping into a chair.

"Oh, don't be silly. It's just that I thought maybe you all were customers. Business has been slow today." Tess walked to a bookshelf to return a book to its spot. "People don't know whether to offer condolences or congratulations to you all. Condolences don't seem fitting since it's common knowledge you and Lenny were getting a divorce, but congratulating someone on the death of her estranged husband or son-in-law seems crass, even if it does mean an end to the custody battle. At least that's my theory on why so many people are staying away."

Lou was almost to her office when she turned around. "It's just like him to get revenge on us even in death. I wonder how much longer that man's gonna continue to be a burr in our collective butts."

"Mind how you talk, Mama. You never know when Butterbean's going to be around to hear you."

"Did you accomplish everything?" Tess bumped into a table of books and then went about straightening them.

"Yes, I think so. We're not gonna have any visitation, just the service. I doubt there's anyone in town who would come pay respects anyway, but I hope some people will come to the service. There's nothing sadder than a one-car funeral."

"I expect it will be well attended." Having dropped off her purse, Lou came back out of her office fussing with her hair and straightening her multicolored flowered dress. "People will want to show you their support."

They heard a voice from behind a bookshelf. "And we thank you for your support."

"Mmm, Bartles & James. Now those are good wine coolers," Tess said.

Martha Maye sat up and twisted around in the chair. "Aunt Imy? Are you back there?"

"Yeppie." She peeked around a shelf corner. "Tess put me to work."

"Me too," Pickle said, coming through the back room carrying two boxes stacked one on top of the other, the top one restricting his view. He bumped into the counter and stepped back, doing a little dance to keep the boxes from toppling out of his hands. He managed to maintain control of them, and with the tip of his tongue stuck out in concentration, he worked his way to the side of the store where he set the boxes down, revealing his T-shirt, which said, HARD WORK MUST HAVE KILLED SOMEONE.

"Don't worry, Pickle. Hard work won't kill you. Does it take you long in the morning to decide which shirt to wear?" Martha Maye asked.

"No, ma'am." He looked at her like she had flowers growing out her ears. "I hardly pay any attention to what I put on. If it don't stink and it's in my closet, it's fair game."

"You keep carrying boxes around like that, Pickle. It's good training for the wife-carrying contest." Tess winked at him. "Who won that, by the way? The finals, I mean."

"I heard Johnny Sue and Harlowe won it," Lou said.

"Who're they, Mama?"

"You know Johnny Sue. She's the one everybody says has a butter face."

"A butter face?" Tess asked.

"Everything looks nice but her face." Louetta giggled.

"Oh, Mama. Quit being ugly."

"It ain't ugly if it's the truth."

"But I do know just who you're talking about," Martha Maye added.

"Charlotte came in second in the chicken dance contest," Pickle said proudly.

"Well, bless her heart," Louetta said.

"As soon as Butterbean gets here I'll take you both home, if you want," Martha Maye said to Ima Jean.

"Take home a package of Tennessee pride!" Ima Jean crowed.

"We can do that, too." Martha Maye walked to the window, watching for her daughter. "There's that new officer lady. Looks like she's heading this way."

"I've seen her out there most of the day," Tess said. "She's talking to everybody she sees. Seems friendly enough."

"She may be friendly, but that's not why she's talking to people. Ten to one she's working the case. Johnny told me he put her in charge. Well, I'll be. Here she comes."

"We must be gracious," Lou said, two seconds before the door opened and Velveeta stepped in.

"How's the investigation coming along, Officer Witherspoon?" Martha

Maye asked, as Velveeta walked through the door.

"It's coming." She took in the group standing and looking at her. "One thing's for sure, I'm getting to know folks in this town real fast."

"What can we do for you, Officer?" Lou asked.

"I'd like to ask y'all a few questions if you don't mind."

"Shoot." Martha Maye's eyes went to the officer's service revolver. "I mean, don't shoot, shoot, but go ahead, ask your questions." She clamped her hand over her mouth.

Velveeta's eyebrows rose at Martha Maye's blabbering.

"I swan, Martha Maye. Sometimes I think that mouth has a motor of its own." Louetta gave her daughter a stern look.

Velveeta switched her gaze to Tess. She stuck out her hand. "I'm Officer Velveeta Witherspoon. We weren't formally introduced last night."

Tess shook her hand. "Tess Tremaine. Have you met Louetta Stafford? She's Martha Maye's mother."

"How do, ma'am." She nodded at Lou.

"I do just fine, thank you." Lou's naturally hospitable behavior seemed a little forced.

"Tess, you're engaged to Jackson Wright, is that right?"

Tess smiled at the unintentional pun. "Yes, that's right. Mr. Wright is my Mr. Right."

"Good one." Velveeta walked closer to the three women. "Can you tell me about his relationship with Mr. Applewhite?"

"Relationship? He had no relationship with Lenny." Tess's face showed confusion, and her voice came out a little higher than normal.

"Were they friendly to one another?"

"I wouldn't say anyone I know was friendly to Lenny," Martha Maye interjected. "Folks I know thought he was about as useful as an ashtray on a motorcycle."

"Did you witness any interactions between the two men?" Velveeta asked, continuing to look at Tess.

"Interactions?" Lou squawked. "She just told you Jack didn't have no use for the man—"

"I think I know what she's getting at," Tess interrupted, placing her hand on Lou's arm. "You want to know about last week at the diner, don't you?"

Velveeta scratched her head with the eraser end of her pencil. "I'd like to hear your take on it."

Tess told her the story of how Lenny came into the diner and started harassing Martha Maye. "Jack let him make a fool of himself for a bit, and then he showed him the door. That was basically all there was to it."

"Were any threats made? From either party?"

"Oh, Lenny was just being Lenny." Martha Maye stood with her hands on her hips. "He always had a pebble under his paw. Jack was protecting me, is all. He certainly didn't threaten Lenny, for heaven's sake."

"Did Lenny threaten Jack?" Velveeta asked Martha Maye.

Martha Maye and Tess exchanged a look, and Tess said, "He ran his mouth off, is all he did. Nobody took him seriously."

"So, Lenny did threaten Jack?"

"Oh, I think he said he'd put him in a permanent off position." Tess leaned against a table and crossed her arms. "Something like that. But as I said, nobody thought he was serious." She sat back slightly and knocked a stack of books off the table. "Oh, for heaven's sake," she mumbled, stooping to pick them up.

"Do all y'all have alibis for the time in question?" Velveeta asked, writing in her notebook, as Tess and Lou picked up the books.

"We sure as shooting do," Lou said hotly. "We were all at the Oktoberfest. You can ask anybody."

"I asked Ms. Applewhite last night, and she indicated there was a period of time where nobody can vouch for her whereabouts."

"That's on account of she went home to use the little girl's room, then she came right back. Everyone else was together, I guar-on-tee it." Lou stood and crossed her arms defiantly.

"Why did you go to your mother's house instead of your own?"

"Mama suggested it on account it was closer."

Velveeta nodded and wrote that down in her notebook. When she looked up, she noticed Ima Jean for the first time.

"Oh, hello. I don't believe we've met. Who might you be?"

"I drink Dr Pepper and I'm proud. I'm part of the original crowd."

"This is my sister, Ima Jean Moxley. She lives with me now." Lou came up behind her sister, putting an arm around her shoulder.

Martha Maye sidled up to Velveeta and said out of the corner of her mouth, "She ain't right in the head."

"No kidding." Velveeta walked closer to four-foot-eight Ima Jean, towering over her.

"You were at the Oktoberfest all night, too?"

"Yes, she was," Lou answered for her sister.

Velveeta persisted, directing her question at Ima Jean. "Do you remember being there all night, Ms. Moxley?"

"'Course I do. I'm not crazy."

Velveeta wrote in her notebook, suppressing a smile. "Yes, ma'am."

She turned toward Martha Maye. "You and the deceased were in the process of a divorce, is that right?"

Martha Maye nodded. "Yes, that's right."

"Was it a contentious divorce?"

The ladies exchanged looks, which Velveeta noted.

"I guess you could say it was."

"How so?"

"We were fighting for custody of our daughter."

"Did your husband want the divorce?"

Martha Maye snorted. "He said he didn't, but he never acted like a proper husband, with all the philandering he did."

"I'll bet that was humiliating. Must've made you real angry."

"No," Lou interrupted. "Hell, no. I know what you're getting at, and the answer is no. Martha Maye wanted a divorce, and she wanted custody of Butterbean, but she did not kill Lenny. That's just not logical."

"Oh my gosh." Martha Maye shrieked. "Oh my gosh. Oh my gosh! You still think I did it?"

"Well, you have motive—the divorce and the custody battle—and you can't account for your whereabouts for about thirty minutes right around the time of the murder . . ." Velveeta let the suggestion hang in the air to see if anyone would try to fill the silence.

All four women did. They all began talking over one another.

Lou: "Martha Maye could no more kill someone than she could sing an opera"

Martha Maye: "I was madder than fire at him, but I didn't kill—"

Tess: "That's ridiculous."

Ima Jean: "Sometimes you feel like a nut, sometimes you don't."

"Now you listen here, little missy." Louetta put her hands on her hips and walked toward Velveeta. "I know you're just trying to do your job, and I know you're new in town and don't know no better, but you're about as smart as a mashed potato if you think Martha Maye, or any of us for that matter, had anything to do with Leonard's death. Jack included. Now you best giddyup and get along."

"Okay, okay folks." Velveeta held her palms up to quiet them. "That's all for now. Thank you for your time. I'll be talking to you." She turned toward the door and then turned back around. "Is there anyone you think might have wanted to do harm to the deceased?"

"Harm him?" Martha Maye laughed through her nose. "Nobody had any use for the man. But murder him? No."

"Can any of y'all think of anything out of the ordinary that night? Did you see anyone that stuck out to you?"

"I saw Ernest Borgnine," Ima Jean piped up.

"You saw Ernest Borgnine," Velveeta repeated, looking at the woman skeptically.

"Yeppie."

"In Goose Pimple Junction."

"Sure as eggs is eggs."

"Last night," Velveeta persisted.

"Woman, are you deaf? Isn't that what I just said?"

"Ima Jean, don't be ugly now, she's just making sure she heard correctly what you think you saw," Lou said.

"But she keeps going and going and going."

"Like the Energizer Bunny, right?" Velveeta smiled kindly at Ima Jean. No one smiled back. "All right." On the way to the door, she glanced over her shoulder. "That's all for now. Thanks again."

And with that, she beat a hasty retreat.

VELVEETA SAT on a bench and made note of what she'd just heard. She watched leaves fall to the ground like brightly colored snowflakes, then she walked to the hardware store. She wanted to hit all the businesses in town. The bell over the door jingled as she entered.

"Good afternoon." The man behind the counter was short, fat, and gray, with round eyeglasses that made him look like an owl. He wore an apron with the words "Doc's Hardware."

"Good afternoon to you, too. I wondered if you could tell me if you knew Lenny Applewhite."

"Oh, I don't know that I could say I knew him, but I knew *of* him."

"Oh? Did he come in here a lot?"

The man sat down on a stool behind the cash register, smoothing his mustache. "No. Now that you mention it, he was in only once."

"What did he come in for? Did he make a purchase?"

"No. No purchase."

"Then what makes you remember him?"

"You see . . . he had . . . sort of an altercation."

It would be easier getting answers from a wooden man.

"An altercation? With whom?"

"With the police chief."

"Chief Butterfield?" She was so surprised she almost dropped her pencil.

"Yep."

"What happened?"

"He called him Chief Gutterfield and Chief Mutterfield and whatnot."

"Is that it?"

Could the man be any more obtuse?

"Well, he might have accused the chief of sleeping with his wife. I guess the chief got real angry with him and told him what for."

"What do you mean 'told him what for'?"

He scratched his head. "Oh, I don't really remem—"

"I do," a man in overalls said. He stood in the paint aisle about eight feet from Velveeta. He walked over to her. "I remember 'zactly what he said." The man's head bobbed up and down. "He said one day he would be off duty and he'd teach him a thing or two. Can't say's I blame him. Lenny was talking lower than a mole's belly button on digging day."

"Do you think he was serious? The chief?"

"Oh, I don't know. I guess it was just posturing. Two males after the same female. They gotta butt heads. It's nature's law."

"But he definitely threatened the deceased?"

"The who?"

"Lenny Applewhite," Velveeta clarified.

"Well, yeah. They was both threatening each other, like two bucks vying for a doe." The man scratched his stomach underneath his overalls.

"Okay, sir. Thank you. And your name is?"

"Chester White."

"Okay, Chester White." She wrote his name in her book. "If you remember anything else, you be sure to call me, all right?"

"Sho' 'nuff." Chester shuffled back to the paint aisle.

Velveeta turned back to the man behind the counter, who was now arranging keys on a display. "I'm sorry to say I don't know your name, sir."

"Who, me?" The man pointed to his chest.

"Yes, you."

"You ain't from around here, are you?"

"No, I'm new to town. I'm Officer Witherspoon. And your name is?"

"Doc."

"Doc." She wrote the name in her book. "Do you have a last name, Doc?" *Do you have a family tree that forks, Doc?*

"Hardy," Doc said, more interested in the keys on the swivel display than in the officer or her questions.

"Okay, Doc Hardy. Thank you kindly. You be sure to call me if you remember anything else." Velveeta walked back out into the sunshine thinking Doc was doing well if he remembered to breathe.

She reviewed her notes. So nobody liked Lenny Applewhite, but did anyone really have a motive to kill him? He'd gotten a lot of good guys riled up. Is it possible one of the good guys had been provoked enough to commit murder?

She studied her list of suspects:

Martha Maye: Contentious divorce, custody battle, no real alibi.

Jack Wright: Disliked victim? Threatened him. Wanted to protect Martha Maye?

She tapped her pencil against the notebook, then put the eraser end between her teeth. She stood in the shade of the hardware store's awning, thinking, wondering, hypothesizing. Then she added another name to her list.

Chief Butterfield: Resentful? Protective? Angry?
No concrete alibi.

TWENTY-FIVE

Rheumatism and happiness both get bigger if you keep telling folks about them.

~Southern Proverb

"Aw no, I wouldn't say the chief hated Lenny," Skeeter said, clueless as to the point of his conversation with Velveeta. "He was just an ornery old cuss, and the chief wanted to put him in his place. Make him tow the line. You know how it is."

"Put him in his place," Velveeta repeated. They were at the Muffin Man, eating donuts and drinking coffee. Skeeter clearly thought they were just chatting, but Velveeta was actually pumping him for information. After talking with the men in the hardware store, she wanted to know more about the chief's relationship with the deceased.

"Uh-huh." Skeeter looked out the window behind Velveeta, searching for words. It was a pretty autumn day, and the gingko trees on the town square were a vivid yellow.

"What exactly do you mean?"

"See, there was the time he set him up to get a speeding ticket." Skeeter slapped his leg and laughed. "Oh law, that was a goodun. See, Lenny had been following Martha Maye all over town, and he followed her to that restaurant out on Route 42 where she met Johnny for dinner. You know the one—the Buttermilk Hill Inn. And then he wouldn't leave. He just sat across the room, staring at them."

"So what did the chief do?" Velveeta wrestled with herself, fighting her motherly instinct to wipe the powdered sugar off Skeeter's face.

He shoved the last of his jelly donut into his mouth, chewed, and then dusted off his hands over the table, the powdered sugar still on his lips.

"He called us—me and Hank—and then he set him up."

Skeeter told her about the gravy mishap, the speed trap, and how they gave Lenny a speeding ticket when he crossed into the city limits.

"I have the feeling that it didn't end there." Velveeta's eyes dipped to Skeeter's lips and the donut residue. She swiped at her own lips, but he didn't get the hint.

"Naw." He wadded up the donut papers, the crinkling momentarily drowning out a little girl's whine at the next table. "Lenny was waiting for him up at the station the next day."

"What did he do?" Velveeta shot a look at the mother a table over, whose daughter was throwing a tantrum.

"Aw, it was all posturing. Lenny had to try to reclaim his manhood."

"How did he go about doing that?" She swiped her mouth again. Seeing the powdered sugar on his face made her feel like she had some on hers.

Skeeter continued grinning. "He said we were harassing him and trampling on his civil rights. Can you believe that? His *civil rights*." He shook his head. "With that man, there are biscuits on the griddle but the stove ain't on. Know what I mean?"

"I suppose I do. Is that all he did?"

"No, he called the chief some names, told him to stay away from his wife, said he was giving him fair warning." Skeeter poked his finger toward Velveeta, punctuating each word, imitating the way Lenny had acted. "Then the chief told Lenny that Martha Maye didn't want him around her and he should stay away from her or Johnny would be on him like stink on a pig."

"And?" Velveeta raised one eyebrow.

"Hell, of course Lenny had to go and say the chief was threatening him, said he had witnesses, but he was just running off at the mouth, is all."

"How do you know that?"

"That Johnny wasn't serious?" Skeeter's eyebrows tented.

"Yeah. Maybe he was angry at Lenny for the way he'd been behaving. How do you know the chief wouldn't be all over him, if he thought he had to protect Martha Maye?"

He thought about it for a minute, pursing his sugary lips left then right, then out like a fish. "I guess he might've wanted a dustup with him, maybe, to make sure he stayed away from Martha Maye." His eyes snapped to Velveeta, realization finally dawning on his face. "Aw, no. Hell, no. You don't think the chief killed Lenny, do you?"

"Well—"

"Because that dog won't hunt, missy. Johnny's the police chief, galdernit. He sees that the laws of this town are upheld, and he upholds them himself. He's the most decent, honest man I know, believe you me."

"Yeah, we know how Goose Pimple Junction police chiefs always uphold the law."

"Hey now, that's not fair." His frown turned into a smile when he greeted a woman coming in with her young son. "Hidee, Mizz Rayann."

Velveeta smiled politely and returned her gaze to Skeeter. "How long have you known Johnny?"

"Okay now, I take your point. It hasn't been that long, I'll give you that, but I know these things." Skeeter tapped his temple. "I can tell about people. I have the touch. And I can tell you, Johnny ain't no killer."

Velveeta looked at him skeptically. He stared back at her defiantly. The mother in her overcame the cop in her, and she said, "Oh, good grief, Skeeter, you're a cop, not a clairvoyant." She couldn't hide her annoyance as she stood to go. "And for heaven's sake, wipe that powdered sugar off your kisser."

VELVEETA KNOCKED on Jackson Wright's front door. As it opened, the first thing she saw was a big black nose followed by the head and then the body of a white and light-brown basset hound, whose tail wagged her whole body as she stood at Jack's ankles. She let out one lone bark.

"Ezzie, hush your mouth." Jack's eyes went from the dog to Velveeta. "Well, if it isn't the Junction's newest law officer."

"Hello, Mr. Wright." She stuck out her hand. "Officer Witherspoon."

"I remember you." He nodded, shaking her hand.

"Do you have a moment? I'd like to ask you a few questions."

"Sure, c'mon in." He held the door open, admonishing Ezzie to get out of the officer's way.

He led her into the living room, Ezzie sniffing Velveeta's feet. She sat down on the couch, and the dog jumped up with her. Ezzie charmed the officer, earning some head pats.

"Ask away," he said, sitting in a chair to her right. "Just say the word if she bothers you." He nodded at Ezzie, who put her head on her paws, her big droopy eyes pleading with him to let her stay where she was.

"I'm investigating the murder," she began, looking directly at him. "I don't see any sense in beating around the bush. First off, do you have an alibi for that night?"

"I do." He nodded his head. "I was at the Oktoberfest with Tess, among others, all night."

She scribbled in her notebook. "What was your opinion of Lenny Applewhite?" she asked, still writing and not looking up.

Jack didn't skip a beat. "If stupid could fly, he would have been a jet. A rusty, dirty old jet."

Her head snapped up. "The man is dead, you know," she reprimanded him.

"Sorry. May he rest in peace." Jack didn't look particularly sorry.

"What was your impression of his relationship with Martha Maye?"

Jack crossed his leg and brushed some lint off his pants as he thought about her question. "I didn't exactly see it firsthand, so I'm only going on hearsay, but I'd say it was about like you'd expect for two people going through a divorce. But did she kill him? No, ma'am."

"She had motive, and she was alone for about thirty minutes, right around the time of the murder," Velveeta pointed out.

Jack snorted on an exhale. "Martha Maye is a God-fearing, good Christian woman, Officer. She wouldn't go back on her raising. Not in a million years."

"A mama bear can be quite ferocious when her cub is threatened."

"Martha Maye wouldn't handle it that way. She just wouldn't."

"How long have you known her, Mr. Wright?"

"It's Jack. And I guess I've known her for about four months now. Not a great quantity of time, but it has been quality time, and I know her."

"What about Chief Butterfield? He's got some unaccounted time and a motive, too. He's new in town. Not many folks know much about him."

"No, but my spidey sense says he's not a killer, either. You're grasping at straws, Officer."

"Spidey senses aren't admissible in court." Her smile was condescending. "So who did it?" She crossed her beefy legs, staring intently at him.

He sat forward, putting his elbows on his knees, looking her in the eye. "I have no earthly idea."

She studied him silently for a long moment, sizing him up. "What do you do for a living, Mr. Wright?"

"Jack. And I'm a writer."

"What do you write?"

"Mysteries." He sat back.

"Mysteries? Murder mysteries?" She made more notes in her book.

"Officer, I solve murders, I don't commit them."

"You don't write your own murder scenes?"

"Sure I do, but last time I checked, it wasn't against the law to *write* about killing someone."

"But it might be good practice for the real thing, hmm?"

"Oh, for crying out loud, you can't seriously think I killed Lenny Applewhite." Ezzie had fallen asleep, but Jack's tone of voice roused her. She looked up at him with her ears down.

Velveeta smiled sheepishly. "You're right. I don't. I'm just fishing." She looked at the picture of Tess on the side table. "She's pretty. Looks kind of like Princess Diana, doesn't she?"

"She's beautiful inside and out," Jack said, beaming.

"Did I hear y'all met on account of a murder?"

"I guess you could say we fell in love during the course of an unofficial investigation." Jack told the officer about the murder of Louetta's father, about all of the mayhem that occurred because the killer's family didn't want the murder solved, and how he and Tess eventually figured it all out. "I'm writing a book about it right now. I think I'll call it *Murder and Mayhem.*"

"So what you're telling me is, you solve murders and write about murders, but you don't commit murders. That about cover it?"

"Yep, cover to cover." He flashed her his devilish smile, complete with dimples.

"So who do you like for this murder?"

He took a slow, deep breath, looking out the window and thinking about the question. Finally, he said, "I told you I don't know, and I don't, but I'd be game to help you figure it out."

"I just might take you up on that." She got to her feet.

"I could ask around the Mag Bar," he offered. "Lenny picked up a lot of women over there. Could be somebody's better half got wind of it and wanted revenge."

"Okay, ask around unofficial-like. Maybe someone will tell you something as gossip they wouldn't tell me as an officer of the law."

"You got it."

"But don't go off half-cocked and do anything crazy on your own," she warned.

"Gotcha. If I want to do anything crazy, I'll call you first."

VELVEETA WALKED into the police chief's office and sat opposite him, plopping her notebook on the edge of his desk.

"What's up, Officer Witherspoon?" he asked, looking up from the reports he was working on.

"Truthfully, Chief, right now Martha Maye and you are my chief suspects. No pun intended."

Johnny sat back in his chair and laced his fingers over his stomach. "Zat so." He said it as a statement, not a question, propping a foot on his knee. "The truth's out there. You just have to look past the obvious."

"I know what you're saying, Chief, but I have to wonder again if you're being objective." Her posture was ramrod straight, but she was a hefty woman, and fat bulged around her midsection.

"You can wonder all you want, but that won't put yeast in the biscuits." Johnny folded his hands on top of his desk and leaned toward Velveeta. "You're new here and don't know me all that well, but I'm telling you, you're wasting daylight looking at me or Martha Maye for this."

"Tell me again where you were for those unaccounted minutes?"

He took a drink from a bottle of Orange Crush on his desk, set it down, and looked her in the eye. "I had responded to a call from Slick and Junebug about a theft at the diner. I left there, took a swing around town, checked in with some of the other officers, and then got the call about a body on Marigold Lane."

"You were alone in your car for much of that time, is that correct?" She scribbled in her notebook.

"Correct."

"You responded pretty darn quick to the call, Chief. How'd you get there so fast?"

The innuendo sat in the air like a dirigible. Johnny took another swig from the Orange Crush bottle, his eyes never leaving Velveeta's. She shifted in her seat but stayed silent, waiting for his answer.

Finally he set the bottle on his desk. "Officer, I've already answered that question. Now you can either believe me or not, but I'm telling you, I do not go to church on Sunday and steal chickens on Monday. You're barking up the wrong tree, and in the meantime, those valuable first hours are slip sliding away along with the killer."

"With all due respect, Chief —" She stood up, towering over him.

"Oh now, come on. It's been my experience that when people say that, there isn't any respect in the equation," he cut in with a good-natured, but pointed, tone.

"With all due respect," she repeated, "you hired me to do a job. I'm doing it the best way I know how. These are the facts: you have some time you can't account for; your girlfriend's soon-to-be-ex-husband was a burr in your butt; you were heard threatening the man. That gives you means and motive."

"Oh, good heavenly days, you can hardly call her my girlfriend." He stood now too, meeting her eyes.

"And Martha Maye has at least thirty minutes she can't account for." Velveeta ignored the interruption. "She was involved in a nasty divorce, and her husband was threatening to take her child away. That gives *her* means and motive. So you'll have to excuse me saying, but you and Martha Maye are the two most likely suspects. There's no way I can sugarcoat that just because you're my boss and just because you say y'all didn't do it."

"Officer, you're right. You shouldn't take my word for it. But think about it. Why would Martha Maye or I go against our character and risk losing everything over a pipsqueak like Lenny? He wasn't a threat. He wasn't gonna win custody. He wasn't my rival for Martha Maye's affections. He wasn't anything but a nuisance, and you may swat at a gnat, but there's no need to kill it. This was either premeditated, or a heat-of-the-moment thing, or a robbery, and none of those scenarios fit Martha Maye or me. I wish to high heaven I knew who they did fit, but it isn't either of us."

"I take your point about the premeditation, but the heat of the moment is just that. How can I be sure of what anyone would do in a moment of rage? You never know what's on the inside of a person. That's my philosophy."

"Besides the fact that we're both Christians and could never mur—"

"Are you gonna try and tell me there ain't never been a Christian who committed murder?"

"Of course not, but there are some Christians with a faith deep enough and a soul pure enough that committing murder is so far out of the realm of possibility, it's in a different county. I'm telling you Martha Maye and I are those souls."

"You know I still just can't take your word for it." Velveeta didn't really know why she was pushing so hard on the idea of the chief or Martha Maye being the killer. In her heart, she believed him, but she was a by-the-book kind of person, and she needed solid reasoning to eliminate a suspect, not a feeling.

As if the chief read her mind, he said, "What's going on with forensics?"

"Nothing back yet, Chief."

"Keep me informed," he said curtly, dismissing her and sitting back in his desk chair.

Velveeta walked through the building looking for Hank Beanblossom. She found him sitting in the break room with a small bag of Cheetos in his hand and a Mtn Dew on the table in front of him.

"Hank, you got a minute?"

"Sure, Vel. What's up?" He chewed a handful of Cheetos and licked his orange fingertips. "You don't look too good. I've seen better heads in a cabbage patch."

She grabbed a heavy plastic chair, dragged it away screeching from the table, and dropped into it with a *thud.* "I can't clear the chief and/or his girlfriend for Lenny."

Hank swallowed a mouthful of Cheetos too fast and began coughing. He fisted his orange-fingertipped hand over his mouth. When he finally recovered, he croaked, "You got evidence?"

"No. Not yet, at least." She sat with her head propped on her fist, feeling completely dejected. "But they both have means and motive. They were both close to the suspect. How can I ignore that?"

"Don't suppose you can. You talk to the chief about it?" He licked the orange residue off his fingers.

She nodded miserably and handed him a napkin. "Just got through. He denied it, of course. Said I was wasting valuable time."

"Well, Velveeta, I gotta agree with him. I just don't see either one of them as capable of murder." He wiped his fingers on the napkin and wadded it up along with the snack bag.

"The thing is, all y'all are too close to the subjects. I'm the only objective one in the bunch. People always say they know someone, but the only one who *truly* knows a person is hisself. I'm looking at the facts and not the person. I can't let emotions get in the way of finding a killer."

He raised his arm and shot the handful of trash in a high arch into the garbage can, grinning when it made it in. "Maybe that's your problem. Seems to me a good detective takes all kinds of things into account, but it sounds like there isn't enough to even take to a prosecutor on the chief or Martha Maye, so all I'm saying is look around. There's something you're not seeing yet." He took a sip from the soda can. "Take my word for it. There's something else."

"To tell you the truth" — she looked over her shoulder to see if anyone else was around, then continued —"in my heart of hearts, I don't think either one of them did it, but I don't see how I can rule them out just because people vouch for them, or because I think they're too nice to be murderers. I gotta be objective."

"Then do what you gotta do, but while you're doing it, be thorough. And hold on to common sense." He winked at her.

After talking with Hank, Velveeta went out to the front desk where Teenie had taken over for Bernadette.

"Teenie, let me have the key to the evidence locker. I'm going to go take a look at what we got. Maybe just staring at the clothes will give me an idea. A clue of some sort."

Velveeta disappeared to the back room but returned a few moments later.

"Teenie, where is the evidence?"

"It's back there in the locker." Teenie gestured with her thumb toward the evidence room. Then she turned and saw Velveeta's face. "Isn't it?"

Velveeta stalked to Johnny's office and stopped in the doorway, hands on her hips. "Chief, where is the evidence?"

Without looking up from his papers he said, "Wherever you locked it up, I assume." His head snapped up. "Isn't it?"

Velveeta sank against the doorframe and rubbed her forehead. "Negative. It is not."

TWENTY-SIX

 Don't blame the cow when the milk gets sour.

~Southern Proverb

"What did you do with it?" Velveeta, over her momentary shock of the lost evidence, stood defiant in the chief's doorway with fire in her eyes, her arms crossed in front of her.

"Have you lost all your mind?" Johnny stood up, propping both hands on his desk and leaning over them, his voice raised. "I didn't do anything with it. What're you talking about?"

"I'm talking about the evidence bag that should be over in the evidence locker except it isn't. And I have to wonder. Who has access to said evidence? And who stands to gain the most if it's lost?"

"Oh, for land's sake. Now you've gone too far." Johnny sank back into his chair. "I'm telling you flat-out I didn't take it. If anything, that evidence would clear me."

"But maybe it wouldn't clear Martha Maye." She was at his desk now, accusation on her face, stance, and voice.

"Teenie!" he bellowed.

She meekly peeked around the doorjamb. "Yes sir?"

"Put out an all-call. I want everybody in here in fifteen minutes. I mean *everybody*."

Teenie disappeared without a word. Velveeta spun on her heel and followed her.

Fifteen minutes later, Johnny stood in front of his police force. "There's only one thing that Officer Witherspoon has said to me today that makes any sense." He slowly made eye contact with each of the seven officers.

"She said you never can truly know a person. The first thing I thought when she told me the evidence was gone from the Lenny Applewhite case was that I don't know my force like I thought I did, because I never would have imagined any one of you could have pulled a bonehead stunt like this." Johnny began pacing back and forth in front of them, hands on his hips. He stopped in the center of the room and held up one finger.

"This is a one-time-only get-out-of-jail-free card. Whoever took that evidence has until midnight to get it back in that room, no questions asked. After that, when I find out who took it—and I will—I will arrest your sorry butt and throw it in the pokey. Friend or not. Understood?" He stopped pacing and glared at the officers.

They all mumbled, "Yes, Chief," and "Roger that," and one said, "Solid copy."

Velveeta spoke up. "Chief, that evidence is corrupted now. We can't be sure of what has been done to it or with it. Them's tainted goods now."

"But I'm confident it has something to tell us. It's police property, and I want it back. Pronto."

He looked at his watch. "I'm leaving for dinner. I'll be back at twenty-four hundred hours. That stuff had better be back where it belongs, or heaven help the guilty party when I find him. Dismissed," he barked.

Velveeta stood up.

Before she could say anything, he rolled his eyes and added, "Or her."

"No, Chief. That's not what I was going to say. Before everybody goes, I think there's something we should discuss."

Johnny sighed. "Of course you do."

"If the evidence isn't back by tonight at twenty-four hundred hours, I'd like to suggest that you take a leave of absence until the murder is solved."

There was stunned silence at first, then everybody started talking at once.

Johnny held up his hands. "Pipe down," he hollered over the roar. "Officer Witherspoon has effectively put a motion on the table. Is there any discussion?"

Someone said, "Aw, Chief, we know you didn't do it."

Velveeta shot back, "How? How do you know? And how do you know his girlfriend didn't do it and he isn't trying to protect her?"

"For the last time, Martha Maye is *not* my girlfriend."

"You deny having feelings for her?"

Johnny stared at Velveeta, his jaw clenched tight. He was determined not to show his feelings. He intended to stay professional and unemotional.

"Okay, let me make this easy for y'all. As of right now, I'm officially on a leave of absence. Effective immediately, Officer Beanblossom is in charge. When y'all realize I'm innocent, you let me know." Walking toward the door, he stopped and turned around. "I'll be around if anyone needs me. If something comes up, y'all call me, but I'll not be accused of hindering an investigation." He stalked out of the room to stunned silence. Hank and Skeeter got up and followed. Johnny turned around, put a hand in the air, and said firmly, "Stay."

A few moments later, the back door slammed loud enough to rattle windows.

JOHNNY DROVE straight from the police station to Martha Maye's house, and when the door opened, he was surprised to see a tall, skinny man with a mullet haircut standing in front of him. He didn't know why, but he disliked the man on the spot, and not just because of his haircut.

"Oh, I-I didn't mean to intrude. I just-I wanted to see how Martha Maye was doing. I'm sorry. I should have called first." He looked past the man and saw Martha Maye coming to the door.

"Don't be silly. Come on in, Johnny. I want you to meet Lenny's brother, T. Harry. I didn't expect him in town until tomorrow, but he surprised us this afternoon. T. Harry, this is Chief Johnny Butterfield."

"Actually, it's Chief-on-leave Butterfield," Johnny said miserably, reaching his hand out to T. Harry.

"Nice to meetcha." T. Harry shook Johnny's hand with the strength of a dishrag. "But you don't have to worry about Mayepie here, I'm gonna take good care of her. That's why I came in early." He put his arm around Martha Maye's shoulders.

"What do you mean Chief-on-leave?" Martha Maye asked, ignoring her brother-in-law and moving out of his reach. She wore a red cashmere sweater and jeans that did all sorts of good things for her figure, Johnny thought. He couldn't help but feel a surge of jealousy toward T. Harry's slightly proprietary air.

"It's a long story. I'll fill you in later." Johnny hitched his thumb over his shoulder. "I'll just get going since you have company."

"Oh, Johnny, don't rush off. Why don't you come in and let me fix you a plate? We just ate, but there's plenty left."

"I really don't want to impose."

"You're not imposing, is he, T. Harry?" Martha Maye didn't wait for an answer; she'd already started toward the kitchen.

"Actually," T. Harry started to say.

Johnny cut him off with a hard stare and quickly said, "Well, if you're sure." He followed Martha Maye, while T. Harry lagged behind, mumbling something about more pie.

"Where's Butterbean?" Johnny asked, looking around the bright yellow kitchen. He saw a big Dutch oven and a black pot on the stove and a pie plate full of homemade rolls on the counter. A cake plate holding a pound cake sat next to the sink.

"What's all this Butterbean talk?" T. Harry leaned against the counter, sounding annoyed. "Her name is Carrie."

"She's upstairs doing homework. And T. Harry, around here we call her Butterbean. You'll just have to get used to that."

Johnny looked down so they wouldn't see him smile at her directness.

"Well, aren't you a little spitfire?" T. Harry sidled up a little too close to Martha Maye. "I'd say you've changed for the better since you left my brother, God rest his soul. You always had spirit, but now you got spunk. Spunkiness is next to Godliness." He winked at her, but Martha Maye ignored him.

"Here you go, Johnny. Come sit down." On the table she set a plate loaded rim to rim with pork chops, new potatoes, green beans, fried apples, and hot rolls. "Now you be a clean plater, and you can have some of Mama's pound cake for dessert," she teased, sitting down at the table with him. "Or apple pie. Your pick."

"Humph. Looks like he's a practiced and accomplished clean plater," T. Harry mumbled. When he saw Johnny's glare, he held his hands up in a placating gesture. "I'm not saying you're fat or nothing, but I'll bet when you get on the scale to be weighed, it says 'to be continued.'" T. Harry slapped Johnny on the back in what would have been taken as good-natured ribbing if he hadn't put so much force behind the slap. Johnny didn't acknowledge the sting the man's hand had left behind. Martha Maye missed the gesture because she'd gotten up to pour some tea.

T. Harry sat down at the table. "Martha Maye, that apple pie sure was goood. I believe I could eat another piece. Reckon you could get me some?"

Martha Maye gave him a hard look, but she unwrapped the pie and cut a slice for him. She set it down in front of him and joined the men at the table.

"Mayepie, honey, I need another fork," T. Harry whined.

"Oh, I'm sorry." Martha Maye's voice suggested she wasn't sorry at all. "Help yourself, you know where they are." She turned to Johnny before T. Harry could argue.

"Can I get you anything else, Johnny?"

"I'm good. This is, too," Johnny said with his mouth half-full. "Mmm, mmm, that'll make a Chihuahua break a chain."

"Say, you know what I saw on the way in today?" T. Harry asked.

"What?" Martha Maye said.

"You know those farmer stands out on the highway? The ones that sell on the honor system?"

"Yeah," Martha Maye said, while Johnny nodded. His mouth was too full to talk.

"Well, I saw this dude trying to carry too many watermelons to his car, and he had them stacked precariously-like, and yep, sure enough, one dropped and went splat all over the ground."

"Oh no." Martha Maye sounded uninterested.

"Yep, and what do you want to bet he didn't pay for that'n? I'll tell you what else. Driving in today, I saw a man walking down the road with snakes coiled all over his arms. Can you imagine that?"

"Yeah, that's just Roddey McClansky." Martha Maye answered T. Harry, but she looked at Johnny with amusement in her eyes.

"And guess what else I saw?" T. Harry asked, hardly stopping to take a breath.

Does the man ever shut up? Johnny wondered.

"What?" Martha Maye said.

"The old Marshall farm is for sale. It's a beaut, too. I wonder how much they want for it." T. Harry continued to monopolize the conversation as Johnny ate. Martha Maye got in an "Oh," a "Mmm-hmm," and a "you don't say," but T. Henry was on a roll, while she and Johnny had a meaningful conversation with their eyes.

Finally, Martha Maye said, "I called over to the Stay A Spell Hotel and got you a room, T. Harry. How about you gwon over and get settled in. You must be tired after that long trip, and tomorrow will be another long day what with the funeral and all."

T. Harry frowned. "I'm not that tired, and what'd you get me a room for? I thought I could just stay with y'all."

"I thought it would be better this way, since the house is so small and all." Martha Maye stared back at T. Harry as an uncomfortable silence fell over the kitchen.

T. Harry must have realized Martha Maye had her mind made up, because he didn't argue. "All right. You the boss. Nice meeting you, John," he said, again clasping Johnny too hard on the shoulder as he walked past him toward the front door.

"Nice meeting you, too," Johnny called with a wave T. Harry didn't see. *Even nicer seeing you leave. Shewee, my ears are bleeding.*

A WHILE later, Johnny and Martha Maye sat together on the couch, and Johnny told her what had happened at the police station.

"Oh, Johnny, I'm so sorry. I'm nothing but trouble for you." She reached out and held both his hands in hers, her eyes sympathetic and apologetic.

"Now, you stop that right now." She looked startled and started to pull her hands back. Johnny held them tighter and said, "No, don't stop *that*. I mean stop blaming yourself. This isn't your fault, and I guess now that I've calmed down a little, I have to admit it does make sense. Velveeta's right. I can't be objective about this. Until they're sure you and I weren't involved, I *should* step aside. I should have seen it before she made it an issue in front of the entire force."

"What if they never find the killer? What happens to your job then?" she asked.

"We'll jump that bridge when we get to it." He ran his hand up and down her arm in a comforting way.

"You know what I think we should do?"

That brought all sorts of ideas to Johnny's mind, but he said simply, "What?"

"Let's go over and talk to Jack and Tess. They're good at sniffing out bad guys. Maybe you can team up with them, and just like with my granddaddy's murder, they can get to the bottom of this. And I want to help, too."

"If there's something I can think of for you to do, I'll sure let you know, but you got your teaching, and Butterbean to care for, and the funeral tomorrow. You're going to be busier than a one-legged woman at the IHOP."

That made her smile.

"You know, you're beautiful all the time, but when you smile, man alive, you pretty much turn me into a puddle."

"Oh, Johnny." Her eyes went to her lap, and she tucked her hair behind her ear in a self-conscious gesture.

"I mean it, sweet pea." He stopped when he saw the strained look on her face. "What? What did I say?"

"That's the second time you've called me that." She suddenly had an agitated air, and Johnny didn't know why.

"You don't like to be called sweet pea?"

"No, it's not that. It's just . . ." Her hands were in her lap now, and she fidgeted–almost wringing–them. "It's just . . . someone left a sweet pea on my desk not too long ago." She looked up at him. "It wasn't you, was it?"

"No, Mart. It wasn't me. I swear. Why didn't you tell me before now?"

"Oh, I don't know. It happened the day I called you about Lenny watching me over at school. Remember? You came and took me home and we followed Butterbean on her bike?"

"I remember." Their eyes met, and they both knew the other remembered it was also the day they kissed.

"We kinda sorta had enough going on then." She cleared her throat.

Johnny reached for her hand, squeezed it tight, and leaned toward her. "I've thought a lot about that day."

"Me, too." She leaned in, their faces just inches apart. Johnny suddenly sat up straight. The abrupt change startled Martha Maye, and she moved back.

"Is that the last gift you got?" he asked. "The sweet pea? Have there been any more?"

Again she diverted her eyes to her lap and smoothed a crease in her skirt. "Actually, no. And yes."

"I beg your pardon?"

"No, it's not the last gift I got. Yes, there've been more."

"Good night, nurse," Johnny swore. "Why don't you tell me these things when they happen, Mart? I'm the blessed police chief. How can I protect you if I don't know all that's going on? When did you get something else?"

"The night Lenny died," she said softly.

"Oh."

"Yeah, oh. It was a pumpkin with a heart carved out of it. I figured it was from Lenny, and that's why he was at my house. I didn't think I needed to worry about it any more. Since he's . . ."

"On the dance floor for the last horizontal tango?" Johnny finished for her. Martha Maye grinned and he said, "There it is again. That beautiful smile." He leaned in again and put his hand to her face, caressing her cheek with his thumb. "I'd like to do that more often."

She looked at him questioningly, and he clarified, "Make you smile." He came closer still. With his lips against hers, he added, "And I'd like to do this more often, too."

TWENTY-SEVEN

All the buzzards will come to the mule's funeral.

~Southern Proverb

"I'm ready." Butterbean came into her mother's bedroom and plopped down on the bed, looking sadder than a weeping willow in frost.

"Don't waller around like that, you'll mess up your dress," Martha Maye snapped. She saw the hurt look on Butterbean's face and went to her, smoothing her hair.

"You all right, peaches?" Martha Maye cupped her daughter's chin, forcing her face upward so she could look into her eyes.

"I'm all right, Mama." She pulled her eyes away from her mother's and fidgeted with the blue bow on the front of her dress. Without looking up, she asked, "Are you sad, Mama?"

Martha Maye sat down and wrapped her arms around her daughter. "Yes, sweetie, I *am* sad. I may have been divorcing your daddy, but he was still your daddy, and I'm sad he's gone. I know you are, too. You just come talk to me anytime you want, okay? It's important for you to get your feelings out, and it's important for us to always speak our minds with each other."

Butterbean nodded, and Martha Maye kissed her daughter and went to the mirror to put on her lipstick.

"Mama, do you like Chief Butterfield?" Martha Maye met her daughter's eyes in the mirror. "You know, do you *like*, like him?" Butterbean stood uncertainly beside the bed, nervously twisting her fingers around the big bow at her waist.

"Well, Bean, I suppose I do. Is that all right with you?" She leaned close to the mirror to apply her lipstick.

"Uncle T says it's unseemly for you to be dating so soon after Daddy died."

"Oh he does, does he? I'll have to remind T. Harry to keep his straw out of my Kool-Aid."

"He says your business is his business. He says he's the head of the family now. He says he has to watch out for us."

Martha Maye capped the lipstick tube and set it down. She turned and grabbed Butterbean's arms, pulling her to the bed again, where they sat facing each other.

"Honey pie, it's sad, and I know it's not something you'll fully understand for quite a while, but your mama and daddy's marriage has been over for a long time. I'm not promiscuous, and I wouldn't do anything to bring shame on this family, but I do like Johnny an awful lot, and I think he likes me back. Right now we're just two good friends, but I'd like to see if we can be more than that. There isn't anything wrong with me doing that. You understand?"

Butterbean nodded and Martha Maye added, "The heart wants love, the soul wants friendship. I forget who said that, but it's true."

"I saw you two kissing," Butterbean said accusingly.

"Oh honey, that's what grown-ups do when they like each other, but good Southern girls don't sleep around, and you have my word on that, okay?"

"Okay, Mama."

After several moments of silence, Martha Maye said, "You know, I probably should have waited until the divorce was final to kiss Johnny. I'm sorry I didn't wait, but me liking Johnny doesn't mean I'm not sad your daddy is gone."

Butterbean nodded but was unable to look at her mother.

"You ready to go?" Martha Maye stood up and smoothed her skirt with her hands.

"I guess so."

On the way out the door, Butterbean said, "Mama, what's 'miscuous'?"

"THERE ARE more people here than you can shake a stick at," Martha Maye whispered to her mother as they waited for the funeral service to begin. "More than I expected, that's for sure."

"It was good of everybody to come. Are you sure you don't want to be seated last?"

"I'm sure. It doesn't seem proper to play the grieving widow, and I don't want to parade Butterbean down the aisle in front of everyone."

Lou craned her head around to see who was in attendance. "Looks like all the Nosey Nellies in town have come to gawk, but all your friends came for *you*, darlin', not Lenny."

"Do you see Johnny?"

"Yes. He's sitting with Tess and Jack." She patted her daughter's hand and held onto it. Butterbean took her mother's other hand.

Martha Maye felt bad that T. Harry and Butterbean were the only ones who were mourning. *But he made his bed. Now he's gotta lie in it.* She looked at the casket and heard Lenny's voice in her head say, "Literally."

She couldn't help but chuckle.

LATER THAT day after dark, Johnny and Jack drove down the deserted country road toward the Magnolia Bar, talking about the funeral. "It was more than he deserved, I can tell you that," Jack said.

They pulled into the bar's parking lot, gravel popping under the tires. As the headlights swept over the lot, they illuminated Pickle pulling away in his red pickup truck.

"What in tarnation is Pickle doing in a bar parking lot?" Johnny asked, craning his neck to watch the taillights on Pickle's truck grow smaller and smaller.

"Good question." Both their eyes searched the parking lot to see if anyone else was around, maybe meeting Pickle, but they saw only empty cars.

"You don't suppose he was buying weed or something, do you? The Mag Bar attracts all kinds." Johnny parked the car.

"I don't think so." Jack looked to the side and behind him, "Besides, there's nobody else around."

"I tell you what," Johnny said as they got out of the car, "I'll be speaking to Pickle about this the next time I see him."

They walked into the Mag Bar, looking like two friends wanting to kick back with a couple of beers, which they were, in fact, but they were also there for information.

"Help ya?" Bartender Cash Wily asked, slapping two napkins on the bar, as the men sat down on stools.

"Two Blue Moons." Jack looked at Johnny for approval, and he nodded.

When Cash put the bottles in front of the men, he said to Jack, "You only hang out with lawmen these days?"

Jack gave him a confused look, and the bartender said, "You's in here the other night with Officer Beanblossom. Looks like you moved up the totem pole bringing in the chief. You gonna come in with the mayor next?"

"Oh." Jack nodded. "He's actually a civilian at the moment." He bobbed his head toward Johnny.

"Zat so?" Cash said.

Both men nodded.

"How come?"

"Conflict of interest," Johnny said. "I'm just taking a short leave." He took another pull from the bottle. "Ah, that tastes good. My mouth was as dry as Melba toast."

"Conflict about what?"

Johnny looked uneasy, so Jack answered. "Has to do with Lenny Applewhite."

Cash wiped a glass clean and grunted. "You ask me, I say it was a jealous husband who killed Lenny."

"Yeah?" Jack said.

"Yep. Lenny was in here practically every night picking up women. Some were married." He shook his head. "The stories he used to tell me."

Jack and Johnny exchanged looks. "Like what?" Jack said.

Cash leaned on his forearms toward the men so he could talk confidentially. "This one woman he picked up, he mentioned to her to stop by Big Darryl D's sometime and he'd get her a real good deal on a car." Cash's eyes scanned over both men's shoulders, and he looked side to side to see if anyone was listening. The bar was busy, but no one was close by. Deciding it was safe, he continued.

"So she shows up—*with her husbin.*" He waited for the men to react, and they didn't disappoint. Jack dropped his chin and gave Cash a look of disbelief. Johnny, who had just taken a pull from the bottle, almost spewed beer in the bartender's face.

"Yep. She showed up with her old man over to Big Darryl's. So Lenny, the old dog, he gets Darryl D to yack at the husbin while he takes the wife for a test drive. And I do mean, he took *her* for a test drive." Cash's eyes went big in the telling, and he nodded with a know-what-I-mean look.

"In the car?" Johnny squeaked.

"While the husband waited back at the lot?" Jack's eyes bugged out like a bullfrog's.

"Yup. That's old Lenny for you. Or I should say, *was* Lenny."

"Did the husband find out?"

"Don't know. But she wasn't the only one he did crazy stuff like that with. Maybe one of them husbins got wise to him. You know?"

"Can you give us some names?" Johnny asked.

"Thought you weren't on the case no more." Cash stood up straight, his distance showing his reluctance to cooperate.

"Unofficial investigation. I've got to clear my name. Don't worry, I won't say where it came from."

Cash reached for a glass to dry, appearing to think it over.

"I gotta know, Cash," Johnny said. "I swear I'll leave you out of this."

The bartender hesitantly scratched three names on a napkin and slid it across the bar to Johnny. "There were more, but those are the only names I know."

Johnny looked at the napkin and then back at Cash. "You have got to be kidding me."

"Nope."

"What?" Jack leaned over to get a look.

Johnny handed him the napkin. "I know two of these women." He took a pull on his beer. "Well, not *know* know them, but I know who they are."

"That Lenny." Cash shook his head. "I'll say one thing for him. That man could sell socks to a rooster. But honestly, he didn't have to try all that hard with women. Can't explain it, don't understand it. There was just something about him the girls liked. It was like watching moths to a light."

"Until they got to know him," Johnny said.

Cash pointed to Johnny. "You got that right."

"Maybe one of the women had a score to settle," Jack suggested.

"Wouldn't surprise me. Of course, could be his old lady found out about his philandering ways."

Johnny slammed his hand on the bar. "No. It could not be, and don't you go spreading unfounded rumors like that."

Cash studied Johnny for a moment and then wandered off to help another customer, looking glad for an excuse to leave the conversation.

"How do you want to approach these women, Johnny?"

"Let's call on them tomorrow night right after supper. I want to talk to them with their husbands there. It will be interesting to see how *both* of them react when we bring up old Lenny's name."

After a moment of silence, Jack asked, "So what do you think of

Lenny's brother?"

Johnny turned the bottle in his hands in a slow circle, thinking how to answer. The jukebox played Lewis Grizzard's "If Love Were Oil, I'd Be About a Quart Low."

"I think he's as useless as pockets on a cow. I think Martha Maye and Butterbean are the best things that ever happened to the sorry lot, though I don't see how she ever got mixed up with them in the first place."

"He seemed like a decent enough fellow to me," Jack said. "I didn't talk to him all that long, but it looked like he took good care of Butterbean and Martha Maye. You've got to give him credit for that."

Johnny grunted. "I don't trust him any more than I could throw him. There's just something about him that isn't quite right, and it's not just on account he's an Applewhite." Johnny shook his head in disgust. "Maybe it's coply intuition, I don't know. I do know I'm going to be glad to see his taillights, I tell you that."

"You didn't hear?"

"Hear what?"

"T. Harry's sticking around a while. Says he wants to look after *the girls*."

"Isn't that a fine how do you do."

Cash came back and stood warily in front of them. "'Nother one?"

"I'll take one," Jack said. "Johnny's driving. He's reached his limit."

"You know." Cash popped the top on the bottle. "I thought of something else."

"Oh?" Johnny raised his eyebrows.

"There were some dudes in here looking for Lenny—two, maybe three times. Real rough looking. He never was here when they were. Wait, maybe he was here once, but he beat feet. Anyway, they didn't hook up with him far's I know."

"Any idea who they were?"

"No idea. They weren't local, I know that. They didn't offer names. Just asked about Lenny."

"Well, well, well," Jack said, turning to look at Johnny. "Add that to the stew and mix real good."

TWENTY-EIGHT

All the buzzards will come to the mule's funeral.

~Southern Proverb

The sound of Muzak and a creaky grocery buggy wheel couldn't drown out a distressed mother's voice.

"Cinnamon! I'm not playing. I'm about to embarrass you."

The man wearing overalls and an oversized jacket heard the mother yelling to her daughter one aisle over. He leaned into the grocery shelf full of cookies, pretending to examine them carefully, eased the package of Double Stuf Oreos into his jacket, then stood up straight, adjusting his coat.

"Put that back, puddin'. I don't have money for that," he heard the mother say,

wondering for a moment if the woman was talking to him. Over his shoulder, he saw Pickle and his mother rounding the aisle, although it appeared they hadn't seen him yet. He turned his back, flipped his coat collar up, and pulled his hat down over his brow, praying neither one would recognize him. He began to nonchalantly make his way out of the aisle.

"Let's get some Nilla wafers so I can make 'nana puddin'," Pickle's mother, Caledonia, said.

"Yeah, I love nanny puddin', Mama."

"I know it, son. Pretty soon you're gonna eat us out of house and home."

Overalls edged down the aisle, feigning interest in all things cookie. He heard the young mother's voice again.

"Why, hello, Ms. Winchester. Hireyew tonight?"

"You're that new officer, right?" he heard another woman say.

"I am that. I'm off duty now. You can call me Velveeta. "

"And you can call me Honey. Did y'all catch him yet?"

"You mean Mr. Applewhite's killer?"

"Yes. When I think it happened just a few feet from my house, lawzie, I just get the heebie-jeebies. Did you catch him?"

"Not quite, ma'am, but I'm hot on her trail. His. His or her."

"Her? You said 'her' first. You think the killer's a *her*?" Honey was loud, and her voice rose a few decibels at the end.

"I really can't comment, ma'am."

Overalls leaned into the display of chocolate MoonPies, as he sensed Pickle and Caledonia passing behind him.

"A her." Honey said it as though she were talking to herself more than to the officer.

"Yes, ma'am. But don't you worry. I'm all over it like a bad rash on a big butt."

"Oh my."

Velveeta let out a big laugh.

"What's so funny?"

"Your hand went unconsciously to your behind when I said that, bless your heart."

"Oh, for heaven's sake."

"But I've said too much, ma'am. I really can't say any more. Just rest assured we'll apprehend the person responsible for the homicide. Don't you give it another thought. You're perfectly safe here in Goose Pimple Junction."

Looking over his shoulder, he saw Pickle and Caledonia turn the corner. He thought the officer and Honey were through talking but then heard Velveeta's voice.

"Say, where were *you* at the time of the murder? You didn't happen to see anything that night, did you?"

"Me?" Honey asked. "No, I wasn't home when it happened."

"Just exactly where were you, ma'am?"

"Ma'am? Me?" Honey said again, then under her breath, *When did I go from Miss to ma'am?* "I was at the Oktoberfest, of course."

"All night?"

"Yes, I was there with my daughter and Martha Maye and her daughter. And Lolly."

"What's a Lolly?"

"It's a he. Pete Lallouette, the fire chief."

"Ohh. All right then." There was a pause. "Well, I gotta get these youngins home. Nice talking to you."

"You too, Officer." After a pause, she added, "Velveeta."

Overalls decided to move quickly, intending to leave the store before he was seen. As he reached the end of the aisle, suddenly a little girl flew around the corner, slamming into him, causing the cookie package to rustle. His hands went out instinctively to the little girl, to keep them both from toppling over, and when he did so, the cookie package fell to the ground. She looked up, wide-eyed, into his eyes.

He quickly mumbled, "You ought not run in the store." He scooped up the cookies and walked away as fast as he could.

Behind him, he could hear the little girl saying, "Mama, that man had cookies in his belly."

"Cinnamon, whatchew talking about, child?"

"WHO'S FIRST on the list?" Jack asked Johnny, as he buckled his seat belt.

"Molly Ann Adair and her husband Stanley. They live in a small house up in Spring Hill. I've run into him a time or two. He should remember me."

"By gonnies, they live so far out they just about have to pump sunshine in."

"Oh, Jack, it's not that far out."

"It's halfway to Bristlebuck. I call that a pretty fer piece."

"Sit back and enjoy the ride."

When Johnny pulled in front of the Adairs' house, he said, "See? It wasn't that bad."

Jack pretended to be asleep, and Johnny punched him in the arm.

"All right, all right, I'm up." Jack opened the door and started to get out of the car.

"Jack, would you mind if I call Martha Maye right quick?"

Jack had already swung his legs out, but he twisted in the seat to look at Johnny. "'Course I don't mind. Want me to go on up to the house? Give you some privacy?"

"Naw, you don't have to do that." Johnny punched in the numbers on the phone. "I just want to make sure she's doing all right. I haven't seen her since the funeral yesterday and haven't been able to reach her all day."

Jack nodded as Johnny held the phone to his ear. A few seconds later he said, "Martha Maye, this is Johnny. Just wanted to see how y'all are doing. I hope you and Butterbean are all right. Give me a call when you get a chance." He punched the phone with his thumb, disconnecting the call.

"Third message I've left today." He looked at Jack. "You don't suppose she's avoiding me, do you?"

"No," Jack said firmly. "I do not think that."

"There's a killer on the loose. You don't suppose —"

"Nope. Don't think that, either."

"What're you smiling at?" Johnny asked.

"You. You're so darn cute when you're smitten."

As they walked up to the house, Johnny noticed a blue minivan with a DO NOT DISTURB bumper sticker parked in the driveway. The yard was well maintained and manicured, which was more than he could say for Molly Ann when he stepped up on the porch and got his first look at her. It was a beautiful fall evening, and Molly Ann and Stanley were sitting on the glider on their front porch, amid potted chrysanthemums and asters.

The couple appeared to be in their thirties, and Molly looked like she had lived every one of those days to their fullest. At first glance, Johnny thought she was pretty enough, but then he noticed her bleached blond teased hair, her face caked with too much makeup, and leathery skin that suggested she'd spent too many summers in the sun. The lines above her upper lip told Johnny she was a smoker. Even though she looked a little rough, it appeared to Johnny that she'd married down.

"Evening, Chief." Stanley didn't bother getting up with his wife when the men stepped onto the porch.

"Evening, folks," Johnny said, taking in Stanley's denim cutoffs and white T-shirt with the sleeves ripped off. "This here's Jackson Wright. Don't know if y'all have met."

"No, can't say's we have. Nice to meet you, Jackson."

"Likewise." Jack nodded at Mary Ann and shook Stanley's hand.

"This isn't official police bidness, is it, Chief?" Molly Ann motioned to two old lawn chairs with heavy steel frames covered by sturdy nylon webbing in which the men could sit. Johnny watched her as she sat down, her nervous eyes darting every which way.

"No, of course not. Fact is, I'm on a leave of absence from the department."

"Y'are? How come?" Stanley asked, gently moving the glider up and back with his foot.

"I guess you heard about the murder over on Marigold Lane." Jack and Johnny had previously agreed that Jack would watch Stan's reaction and Johnny would watch Molly Ann's. But Johnny tried to register both of their expressions when he said, "You know—Lenny Applewhite?"

"Yeah, we heard about it," Stanley said indifferently. "But I thought you said y'all weren't here on official bidness. Asking folks about murder sounds official to me, don't it to you, Moll?" Stan nudged Molly Ann's leg, clad in skintight jeans. She nodded, her eyes flitting from Jack to Johnny. She chewed on a hangnail.

"I can see where y'all might think that." Johnny looked at Jack.

"Thing is," Jack said, "we're just out talking to folks, trying to find any little clue, so we can catch a killer."

"So you're going to every house in Goose Pimple Junction?" Stanley asked suspiciously, absentmindedly scratching his protruding stomach.

"'Course not," Johnny said. "We saw y'all out on the porch here, thought we'd just stop and see if y'all had any thoughts on the subject."

"Nope, sure don't." Stanley looked at his still silent wife.

"Did y'all attend the Oktoberfest?" Jack asked.

"Uh, yeah, we were up there for a while. Ate some supper, then came home."

"But y'all did know Lenny Applewhite, didn't you?" Johnny pressed.

Both husband and wife shook their heads, but Stanley spoke for both of them. "No, can't say that we did. I may have seen him around town once or twice, but don't believe I ever met the man. Honey, did you know him?"

Molly Ann had been nodding to what her husband was saying, but then switched to studying her nails. "No, I don't think so." Then, giving her gravelly voice its full strength, she said, "Where are my manners? Can I get y'all a beverage? Co'Cola or Mtn Dew maybe?"

"No, ma'am, we won't trouble you for that." Johnny held up a hand.

"Ale-8? RC? How about a Dr Pepper?"

"No, ma'am. Thank you." Johnny pursed his lips and looked questioningly at Molly Ann. "You never met Mr. Applewhite?"

"Well, I *might* have met him up at the Mag Bar. His name does sound kinda sorta familiar." She tried to look uncertain but failed. She stood up and forced a smile. "How about an ice-cold Yoo-hoo?"

"No thanks. Can you tell me where y'all were between eight and ten that night? The night of the murder?"

Husband and wife looked at each other. "Yeah," Stanley said, "We can tell you."

They waited. Finally, Johnny said, "Well?"

"Oh. We were eating and socializing and participating in the wife-carrying contest. Don'tcha remember, Jack? Our turn was before yours, maybe you didn't see us, but I know plenty other people did."

"Yeah, I do remember, now that you mention it. Y'all look a might different than you did that night."

"He was Popeye, and I was Olive Oyl," she explained to Johnny.

Johnny stood up and Jack followed. "I see. Okay then. We'll get out of your hair. If y'all think of anything pertinent to the case, you be sure to call me or the house, you hear?"

"Sure thing, Chief," Stanley said.

"Toodle-oo." Molly Ann wiggled her behind as she leaned on the porch railing and waved to the men, giving them a good look at her cleavage. "Y'all don't be strangers."

Jack and Johnny waited to speak until the car doors were closed. The second they were both in the car, Jack said, "She was lying through her yellow teeth."

"She sure was, but I've got to say I don't think Stan was lying. So if he doesn't know about his wife and Lenny, it would be a pretty human thing for her to lie to keep him from finding out. And they do have an alibi."

"So they say. Right now all's we can be sure of is they were there for the wife-carrying contest. I'm going to see if I can get Hank to confirm their alibi."

"Sounds good."

Johnny started the car, both men waved to the Adairs, and Johnny drove off. After a few moments, he said, "Know what my mama used to say?"

"Hard telling," Jack said.

"Tomorrow's ash cake is better than last Sunday's pudding."

"And her point would be?" Jack asked.

"Folks always want what they don't have."

"Words to live by." Jack nodded. "Who's next on the list?"

"Nettie and Sonny Luckett, back in town, over on Walker Street."

"Hmm. If Goose Pimple Junction had a rough neighborhood, that would be it."

"Then this should be fun."

TWENTY-NINE

When you are standing on the edge of a cliff, a step forward is not progress.

~Southern Proverb

Johnny and Jack wound their way through the crowd of kids playing freeze tag in the Lucketts' front yard. Jack knocked on the screen door, and Nettie Luckett, a blonde who might have been attractive if she didn't have such a huge nose, opened the door a few seconds later. She took one look at the chief and her face lost all its color.

"Oh Lord. Who died?" she said, with her hand over her mouth.

"Nobody died, Mizz Luckett, we just want to ask you some questions."

She took a deep breath and laid her hand over her heart. "For crying out loud, you about scared the living daylights outta me."

"Sorry, ma'am, didn't mean to. This here's Jackson Wright. May we come in and set a spell?"

"Oh! Of course, Chief. Where are my manners? Come right on in."

As the men came into the house, she looked past them to the kids in the yard and hollered, "Jenny, you leave your brother be." She let the screen door slap closed, mumbling about dang kids, and led the men to the family room at the back of the house, where Sonny Luckett watched *Wheel of Fortune*. The room looked lived in, and Sonny fit right in with the décor. Johnny detected a faint smell of marijuana.

"Cut off the TV, Sonny, we got kumpny."

Sonny did as he was told and pulled his La-Z-Boy up to a sitting position. "Somebody die?" He stubbed out a cigarette in the ashtray next to him.

Jack and Johnny both assured the Lucketts that nobody had died; they just wanted to talk.

"I hear tell you ain't the po-leece chief right now," Sonny said.

"That's correct." Jack and Johnny sat on the sofa next to Sonny's chair. "Jack and I are conducting an unofficial investigation into the murder of Lenny Applewhite."

"Lenny Applewhat?" Nettie spoke a little too loudly.

"Applewhite," Johnny said. "We were told y'all might've known him."

"Well, I don't know who told you that. We don't get out much, and I can assure you we never had no Lenny Applewhatsits over to the house." Nettie laughed a nervous woodpecker kind of laugh, as Sonny pulled the lever on his La-Z-Boy, returning the chair to the reclined position. He took a drink from his can of Coors Light, swiped his hand over his mouth, and wiped it on his dirty shorts.

"Unless the feller was at one of them Bunco nights you go to all the time," he said to his wife.

Even though Sonny had said it jokingly, she visibly pretended to ponder that question, her index finger propped on her cheek. "No. No, can't say that I knew the man. I wish I could help."

Their daughter appeared in the doorway. "Mama, I'm going over to the diner with Julie, 'kay?"

"How you getting there?" Nettie blew a puff of smoke from the cigarette she held in one hand, the other hand propped on a hip.

"Julie's gonna pump me on her bicycle."

"All right, just be home before the street lights cut on."

"Aw, Mama, do I have to?"

"Naw. You can stay home if you'd rather."

"All right, all right." The girl stomped away.

Johnny looked pointedly at Nettie. "We were told maybe one of y'all met him up at the Mag Bar and thought maybe you could tell us something about him."

"Well, honey, it looks like you came to a goat's house for wool." She smiled sweetly.

"Come again?" Jack said.

She made her eyes big in a transparent attempt to look innocent. "Y'all have come to the wrong house if you think we can tell you anything about that man. We must not have run in the same circles."

"Aw, Net, don't go acting all highfalutin. Fact is, boys, we's just a couple of homebodies. Nett here only goes out on her Bunco nights. That's as far as our *circle* goes." Nettie shot him a stink eye.

"I don't get a chance to meet many folks," Sonny explained. "I'm a trucker, and I'm either on the road, or I'm home resting up to get back on the road. Nettie doesn't have time to meet nobody. Between taking care of the kids and her sick mama, and her occasional Bunco night, she don't get out much, neither."

"Do you remember where you were on the night of the Oktoberfest?" Jack asked.

"I's on the road, heading for the armpit of America—Peoria. Where were you, Nett?"

Nettie swiped a hand under her nose. "I would have had to have been home with the kids, of course."

"Ma'am, are you sure you never met Mr. Applewhite?" Johnny leaned forward, his elbows on his knees. "I was under the impression you knew him. He had brown eyes and brown hair, and wore muttonchops, although I hear tell women found him attractive. He was a little thick around the middle, but that didn't hurt his popularity with the ladies any, or so they say. You sure you don't know him? Feller I talked to said he thought for sure you knew him."

She looked everywhere around the room but at the men. She rearranged some knickknacks, scratched her nose, and puffed her cheeks out like she was thinking hard. They stayed silent, and she cracked in under a minute. "Oh! Oh, *that* Lenny Applewhite."

Jack and Johnny glanced at each other, a silent laugh passing between them. "So you *did* know him?" Johnny said.

"Uh, not *real* well, but now that I think about it, I think I seen him once or twice."

"Where?" Sonny demanded. "Where did you *see* him?"

"Now, honey, it's nothing to get all riled up about. I believe I met that man at the Piggly Wiggly." She brought her hand up to her mouth and tapped her lips with her finger while she looked off into space, apparently trying to remember where she'd met Lenny. "Or maybe it was over to the school. Yeah, that might've been it."

"I see. You're out philandering while I'm working my butt off trying to provide for you and the kids—"

"Aw, hon, it ain't like that at all—"

"Okay, folks." Johnny put two fingers in his mouth and whistled loudly. They shut up. "Is there anything you remember about Mr. Applewhite that might help us find his killer? Maybe he mentioned someone, or something he was doing. Can you think of anything that would point us in a specific direction?"

"I'm sorry, Chief, I just didn't know the man that well. We didn't talk much."

Back in the car, Jack and Johnny shared a laugh over Nettie Luckett's comment.

"I'll bet they didn't talk much," Jack said, strapping his seat belt on.

"Oh, she probably just *disremembered*." Johnny put the car into drive. "Bunco nights. Something tells me Mr. Applewhatsis *was* a part of those *Bunco* nights."

"Yeah, but what do you bet if we asked Nettie the rules of Bunco, she wouldn't be able to tell us?"

"Bunco night," Johnny echoed, laughing and shaking his head. Then he rolled through a stop sign to make a right turn toward the last couple's house.

THIRTY

You can't unsay a cruel word.

~Southern Proverb

"It's getting late. Who's next?" Jack asked.

Stopped at a traffic light, Johnny got out his cell phone. As he punched in numbers, he said, "Rita Grayson. Cash indicated she was the woman who bought a car from Lenny. But first I'm—"

"Gonna try Martha Maye again," Jack said along with Johnny.

"I know it's getting kind of late," Johnny said, holding the phone close to his ear but away from his mouth so he could talk to Jack, "but I want to see all three women on the list tonight." The light turned green and they continued on their way.

Jack nodded his head as Johnny disconnected the call.

"Still nothing?" Jack asked.

"Nope. You think I should worry?"

"Want me to get Tess to check on her?" Jack asked.

"Sure," Johnny said miserably, as he made a left turn.

Jack quickly called Tess as they pulled up to Rita Grayson's house, and Johnny raked his eyes over the scraggly grass, the overgrown bushes, and the house in need of paint. An adolescent girl with a dirty face opened the door when Johnny rang the bell.

"Is your mama home?" Johnny said through the screen door.

"How come?" The girl had an attitude. "You gonna arrest her?"

"Do I have cause to arrest your mama?"

She shrugged. "I dunno." Then she called over her shoulder, "Mama! It's the law." She turned back to the men, eyeing them suspiciously.

"The law?" a woman's voice said. A thirty-something redhead who wore clothes a size too small appeared at the door. "Yeah?" she said, chewing open-mouthed on a piece of gum.

"Mrs. Grayson?" Johnny asked.

"Who wants to know?"

Johnny wore his GPJPD Chief's hat, although he wasn't wearing his chief's badge since he was on leave of absence. Still, Johnny thought she knew who he was; she was just being difficult.

"I'm Johnny Butterfield, and this is Jackson Wright. We'd like to speak to you and your husband for a bit if you don't mind."

"What if I do mind?" She popped her gum and then blew a big pink bubble.

"Ma'am?"

"What if I mind?" She propped a hand on her hip.

Johnny put on his most endearing smile. "Now why would you object to speaking to two fine gentlemen such as us?"

"I ain't done nothing," she said, shrugging.

"No, ma'am, we're not here because any of y'all did something. We just want to ask you some questions about Lenny Applewhite. I hear he sold you a car."

"That's in my behind," she said, smacking her gum.

"Yes, ma'am, we realize it's been a few weeks, but the fact is the man was murdered, and we'd like to see if you can tell us anything that would help us find the killer."

Reluctantly, she stepped aside. "I don't know what I can tell you, but come on in." She led them to a kitchen where a haze of smoke hung in the air and dirty dishes overflowed from the sink. Flies buzzed around a dish with some uneaten cake. She motioned to the chairs around the table as she brushed crumbs off one of the seats and began gathering up papers, mail, and more dishes from the table.

"Can I get y'all something to drink?" she asked as they sat down. "I got just about anything. Coffee?" She opened the refrigerator. "Co'Cola? Beer?"

"No thank you, ma'am." Johnny said, noticing a sour smell.

"I'll pass too, thanks," Jack said, glancing around the stuffy kitchen.

"You don't talk much, do ya?" Rita eyed Jack.

"Oh, I can talk a blue streak when I want," Jack said, flashing his lady-killer smile.

"Ma'am, is your husband at home?" Johnny asked.

"Harlan!" she bellowed so loudly both men flinched a little.

A male voice came back impatiently. "What?"

"Get your butt down here." A few seconds later, a skinny, ferret-faced man appeared at the doorway, wearing a pair of athletic shorts and a torn T-shirt. His stark-white feet were bare, and he had tan lines where his socks would be.

"What's so important I had to quit watching the game for?"

"Harlan, this here's Johnny Butterfield, and his friend, Jackson, uh …"

"Wright," Jack supplied.

"Right. Jackson Wright." She giggled at her pun. "They want to ask us a few questions about that salesman over to Big Darryl D's what got hisself killed. You know the one?" She put a cigarette between her lips and struck a match to light it. He nodded, and she pointed a thumb at her husband and addressed the men. "This here's Harlan."

"How do, sir." The men exchanged nods.

"Here, hon, have a cold one."

"Just one? Do those come like a dead man? One to a box?"

Johnny cleared his throat. "Uh, folks," he said, eager to ask his questions and not be an audience to the Bickersons. "What can you tell us about the deceased?"

"He's graveyard dead," Harlan said.

"Besides that," Jack said, not smiling.

"He sold us an old rattletrap, I can tell you that. Other than selling us the car, we didn't have any dealings with him, did we sugar puss?"

"How did you know he was dead?" the woman asked her husband.

"I can read." The man was indignant.

"Did he cheat you on the car?" Johnny asked. *Or did your wife do all the cheating?*

"Yes," Harlan said.

"No," Rita said at the same time.

"Well, which is it?" Jack asked, looking from one to the other.

"Oh." She waved her cigarette-holding hand in the air, causing some ash to drop on the floor. "It needed a new distribution cap and a new doohickey — what was that thing called, Har? A Cadillac whatchamacallit?"

Harlan mouthed the word *women* to Jack and Johnny and drew a circle in the air with his finger next to his temple. "A catalytic converter," Harlan said, shaking his head. "And it's a distributor cap, woman. How many times were you dropped on your head as a child?"

"Yeah, a catalytic converter, that's it," she said, ignoring her husband. "But now that we got all that fixed, it runs real nice."

"Humph," Harlan grunted.

"Did he do that often? Sell clunkers to folks?"

"It wadn't no clunker, I'm telling you!" Rita protested.

Johnny waited a beat, then said, "Do you know if he sold many cars that had things wrong with them?"

"How would we know? We just bought the car and never saw the man again," Harlan said.

"Did *you* ever see him again?" Jack asked Rita.

"No," she said quickly, before shooing a fly from her husband's can of beer and putting it to her lips.

"Have y'all heard about anyone being mad at him? Anyone he might've argued with?"

"I hear *you* had a right smart argument with him." Harlan looked pointedly at Johnny.

"That's true," Johnny allowed. "As you know, the man could be real irritating. Half the time I think he was walking on a slant."

"You mean drunk, Chief?" Rita asked.

"Yeah, that's exactly what I mean. What do you think? Was the man an imbiber?"

"I wouldn't know." Rita turned toward the sink and moved a few dishes around.

"Oh yeah? A little bird told me he saw you talking to Lenny Applewhite over at the Mag Bar."

Rita turned back toward them. Harlan's head snapped up, and his beady little eyes bored into his wife's. "Is that right?" he said very slowly and deliberately.

"Well, sure hon, I told you that," she said nervously. "That's how come we went to Car Country to buy the car. I told you about me meeting him." Rita talked fast, suddenly intent on getting the dishes washed.

"Back to the question, Mrs. Grayson." Johnny stood and leaned against the counter next to her. "Did anything come up during your talks with him? Do you know of any women he might've been seeing? Someone who had a beef with him? Anyone he might've cheated? Just any little thing you can remember that might seem inconsequential, but might actually be a lead."

Rita shook her head, and when Johnny stopped talking, she said, "Nothing I can think of, but we really didn't talk all that much."

"I'll bet," Harlan snorted.

"Maybe you know of some women he'd been seeing? One theory we're working is that a jealous husband found out about his wife and Lenny," Jack said, looking straight at Harlan to see his reaction to the jealous husband theory, "and the husband went after him for revenge."

"Don't look at me," Harlan said. "No need for me to be jealous."

"Why is that, Mr. Grayson?" Jack said.

"Shoot, Rita was too old for Lenny Applewhite. She's almost past her expiration date."

Rita's face flushed bright red, and her eyes turned cold as she returned her husband's gaze. "I thought you didn't know the man," she said with measured calm.

"I didn't, but I heard a thing or two about him. Saw him at Big Darryl D's." Harlan's smug smile registered his happiness that his comment had gotten to Rita.

Johnny got to his feet, not entirely sure they should leave the happy couple by themselves, but he'd been watching them and didn't think they were hiding anything except Rita's affair.

"Do you both have an alibi for the night of October twenty-second?"

"Sure we do. We were up to the Oktoberfest, like everyone else in town. I was a gangster" — he nodded at his wife — "and she was a Playboy bunny."

"Y'all call me" — Johnny got a business card out of his wallet, scribbled something on the back, and placed it on the kitchen table — "if you think of anything, all right? The station's number is on the front and my cell is on the back."

"Yeah, we'll think real hard on it, and if anything comes to mind, my waff'le call you."

"Thanks for your time, folks." Johnny put his hat on as he reached the door.

Walking to the car, Jack had a perturbed look on his face.

"What?" Johnny asked.

"His waffle's gonna call you?"

Johnny smiled, opened his car door, and looked over the roof of the car at Jack.

"Wife. His wife will call."

Jack nodded and looked as if a light bulb had come on in his head. "You learn something new every day, huh?"

As they drove away, Jack called Tess again. "Hey, darlin'. Did you talk to her?" Johnny hit the turn signal and stopped at a stop sign.

"Okay." Jack listened some more. "And where's she —" More listening, and then, "Okay. Mmm-hmm. Thanks a lot, sweetheart." He hung up and said, "Martha Maye's fine. She's been at Lou's most of the night."

Johnny checked his phone to see if he'd missed any calls while they were talking to the Graysons. "So why didn't she call me back?"

"*That*, Tess didn't ask, but she did tell her you've been trying to reach her, and she said Martha Maye acted surprised."

"I don't know why she'd be surprised. I've left three messages."

"You need to talk to her face to face," Jack advised.

"What if she's avoiding me?" Johnny asked, looking worried.

"Then you'll know. Some smart folks can't tell a rotten rail without sitting on it."

THIRTY-ONE

Trust everybody, but brand your cattle.

~Southern Proverb

B right and early on the Saturday following the Oktoberfest, Johnny sat in a window booth in the back of Slick and Junebug's Diner, watching folks in the restaurant and out on the street. The usual smell of grease hung in the air, just enough to make a stomach rumble. He saw Junebug coming toward his table with a coffee pot in her hand, and he smiled at her.

"What'll it be today, Chief?" She turned his coffee cup over and filled it as she talked.

"I have a hankering for some of Slick's waffles, Junebug."

"Then that's what you shall have, darlin'." She paused for a moment, seeming unsure of something. "It *is* okay to call a chief of police *darlin'*, isn't it?"

"As a general rule, no, but I'll make an exception for you." Johnny gave a lopsided grin to the older woman, who was clearly pleased with his answer.

"Oh, you." She shoved his arm and started to walk away, then took two steps backward and cocked her head. "Side of bacon, too?"

"Of course."

"I'll go get your checkerboard and grunt and be back in a flash."

Johnny looked around the restaurant, studying the faces and thinking. It was entirely possible that a killer was in the room. He looked at the goings-on out on the street and was glad to see Louetta Stafford, in her lime-green skirt, hot-pink blouse, and orthopedic shoes walking with purpose up the sidewalk and into the diner. He'd hoped to run into her so he could try to find out what was going on with Martha Maye. He hadn't talked to her since right after the funeral service. Lou looked around the diner, saw Johnny, and headed straight for his booth after sparring briefly with Clive and Earl.

"Morning, Chief. I didn't expect to see you here, but I'm glad y'are. Do you mind if I join you?"

"Morning, Lou. I'd be offended if you didn't. Hireyew?"

"I'm still on the north side of the grass, but just barely." Her hefty pink purse preceded her into the booth, and she slid in, taking in and letting out a deep breath once she was settled.

"Aw, you look like you're doing better than that."

"Well, I can't say much for your eyesight, but you're sweet as a four-sugar-cubed cup of coffee." She leaned toward him and added with a wink, "And you're easy on the eyes, too."

Johnny laughed. "And how're Martha Maye and Butterbean?"

"It'll take some time for Butterbean," she said, sadness registering on her face. "Martha Maye's fine, but she seems to have her hands full with Lenny's brother. I swan, she got rid of one Applewhite and now another one's hanging on like a tick on a fat dog."

"How long's he sticking around for?" Johnny sat upright when he saw Junebug approaching with his waffles and bacon. His frown at Lou's statement turned into a grin aimed at Junebug when she set down his order.

Lou leaned over the table, eyeing the waffles. "Ooh law, that looks delish. Junie, give me an order of them, too. Hold the bacon. A girl's gotta watch her figure."

"Sure thing, Louetta. Hey, I don't believe I've seen Martha Maye since Lenny was funeralized. She doing all right?"

"I was just telling Johnny that she's doing fine, but I'd like to think up a way to run that T. Harry outta town."

"How come?" Junebug scooted in next to Johnny and propped her chin on her hand, looking intently at Lou.

"He won't give them a minute's peace. He walks them to school, and he walks them home. He stays for dinner, and he stays all evening. He says he wants to make sure they're okay before he leaves town, but to tell you the truth, I think they'd be more okay *if* he left town."

"That's just terrible. Why don't she just tell him to get?" Junebug's eyes went to Slick, who stood in the window that separated the counter from the grill. She waved away his stink eye.

"She's too kindhearted, Junebug. You know Martha Maye."

"Shoot. She should just tell him to cut his own weeds."

"That's just it. He thinks Martha Maye and Butterbean *are* his business."

"Why don't you have a talk with him, Chief?" Junebug nudged his arm.

Johnny swallowed a big bite of waffle. "I don't have cause to talk to him. I'm on leave from the department, and even if I weren't, there's been no complaint."

"I didn't mean talk to him as the chief. You're Martha Maye's friend. Friends don't let buttheads take over a friend's life."

"Oh, I don't know, Junebug. I'd feel like I'd be overstepping my bounds if I did that without Martha Maye asking me to."

"She can't ask you if you don't talk to her. When's the last time you two talked?" Louetta took her fork and cut a piece of Johnny's waffle.

"Not since the day of the funeral—"

"You oughtta call her, Johnny, you know she's sweet on you," Lou said around a mouthful of waffle she'd stolen from Johnny's plate.

Johnny blushed and looked at his plate. "I did call. Left messages, even asked T. Harry to have her call me back, but she never did."

"You try again, you hear? Or stop by and see her. I know she wants to see you."

"Are you sure? And are you sure she's all right? I mean, you did see her yesterday, correct?"

"Yes and yes." Louetta took another big bite of Johnny's waffle, closing her eyes in ecstasy as she chewed and swallowed.

AFTER BREAKFAST, Johnny did what Louetta suggested and headed to Martha Maye's house. Waving to Estherlene, who was in her front yard raking leaves, he pulled into Martha Maye's driveway and parked.

"Hidee, Chief," Estherlene called to him, leaning on her rake.

"How-do to you, Mrs. Bumgarner." He tipped his hat and walked up to her.

"Oh, pooh. Don't you *Mrs.* me. Makes me feel so old. Call me Estherlene." She flashed a big smile that made Johnny think how beautiful she must have been in her younger days. She was over twice his age, but still a somewhat attractive woman.

"Aw, you're in the prime of your life, Estherlene."

"Well, bless your heart, aren't you sweet for noticing," she cooed.

"You ought to get Hector to take you out dancing. They've got live music over at the Mag Bar, you know."

"The Mag Bar?" She flopped a dismissive hand in the air. "Oh no, that's not somewhere I'd ever frequent."

Johnny nodded. "You doing this all by yourself?" He motioned with his eyes at the leaves.

"Yeah," she sighed. "Hector has a bad leg, so it's hard for him to help out. I don't mind. A little fresh air and exercise is good for a body." Johnny nodded and she said, "Say, Chief, how's the investigation coming along? Did you catch that hooligan?"

Johnny turned toward Martha Maye's house, looking for any sign of her, then turned back to Estherlene to answer her question. "To tell you the truth, I don't know. I'm on a leave of absence at the moment."

"A leave of absence? What do you want to do a fool thing like that for at a time like this? We got us a psychopath, a lunatic, a miscreant, and you pick *now* to take a leave of absence? Have you taken leave of your senses? I'm half scared outta my brain, and you're on vacation?"

He cleared his throat. "Uh, no ma'am, and I really shouldn't discuss it—"

"Maybe I can help, Chief. Did you know I have a touch of that there clairvoyant ability? And I'm not one of them fortune-teller hacks. I got a gift. I got some of that extrasensory perception, you know? I just *know* things. I don't know where it comes from, stuff just pops into my head. I bet if I went to work with you, we could crack the case. Hector says I got one of them pornographic memories, and maybe I do—"

"I'm pretty sure you mean *photographic* memory," Johnny said, biting the inside of his cheek to keep from laughing.

"Whatever. I'm telling you, me and you team up together and we'll catch us a hooligan. Why, I—"

"I'll keep that in mind, Estherlene," Johnny broke in. "Are you sure you didn't see anything that night? Maybe a car, or something that didn't seem important at the time?"

She looked off toward the spot where they'd found Lenny's body. "Hmm, now that you mention it, I think there *was* a truck parked up the block." She pointed toward Honey's house. I think it was green or blue, but with it being dark and all, I couldn't say for sure. All's I know is, it was a dark color."

Johnny pointed at the green pickup truck parked in Martha Maye's driveway. "It didn't look like that one, did it?"

Her eyes went to the truck. "Hmm." She tapped a finger on her top lip and stared at the truck, thinking hard. "It just might've, now that you mention it. I tell you what, I'll put my thinking cap on, along with my oracular hat, and I'll let you know what I come up with. Isn't that Lenny's brother's truck? You don't think the killer was his own brother, do you?"

"Anything's possible," Johnny said. "And actually, you should call Officer Witherspoon. She's in charge of the investigation, cause like I said, I'm not working right now." He gave her a chagrined smile. "But listen, I was wondering, have you seen Martha Maye today? I need to speak with her."

"Today?" She gave it some thought. "I don't believe so. Is she missing?"

"Not that I know of. I'll just go to the door and she if she's home."

"Alrighty dighty. Nice chatting with you, Chief." She resumed her raking. "You let me know when you want me to come in on the case. I'm raring to go."

Johnny waved her off and rang the bell. He didn't have to wait long for the door to be answered. Unfortunately, T. Harry did the answering. He didn't try to hide his lack of enthusiasm at seeing Johnny.

"John." His voice was monotone, face devoid of a smile. "What can I do for you?"

"T. Harry." Johnny nodded once. "Is Martha Maye at home?"

"She's busy at the moment." T. Harry kept the front door half-closed, and his body took up the rest of the doorway so Johnny couldn't look past him.

"Would you mind telling her I'm here and would like to speak to her for a few moments?"

"Yes." T. Harry pulled the front door almost closed, standing in between it and the screen door he held propped open with his knee. He stood with his arms crossed, trying to look menacing. He smelled of beer and cigarettes.

"Yes, you'll tell her, or yes, you mind?" Johnny tried his best to keep a friendly tone of voice. He moved slightly to the right so he could look directly at T. Harry through the opening.

"Yes, I mind. She's undisposed at the moment."

"Oh." Johnny scratched his head and put his hands in his pockets, trying to decide how to proceed. He felt like he was trying to get past a border guard. "Well, when she's *indisposed*, would you please tell her I stopped by and I need to speak with her?"

"Sure thing." T. Harry backed up and took his foot away, letting the screen door slap shut seconds before he closed the front door firmly in Johnny's face.

"You have a real good day," Johnny said to the closed door.

T. HARRY walked into the kitchen where Martha Maye was making lunch. The radio was on, and her hips were swaying in place as she sang along to Shania Twain's "When You Kiss Me."

"T, was someone at the door?" she said over her shoulder.

"Naw, it was just some of them Jehovah's Witnesses." He came up beside her and took a pinch of egg salad from the bowl. He put it in his mouth and then wiped the leftover from his finger on the tip of her nose.

"T. Harry! Stop carrying on like a fool!" She wiped her nose with a dishtowel and went back to making the sandwiches.

"I have an idea," T. Harry said, sitting down at the table. "What say you, me, and Butterbean take a drive out to the country to look at the pretty leaves?"

"I doubt Butterbean would find that a very appealing afternoon activity," she said, cutting a sandwich.

"Well, maybe she could stay over at Honey's and play with Maddy Mack while me and you go."

"You and I. You and I. You and I. You and I." It came out harsh and exasperated. She gentled her tone. "And I don't know, T. I kind of want to spend time with Butterbean and not go off without her—"

"Then we could take her to a movie," he interrupted. "Or we could take these samiches and go out to the country for a picnic."

"I think I'd just like to stay at home today, but thanks for the offer. There's no reason you can't go do something, though. You don't have to stay here and entertain us." She'd finished making three sandwiches, and she licked her fingers clean. "What?" she asked, looking curiously at him.

"I was just thinking how pretty you are."

"Oh, T. Harry, stop that foolishness." It wasn't said in a flirtatious tone, but in more of a don't-go-there kind of tone. "Butterbean!" She stuck her head out the kitchen door. "Lunch!"

Butterbean came into the kitchen looking glum. She flopped into a chair without saying a word.

"Wash your hands, pumpkin."

Butterbean went to the sink, while Martha Maye added potato chips to the three plates, set them on the table, and sat down.

"Say, Carrie," T. Harry pretended he just had a thought, "how about we go hiking today? I'll make a list of things we have to find in the woods, and we'll have ourselves a scavenger hunt. What do you say?"

Martha Maye's mouth dropped open, but she stayed quiet when Butterbean perked up. "Yeah! That sounds like fun."

"All right. That's what we'll do. And Marty, why don't you pack us up some cold chicken and tater salad, and some of them oatmeal cookies, and we'll have us a picnic dinner."

"Yeah, Mama! That sounds real nice." Butterbean clapped her hands together in delight. It was the liveliest Martha Maye had seen her daughter act in a week, and she couldn't say no.

"You could sell country to cornbread," Martha Maye told T. Harry.

"Thank you kindly, Marty." He beamed at them both.

JOHNNY WALKED into A Blue Million Books later that afternoon in a foul mood, but he had to laugh when he saw the back of Pickle's T-shirt. It read, LEGALIZE POT PIE. Then he remembered seeing Pickle in the Mag Bar's parking lot.

"Hey, Pickle."

"Hidee, Chief." Pickle was three steps up on a ladder and turned his head to speak over his shoulder but kept at his job of dusting.

"Glad I ran into you. There's something I wanted to ask you about."

"Yessir?" Pickle stepped down and turned toward him. Johnny could now see a picture of a steaming hot pot pie on the front of the boy's shirt.

"Did I see you over at the Mag Bar the other night?"

Pickle's brow wrinkled. "Uh, could be."

"Either you were or you weren't, son." He stepped closer to him. "The thing is, I can think of no good reason for you to be there, and I can think of lots of bad reasons." Johnny put his hand on Pickle's shoulder and looked him in the eye. "As a friend, I'm telling you, if you're buying *pot pie*, you need to know it ain't *legal* yet, and you'd best stop right quick. I won't ask you to incriminate yourself, but if I see you over there again, I *will* stop you and search your car and your person. Is that clear?"

Pickle looked like a bobblehead doll as he nodded. "But—"

Johnny squeezed his shoulder in a fatherly gesture. "No buts. Teenage years can be hard; just don't go doing anything stupid. You understand my meaning?"

Pickle nodded again, and Johnny said, "Is Louetta around?"

"Yessir, she's in the back, but—"

"Back to work, Pickle." Johnny walked toward the back of the store and called out for Lou from the counter. She came out of her office patting her hair in place.

"I thought that was your voice I heard. Well? Did you talk to her?"

"I tried, Lou. I couldn't get past the sentry." Louetta looked puzzled, and he added, "T. Harry. He said she was indisposed and shut the door in my face."

"Oh, that man. I'd like to snatch his arm out and beat him with the bloody stump."

"Louetta Stafford!"

"I'm telling you, Johnny, I got a bad feeling about him. So whatchew gonna do now, just let him chase you away?"

"I went back by the house a few minutes ago, but no one was home. I stopped in at Honey's, and she said she didn't know where they were."

"That can't be." She picked up the phone and punched in some numbers. She ended the call and punched in seven new numbers. "I don't know why she got a cell phone. She hardly ever keeps it on."

Drumming her fingers while she waited for an answer, Johnny watched as her expression changed from irritated to worried. He heard her say, "Martha Maye, this is Mama. You give me a call the minute you get home, you hear? I'm worried about y'all. Call me, now."

When she hung up the phone, he said, "Where could they have gone?"

"I surely don't know, but do you know when the last time I couldn't find my daughter was?" She walked to the window, and he followed her.

"No, ma'am, I reckon I don't." He patted her back consolingly as they looked out the window.

"It was the day she and Tess were kidnapped. Does that tell you anything?"

"Yes, ma'am. It tells me you usually can find her, but today you can't. It's not time to panic yet, you hear? Don't go getting your socks on over your boots."

She nodded and gave him a hug.

"What are we going to do?" She pulled back from the window, rubbing her forehead.

"You're going to stay here and mind the shop, and I'm going to go out and look for them. I'll call you the minute I find them."

"Bless your pea-pickin' heart. You're good people, Johnny."

"Thank you, Lou. Maybe you could put in a good word with your daughter?"

THIRTY-TWO

You can't tell much about a chicken pie until you get through the crust.

~Southern Proverb

Johnny cruised through town, stopping periodically to ask someone if they'd seen Martha Maye or T. Harry's green truck. After thirty minutes with no success, he headed south on a road leading to farmland. He racked his brain thinking where they might have gone, but he came up blank. He told himself to calm down. It was pretty obvious T. Harry had a crush on Martha Maye, but he couldn't see the man hurting her or Butterbean.

After twenty miles, he did a U-turn and headed back toward Goose Pimple Junction. He propped his elbow on the door and rested his head on his hand. Estherlene's earlier comment about possibly seeing a green pickup truck had been bothering him all day. T. Harry had a green pickup truck. But Martha Maye said he hadn't come to town until two days after the murder. He couldn't remember where she said T. Harry lived. *Could he have possibly snuck into town, killed his brother, and snuck back out? But why would he kill his brother?*

He didn't like the thoughts he was having, or the possibility that Martha Maye was very likely with someone nobody in town knew very well, and he *really* didn't like the fact that no one knew where she and Butterbean were. *Why hadn't she called someone? And why hadn't she returned my calls?*

He rode back through town and then took a road that led north. He stopped at a few houses to ask if they'd noticed a green pickup truck drive by, but as one person put it, "We're in the country. There's a green pickup truck for every four people in town." He got tired of explaining he was on a leave of absence and saying no, they hadn't caught the murderer.

Feeling defeated, he rode back into town at dusk. He decided to go by Martha Maye's house one more time, and then he would go to the station and call the staties for help. Chief or no chief, he could call in a few favors.

He turned onto Marigold Lane and relief washed over him. The green truck sat in the driveway, and lights were on in Martha Maye's house. He parked his car behind the truck and jumped out, stalking to the door and pounding on it. T. Harry opened it.

"T. Harry," Johnny said flatly. He was breathing hard and hoping his eyes conveyed as much anger as he felt.

"John," T. Harry said for the second time today. Johnny heard the disdain in the man's voice.

Johnny took a deep breath. "T. Harry. I'd like to speak to Martha Maye." He held up a hand signaling T. Harry not to say another word. "I mean to see her tonight. If she's *indisposed* again, I'll wait." He opened the screen door wider. "I mean to see her tonight, even if it harelips the governor. Now I'll wait right here while you go get her." Johnny held onto the screen door and glared at T. Harry.

"Harelips the governor? Whatchew talking about?" T. Harry tried to step outside and close the front door behind him. Johnny put his hand on his chest, stopping him.

"It's an expression. Now. Go. Get. Her." Johnny matched his tone with the look in his eye. Tired of playing nice, he was not leaving without making sure Martha Maye and Butterbean were all right.

"Hey now, don't have a duck fit. I think Martha Maye's in the sh—"

He didn't get to finish his sentence because Martha Maye appeared behind him. "Johnny! It's so good to see you!" She pushed past T. Harry and took one look at Johnny's face. "Is everything all right? Is Mama . . . Aunt Imy—"

"Everything and everybody's fine, Martha Maye," Johnny assured her. "We were just worried about you because nobody knew where you were all day."

"Oh!" she clamped her hand over her mouth. "I'm so sorry. You're right, I shoulda called Mama and them and said we were going on a hike and a picnic. T. Harry rushed me so much, I guess I just forgot. I'm so sorry. I really didn't mean to worry y'all. Why didn't y'all call my cell?" She pulled it out of her pocket. "Oh. It's been turned off. Hmmm. Wonder how that happened."

Johnny was struck by how lovely she looked. It had been a while since they'd spent any time together. He'd missed her and couldn't believe how grateful he was that she was all right. Glancing past her, he saw T. Harry leaning against the doorway to the kitchen, watching them and listening in. He looked back at Martha Maye.

"Martha Maye, do you suppose we could go for a short walk? Just you and me?" He hitched a thumb over his shoulder.

Her smile washed all his worry away. Suddenly everything was right with the world.

"Sure, I'd like that." She turned to her brother-in-law. "T. Harry, you mind staying here with Butterbean while we go out for a walk?"

T. Harry looked at his watch. "I don't know, it's getting kinda late, Marty—"

"Hey, if you need to leave, go ahead. Martha Maye and I can sit here and talk," Johnny offered. He could see T. Harry's thoughts all over his face. T. Harry was kicking himself for falling into that trap.

He recovered quickly, though. "No, no, y'all gwon. I'll stay with Carrie until you get back." T. Harry made a shooing motion with his hands. "Just don't be long."

Martha Maye shot him a smile, and Johnny felt himself begrudging him. *She shouldn't grace that no-good lying ferret face with one of her smiles.*

As Johnny closed the door behind them, Martha Maye said, "How've you been, Johnny? It's been a while since we talked. I was getting worried about you."

"Really? I called you a couple of times and even left messages. And I left one with T. Harry today. Didn't he tell you?"

She looked confused. "You did? When?"

They walked past Estherlene's house and waved at her in the front window. Estherlene made a motion with her hand to her ear miming, *"Call me."*

"I wonder why she wants me to call her," Martha Maye turned her head to look at the woman as they kept walking.

Johnny waved, and said, "She might've meant me. She wants to help on the investigation."

"Oh." She glanced up at him. "Anyway, when did you call, Johnny?"

"Uh, I guess the first time was the day after the funeral."

"And you left a message with T. Harry? How odd. He never gave it to me."

"Must've slipped his mind," Johnny said, trying to keep the sarcasm out of his voice.

"Hmm, I guess so. His brother was just killed, after all. I guess he's had a lot on his mind."

"How long's he staying in town? Doesn't he have a job to get back to?"

"He hasn't actually said how long he'll be here. He's a self-employed carpenter, so he can take off pretty much whenever he wants. I guess he could find work here, too, if he was so inclined. I keep assuring him we're fine, and to tell you the truth, I wish he'd gwon back home, but I don't have the heart to tell him so. He's been so good to us."

"I could tell him," Johnny said through thin lips.

"No." Martha Maye shook her head. "I just couldn't hurt his feelings."

"Are you sure you trust him, Mart?" Johnny glanced sideways at her.

"He's family, Johnny. Of course I trust him. Why on earth wouldn't I?"

"Tell me something." He took her hand and kept walking, trying to act like it was a perfectly natural act, and praying she wouldn't pull it away. "Did he tell you I came by the house this morning?"

She stopped walking and looked up at him. "You were by this morning?"

"Yep. He didn't tell you, did he?"

"Well . . . no. I thought I heard someone at the door, but he said it was the Jehovah's Witnesses." Looking up at the almost-black sky dotted with stars, she said, "I can't believe he lied to me."

She sounded so hurt, Johnny just wanted to wrap his arms around her, which is exactly what he did. He was relieved when she didn't pull away. Actually, she held on tight.

"Oh, Johnny, it's been a rough couple of months, what with one thing after another, but I never dreamed my brother-in-law would lie to me. Why would he do that?"

"He's not worth a hat full of rotten eggs, Martha Maye." He smelled her sweet perfume and felt her hair tickle his chin. "I think he's got a thing for you," Johnny said softly, still holding her. When she was silent, he went on. "I see how he looks at you, and he hasn't been civil to me since the minute I met him. The fact that he's not giving you my messages and he's been trying to keep us apart just clinches it for me."

She pulled back and looked into his eyes. "Johnny, I'm scared. After what happened with Henry Clay and now T. Harry, my goodness, what a horrible judge of character I am!"

They began walking again, holding hands and leaning in close to each other, Martha Maye seeking reassurance and Johnny offering it.

"You're just a good person who doesn't see the evil in people. You want to believe what you see is what you get, because that's the way you are, honest and true, but some folks aren't like that. Most of the time, you can't tell much about a chicken pie until you get through the crust."

Softly, she said, "Are *you* who you say you are, Johnny?" Her question cut through him as if she'd hacked at him with an axe. He stopped walking again, pulling on her hand so she faced him. With his hand under her chin, he tipped her head so she'd look at him. "Martha Maye, I swear to you I am what you see. I don't have a dark side, I don't have any secrets, and I certainly don't have a mean streak. I will not lie to you, and I promise you never have to be afraid of me."

She nodded, and they walked on in silence. He looked up at the sky and saw the prettiest sliver of a moon and a bright star next to it. He pointed to it. "Look, that's Jupiter."

"Oh, it's beautiful. I'll have to tell Butterbean. She'll love it." Her head snapped to Johnny, a terrified look on her face. "You don't suppose he'd do anything to Butterbean, do you? I left my baby with that liar!"

"Come on, we'll go back. It'll make you feel better. But no, I don't think Butterbean's in danger. You said yourself he's been good to y'all, and Butterbean is his niece. I don't see him hurting her."

They were quiet again as they passed several houses, and then she said, "What am I going to do, Johnny?"

"About T. Harry?" Johnny grabbed her hand again. He was finding it hard not to touch her.

"Yeah. I'm not saying he's dangerous or anything, but what you told me tonight gives me the creeps. I don't think I want to be alone in the house with him anymore."

Johnny nodded and said, "Here's what we'll do: I'll come in with you while you tell him you need to go stay at your mama's house. You could tell him it's on account of your aunt. Make something up. Just go to Lou's. If you're not at home, he can't hang around, and Louetta certainly won't put up with his foolishness."

"Do I really have to go to Mama's? You think that's necessary?"

"Yes, I do. Tell him you need to pack, and then show him to the door. I'll leave, too, but I'll stick around outside your house until he's gone tonight. Then you pack a few days' things for both of y'all and go to your mama's house."

"What if he comes over to Mama's?"

"Ha! Like I said, Lou won't put up with his shenanigans. Once he sees he can't follow y'all around like a lost puppy, maybe he'll get bored and go home."

"And if he doesn't?"

"Then he and I will have a come-to-Jesus talk. You may not want to hurt the man's feelings, but if he keeps carrying on, I *will* be talking to him."

She nodded.

Johnny said, "You cannot get the water to clear up until you get the pigs out of the creek." She didn't laugh, but she smiled. That was enough for Johnny.

They got back to Martha Maye's house and stood on the front porch. Martha Maye took her hand from his and reached for the door. Seeming unsure of what to do next, she turned back to Johnny, then reached for the doorknob again.

"Uh," Johnny said at the same time she said, "Well . . ."

They both cracked up laughing, and Johnny caught her hand in his. Their laughter died down, and he brought her hand to his face and kissed her knuckles.

"Thanks for the walk, Johnny, and the advice."

"I am so relieved you're okay," Johnny said, holding her hand to his chest. "How about I come in with you while you get rid of T. Harry. Then I'll sit out in my car over there until I see him leave." He thought a minute and then said, "No, I'm gonna sit out there until you and Butterbean get in your car to go to your mama's, then I'm gonna follow you. Just so you know and don't think I'm stalking you or anything."

"Well, if I had to have a stalker—" Johnny's kiss cut off Martha Maye's sentence.

He pulled back a little and said, "I've thought of nothing but you, Martha Maye. I can't get you out of my mind."

"Do you need to?" she asked, kissing his cheek and then the spot right under his ear.

He closed his eyes and relished her touch. "Sooner or later, I'm gonna have to get back to work—"

The front porch light began flashing on and off.

"Oh, for heaven's sake," Martha Maye said. "I'm not a teenager, and T. Harry isn't my daddy!"

"Mart, he's showing such possessiveness, I don't want you wasting any time getting rid of him."

She nodded. "All right, but you don't have to wait in your car. You wait inside the house, okay?"

He kissed her again. "Ready?"

"Ready as I'll ever be." She'd opened the screen door and was just about to open the main door when Johnny said, "And just in case he asks, I'm taking you and Butterbean out trick-or-treating on Monday night."

She smiled and said, "Thank you, Johnny. That'll be real nice."

THIRTY-THREE

The cotton patch doesn't care which way you vote.

~Southern Proverb

"Happy Halloween, lady policeman. Hireyew doing today?" Junebug greeted Velveeta as she sat down at the diner counter on Monday morning.

From the kitchen, Slick yelled, "That's an oxymoron, Junie. She can't be a lady *and* a police*man*."

"Oh, shush. You're an ox and a moron. Just concentrate on slinging hash and let me talk to the customers."

Velveeta stared at Junebug wide-eyed and open-mouthed.

"Oh, don't look at me that way. Slick and I banter about all the time. He knows he's the mint to my julep. Just like I'm the macaroni to his cheese." She called over her shoulder, "Right darlin'?"

"You're the cream to my coffee," Slick hollered through the open window.

Junebug turned to Velveeta. "See? It's just our way." She slung a dishtowel over her shoulder. "Now, what can I getcha, sweet thing?"

"Just coffee, please."

"How about a donut to go along with the joe?" Junebug suggested. She plucked a chocolate iced donut with orange and black sprinkles out of a glass cake dome. "It's on the house."

"Well, if you insist," she said, as Junebug put it in front of her.

Junebug placed a cup and saucer in front of Velveeta, went for the coffee pot, and returned to fill the cup. "Did you catch that nefarious criminal yet?"

Slick called out, "Junebug, do you know any criminals who *aren't* nefarious?"

"Oh, shush, you," Junebug said over her shoulder. "Or I'll come back there and fix you a knuckle sandwich."

Velveeta shook her head, chuckling. "No arrests yet."

"Y'ont cream, or do you like it unadulterated?" Junebug asked.

"Just sugar, thanks." Velveeta looked around the diner, then back at Junebug.

"Listen, I'm trying to track down the chief's whereabouts on the night of the murder. He said he answered a call about a theft here?"

"Yeah, honey. He sure did. He was here for about, oh, I don't know. Hey Slick, how long you think the chief was here the night of the Oktoberfest after those hooligans nearly robbed us blind?"

Slick came out of the kitchen wiping his hands on a towel tucked into his pants. "Oh, I'd say about thirty minutes."

"Did he say where he was going after that?" Velveeta studied Slick and then Junebug.

"Naw, can't say that he did." Slick rested a hip against the counter in front of Velveeta.

"You can't think the chief had anything to do with the murder." Junebug's hands fisted on her hips.

"I don't, but I do need to establish his alibi so it won't look like I didn't investigate this fully. I have to be able to cross him off the suspect list legitimately."

"Oh. Well, we can vouch for about thirty minutes that night, right around eight, eight thirty."

"Okay." Velveeta took a sip of coffee and watched Slick return to the kitchen, his gray ponytail bobbing as he walked. "Where are Clive and Earl today?"

"It's free samples day over at Piggly Wiggly. They go shopping every Monday so they can eat for free."

Velveeta broke the donut in half, dunked it in her coffee, and slurped the coffee off the end before she bit off a piece. "I was wondering, Junebug. Did Lenny ever come in here with anybody other than his wife and child?"

"Not so's I noticed. I'm not here all the time, but purt near."

"I just don't know where to go on this. Nobody saw anything, the evidence is missing, and my only suspects are ones other people tell me are the salt of the earth and couldn't be murderers. I found nothing in his hotel room." She put her head in her hands. "I just don't know how to proceed."

"What does your gut tell you to do?" Junebug asked, wiping off the counter.

"I don't know. I don't think I have enough for it to tell me anything yet."

Junebug ducked her chin and looked at the officer under raised eyebrows.

Velveeta nodded. "Okay," she lowered her voice to almost a whisper, "I guess I like Martha Maye for it. She hated the man, and she can't account for her whereabouts for about thirty minutes that night. A mama bear will do anything to protect her baby bear. She has means and motive, and the murder weapon was her kitchen knife. How can I ignore that?"

Junebug crossed her arms and looked thoughtfully at Velveeta. She propped an elbow on the counter and sat her chin in her hand as she thought about the question. Finally, she propped her elbows on the counter and leaned toward Velveeta.

"There's something to be said for hunches. They ain't scientific, but a lot of times they pan out." She leaned in even more and lowered her voice before continuing. Her face and tone suggested she was deadly serious.

"But I'm telling you, sugar, I've known Martha Maye since she wasn't no bigger 'n a beef roast. She doesn't hate anybody, and if she's capable of murder, I'll eat Slick's liver 'n onions. And honey, let's just say there ain't no flipping way on either account. I'd sooner believe Elvis was a woman than believe Martha Maye is a murderer." She shook her head and grimaced. "Mmm, it pains me to say that, 'cause I do love my Elvis, and I do hate Slick's liver 'n onions—"

"Hey!" Slick protested from the window.

"Oh, that ain't no state secret, bless your heart, and it ain't nothing against your cooking, neither. I'm just talking 'bout liver in general." She looked back at Velveeta. "What I'm saying is, my belief in Martha Maye is that strong."

Velveeta nodded and slowly chewed the last bite of donut.

"You know, I don't mean to be telling you your bidness or anything," Junebug said, still leaning on the counter and talking to Velveeta conspiratorially, "but I saw Martha Maye's costume that night." Velveeta's eyebrows formed a V, and she listened intently to Junebug. "Now think about it. That dress talked as she walked. She couldn't have sneaked up on anybody, and if Lenny knew she was there, there woulda been a struggle and she woulda gotten grass or dirt or hair or something on it. How in the world could she have killed Lenny while she wore that froufrou white dress?"

Velveeta's eyes got big. "She couldn't have," then looked as if a light bulb had gone off in her head.

"Now let's look at it with a different set of eyes." Junebug came around the counter and sat on the stool next to the officer. The women faced each other. "Supposing she didn't have the dress on. Could she have changed clothes, come upon Lenny, killed him, changed back into that white Southern belle dress, and gotten back to the Oktoberfest all in — how long was she gone?

"Thirty minutes." Velveeta nodded. "You're right. Thank you, Junebug. You're the best."

"If you ask me, this murder didn't have anything to do with Goose Pimple Junction. Who here would know him enough to care if he were alive or dead? It don't add up."

"That's why I keep coming back to the chief or Martha Maye."

Junebug shook her head. "You gotta think outside the box, sugar."

Velveeta cocked her head.

"Think about the man's life before he got here. Have you looked into that at all?"

Velveeta downed her coffee, slapped a five on the counter, and hurried to the door.

"Hey! I said the donut's on me!"

"Keep it! I owe you more than that for helping me get my head on straight."

And she took off down the street like a lion charging toward its prey.

Big Darryl D stood when he saw Velveeta Witherspoon get out of her car and head for the showroom. He pasted on a smile as she pushed through the door.

"How do, Officer. What can I put you in today?"

"I'm not here to shop. I'm here to ask you some questions about Lenny Applewhite."

Darryl D put on his hangdog face. "Yes, yes, such a shame, wasn't it?"

"What kind of an employee was he?"

"The man was a born salesman. He sold a lot of cars in the brief time he was here, God rest his soul."

"How did he come to work here?"

"He showed up one day outta the blue. Said I needed him. Like I said, he was a salesman, and I bought what he was selling and hired him that very day."

"Anything you can remember that was strange or out of the ordinary concerning him?"

"Yes, actually there is. I got in a car one night to go home and he was sleeping in the backseat."

"The backseat?"

"Yep. About scared the life outta me, let me tell you. I screamed like a girl."

"Did he say why he was sleeping in the car when he had a hotel room?"

"All's he would say is he was having 'people problems.'"

"People problems?" Velveeta quirked her brow.

"Yep. As I pulled out of the lot that night, a big black SUV rolled up, two men inside. They looked real suspicious, but when I told them we was closed for the night, they just kinda looked around the parking lot and then drove off without a word."

"And you think that was related to Lenny?"

"Yep. He saw them coming, took a dive in the backseat, and told me to drive."

"But you have no idea what they wanted?"

"No earthly idea."

"Can I have a look around his office?"

"Sure. It's just as he left it. I haven't touched a thing."

MARTHA MAYE stood in front of her mother's refrigerator looking into the freezer. "There aren't any waffles, Butterbean, and no cereal, either. How about I make you some eggs?"

Louetta walked into the kitchen dressed in a bright orange blouse and black pants, her hair coiffed nice and big, and her face made up for the day. "No cereal? That can't be. I just bought some the other day."

Ima Jean followed Lou into the room. "I go cuckoo for Cocoa Puffs."

"Yeah, well, somebody else did, too, Aunt Imy. I'm telling you, we're out." Martha Maye opened the refrigerator and pulled out a carton of eggs and a package of bacon.

Lou went to the pantry to look for herself. She stood in front of it, hands on her hips, shaking her head. "The peanut butter's gone, too." She moved a few things and said, "And my two cans of peaches and some granola bars. What in the land of cotton is going on?"

"I don't know, Mama, but I don't have time right now to figure it out. I gotta get Butterbean some breakfast and get us both to school."

"Here, honey, I'll make my special ghostie eggs for both of you. You have to have ghostie eggs on Halloween morning, for Pete's sake. You go finish readying yourself while I fix breakfast."

Martha Maye gave the carton of eggs to her mother, who took over breakfast preparations.

The bacon was almost done, and Lou was cracking an egg into a ghost-shaped hole she'd cut in the bread in the pan when a knock sounded on the back door. When Lou looked up, she saw T. Harry looking through one of the panes of glass that covered the top half of the door. He had his hands cupped around his face to shade the light from his eyes as he peered into the kitchen.

"Oh, for crying out catfish. That man's about as sharp as a mashed potato. I'm gonna nip this in the bud right quick." Louetta stomped to the door and pulled it open, nearly knocking T. Harry off balance.

"Good morning, Ms. Louetta. I was in the neighborhood and thought maybe I'd walk the girls to school." He craned his neck around her to see if Martha Maye was in the room. Lou blocked the doorway and kept him from entering. She had a look on her face that could wilt a daisy.

"Listen up, T. Harry. I want you to stop all this foolishness. I mean it. You've taken real good care of our girls, and I know they 'preshade it, but it's time for you to get in your car and drive on back home."

T. Harry sniffed the air. "Say, is that bacon I smell? And coffee?"

From behind Louetta, Ima Jean said, "The best part of waking up is Folgers in your cup."

"T. Harry." Louetta glared at him. "I want you to read my lips and mind my words. Go home. The girls are fine now. We're all watching out for them, and we'll take real good care of them." She propped her hands on her ample hips. "Get in your car and go home. *Now.*"

"Have you driven a Ford lately?" Ima Jean piped up again, peering over Louetta's shoulder.

"Ms. Louetta, you ain't got no call to talk to me like that. Butterbean's my niece, and if I want to spend time with her, I can—"

Once again, Lou didn't let him finish.

"Act like you got some raising, boy. I only met your mama once, God rest her soul, but I think she'da raised sand if she ever saw you carrying on this way."

That did it. T. Harry let out a big sigh and held up his hands in surrender. "All right. All right. I'll go. May I please say good-bye to Martha Maye and Butterbean?"

"Make it snappy." Lou reluctantly stood aside so he could come into the kitchen.

Ima Jean handed him a glass of orange juice. "A day without orange juice is like a day without sunshine."

"BERNADETTE, DO you have the dispatch log from the night of October twenty-second?" Velveeta pulled her jacket off as she approached the desk.

Bernadette, at her computer, hit a few keys and said, "Yep. I'll shoot it over to you."

Velveeta sat at her desk and pulled up her email. The log showed Johnny had talked to Bernadette at 7:55, 8:28, and 8:42. She sat back in her chair and tapped a pencil on the desk. Then she went into the break room, where she found Hank Beanblossom.

"Hank, I got a hypothetical for you. Let's suppose I liked a person for a murder—"

"Okay, who?"

"We're just supposing. *Hypothetical* like. Suppose this person talked to someone off and on for about two hours at intervals no more than thirty or so minutes."

"Okay . . ."

"Do you see any way this person could have lost his mind and killed someone with a knife and then gotten back to his normal self, normal voice, normal demeanor, talking that frequently to someone else?"

Hank thought about it for a minute, biting his lip in concentration. "I reckon it'd be awful hard to do, especially since I talked to the *hypothetical person* a couple times myself during that window."

"I think it'd be impossible, too, and I don't see how Martha Maye woulda had time to do it, either. She was only gone thirty minutes, tops, from the Oktoberfest, and she had that costume on. There wasn't any blood at the scene, but still, you'd think the killer would have gotten something on his or her clothes."

"Well, the blade killed him instantly, so there really wasn't a lot of blood. And we know the killer snuck up on him, on account he had to have been urinating in the bushes, what with his ding-a-ling sticking out of his zipper and all, so there probably wasn't much of a struggle. Even so, it would be practically impossible for Martha Maye to do it in such a short time, especially given her getup."

"Have you ever worn one of them hoop skirts and a long frilly dress like that?"

"Nope, can't say that I have."

"To tell you the truth, I haven't either, but thinking about it, I just don't see how it would be at all possible. Not to mention it would have been next to impossible to sneak up on him in that dress that went *swish swish* with every move she made."

"So you've crossed the chief and Martha Maye off the list."

"You knew I was talking about the chief from the get-go. How'd you know that all along?"

"I'm not as dumb as I look," Hank said.

"That would be impossible," Velveeta said over her shoulder on her way to find the chief. "Bless your heart."

THIRTY-FOUR

Hospitality is making your guests feel at home, even if you wish they were.

~Southern Proverb

"**S**o she came to my house and said she had talked to Junebug and looked at the dispatch log. Said she'd done some pondering, and checking, and she apologized for putting us through the wringer. Said we were both free and clear of any suspicion. Said she has another theory she's working on."

Johnny told Martha Maye about the day's interesting turn of events as they walked along the sidewalk, trailing Butterbean and Maddy Mack, who were trick-or-treating.

"That's great, Johnny. I'm so glad you got your job back, and more importantly, your good name."

"And even more importantly, it sounds like you got rid of T. Harry." Johnny gave her a sympathetic look. "I ran into Louetta today, and she told me about her talk with him."

"Yeah, she took care of it all right. I feel bad for him, but after finding out about his duplicate behavior, I don't feel too awful bad."

"Duplicitous," Johnny gently corrected.

Martha Maye bumped sideways into him. "Yeah, that's what I mean."

Johnny put his arm around her shoulders and gave her an affectionate squeeze. "Did your mama tell you she invited me to dinner tonight?"

Martha Maye watched the girls run across a lawn to knock on another door. "She did, but if she hadn't, I would have. Mama puts on the best Halloween party you ever did see. I hope you're hungry. She'll expect you to eat until you burst."

"I'm always hungry, but I'll pass on the bursting." Butterbean screamed, and the light from the flashlight in his hand jerked toward the sound. Martha Maye took off at a dead run, but Johnny beat her to the two girls, who were jumping up and down, clinging to each other, half-laughing and half-crying. Pickle stood inside a Rubbermaid trash can, his skinny legs sticking out of the cutout bottom. He held the lid in his hand. He wore the black trashcan like it was a pair of overalls.

"What in the world?" Martha Maye started to say.

"Mama! We came past this trashcan—least we thought it was a trashcan—and Pickle jumped out and scared the living daylights out of us."

"Him is mean!" Maddy Mack glared at Pickle, who was still laughing at his practical joke.

"Aw, I'm sorry." Pickle didn't look sorry. "But y'all gotta admit that's a good trick."

"That is a good trick," Johnny said. "I'll have to remember that next time I'm on surveillance."

"Surveillance?" Maddy Mack's face screwed up in confusion.

"Like a stakeout," Johnny explained.

"You've been on a stakeout before?" Butterbean asked, full of awe and wonder.

"Sure. A couple of times."

As Johnny recounted one stakeout he'd been on, Pickle quietly crouched back down on the grass, pulling the trashcan lid over himself like a turtle. Then he pulled his arms through the cutouts and tucked them inside. It looked like a trashcan was simply sitting on the lawn. When Johnny finished his story, Pickle jumped out like a jack-in-the-box, scaring the little girls again and sending them into another round of screams.

"Aw, come on, that couldn't have scared you! You knew I was inside there."

"Okay, y'all, everybody move it. Let's head to Mama's for dinner. I can practically smell the cornbread from here." Martha Maye herded them all toward Lou's house in typical teacher mode.

"Hey, looka there!" Pickle said. "Hi, Mama! Hey, Peanut!"

"Ugh, Peanut," Maddy Mack said to Butterbean. "He's so ugly he could trick-or-treat over the phone."

"Shh, now, none of that, girls." Martha Maye swatted at the girls behinds. "Hello, Caledonia. Hi, Peanut. You sure are a scary vampire," Martha Maye said.

"He scared us!" Butterbean said to Caledonia, pointing to Pickle.

"What did he do, darlin'?" Caledonia looked from Butterbean to her son. "What did you do, Pickle?"

Pickle started to crouch back down and show his mother his trick, but Martha Maye stopped him. "Show her later, like when the girls aren't in the vicinity. Caledonia, will you and Peanut join us for supper? I'm sure Mama fixed enough to feed Pharaoh's army."

"That would be lovely," Caledonia said.

"Where's Philetus tonight?"

She shook her head. "Working. He's always working, isn't he, Peanut?" Peanut was no longer at his mother's side. He was running after the girls, who were going to trick-or-treat at the last few houses.

When they finally got to Louetta's house, Martha Maye led them through the extensively decorated living and dining rooms and into the hub of activity—the kitchen. Louetta had placed jack-o'-lanterns all over the living room. Some lined the mantle, some were on the coffee table, some went up the stairs, and some stood sentry in the doorways. Witches, ghosts, and monsters decorated every table in the room. In the dining room, five tissue paper ghosts hung from the chandelier, and pumpkins with faces made from vegetables sat on the table as a centerpiece. For hair, they had broccoli, unshelled peanuts, or Brussels sprouts; red peppers for lips; tiny white potatoes for eyes; string beans for eyebrows; tomatoes for ears. The antique sideboard showcased five different desserts.

Ima Jean, Louetta, and Charlotte were in the kitchen, preparing dinner.

"Howdy, y'all. Welcome." Louetta was dressed up like a witch, all in black, complete with striped stockings, a witch's hat, and a fake nose with a wart. "Would y'all like some of my witch's brew?" She cackled like a witch and didn't wait for an answer, but grabbed mugs, and began pouring hot apple cider into them. "I got Polka Dot Punch for the kids, too."

Martha Maye opened the lid of a pot on the stove, her face showing utter contentment as she breathed in the aroma. "Mmm, chili."

"Where's the beef?" Ima Jean said.

"Looks like it's in the chili." Johnny peered over Martha Maye's shoulder into the pot.

"Good Lord, this is a gracious plenty," Johnny said, looking at the food covering every surface of the big country kitchen.

"I had lots of help this year," she said. "Imy and Charlotte have purt near cooked their fingers to the bone."

"Shake and bake. And I hayulped," Ima Jean said.

"So y'all better eat up," Lou continued. "Caledonia, Peanut." She hugged Caledonia. "I'm so glad y'all could come, too. Philetus isn't with y'all?"

"Thank you kindly for having us, Ms. Louetta. No, he's working tonight, as usual. It sure does smell good in here, and everything looks wonderful." She stepped next to Charlotte, who was putting corn sticks into a basket, and pulled her in for a quick side hug.

"Hi, Ms. Culpepper. Where's Peekal?" Charlotte leaned into the hug.

Caledonia looked around the room. "Well shoot, he was here just a minute ago. Peanut, where'd your brother go?"

Peanut shrugged. "I dunno."

"He's probably out front playing his Pickle-in-the-trashcan joke on some poor unsuspecting person," Johnny said.

"I'll go look for him." Charlotte headed for the door.

"No need. We brought in the trash," Jack said, coming into the room with Tess and Pickle. "And by trash, I mean Pickle, not my sweetheart."

"You didn't bring Ezzie?" Martha Maye asked.

"Heavens no, she wouldn't be able to keep herself from all this good food. It would be a calamity."

Lou handed over a cheese ball that looked like a pumpkin, complete with a broccoli stem. "Here, Caledonia, you take this cheese ball to the table. Imy, take the tater salad. Charlotte, grab the macaroni and cheese. Butterbean, you take the mummy pizzas. Madison Mackenzie, take these." She handed her a plate of pigs in a blanket, which were also made to look like mummies.

"Lou, can I just have dessert?" Johnny eyed the huge orange-iced pumpkin-shaped cake, ghost sugar cookies with M&Ms for eyes, spider cookies with candy eyes and chow mien noodles for legs, Rice Krispies treat eyeballs, skeleton cupcakes with white chocolate–coated pretzels for the bones, and cupcakes with candy witch legs sticking upside down out of the icing.

"You can have whatever your little ol' heart desires, Johnny." Johnny's eyes immediately went to Martha Maye.

Jack whispered into his ear, "Man, you got it bad, don'tcha?"

Johnny's face flushed bright red, and he swiped his hand over it.

"Yoo-hoo!" Honey called from the front door. "Can we come in?"

"Absodanglutely." Louetta hurried to greet Honey and Lolly. "Lolly, I'm glad you could make it."

"Thank you kindly for the invite." Lolly kissed her cheek.

"All right, y'all, have a seat and dig in," Lou said, clapping her hands together. Then, "Wait. Let me say grace first."

"I TELL you what," Lolly said after dinner, when everyone sat around in a sugar stupor, "that'll chink your cracks."

"I second that." Jack patted his stomach. "That was flat-cold good. Y'all outdid yourselves."

"Aw, thank you, boys, I—" Lou stopped talking when she saw Ima Jean sit up straight and stare strangely at the dining-room window.

"Ernest Borgnine!" Ima Jean pointed. "Ernest Borgnine! He's here." She got up and ran to the window. Lou followed her, as Jack and Johnny rushed out the back door to see if Ima Jean truly had seen somebody.

"I don't see Mr. Borgnine, Imy. And furthermore, I can't imagine why he would be in Goose Pimple Junction, or looking in our window."

"But he was," Imy insisted.

The men came back inside shaking their heads. "Nobody out there that we could see," Jack said.

"Hey, Pickle, come here a minute, would you?" Johnny said.

They disappeared out the back door and Jack explained, "He's going to set out the trash."

"I beg your pardon?" Caledonia said.

Jack laughed, along with everyone else. "I didn't mean it like that. He's setting up a stakeout, and Pickle's going to help. He looks invisible in that trash can, but even though nobody would guess there's somebody inside that can, he can see out with those peepholes he punched into the side. Maybe he'll see someone. You never know."

Charlotte stood up so fast she nearly knocked over her chair. "I don't want him doing that," she said loudly. "He doesn't know anything about stakeouts. He could get hurt."

"Naw, Johnny won't let that happen," Jack assured.

"Won't let what happen?" Johnny said, coming back inside.

"You won't let Pickle get hurt out there."

"'Course not."

"I don't care." She looked like she was going to cry. "I don't want him out there by himself. I'm going out, too."

"But honey, if you go out, whoever it is might see you, and then Peekal wouldn't be able to catch him," Lou pointed out.

"He's gonna scare the living daylights outta some poor unsuspecting soul." Charlotte ran for the back door, leaving everyone at the table to look at each other in puzzlement.

Louetta broke the silence. "I've been around teenage girls in my time, but that'n is acting crazy as an outhouse mouse."

THIRTY-FIVE

The terrapin walks fast enough to go visiting.

~Southern Proverb

J ohnny was in his office Tuesday afternoon when Bernadette yelled into the intercom, "Chief! Somebody here to see you!"

He pushed the intercom button and, trying not to sound irritated, said, "Send the somebody in, please."

A short man wearing a khaki poplin suit and a salt-and-pepper bottlebrush mustache that matched his hair appeared at the doorway. Johnny stood up to greet him and put out his hand.

"I'm Chief Butterfield."

Shaking the chief's hand, the man said, "I'm Detective Rusty Squares from Nashville. You got a minute to talk?" He handed Johnny his business card.

"Sure thing, Detective Squares. Have a seat." Johnny glanced at the card, noticed the man's last name was actually spelled S-q-u-i-r-e-s, and corrected himself. "I mean, Detective Squires."

The detective nodded. "It's all right. I get that a lot." The man's Southern accent rolled off his tongue thicker than his moustache.

Johnny returned to his seat, folded his hands on his desk, and studied the man. "What can I do for you, Detective?"

"I'm investigating a murder, Chief. I have a forty-year-old victim by the name of Joe Bob Mossbourn, and I'm looking for a person of interest by the name T. Harry Applewhite. I've been searching for him for some time. He's wanted for questioning, and I heard he might be down here."

"Well, he was. I'm afraid you just missed him. I believe he left town yesterday. Hold on." He held up one finger. "Let me make sure of that."

Johnny looked in the phone book, then punched in some numbers. While he waited for the call to be answered, he told the detective, "I'll put it on speaker phone."

"Stay A Spell Hotel, Sydney Greenbottom speaking. How can I help you?"

"Syd, this is Chief Butterfield."

"Howdee, Chief. Hireyew?"

"Fine, fine. You?"

"Not too good, actually. I messed up my leg in an ATV accident."

"Ouch. What did you want to go and do a fool thing like that for?"

"It's my nature, I suppose."

"I see. You best take it easy until it heals. Listen, you had a fella named Applewhite—"

"You mean T. Harry?"

"Yes, that's right."

"Yep. He's in room 301."

Johnny sat up straight. "You mean he hasn't checked out yet?" He picked up a pen from his desk as he talked and clicked it in and out.

"No. He's still here. I saw him drive off about an hour ago."

Johnny scribbled something on a piece of paper. "And you're sure he didn't check out?"

"I'm sure. He said he'd be here indefinitely. I gave him the long-term rate."

"Which way'd he go?" Johnny bopped the pen on the desk blotter.

"He turned left out of the lot, which would take him up toward Helechewa."

"Okay, that'll do it. Thank you a lot. Hey—think you could give me a call when he returns?"

"I s'ppose. But I'll be going off shift after while. I doubt Junior would remember."

"Okay. Just do your best."

He hung up and looked at the detective. "I'd like to talk to Mr. T. Harry myself. Why don't I get an officer in here to help you look. Y'all can bring him in, and we can both get down to business."

"Sounds like a plan."

Johnny pressed the intercom button. "Bernadette, would you have Officers Beanblossom and Witherspoon come to my office?"

Bernadette shouted, "Sure thing, Chief."

Johnny grimaced. "She's good people, but why the woman feels the need to yell into an intercom is beyond me."

A few minutes later, the officers appeared in the doorway. Both men stood for the introductions. "Detective, this is Officer Witherspoon and Officer Beanblossom."

Rusty stuck out his hand and said, "Detective Rusty Squares, nice to meetcha."

They shook hands and Hank said, "Likewise, Detective Squares."

Johnny looked at the detective with apologetic eyes. "Let's get this over with right quick. The name's *Squires*, with an *i* not an *a*."

"Your people aren't the Bugscuffle Squires, are they?" Hank asked.

"Naw, afraid not."

"He's investigating a murder up in Nashville. Wants to talk to T. Harry Applewhite. Syd says he's still in town—"

"But left the hotel about an hour ago," the detective interjected.

Witherspoon narrowed her eyes and asked, "You drive a dark SUV?"

The detective's forehead wrinkled. "No. A Crown Vic. Why?"

"Somebody in a dark SUV was looking for Lenny. Just wondering."

Johnny took command. "Beano, I want you to take the detective around and find Applewhite. Witherspoon, let's you and me go on over to the Mag Bar. I have a few more questions for Cash."

By the time Johnny and Velveeta walked into the bar a little after three, she'd filled him in on her talk with Big Darryl D, and he'd filled her in on his previous talk with Cash and his visits to the three couples' homes.

"I'm really liking those two hooligans in the dark SUV for the murder, Chief. It's the only thing that makes sense."

Johnny nodded and took off his sunglasses as he pushed through the door into the dim interior.

Cash Wily was behind the bar setting up, with his back to them. "We're not o—," he stopped midsentence when he turned and saw who had come into the bar.

"Oh, it's the law. You here on o-fficial or un-o-fficial bidness this time?"

"*Official*," Johnny said. "I checked out all the names you gave me."

"Yeah?" Cash looked indifferent.

"Yeah. Got nothing. You've had some time, and I thought maybe you might've remembered someone else who was in here talking to Lenny."

"Or something else about the two men who came in looking for him,"

Velveeta put in. "Anything come to mind?"

Cash laughed. "Nope. Didn't talk to them but the one time. Y'all want something to drink?"

"I could wet my whistle. Got Mtn Dew?" Johnny asked.

"Sure," Cash got a clean glass, added some ice, and shoved it under the soda dispenser, filling it up. When he turned to set the glass on the bar, his face brightened up. "I know who!" He slapped the bar lightly. "I mean, I don't know who exactly, but I seen somebody."

"Come again?" Velveeta said.

"I don't know the woman's name, but I do remember her hitting on Lenny a bunch of times, but she wasn't ever successful. He always brushed her off like a gnat."

"Can you describe her?" Johnny got out his notebook and pen.

"Well, lessee. She was probably in her sixties, maybe older, it's hard telling not knowing. Blondish hair that looked like a dye job. Wore a lot of spackle on her face."

Johnny looked up with a raised eyebrow.

"Makeup. She was always heavy on the makeup. Dressed younger 'n her age, if you ask me, but not nothing trampy-like."

"Height?"

"Oh, I'm never good at that." Cash held his hand out sideways in front of his torso. "Uh, I guess, right about here. What would that be? Around five-two? She was petite."

"Was she ever with anybody?"

"Nope. Always alone. What made me remember her is she always asked for a Mtn Dew. She didn't drink nothing but the Dew."

"Did she have any distinguishing features?" Velveeta asked.

Cash looked blankly at her.

"You know, a big nose, or no lips, or big boobs, or three eyes?"

"Oh." He nodded. "Yeah, she did kind of have what you'd call *prominent* ears. And big hair. She was real tan too." He rubbed at a spot on the bar, lost in thought, and then added, "And she smoked a lot. Man alive, she sure liked her cigarettes and her Mtn Dew."

Johnny and Velveeta looked at each other.

"You thinking about who I'm thinking about?" Johnny's eyebrows tented as he looked at Velveeta.

"Yeah, but that can't be. Can it?"

"Y'all know who I'm talking about?" Cash's face showed true surprise. "Cool! Do I get a reward?"

"For describing a woman?" Johnny said incredulously.

"You know, maybe a tip or something?" Cash said, with less certainty.

Johnny downed the Mtn Dew, put the glass back on the bar, and said, "Here's your tip: Never slap a man who's chewing tobacco."

Cash scowled at him, and Johnny slapped some bills on the bar. "Just kidding. Here you go. Use it in good health. Thanks for the help."

When they were back in the car, Velveeta said, "Now what? You don't actually like *her* for the killer, do you? That doesn't make as much sense as the two men, Chief."

"As a matter of fact—" Abruptly, Johnny stopped talking. Throwing the cruiser into gear, he said, "Shoot fire. There goes Pickle Culpepper. That's the second time I've seen his skinny butt coming from out back there." He flipped his lights and siren on and tore out of the gravel parking lot after Pickle's truck, spraying dirt and gravel.

"What are you doing?" Velveeta held onto the door as the car fishtailed and then righted. "Coming from behind a bar ain't against the law."

"I have a few questions for him. If he's dealing or buying, I aim to put a stop to it right quick." They caught up to Pickle and pulled off to the side of the road behind his red pickup truck.

Velveeta followed Johnny to Pickle's driver's side window. Pickle looked scared and confused.

"Son, I thought we had an understanding about you being over there at the Mag Bar."

"Yessir," Pickle gulped visibly, his face so white his freckles looked painted on.

"Would you kindly state your business?"

"I'm not doing nothing, Chief. I swear."

"Did you think I was kidding before?"

"No sir, but I ain't done nothing–"

"Step out of the vehicle, son." As Pickle obeyed the order, Johnny glanced at his T-shirt: EASILY DISTRACTED BY SHINY OBJECTS.

"God, give me strength and patience," Johnny muttered under his breath, swiping his hand over his face.

"Chief, I swear! I ain't up to nothing."

"I don't understand what you think he's done, Chief."

"Come with me." Johnny's tone was firm and professional, and he could see he was clearly scaring the fire out of Pickle. *Good.*

Pickle and Johnny got into the cruiser, and Pickle said, "Seriously, Chief. I was just doing a favor for—"

Johnny interrupted him. "Weren't you in trouble with the law once before, not too far back?"

Pickle ran his hands through his hair and held them against his head as if he were holding his brains in.

"Yessir, but I learned my lesson. I surely did." He put his hands in his lap, leaving his hair sticking out in several places.

"Well then, you need your sleeves lengthened a few feet so they can be tied in the back."

"Huh?"

Johnny rolled his eyes and mumbled, "Straightjacket."

"Chief, let the boy talk." Velveeta stood by the open passenger door.

"All right. Out with it. But it better be good."

Pickle took a deep breath and said, "I been trying to tell you. I was just doing a favor for Charlotte. She asked me to deliver a box, and that's all I did."

"A box? What was in it?"

"I don't know, Chief. I never asked. I trust Charlotte. She wouldn't do nothing bad. Honest."

"Who did you give the box to?"

"Nobody," Pickle said, rubbing his eye and blinking fast.

"Pickle ..." Johnny's voice held a warning tone.

"No really, I swear. She said to take the box, put it on the picnic table out there behind the Mag Bar. She said it was for a friend. So that's what I did."

Johnny took a deep breath and stared through the windshield. "Go check it out, Witherspoon, while he and I chat some more."

Five minutes later, Velveeta returned, reporting that there was no box behind the Mag Bar.

"They must've come and got it," Pickle insisted.

"Did you search the area?"

"Yeah, but you know what it's like back there. The bar backs up to woods. Anyone can come and go through there, sight unseen."

"I put it back there. Honest. Am I still in trouble?" Pickle asked.

"For the moment, I'm going to give you the benefit of the doubt. But we're going to follow you to Louetta's. I aim to talk to Charlotte and find out what all these shenanigans are about."

THIRTY-SIX

Lazy folks' stomachs don't get tired.

~Southern Proverb

Johnny parked in Louetta's driveway, and he, Pickle, and Velveeta traipsed up the sidewalk. Ima Jean answered the door.

"How many licks does it take to get to the center of a Tootsie Roll Tootsie Pop?" she said.

"I'm not rightly sure, Ima Jean, but we'd like to speak to Charlotte. Is she here?"

"Charlotte!" Ima Jean yelled, holding the door open. "Kumpny!" The three stepped into the house, Johnny gently pushing Pickle in first.

Charlotte came out of the kitchen, sucking the icing off the candy witch legs from a cupcake. She stopped in her tracks when she saw the three of them, her eyes round as teacups.

"Wha-what's going on?"

"Charlotte, I'd like to ask you a few questions." Johnny looked at Ima Jean. "Do you mind if we talk to her alone?"

Ima Jean shrugged and walked toward the stairs singing, "Have it your way, have it your way."

Pickle rushed to Charlotte. "It's all right, least I think it is. What was in that box you gave me?"

Before she could answer, Johnny said, "Pickle, I'll let you stay, but you're gonna have to let me ask the questions."

"Yessir."

Pickle started to sit on the couch with Charlotte, but Johnny grabbed his elbow and led him to a chair next to the sofa. Johnny remained standing, but Velveeta sat next to Charlotte, who had turned white, making the freckles across her nose more prominent.

"Okay, Charlotte, I need to know what's in those boxes you've been giving Pickle to deliver and who you were delivering them to."

Charlotte's eyes filled with tears. "I can't tell you. If I do, I'll get somebody else in trouble."

"Right now you need to worry about your own self. The more you stall and don't answer my questions, the more I think something funny's going on. I don't want to think poorly about you, but at the moment my curiosity is more than aroused." Johnny spoke kindly but firmly.

She began to cry. Pickle started to get up, saw Johnny's hand in the air and the warning on his face, and sat back down. Velveeta went to the bathroom and brought back a box of tissues.

When her crying had lessened a bit, Johnny tried again. "C'mon, Charlotte, tell me what the devil is going on."

The tears got worse, and she choked out, "I can't, I just can't. We haven't broken any laws."

"You're suspected of criminal behavior. Folks who make a drop behind a bar habitually heighten my natural curiosity. If you've done nothing wrong, it won't hurt to tell us. Now talk to us, Charlotte. That's the only way we can help you."

She cried quietly for several minutes, then finally spoke softly. "I was just trying to help my . . . my granddaddy."

"Okay, that's good, Charlotte, that's a good start, now tell us the rest of it." Johnny squatted down in front of the girl.

She looked at Pickle, and he nodded reassuringly to her.

"Well, since he lost his job as police chief, he hasn't had much money to live on." She blew her nose and looked at her lap. "He gets real hungry, and I was just trying to help him." She sniffed. "I didn't think I was doing anything wrong, even though he asked me not to tell anyone."

"Not to tell anyone what?" Johnny gently prodded.

"I figured if I cut back on what I ate at Lou's house, I could give my granddaddy some of the food I *would* have eaten. You know? If it was gonna get eaten, Lou wouldn't care who ate it, right?" She blew her nose again and looked at Pickle pleadingly.

"So you packed up some of Lou's home cooking, gave it to Pickle, Pickle delivered it to the picnic table behind the Mag Bar, and your granddaddy picked it up. Is that about the size of things?" Johnny said.

"Yessir, it is." She blew her nose into another tissue.

"See!" Pickle leaned forward, hands on his thighs, looking like he was going to spring at any moment. "I didn't do nothing wrong and neither did Charlotte."

Velveeta said, "Why didn't you just ask Lou for the food for your grandfather?"

"He was afraid she hated him on account of what he did, and besides, he told me not to tell."

Johnny looked from Velveeta to Charlotte. "Charlotte, I know you're a good girl, and I don't see anything particularly wrong with what you did. I respect you for keeping your word to your grandfather, but I'm wondering why you thought you couldn't tell us? You said it would get someone else in trouble. Who did you think you would get into trouble?"

Charlotte began crying again, in great big heaving sobs. Velveeta tried to calm her down, but Johnny finally let Pickle sit by her. He held her hand and patted her back.

"I believe there's more in the can, Charlotte," Johnny said soflty.

She looked at the tissue in her hands as she said, "I didn't have enough to give him."

"And?" Johnny said, growing impatient.

"And he didn't have enough money to buy food."

"And?" Johnny said again, but Charlotte was back to crying too hard to answer. She put her face in her hands and cried, while Pickle talked soothingly to her.

Johnny looked at her, then Pickle, and finally Velveeta. Then it came to him. He smacked his forehead.

"Ernest Borgnine," he said as if he were stupefied.

"Who?" Velveeta asked.

Johnny walked to the window to look out onto the street and then back to the three on the couch. His expression had gone from bewilderment to comprehension. "John Ed doesn't have any money, and he's mad at the town for shunning him, so what's he do?"

Velveeta looked up at him, realizing what he was getting at.

"What?" asked a clueless Pickle.

"He steals the town blind," Velveeta said.

Charlotte cried louder.

"Well, Detective, we've been cruising for hours. Up through town five times, out past the city limits north, south, east, and west." Hank

Beanblossom turned onto Marigold Lane for the third time that day. "Past Martha Maye's house three times. We've cruised all the restaurants and bars. I just don't know where else to go."

"I guess we're going to have to sit outside the mo-tel and wait for him to come back."

"Let's swing by Slick and Junebug's first. If we're going to sit in a car for hours, at least we can sit in a car for hours with some good food." Hank turned the car toward Main Street, resisting the urge to put on the lights and siren.

When they walked into the diner, Clive and Earl were on their usual stools. By way of a greeting, Earl lifted a hand about an inch from the counter and Clive nodded to the men.

"Boys, how are you?" Hank took the stool next to Earl.

"I'm fine, but Clive's being sued." Earl hitched his thumb at his friend.

"Sued?" Hank leaned around Earl to look at Clive. "What are you being sued for?"

"His brain is suing him for neglect." Earl slapped his knee and cackled.

"Aw, don't mind him, Officer," Clive said. "His mind is on vacation, but his mouth is working overtime as usual."

"Now, you boys behave. Don't make me load you up in the paddy wagon for disturbing the peace."

"They certainly disturb my peace, each and every day," Junebug said, walking behind the counter to place some orders.

"You'd be lost without us, and you know it," Clive said.

She poked her pencil behind her right ear, turned, and called to Slick, "I need a bowl of red, and two cows. Make 'em cry."

Turning back around to Hank and Detective Squires, she said, "What can I get y'all?"

"Junebug, we need the works to go. Couple a burgers — Rusty, how you like yours?

"The works."

"The works for him, and just onions and ketchup for me. And give us some fries, too." He looked at the domed cake plates. "What kind of pie you got today?"

"Apple caramel, cherry, chocolate, peanut butter, and coconut."

Hank looked at the detective, who said, "Apple caramel without a doubt."

"An apple caramel, a cherry, and two shakes."

Junebug looked up from her order pad. "White cow or you wanna throw it in the mud?"

Hank looked at the detective and said, "Chocolate or vanilla?"

"Oh. Um . . . chocolate."

"One chocolate and one vanilla, Junie."

She hollered in Slick's direction, "All righty, Slick, on the rail. Burn one, take it through the garden and pin a rose on it, burn another one, make it cry and give it a hemorrhage, gimme some frog sticks, and let it walk."

"Be right out," Slick called.

"Tell you what, darlin', set yourselves down while I pack a poke. I'll be right back, y'all. Gonna fix your shakes first."

Rusty leaned toward Hank and asked, "What's she going to do?"

"Fix our shakes."

"No, before that."

"Oh," Hank said smiling, "She's going to pack it all in a sack for us."

"You're not from around here, are you?" Clive asked.

"He's from up north in Nashville. This here's Detective Rusty Squires."

"How do, Detective."

"This is Clive." Hank pointed with his thumb. "And this here's Earl."

"Howdy, boys." Rusty nodded to the men.

"Did you catch that killer yet, Officer?" Clive asked, stuffing a bite of chocolate pie in his mouth.

"Not yet, but we will."

"What about the hooligan who's been taking stuff all over town?" Earl asked.

"We're getting close," Hank said.

"Did you bring in the detective to help out on the cases?" Earl asked.

"Naw, I'm here on my own case."

"You come down here on account of another case?" Clive echoed. "What for?"

"I'm not at liberty to say, sir."

"Well, ain't he highfalutin," Earl grumped. "Up from the big city and all."

"He's just doing his job, Earl. Say, y'all haven't seen Lenny Applewhite's brother T. Harry, have you?"

"Can't say that I have," Clive said, going back to his pie.

"Nope," Earl said.

"If you do, you be sure to give me a call, all right?"

"Is he a wanted man?" Clive wanted to know.

"Naw. We just want to ask him some questions."

"Do we get a reward if we call you?"

"Just the reward of doing a good deed," Hank said.

"Humph," both men said together.

"That don't pay for pie," Clive grumbled.

THIRTY-SEVEN

Don't trade off a coonskin before you catch the coon.

~Southern Proverbs

"We got him, Chief," Hank Beanblossom said as he and the detective led T. Harry into the police station by both arms just after one a.m.

"I's innocent. I didn't do nothing," T. Harry slurred.

"He's plum loopdylegged is what he is." Hank said as they walked past Johnny.

"Copy that." Johnny stood in his office doorway with his hands on his hips.

"We got him when he came back to the motel. I'ma book him for DUI and public intoxication. He blew a .25."

T. Harry broke out in song, slurring the lyrics to "My Heart's Too Broke to Pay Attention."

"Mark Chestnut, you aren't." Hank put a finger in his ear and shook it.

"That's enough outta you," Detective Squires snarled.

"All right, Beano, after you check him into our little hotel, show him to his room. While he's sleeping it off, we got another matter to attend to. Detective, why don't you get some sleep. We'll chat with T. Harry in the morning after he's sobered up."

"Sounds like a plan." Rusty tipped his hat and left the building.

A while later, Hank arrived in Johnny's office, where Skeeter and Velveeta were waiting.

"What's up?" Hank slumped into a chair.

"We like John Ed for stealing the stuff around town." Johnny's chair squealed as he settled in behind his desk.

"Well, spit in the fire and call me Billy Bob," Hank said, looking truly astounded.

"Okay, Billy Bob. Now we gotta find him."

"How do you know it's him?"

"His granddaughter Charlotte spilled the beans. She was a tough nut to crack, let me tell you." Johnny took a swig from the can of Mtn Dew on his desk. "He's been stealing stuff he needs or wants from all over town, and she's been supplementing with Lou's home cooking. Seems he figured the town owed him."

"Plus he prolly just wanted some good old-fashioned revenge," Skeeter speculated.

"That, too. I guess it didn't occur to him to take responsibility for his own self. Anyway, he gave himself a license to steal. But we can't find him anywhere. He sold his house back a few months. Got any ideas?" Johnny looked at each of the officers.

"Mag Bar?" Hank offered.

"Negative. Cash says he doesn't come into the bar. I guess he uses—or used—it as a drop-off point for his food deliveries, but he wasn't a regular customer."

"It's not like he could steal anything in there," Skeeter pointed out. "You order a drink, you gotta pay for it."

"Yeah, but you can steal out of the back room," Velveeta said.

"That"—Johnny pointed at her—"you can do." He leafed through some papers and pulled one out of the stack. "Affirmative. Cash reported four bottles of bourbon missing a few weeks back."

"Shoot, since all the commotion last summer, he ain't been a regular anywhere in town," Skeeter said. "But I heard he kind of holed himself up in old Crate Marshall's place. After Tank died, the house has been empty. Doesn't have electricity or gas, but it's a shelter."

"He'd hear us coming a mile away up at that place." The room was silent for a bit. "I think we have to set him up."

"How?" the three officers said together.

"Charlotte let it slip that sometimes she'd leave Lou's back door unlocked, and in the middle of the night he'd come over and help himself to the contents of the kitchen. I think he mostly came for refrigerated stuff at night. Food she couldn't leave in the drop box."

"So old Ima Jean wasn't as crazy as everyone thought she was, huh?"

"It appears not. I say we get Charlotte to tell him she'll leave the door unlocked and we let him steal his last meal." Johnny absentmindedly twirled a pencil around his fingers.

"Then we wait for him at Lou's?" Hank said.

"Then we wait for him at the old Marshall place. He'll walk right to us with the evidence in his hands. I don't want to cause a scene at Lou's, especially with Charlotte living there."

"Okay, when?" Velveeta looked like she was ready to go right then and there.

"Charlotte said the food she just sent him should last a few days. Let's do it on Thursday night."

"Roger that." Hank's usual easygoing nature had turned all business.

"Meantime, if you see him, watch him, but don't bring him in. I think we'll get him to tell all if we catch him red-handed." Johnny put his pencil on the desk and stood up.

The officers filed out, but Johnny called out, "Officer Witherspoon?"

Velveeta peeked around the doorway. "Yes sir?"

"Anything on that theory of yours?"

"Negative, sir. I'm still working it."

He nodded, and she left him alone in the room once again.

Johnny stood up and shoved his hands in his pockets, looking out his office window to the light pole across the street. His mind kept going over Cash's description of the woman at the bar. *It couldn't be.* But things she'd said kept running through his head like a news crawler. *But she out and out lied to me about never going to the Mag Bar.*

He picked up the phone. "Jack? Johnny here. Yeah, sorry for calling so late. Can you meet me up at the diner in the morning?" He listened for a few seconds. "Negative. I gotta go home and get some sleep. It'll keep until tomorrow. About seven? All right. See you then."

JACK WAS waiting in the back booth when Johnny arrived at 7:02. "Morning, gentlemen." Johnny breezed past Clive and Earl at their regular places. "Do y'all sleep here?" He'd said it as more of a statement than question, but the men nodded.

"We might if Slick stayed open twenty-four hours."

"Thank the good Lord he don't," Slick said.

Johnny waved to Slick in the kitchen, squeezed past Willa Jean taking an order, patting her on the shoulder, and walked to the back booth to join Jack.

"You look like you were pulled through a knothole backward." Jack's wrinkled brow showed his worry for his friend.

"Kinda feel that way, too," Johnny said, running his hand through his short, dark hair.

Willa Jean finished at the other table and came to their booth, eyeing Johnny carefully. "You look more miserable than a horse in a hayless barn."

"Aw, not you, too. I don't look that bad, y'all."

Willa and Jack looked at each other and then back at Johnny. They said in unison, "Yes, you do."

"I'm going to get you some of my fresh-squeezed OJ. Y'ont anything else?"

"Thanks, Willa Jean. How about some scrambled eggs?"

As soon as she walked toward the kitchen, hollering, "Gimme two and wreck 'em," Johnny said, "I got a problem."

"I can see that," Jack said. "I thought everything with you and Martha Maye were okay now."

"They are. This is a work problem. I think I know who killed Lenny, but I can't prove it."

"Go on," Jack said. "Wanna tell me who we're talking about? Hey, by the way, did y'all find T. Harry?"

"Yeah, Beano and that detective from Nashville brought him a few hours ago. He's over to the station percolating, but I don't think he killed his brother."

There was a commotion at the door of the diner, and the men looked up to see Skeeter Duke rushing toward them.

"Chief! Hank says the detective arrived and T. Harry's ready to talk. You'd better get over there right quick."

"Aw, criminy. I'm sorry, Jack. I've got to go. Will you be around later?"

Jack sighed heavily. "Yeah, just give me a call. I'll be home."

As Johnny slid out of the booth, Jack said, "Don't suppose you could give me a name instead of keeping me in suspense."

Johnny grinned, slapped his friend on the back good-naturedly, and said, "Negative, buddy, but I'll say this: it will surprise the fire outta you."

"I've not known you to be a cruel man until now."

T. Harry's red hair was mashed down on one side and stuck straight out on the other. Dark circles underneath his bloodshot eyes, on an otherwise pale face, almost made him look like he had two black eyes.

The minute Johnny walked in, T. Harry growled, "I shoulda knowed he's behind this. I don't want to talk to him."

"Well, that's just too damn bad, Applewhite," Detective Squires said. Johnny pulled out a chair and sat down beside him.

"I want a lawyer," T. Harry shot back.

"Sir," Rusty leaned toward him, "you're not under arrest for anything except being loaded up on loud-mouth soup. That's a fact, and no lawyer in the world can get you out of that rap. Right now, we simply want to ask you a few questions. Are you telling us you've done something for which you need a lawyer?"

"I ain't done nothing. Don't go putting words in my mouth."

"Mr. Applewhite, do you know a Mr. Joe Bob Mossbourn?"

T. Harry stared at him. "Yeah, I knew him. That man didn't have the sense God gave an animal cracker."

The detective scribbled on the paper in front of him. "How do you know Mr. Mossbourn?"

"We were acquaintances, that's all." T. Harry's chin jutted into the air.

"How were you *acquainted*?" Rusty pressed.

"I don't recall," he said, studying his fingernails.

"Can you explain why you keep referring to the man in the past tense?"

T. Harry's eyes nervously darted around the small, dingy room. "Well . . . well, *you* were talking like that."

"No sir." Rusty sat back. "I never said anything of the kind. You're the only one who has talked about him in the past tense. I think that's because you know the man's dead."

"He's dead?" T. Harry tried his best to act shocked and surprised.

"I wouldn't count on a career in motion pictures," Rusty said. "Now admit it. You knew he was dead, and maybe the reason you knew he was dead, was because you killed him."

"Aw, no. Hell no. You ain't gonna get me to admit no such thing."

Rusty said nothing. He and Johnny stared at T. Harry, which had the desired effect. T. Harry began babbling away.

"I'm telling y'all, I didn't kill nobody. Besides, I was here in Goose Pimple Junction. I couldn't have killed him."

"I don't recall saying when the man was killed," Rusty said with a grin.

"See, I've been here for a few weeks now, so whenever it was, I was here."

"T. Harry." Johnny stood and pushed his hands in his pockets and leaned against the wall. "You said you came to Goose Pimple Junction the day before your brother's funeral. That's only a little over a week."

"I– I–" T. Harry stammered.

"Because if you were here in town when your brother was killed," Johnny moved beside T. Harry, towering over him, "I might have to look hard at why you didn't tell anyone and why you felt the need to pretend you had just came to town. I'd say that's mighty suspicious behavior right there, wouldn't you, Detective?" He turned from the detective back to T. Harry. "Maybe you killed your brother."

"Now that's just a bald-faced lie."

"I think Mr. Applewhite here is in what you call between a rock and a hard place. Either he was in Nashville and he killed Mossbourn, or he was here and he killed his brother," Rusty said. He leaned toward him and got within an inch of his face. "Which is it, hotshot?"

"Okay, okay, here's what happened. I was in Helechewa for a few weeks before Lenny died."

"Why were you in Helechewa? Why would you be in a town just thirty minutes away and not tell your brother or your sister-in-law?"

"Okay, I'll tell you, but I want immunization."

Johnny sat back into his chair and looked up at the ceiling as if praying for help. He brought his gaze back to T. Harry. "You want a flu shot?"

"No. I want—you know, that thing where's I tell you something but I don't get persecuted for it."

Rusty shook his head at T. Harry's stupidity and said to Johnny, "I'll bet he inspired the slogan, 'A mind is a terrible thing to waste.'"

"That would be a pretty safe bet," Johnny said. "I think he's right, though. I think he needs immunization. Immunization from stupidity."

"What say I take him back to Nashville with me tonight? I got a witness who can identify him."

"Wait! I'm trying to confess, if y'all will just pipe down long enough. I didn't kill nobody, and I wasn't in Nashville because I been in Helechewa for a few weeks on account of needing to be near Goose Pimple Junction so's I could woo Martha Maye. I've been leaving presents for her. Just ask her."

THIRTY-EIGHT

In your life, you've got to eat a peck of dirt.

~Southern Proverb

"It was you?" Johnny shot up and lunged for the man.

T. Harry jumped up and backed into a corner, shrinking away from the mountainous police chief. Rusty stepped in front of Johnny before he got to T. Harry.

"Everybody just simmer down," the detective said, waving off Johnny and pushing T. Harry back into a chair. "Simmer down, now. Let's hear him out." They all settled into their seats, and T. Harry ran his hands through his hair, taking a relieved breath and letting it out melodramatically.

"Yeah, it was me. And last time I checked, it wasn't against the law to leave presents for a woman. Lookit, it's like this: when Lenny told me Martha Maye had left him, I rejoiced." T. Harry swiped a hand under his nose and sniffed. "He wasn't good enough for her. When he told me he knew where she and Butterbean had gone, I thought it was my chance to win her heart. I'm good at romancing a woman." He looked straight at Johnny, an arrogant expression on his face.

"So I came to Helechewa and scooted on over to Goose Pimple periodically so's I could leave her presents. I wanted her to feel flattered." He got a faraway look in his eyes. "I wanted to spoil her, create an air of mystery about a secret admirer. I was planning on revealing it was me and telling her how I felt about her." His face hardened. "Then Lenny told me *he* was trying to win Martha Maye back, but I knew he didn't deserve her. So I started sending them other gifts, so's she'd think it was Lenny, and she'd be mad at him, and she'd go through with the divorce."

"So you sent a woman a bunch of presents–big deal," Rusty said. "Why do I care about that?"

"Because that means I was in Helechewa, and not Nashville," T. Harry said, as if the man were a waste of skin.

"Gimme the dates and the name of the hotel," Rusty said, sounding bored. He slid a sheet of paper and a pen across the table.

T. Harry scribbled on the paper and slid it back.

"Sit tight." He left Johnny and T. Harry alone in the small, windowless room.

For the entire five minutes Rusty was gone, Johnny sat with his arms crossed, stone-faced, glaring at T. Harry.

T. Harry alternated between glaring back at Johnny, picking his nose, and studying his nails. He sighed in relief when Rusty came back into the room.

"Dates don't add up, Applewhite," Rusty said. "Right now, I'd say you look awful good for Joe Bob—"

"And the stalking, *and* your brother," Johnny added.

Rusty tossed the notepad on the table. "You can prove you were in Helechewa before your brother died, but that's all you can prove. Joe Bob was killed before that. It looks to me like you killed him and had to get the heck outta Dodge, so you came to Goose Pimple Junction to woo your sister-in-law, or maybe that was just a ruse. Maybe you'd planned on that being your alibi all along, but since you're a T1 line of pure stupid–or you think we are–it didn't work out quite like you planned."

"And when Lenny sued for custody of Butterbean," Johnny cut in, "you saw how upset Martha Maye was, and you set him up and killed him. Is that how it went down, T. Harry?" Johnny demanded.

T. Harry leaned back, balancing the chair on its back two legs. "No. Don't think I'm not dumb." He let the chair tilt forward to fall on all four legs and leaned toward the men, pointing. "I didn't kill nobody, and you ain't gonna make me say I did. I can prove my whereabouts the night Lenny died. I was at Humdinger's all night."

"You know, you keep coming up with stories, and we're just going keep checking them out and proving you wrong," Rusty said. "Why don't you just stop this foolishness right now and save us all some time? I've got a witness who says he saw you and Joe Bob arguing the night before he was murdered, and I've got another witness who will testify that you were more than an acquaintance of Joe Bob's. He will also testify that you hated the man because he bullied you."

"Oh, for crying out—"

"You know what I think? I think he *was* more than just an acquaintance. I think your drinking buddy humiliated you on a daily basis and you'd had enough." Rusty's voice got louder as he got in T. Harry's face.

"I'll even allow that Joe Bob was a spur-of-the-moment thing," the detective continued, "But you coming here and killing Lenny, that definitely sounds to me like premeditated murder."

T. Harry's face drained of what little color it had. His disheveled red hair looked like it was on fire on top of his stark white face. His eyes darted from man to man, and he jiggled his right leg nervously.

"I know you did it, Applewhite," Rusty said.

"You don't know squat," T. Harry said. They glared at each other.

"I know you're going to get the chair, and when you do, I want you thinking about what Joe Bob lived in his final moments when you had that bag wrapped around his face, cutting off his air supply. Think about his slow, painful death as he struggled with you—"

"I can prove I didn't do it," T. Harry blurted out. "Check when Martha Maye got the first present. That'll prove I was here and nowhere near Nashville."

"I still don't recall telling you the date of Joe Bob's untimely death."

"Uh . . . It don't matter. I know I didn't kill him, so I had to be here. Check the dates with her. Ask her when she got the first present."

Rusty shook his head several times like he was trying to clear the cobwebs from his brain. "You had to be here *when*? You're trying my patience with your stupid talk."

Johnny got up and said, "Sit tight. I'll call. I'm in danger of secondhand idiocy, breathing too much of his air. I'll check out Humdinger's, too."

Johnny left the room and went to his office, where he called Martha Maye and asked her for the dates when she first received a gift from her secret admirer. She promised to call him back when she'd pinpointed the date.

He picked up the phone and dialed again.

FORTY-TWO MINUTES later, Johnny walked back into the room where they were questioning T. Harry. He handed the detective a piece of paper, sat, folded his arms across his front, and smiled a cheesy grin at T. Harry.

"Well, well, well, Applewhite," Rusty said. "Sounds like you thought we were all icing and no cake. I guess you didn't count on FTD records."

T. Harry's face showed a hint of surprise but quickly changed to a frown, as if he didn't understand the detective's meaning.

"The date of the first gift is irrelevant."

"Huh?" T. Harry looked genuinely confused.

"The first gift was a bouquet of flowers. Sent by FTD. They have things called records." Looking bored, Rusty doodled on a pad of paper.

"Uh—"

"Yeah, 'uh.'" Rusty talked conversationally now, as if they were just shooting the breeze. "The flowers were ordered, not delivered by you personally, so they don't give you an alibi for Joe Bob, and no one remembers seeing you at Humdinger's, which means you've got no alibi for either murder."

"Maybe you were mad at the way he treated her. Maybe you confronted him on her lawn and things got out of hand. Maybe it was premeditated, maybe it wasn't," Johnny said.

"Unless you've suddenly remembered something else you were doing at the time of those murders." Rusty tapped his pen on the table. "You'd best start saying your prayers, son, because you're looking guilty as sin." He got up, placed both hands on the table in front of T. Harry, and leaned toward him.

"I think you've been wasting our time here. I think you did know when Joe Bob was murdered because *you* killed him, and I think it was premeditated, and I think if you killed *one* man, what's another? I think you killed your brother, too, which means the prosecutor will most likely go for the death penalty. I think—"

"I did not!" T. Harry blurted, wiping his nose with the back of his hand. "I only killed Joe Bob." He looked up, startled. "I mean, I mean—"

"That," Johnny said to the detective, over T. Harry's backpedaling, "is an example of how the dinosaurs survived for millions of years with walnut-sized brains."

THIRTY-NINE

If you buy a rainbow, don't pay cash for it.

~Southern Proverb

"How'd it go with T. Harry?" Jack asked, as Johnny stepped past him into his house that night.

"He's the one's been leaving those gifts for Martha Maye." Johnny said, reaching down to pet Ezmeralda.

"Seriously?" Jack had been leading the way to his kitchen but stopped dead in his tracks and turned toward Johnny.

"Yep. Says he started out with the intent of establishing an alibi and also trying to woo her. Kill two birds with one stone, pardon the pun. He fancied himself a Romeo. Thought she'd be flattered."

"Good night, nurse." Jack whistled, then turned and headed again for the kitchen. Johnny and the dog followed.

"Then when Lenny showed up trying to win her back, he worried about them being reunited. Thought she'd assume the good gifts were from Lenny. So he switched to distasteful gifts, thinking she'd suspect they were from Lenny, too, which would cause her to go ahead with the divorce."

"Ha! He didn't count on Lenny being his own worst enemy. You said something about an alibi?" He motioned for Johnny to take a seat at the kitchen table.

"Yeah, that's the best part."

"What's the best part?"

"Turns out he killed somebody up in Nashville. The detective pelted him with accusations, and T. Harry thought he was digging himself out of a hole. He thought by admitting to the gifts, he was helping his case. When the detective accused him of doing the murder in Nashville and his brother's, too, and when he mentioned the death penalty, T. Harry blurted out a confession. Once the syrup was out of the bottle, he couldn't get it back in."

Jack whistled softly. "His lips probably moved faster than his brain."

"Easy to do. A turtle could walk faster than he can think."

"Want some coffee?"

"No, thanks." Johnny shook his head. Ezmeralda stood right in front of him, her tail wagging so hard her butt moved with it, her big sad eyes pleading for more attention.

"You think he killed Lenny?" Jack took a seat across the table from Johnny. He snapped his fingers, pointing to Ezmeralda to sit down and leave Johnny alone.

Johnny shook his head and rubbed Ezzie's big velvety ears, both of them ignoring Jack's command. "No, he told enough lies to ice a wedding cake, but his alibi holds up on that, although I did a bit of bluffing and told him nobody saw him there. The bartender over at Humdinger's says he was there all night. Came in early and left late. Played pool and darts and drank himself purt near under the table. I'll ask for a few more people to corroborate, but he didn't do it."

"So are you ever going to tell me who you think *did* kill Lenny? You left a fool in suspense, you know."

"Jack, I don't see how I can prove it, but I'm more sure than ever that I'm right." He sat up from petting Ezzie and leveled his gaze at Jack, radiating seriousness. "I think it was Estherlene Bumgarner."

"No way." Jack sat back as if he'd been slapped. "What kind of Halloween candy you been eating?"

"I'm as serious as a five-alarm fire, Jack."

Jack's eyes were huge as he let the theory settle in. "What on earth brought you to that conclusion? What did she have against Lenny?"

"A few things." Johnny stood and began pacing the room. "First off, on the night of the murder, she said she didn't see anyone or anything outside, but that doesn't add up. You know how she sits in that front window and watches over the street like a sentinel. She knows everything that happens on Marigold Lane. How come that one night she didn't see a thing? She was there, and she was awake. I don't buy for one thin second that she was in the bath that long."

"Okay, that's a little odd —"

"Another thing," Johnny interrupted, pacing to the doorway and back, "is the other day she suddenly remembered seeing a car the night of the murder and said it looked like T. Harry's."

"How can you be so sure it wasn't?"

"At the time she told me that, I wasn't sure. I was thinking it made sense. I could see how T. Harry must have lied about when he came to town—which he did—which suggested he killed Lenny. But it niggled at me, and it bothered me that she said she didn't see anything that night but then all of a sudden remembered seeing T. Harry's car."

"People do remember things later—"

"And now we know for sure it couldn't have been his car if he was at Humdinger's all night."

"So Estherlene was mistaken." Jack shrugged.

"But she lied about something else."

"What?"

"She told me she'd never been to the Mag Bar, but she fits the description Cash gave me for a woman who repeatedly tried to hit on Lenny. Cash said the woman was in her sixties, maybe older, about five-two, very tanned, big hair with a blond dye job, and she had big ears but wasn't entirely unattractive. He said Lenny shot her down every time. Barely gave her the time of day."

Jack shook his head. "Estherlene isn't in her sixties. She's older than that. She claims she's middle-aged, but she's been around since Jesus was a baby."

"Yeah, but she doesn't look it, you know? Nature's been kind to that woman."

Jack blew out a breath. "A person will go to Hell for lying just the same as stealing, but like you said, you don't have proof she did anything more wrong than that. You got nothing other than a gut feeling and a few lies, about which she could just say she was mistaken. Sounds pretty flimsy to me. You don't even have a motive."

Johnny sat down and leaned toward Jack. "I agree, but I know I'm right. I just have to find evidence."

"I hate to tell you, my friend, but that's going be harder than baptizing a cat."

Ezzie's head popped up.

"Unit one, are you in place?" Johnny said into his two-way radio.

Velveeta's voice came back, "Unit one, ready to roll."

"Unit two? Ready?"

"Unit two, in place," Hank answered.

"All right, everybody stay alert." Holding the handset, Johnny paced the old farmhouse from the living room, to the kitchen, and back again. He couldn't sit still. Velveeta was holding watch in the front and Hank was in the back. Johnny couldn't see them, but he knew they were there.

He'd gotten a reluctant Charlotte to tell her grandfather that Louetta had baked a pan of lasagna and a key lime pie. She told him she would cut a portion from each and leave it in the back of the refrigerator, then leave the door to the house unlocked. No man in his right mind could say no to that. He felt bad about making Charlotte lie to her grandfather, but he'd managed to convince her it was the right thing to do.

The old Marshall house was never locked since Tank died a few months before. Johnny had the electric company turn on the power to the farmhouse. His officers were in place. All he could do was wait. And pace.

At 1:29 a.m., the radio burped. "Chief, suspect spotted coming through the backyard. Repeat. Suspect is coming to you."

Johnny had finally stopped pacing. Now lying on the sofa, his thoughts had turned from John Ed to Martha Maye. When he got the call, he sprang up, instinctively put his hand to the revolver at his waist, and edged to the doorway of the kitchen. He flattened himself against the wall and waited.

The sound of the back door squeaking open was quiet but clear. The floorboard creaked, and then he saw the dim glow of a flashlight. He slowly stepped into the kitchen, pointed his revolver at the figure, and said, "Ernest Borgnine, I presume."

John Ed whirled around, dropping the lasagna he'd been about to put on the kitchen table. Johnny heard the front door open and footsteps pounding toward him, just as the back door opened and Hank stepped in, holding a bright light and a video camera aimed at the former police chief.

"Smile, you're on candid camera," Hank said, no hint of a smile on his face or in his voice.

"You know what to do, John Ed." Johnny flicked the switch to turn on the lights. Everyone squinted a little, their eyes unaccustomed to the brightness.

"What are you—you ain't—I didn't—" John Ed looked from face to face.

"You're wanted for questioning in a number of thefts around town, Mr. Price. Not to mention breaking and entering." Johnny swept his gaze around the room, indicating the house.

When John Ed didn't move, Johnny said sadly, "Turn around and assume the position."

John Ed sighed heavily and did as he was told, putting his hands against the refrigerator, and Johnny kicked at his left leg to widen his stance before frisking him.

"You have the right to remain silent." Johnny patted him down, watching carefully where they stood because of the spilled lasagna on the floor.

"Anything you say or do can and will be used against you in a court of law." He took handcuffs off his belt and brought John Ed's hands behind his back.

"You have the right to speak to an attorney." Johnny cuffed John Ed's hands.

"If you cannot afford an attorney, one will be provided for you. Do you understand these rights as they've been read to you?" Johnny turned John Ed around so he was facing him.

"Yes," John Ed said morosely.

"Put him in the car, Officer Witherspoon. Let's get him to the station."

Back at the police station, Velveeta said, "Can I question him about Lenny's murder, Chief?"

In order to rule out John Ed as a suspect, Johnny allowed her to question him. He sat in the room and listened.

"We've got you for multiple counts of theft, Mr. Price, and I gotta tell you, I'm liking you for the murder of Lenny Applewhite—"

"That's ridiculous!" He slapped his hand on the table.

"You were out sneaking around night after night, on the prowl. Maybe you were stealing something from Ms. Applewhite's residence and Lenny found you out."

"Look, I'll admit I allowed the town to help me out in my time of need—that's the least I could expect after all the years of service I gave to this community. But murder? You're crazier than a run-over dog. I had nothing to do with that. I want a lawyer."

"That's the end of cheap talk." Johnny opened the door and motioned Velveeta out. "Let the man call a lawyer."

TWO HOURS later, after John Ed had talked with a public defender, Louis P. Howe, they all reconvened in the interrogation (also known as the break room), and Velveeta continued her questioning.

"As you are undoubtedly aware, Mr. Howe, it's pretty obvious your client is the one who's been stealing the town blind."

"They owed me, dabnamit," John Ed said heatedly. "I'm as broke as the Ten Commandments—"

"Hush your mouth, John Ed," Mr. Howe cut in, but John Ed couldn't help himself.

"And all this town did was turn their backs and stick up their noses at me. It's disgraceful."

Velveeta cleared her throat and asked, "So the next question is, do you have an alibi for the night of October twenty-second, Mr. Price?"

"I do. I was with someone from eight o'clock on."

"Who?"

"I'd rather not divulge that information."

"So you *don't* have an alibi, is that what you're saying?"

John Ed glared at them, leaned in to confer with his lawyer, and finally mumbled, "I was with Christine White."

"Teenie?" Johnny shot up, his face showing distrust.

John Ed's expression went from defiant to sheepish. "Yeah. We been seeing each other for a while now. She didn't care if folks knew, but I didn't want anyone to know on account of how everybody felt about me. She'd just get dragged down with me. Didn't your mama ever tell you that you are the company you keep?"

"Velveeta, go and invite Ms. White to join us, if you would. Get Skeeter to take over for her on dispatch."

Velveeta left, and Johnny pulled a chair out across from John Ed. "You vandalized those gardens and took people's pumpkins, too, didn't you?"

John Ed snorted. "Do you know what it's like to be shunned by the very people you served and protected for over thirty years?"

"Mr. Price," the lawyer said, as Johnny stared sternly at John Ed.

"And none of it would have happened without that Miss Priss, Tess Tremaine. She deserved more than a few dead flowers," he sneered.

Johnny stared at John Ed, his face full of disgust but also pity. "Trying to understand some folks is like guessing at the direction of a rathole underground," he said more to himself than to John Ed.

"Mr. Price, please don't divulge any more information without consulting with me first," Mr. Howe huffed.

Teenie and Velveeta came into the room.

"John Ed," Teenie said, her face tight. She swallowed hard.

"Now, Teenie, it's all right—"

"Hush up, both a you. We'll tell you when to talk," Velveeta snapped. She led Teenie by the elbow to the seat next to the lawyer, with John Ed on his other side.

"Teenie, where were you on the night of October twenty-second?" Johnny asked.

"Well, uh . . ." she stammered.

"Tell them, Teenie," John Ed said softly, looking at his folded hands on the table. "It's okay."

"I was at home all night," she answered timidly.

"Were you alone?" Johnny asked.

She started to glance at John Ed, but Velveeta pointed her first two fingers at Teenie and then at herself. "Eyes right here, Teenie. Answer the question."

"I was . . . I was with—" she cleared her throat, then said softly, "I was with John Ed."

"All night?"

"Yessir. All night." She looked everywhere but at Velveeta or Johnny.

"From when to when?" Velveeta asked. "And can anybody else verify?"

"He came over about nine o'clock, I guess."

"Why do I have the feeling you had something to do with the missing evidence bag?" Johnny stood in front of Teenie with his arms folded. "You had access to the key and a shift when nobody else was around."

When she said nothing, Velveeta said, "Did you take the evidence, Teenie?"

Teenie began to cry softly, her head bowed. She nodded.

"Why, Teenie? Why would you impede an investigation by stealing key evidence? Why would you risk losing your job?" Johnny stretched both arms wide. "All for a man?"

She sniffed and ran her hand under her nose. "Somebody convinced me John Ed might've had something to do with it. I just panicked. She told me to take the evidence so they couldn't prove it was him."

"But if he was with you that night, as you just said, how could he have been the killer?"

"Well, he was a little late," she said. "And wouldn't say where he'd been." She pulled a tissue from under her rolled-up sleeve and dabbed at her nose. "She sounded so sure, and everyone knows she sees everything that happens on Marigold Lane. I guess I wasn't thinking too straight."

Johnny's face stayed neutral, but his eyes lit up.

"That's certainly stating the obvious. But who? Who is this 'she' who told you John Ed might be the killer?" Velveeta asked.

Simultaneously, Johnny and Teenie said, "Estherlene Bumgarner."

"She did it, Jack." Johnny arrived at Jack's house bright and early Friday morning, after having been up most of the night dealing with John Ed and Teenie.

Jack scrubbed his sleepy face with his hand and said, "Come on back. I'll get us some coffee."

While Jack made coffee, Johnny sat at the table. "I'm sure of it, Jack."

"Why?" Jack asked. "What happened?"

"She told Teenie White that she was sure John Ed was the killer."

"How can you be sure he wasn't?"

"Because he was at the diner swiping stuff between seven thirty and eight, then he went home to stash his goods, and then he showed up at Teenie's around nine." He ran his hand over his face, his whiskers sounding like sandpaper. "Turns out Estherlene convinced Teenie that John Ed was guilty, and she believed it since he was late to her house and wouldn't tell her where he'd been."

"Why was John Ed not getting fed by Teenie? Why'd he have to steal it?"

"You ever had Teenie's cooking? Her cooking's so bad you couldn't poke a fork through the gravy."

"That bad?"

"Yep. So Estherlene got her to take the evidence. Teenie said she never opened the bag, and she turned it over this morning. Velveeta and I went over it with a fine-toothed comb, and we found a few hairs we're sending off to forensics now. Maybe we'll get a match, maybe we won't, but I want to move on this. I don't want to wait. Once she hears we've talked to John Ed and Teenie, she could get nervous."

"You could get a search warrant. Have a look around." Jack got mugs from the cabinet and joined Johnny at the table.

"I tried," Johnny said miserably. "Judge Shelby said we didn't have enough to warrant one. No pun intended."

"So why are you here? Why aren't you getting the police force involved? Surely y'all can think of something."

He leaned in across the table, so Jack could hear when he whispered, "I'm thinking of breaking in. I can't involve the force in an illegal activity."

"What for? If you find anything, it won't be admissible. You could jeopardize the whole case."

Johnny nodded miserably. "But at least I'll know. It's killing me to think Martha Maye and Butterbean might be living next door to a cold-blooded killer."

They were silent for a minute, the only sound that of the coffee maker. Finally, Jack spoke.

"If a regular citizen were to search her house and found something suspicious, you would at least know you're on the right track."

"Of course I'd have to arrest said person for breaking and entering." Johnny raised an eyebrow at his friend. Laughing, and making fun of T. Harry, he added, "I suppose I could give you *immunization*."

But Jack wasn't laughing. "If you're sure about this, I'll do it," Jack offered. "I'll go in."

FORTY

Every tub has to sit on its own bottom.

~Southern Proverb

"Estherlene goes grocery shopping every Saturday morning," Martha Maye had said. "It's senior citizens' day at Piggly Wiggly."

So armed with that information, Johnny and Jack had been in Martha Maye's house for an hour Saturday morning, drinking coffee and waiting for Estherlene to leave for her weekly shopping excursion. Martha Maye didn't know what was going on, and the suspense was killing her.

When the two men were practically floating from all the coffee, Estherlene finally left her house. The men waited for five minutes until Velveeta called to tell them Estherlene had arrived and was inside the store. Then Jack scurried next door, and Johnny paced in front of the window, where he could see out onto the street.

"Johnny, would you sit down? You're making me a nervous wreck," Martha Maye said.

"You're sure Hector isn't home?" Johnny asked for the third time, stopping to peer out the window.

"That's what Estherlene told me over the phone. I called over there the other day to see if he wanted some of my leftover corn sticks. He likes to break them up into a glass of milk. Makes me sick to my stomach, but I didn't have any—"

"So a fishing trip?" Johnny prodded.

"Oh. Yes. She said he'd gone on a fishing trip with some buddies. She hinted they were having some marital discord right before he left, and she didn't sound like she planned on seeing him anytime soon. Why don't you sit down for a bit?"

"I don't want to take my eyes off the street. I can't take the chance of Jack being discovered in that house."

"You've had quite a week. Are you getting enough rest?"

He turned from the window to look at her. "I got caught up on sleep last night. I'm healthy as a hog."

"Did you have breakfast? I can fix you something."

"Martha Maye, I'm fine, I promise. Tell me about your week. I haven't seen you much with all that's been going on."

"I know. It seems like the town is overrun with hooligans. I still can't believe T. Harry was the one leaving me all those disgraceful presents. And Mr. Price was stealing the town blind. Gosh, you just never do know about folks, do you?"

"Mama said there'd be days like this," Johnny said wryly.

"You know what my mama says?" Martha Maye didn't wait for a reply. "She says turnip tops don't tell you the size of the turnips."

"Your mama's a wise woman."

"So you had to fire Teenie?"

"'Fraid so. I decided not to press charges, though. I think her real crime was stupidity, and you can't jail someone for that." He chuckled. "If you could, our prisons would be overflowing. It's time she retired anyway."

"What about John Ed?"

Johnny let out a long breath. "I expect he'll get some jail time. Maybe he'll get out after a few months. I don't know. What I do know is every tub has to sit on its own bottom."

"Mama used to tell me that, too. She'd say it when I wanted to blame someone else for my problems."

"Your mama's a remarkable wo—"

Johnny stopped talking when his cell phone rang. "Hold up, it's Jack." He swiped his finger across the phone's screen and said, "Jack?"

As he listened, his eyes widened and his mouth formed an *O*. "Good golly, Miss Molly." His hand flew to the top of his head as Jack continued to talk a blue streak. Martha Maye could hear the voice on the other end but couldn't hear exactly Jack was saying. Johnny appeared to be frozen in place, then bolted for the door.

"What is it?" Martha Maye ran after him.

As Johnny punched some numbers into his phone, he said, "I gotta get over there. You stay here. I'll explain soon's I can." He flew out of the house, holding his phone to his ear.

Martha Maye stood at the front door after Johnny left, wondering what she should do. Then she heard approaching sirens.

"Good heavenly days," she said, staring at the flashing lights coming up the street.

VELVEETA SAT with her children in the window of the McDonald's across the street from the Piggly Wiggly. She wasn't on duty but had volunteered to stake out the grocery store and let Johnny know the moment Estherlene arrived and the moment she left.

She'd been watching the grocery store more than her children, and Cinnamon's whine brought her attention back to the table.

"Mama, he stole my French fry," she wailed.

"Roscoe, give your sister a fry back."

"You want this one?" he asked his sister, opening his mouth wide to show her the mostly chewed-up fry.

"Ew! No!" Cinnamon cried. "Mama!"

"Roscoe, I done told you to stop. Keep it up, and you're gonna get a switching."

Roscoe rolled his eyes and then stuck his tongue out at his sister.

"Son, you roll those eyes at me one more time, and I'll roll that head of yours."

Roscoe sulked, and the three ate in silence for a few moments, while Velveeta continued to watch the door of the Piggly Wiggly. She could see Estherlene's big Buick LeSabre parked near the front of the lot. She looked at her watch and thought it should be about time for Estherlene to be finished with her shopping.

Suddenly, she heard a splash and felt cold wetness seep across her leg. Gasping as she jumped up, she watched orange Hi-C spill across the table, dripping onto the floor.

"Roscoe!"

"I didn't do it, Mama, I didn't," Roscoe cried.

"Oh yes he did," Cinnamon said. "He was stealing another French fry, and he knocked it over. It serves him right."

"Uh-uh, she stole one of mine, and she knocked it over."

"Lands sakes, y'all are both one fry short of a Happy Meal. Literally and figuratively," Velveeta added under her breath. To the children, she said, "It don't matter who knocked the drink over. We gotta get it cleaned up." She stalked off to gather more napkins.

She was in the midst of cleaning up the spilled mess when an employee came over with a mop and bucket. "I'll get it for you, ma'am."

"Oh, thank you," she said, moving out of the way. "Roscoe, tell the nice lady thank you for cleaning up your mess."

"Thank you, 'ady."

The woman finished mopping, and Velveeta gathered up the wet napkins and took them to the trash bin. She filled Roscoe's cup with more Hi-C and came back to the table. After she straightened the hamburger wrappers and set the French fry containers back in front of her children, she sat back with a tired sigh. As the kids began to eat again, she looked around the room and then outside. Her eyes settled on the Piggly Wiggly sign, and she suddenly remembered Estherlene. She quickly looked at the spot where the car had been parked. It was gone.

Her eyes searched the lot frantically. Estherlene couldn't have come out and driven away that fast. *The car must be there somewhere.* She'd only been distracted for a minute. But she finally had to accept the truth. She'd looked away for longer than a minute, and she had messed up. Big time.

She scrambled through her purse for her cell phone.

Johnny flew across the lawn and into Estherlene's house, calling dispatch for backup and an ambulance, half-disbelieving what Jack had told him. But when he entered the room at the top of the stairs, his heart sank.

A bearded, gaunt Hector Bumgarner sat at the edge of the bed wearing nothing but boxer shorts and a leg iron. He was tethered to the bed and sitting on grimy bedclothes that reeked of urine. His ribs were visible through his skin. The room's window had been covered with plywood.

"Well, don't that knock your shirt in the dirt." Johnny gaped. "I guess he did have something wrong with his leg. Really wrong."

"I got him some water but didn't touch anything otherwise," Jack said. "I knew you'd need to see everything as I found it. He says he's not sure how long he's been in here, but the last civilized day he remembers was sometime in September. I didn't get to look around much. I'll do that presently." Jack walked off down the hall.

"What month is it?" Hector asked with a raspy throat.

"Holy crap," Johnny muttered. "Why'd she do this to you?"

"'Cause she's batshit crazy, that's why!" the man rasped just before Nosmo King and his partner, Cathy Lawson, swept in.

"Hold it, y'all," Johnny said. "Back up one minute." He took out his iPhone and opened the camera app. He took several pictures of the room and of Hector and then said, "Okay, go ahead and treat him, but disturb as little as you can in this room."

Jack yelled for Johnny, who followed the sound of his voice to the master bedroom. Jack knelt in front of the closet and had laid out a towel on the ground. On top of the towel was a pair of pants smeared with bloodstains. "The pants were wrapped up in this towel. She'd stashed it in the back of her closet."

"Well, I'll be," Johnny said, standing with his hands on his hips, not quite believing what he saw. He leaned down closer to the pants. "Looks like she wiped the knife across her pants, doesn't it? I always thought she was neither left-brained nor right-brained, but come on." He donned a pair of latex gloves.

"Looks like we got her," Jack said. "Your gut was right, Johnny."

"Sometimes I hate my guts," Johnny said. "Leave everything just like that, Jack. I've got to get folks in here to examine the crime scene. What's that?" Johnny pointed to a piece of paper sticking out of Estherlene's pants pocket. He carefully reached in and removed it.

"It's some kind of a letter." Jack stood to look at the note Johnny held. "It's addressed to Butterbean. What in the—"

"We'll bag it and mark it as evidence."

"But don't you want to know what's inside it?"

"All in good time, my friend." Johnny turned toward the door and hollered, "Hank!"

Hank came around the corner into the room.

"Go cut your lights and move your cruiser around to Walnut Street. Tell Nosmo King to load Mr. Bumgarner as fast as possible and get him to the hospital. I don't want to scare off Estherlene. Everything has to look normal when she comes home from the grocery."

"Solid copy," Hank said, running off to carry out his orders. Johnny's phone rang. It was Velveeta.

She was talking a mile a minute before he could even say one word. "I'm sorry, Chief. I don't know how it happened. I didn't think I looked away that long. If stupidity were a crime, I'd be number one on the Most Wanted List. I am so sorry. Roscoe was bugging his sister, and then he spill—"

"Velveeta!" Johnny snapped. "Just tell me the time, don't tell me how the dang watch works!"

"She's gone. Somehow I missed her coming out. I was cleaning up a spilled drink, and the next thing I knew, her car was gone."

Johnny ran down the stairs and out to the front lawn, scanning the area. And then he saw it—the nose of Estherlene's old maroon Buick LeSabre, stopped at the corner. He could just make out the silhouette of Estherlene's big hair. She was leaning forward, craning her neck, trying to see what was going on at her house. Johnny took off running.

ESTHERLENE HAD thoughts of making pickles as she headed home from the Piggly Wiggly, drinking from a can of Mtn Dew and tapping a beat on the steering wheel. She got ready to turn onto Marigold Lane when the flashing lights caused her to stop. A police car and ambulance were in front of her house. *Great day in the morning! How in the world did they find out?*

She'd been so careful. Everything had gone so smoothly. Nobody had missed Hector.

She saw the chief's massive body fly out of her house and stop on the porch. She saw him scanning, searching. She saw him find her car, and their eyes locked for a few frozen moments. When he started running across the lawn, she stepped on the accelerator and peeled rubber.

FORTY-ONE

A one-eyed mule can't be handled on the blind side.

~Southern Proverb

Johnny reached the edge of the lawn, heard the squeal of tires on pavement, and saw Estherlene speed off. He wasted no time. In a flash, he jumped in his car, backed it out of Martha Maye's driveway, and flipped on the lights and siren. Estherlene had a good fifteen-second start on him, but there were two ways to go: to town or to the countryside. He figured she'd head into the countryside where she could drive faster. In his rearview mirror, he saw Hank Beanblossom also in pursuit, as he turned left, then right, and left again, blowing through stop signs. Once he left city streets and turned onto a county road, he called Bernadette.

"I'm in pursuit of a 1974 maroon Buick LeSabre, going south on Route 42. Anyone in the vicinity, please respond. Subject is a suspect in a homicide."

"Ten-four, Chief. You watch yourself now." He heard the call go out over the radio and prayed someone was on Route 42 coming north.

Johnny remembered seeing the frightened look on Martha Maye's face just before he pulled out of her driveway. *No worries, Bernadette, I got a mighty good reason to be careful.*

Route 42 was a curvy, hilly road with a speed limit of forty-five on the straight patches and twenty-five on the curves. Johnny barreled down the road at sixty, taking the curves at thirty-five with Hank right on his bumper. He'd seen Estherlene up ahead, but now he lost sight of her taillights. He guessed she was maybe a quarter of a mile up ahead. He punched the accelerator and heard a warning in his head: *You can't catch her if you wrap your car around a tree.*

Speeding past farms, Johnny barely noticed cows behind barbed wire fencing, grazing amid hay bales. Purple asters and ironweed growing wild alongside the road blurred as he raced down the sun-dappled country road. He passed empty cornfields on his left, and to his right jimsonweed and chicory mingled with pumpkin patches still dotted with orange. The road was resplendent with greens, oranges, reds, yellows, maroon—his mind screeched to a stop.

Maroon. He'd just passed a flash of sunlight gleaming off of something maroon.

He'd lost sight of Estherlene's car, which was hard to do, considering it was the size of a barge. When he saw the color maroon and the flash of light out of the corner of his eye, he knew she must've ducked into one of the farm driveways. Seconds after he came to this realization, he heard a crash. In his rearview mirror, he saw the LeSabre had T-boned Hank's cruiser and was pushing it—and Hank—off the road.

Johnny made a split-second decision. He pulled the steering wheel to the left and slammed on the brakes, feeling his car skid. He veered sideways, coming to a stop diagonally across both lanes of the country road. Estherlene had succeeded in pushing Hank's car off the road and into the ditch. Johnny could see the smoking car, nose down amid the ragweed and goldenrod.

Now she backed up, turned, and headed straight toward Johnny.

As Estherlene's car barreled toward him, he flashed back to playing chicken as a kid. He could see his friend Peter coming at him on his ten-speed bike. Peter thought Johnny would dodge, and Johnny thought Peter would chicken out. Neither did, and they'd crashed head on.

As her car sped toward his and he realized she wasn't going to stop or veer around him, his hand flew to the gearshift, but he was out of time. He felt the impact as her car slammed into the side of his cruiser. Big hair, blue sky, orange and yellow leaves, the white of the air bag, and the image of Martha Maye's smiling face were the last things he saw before blacking out.

JACK, TESS, and Honey were at Martha Maye's house when she got the call. As soon as Johnny had left to find Estherlene, Jack called Tess, asking her to come be with Martha Maye. Honey had come over when she heard the sirens and saw the commotion. The little house was full of tension as they waited for word from Johnny telling them everything was all right.

When the phone sounded, Martha Maye lurched for it, answering it on the first ring. She listened, said, "Thank you," and then hung up and headed for the door.

Tess and Honey were at her side in a flash. "Wait. What happened?" they asked together.

As if in a trance, Martha Maye patted her pockets, realizing she didn't have her keys. "I have to get to the hospital. Johnny's been in an accident." Her face was tight with fear. "I have to get to the hospital," she repeated.

"Okay, Martha Maye, settle down, we'll get you there," Jack said. "What did they tell you?"

"Johnny's been in an accident," she repeated, too stunned to say anything else. She went to the kitchen and came back with her purse.

"Hold up, Martha Maye! Don't get your cows running. Johnny's a tough old bird; he'll be all right." They all rushed after her. "Let's get you there in one piece, okay?"

When they arrived at the hospital, Hank was sitting sideways on a gurney in the hallway, one leg dangling off, the other in an aircast on the hospital bed. He had cuts and scrapes all over his face. Stitches sewed together a five-inch gash over his right eye. His arm was in a sling, and when he saw Martha Maye, he swung his injured leg down and limped toward her and her entourage.

"Hank, how is he?" she asked, grabbing his good arm.

"I'm fine, thanks," he said, as he smiled and hugged her.

"Well, shoot fire, I'm sorry, Hank. It's just that I can see you. You're alive and walking." She swallowed hard. "What about Johnny?"

Hank led them to a waiting room set aside for consultation with family members. They all crowded into the little room, and Hank sat down gingerly.

"I'm not gonna sugarcoat it, Martha Maye. It's bad. He was unconscious when they brought him in. He's in surgery now. He has a subdural hematoma, which is something like a tear somewhere up here" — he motioned to his head — "and there was hemorrhaging compressing his brain. He also has a break in his right tibia. Plus some minor sprains and lots of scrapes and bruising."

"How did it go down, Hank?" Jack asked.

"She T-boned both of us. First she backed into me as I passed the drive she'd ducked into. I figure she was waiting for Johnny and didn't know I was behind him. She was just gunning it out onto the road when I started to pass. She wasn't going that fast, but she floored it after she rammed me and pushed me into the ditch. And then she righted her car and drove smack dab into the side of the chief's car."

"Where was he at that point?"

"He'd pulled his car diagonal across the road to try to block her in. I could hear sirens coming from town. She knew her goose was cooked. She lit into him at maybe fifty miles an hour and kept going. Man alive, that LeSabre is like a tank. Skeeter was right behind us, as was Northington, and they got there and took over. Skeeter chased her, and she was going too fast for that curvy road. She went into a curve and didn't come out."

"What do you mean?"

"Let's just say she owes Old Man Crider a new fence."

"How's Hector?" Honey asked.

"He's got a tough row to hoe. He's dehydrated and malnourished. Looks like he'll be in the hospital for quite a while."

"That poor man." Martha Maye shook her head. "And what about Estherlene?"

"She's got a sprained ankle, but other than that, she's fit as a fiddle. Velveeta's upstairs now questioning her."

"Velveeta's done questioning," the officer said from the doorway. All heads turned toward her. "Hey, y'all. I was passing by and heard you talking. Martha Maye, I'm so sorry. I feel like this was all my fault. If I hadn't looked away, maybe none of this would have happened. I'm sick about it. I'm so, so sorry."

Martha Maye went to Velveeta and patted her arm. "Hush now. You just make sure the case against her is airtight. You hear?"

"Oh, it's airtight. She confessed to everything. Didn't have much choice. We had her dead to rights. Apparently, she'd been after Lenny for a while. He wasn't interested and kept blowing her off. Said he liked a woman whose skin fit her better."

"That sounds like Lenny. But how did she get in my house? She killed him with my kitchen knife, after all."

"Yeah, she said she saw someone over there, and she thought it was Lenny."

"Lenny was in my house?"

"I'll bet it was T. Harry," Jack cut in.

"No, I'm thinking it was Lenny," Velveeta said. "She said she walked through the backyards and saw the back door open, so she went in. She found a pumpkin with a heart carved out of it, along with a note sitting on the table, but no Lenny. She figured he'd left it, and figured the note was for Martha Maye, so she put it—"

"In her pocket," Jack interrupted. "I found it in the bloody pants in her closet. It was addressed to Butterbean. I turned it in as evidence."

"Oh my goodness." Martha Maye's eyes teared up.

"Estherlene must've been blind with jealousy and rage," Velveeta continued.

"What on earth for?" Martha Maye cried.

"Like I said, she'd been after him for weeks, but he always shot her down. The last time he said no, he wasn't exactly whatcha call a gentleman. He told her he'd rather stare directly at the sun with binoculars than have carnal knowledge of her."

"Oh my."

"Yep. That didn't sit too well with her, which was why she was going over to find him. She'd gotten it in her mind to blackmail him. She knew about all the women he'd picked up at the bar, and she was going to threaten to tell you, Martha Maye, and/or the judge. She was going to force him to sleep with her or else. But once she found him, her plans changed."

"Lawzie, that woman was ate up with him." Martha Maye, eyes wide, shook her head.

"She said she walked back out and around the side of the house, where she found him and confronted him. He told her, uh …" Velveeta looked at her notes. "She looked like three pounds of ugly in a two-pound sack." She looked up. "And then he turned his back on her and began to urinate in Martha Maye's garden—you know, the one by the front door. She stabbed him in the neck and walked away."

"Wait a minute, how'd she get the knife?" Tess asked.

"Oh yeah. When she was hunting for him over at Martha Maye's, her emotions got to a fever pitch. She thought he was dodging her and she snapped. Said she was then determined to either sleep with him or kill him. So she grabbed a knife out of the drawer right before she went looking for him. We got her for premeditated murder. Boom."

"Just like that?"

"Yep." Velveeta nodded her head. "But there's one thing she wanted to know. She asked me how Johnny knew to go inside her house? How did he know Hector was in there?"

Jack's face turned red. "Uh-oh. I guess I'm guilty of breaking and entering."

"Yeah, well, remind me to arrest you later, okay?"

Everyone laughed.

"Kind of ironic, isn't it?" Jack said.

Tess cocked her head. "Why?"

"The lady-killer was killed by a lady." Jack flashed his own lady-killer smile.

"Oh, for heaven's sake." Tess groaned and dropped her face into her hands. "I'm not sure you could call her a lady." Then she sprang back up. "But wait a minute."

"What?"

"Why did she lock up her husband?"

"No good reason, really. Said she could no longer tolerate the man. Simple as that. She said, and I quote, 'He's dumb as dirt and twice as ugly.'"

"Wow. I'm glad I never ticked her off," Martha Maye said.

"Yeah. She said all he did all day was sit around and fart, burp, complain, and make fun of her, and she was sick of it."

"Hmm, I don't think she oughta eat nuts," Hank said.

Everyone looked at him as if he'd suffered a brain injury himself.

"For her, it's practically cannibalism."

EPILOGUE

Life is what you need. Love is what you want.

~Southern Proverb

ive months later

Lou's backyard looked magical. Dogwood and redbud trees full of white and purple blooms dotted the lawn. Glowing white paper lanterns of all sizes hung from the fifty-year-old maple tree in the center of the yard, with a carpet of red tulips underneath. Clumps of white daffodils and narcissus with orange and yellow centers mingled with forsythia in full bloom. The scent of lilac was in the air. It was a beautiful April night in Goose Pimple Junction.

As dusk descended on the celebration, the lush green lawn twinkled with tiny tea lights scattered on pink-clothed tables. Mason jars with raffia bows were filled with bouquets of hydrangea, ranunculus, and peonies and tied to the backs of white chairs at the tables. Big vases of white hydrangeas sat on the tables as centerpieces.

But the prettiest things in Lou's backyard were the two brides glowing with happiness.

"This is a gracious plenty," Jack said, beaming at Tess. "Lou, you've outdone yourself," he told her as she handed him a plate filled with another helping of country ham biscuits and corn pudding.

"Well, good green lands, it's not every day my daughter gets married." She propped her hands on her hips and looked with mock sternness at a beaming Martha Maye. "But this better be the last time."

Jack clapped Johnny's shoulder and said, "Oh, I think this one's going to stick. I've never seen a happier man" — he smiled at Tess — "except when I look in the mirror."

Tess kissed his cheek. He put his arm around her, and she snuggled into him.

"I'm just so happy for all y'all I could bust," Lou said.

"I'm happy for us, too. Life is good and everything is satisfactual." Martha Maye beamed up at Johnny, who wrapped her in his big arms, momentarily lifting her off her feet.

"Thank you for having the reception here, Lou," Tess said. "I can't imagine a better place."

"I started planning for this the minute I heard y'all were having a double wedding."

"It's two, two, two mints in one," Ima Jean said, joining the group.

"Imy, Charlotte, and I have been a bunch a baking fools."

"We bring good things to life!" Ima Jean said.

"It sure is nice eating somebody else's cooking for a change," Slick said from the buffet table.

"He's been grazing here so long I'm going to have to roll him home." Junebug swatted his arm playfully.

"And didn't the reverend do up a lovely ceremony?" Martha Maye added.

"That he did," Lou agreed.

"Aw, look at that." Tess pointed to her son, Nicholas, and Butterbean, who were dancing together.

"He's so good with her," Martha Maye said with a sigh.

Nicholas and Butterbean were not the only two on the makeshift dance floor. Pickle and Charlotte, Caledonia and Philetus, and Honey and Lolly were also swaying to the music.

"I think this is the first time I've seen Pickle when he wasn't wearing a T-shirt," Tess said.

"Yeah, but he still has on his Chuck Taylors," Jack said.

"Lime green, of course," Johnny added.

"C'mon, beautiful," Jack said, tugging Tess's arm. "Dance with me."

"Not so fast, mister," Lou said. "It's time to cut the cake."

"She's so bossy," Jack teased.

The peaceful calm of the wedding reception was broken temporarily when the unmistakable clap of a hand meeting flesh sounded across the backyard. Caledonia had slapped her husband. She stalked off the dance floor and into the house, but Philetus simply smiled, told folks his wife was a little high-strung, and cut in on Lolly so he could dance with Honey. Pickle and Charlotte glared at Philetus and then went to find Caledonia.

After the cake was cut and served, it was time for the brides to throw their bouquets. Louetta, Ima Jean, Butterbean, Maddy Mack, Charlotte, and Honey all grouped together.

"On the count of three," Tess said, turning away from the single girls. "One. Two. Three." The bouquets flew over Martha Maye and Tess's head, into the clump of females.

Honey dove in front of Ima Jean and caught one bouquet, and Butterbean jumped straight up in the air and caught the other one.

"Uh-oh," Johnny said. "That girl is gonna be trouble, I can tell."

"Johnny, why don't you make your announcement now," Martha Maye suggested, pulling on his sleeve.

"Okay. I'd like to announce that Butterbean will not be dating until she reaches the age of thirty."

Everyone laughed and Martha Maye nudged him. "You know that's not what I meant."

He took a deep breath and blew it out. "Okay, Mrs. Butterfield, here goes." He kissed her, then clapped his hands together. "'Scuse me, everyone."

Ima Jean put two fingers in her mouth and whistled. Now all eyes were on Johnny.

"I have an announcement to make. I want everybody to know that not only do I love Martha Maye, but I love our daughter, too, and I'm going to be such a proud father."

A table of church ladies gasped, and one of them said, "Oh law, Martha Maye's with child."

Johnny's face flushed bright red, and he quickly said, "No, I don't mean that. No, no, no, no, no!"

"Well, what *do* you mean, boy?" Clive said. "Spit it out."

"What I mean to say is, in about a month it will be all legal—I'm adopting Butterbean."

Everyone looked at Butterbean, who looked stunned.

"What's the matter, Butterbean? I thought that would make you happy," Martha Maye said, rubbing her daughter's back.

"Well," Butterbean gulped. "I am happy. It's just . . . it's just . . . "

"What? What is it, Bean?" Johnny asked, grabbing her hands and kneeling in front of her, his face full of concern.

"My name. Everybody's going to call me Butterbean Butterfield."

THE END

ACKNOWLEDGEMENTS

I am so thankful for my first readers: Liz Metz, Robert Hoffman, Carmen Pacheco, and Tim Mallory. Their suggestions, enthusiasm, and support were vital to the finished product.

Thank you to my editor, Lindsey Alexander, for polishing the manuscript and cleaning up my mistakes, and to my proofreader, Ellen Mansoor Collier, who caught the nits.

Thank you to John Charles Gibbs, who allowed me to use his painting, *Southern Home* (© www.gibbsgallery.com), for the cover art. His Southern home perfectly matched my vision of Martha Maye's house.

I'm grateful to know Emily Mah Tippetts of E.M. Tippetts Book Designs. Her help in designing the book covers and formatting the books kept me from going crazy. Thank you, Emily.

Thank you to Tricia Drammeh and Ellen Mansoor Collier for their friendship and for saving me money on mental health bills.

Thank you to my sons Jake and Michael and my daughter-in-law Liz for their love and support. There's never been a day when they were hooligans. Well, maybe one or two, but they've more than made up for it. As I said at the beginning of the book, they are my heroes.

Finally, thank you to the readers of this book. I am honored that you spent your money and time on my work. If you liked the book, I hope you will consider leaving a review online.

If you haven't already, I hope you'll check out book one in the series, *Murder & Mayhem in Goose Pimple Junction*. And watch for *Rogues & Rascals in Goose Pimple Junction*, coming soon.

ABOUT THE AUTHOR

Amy Metz taught first grade before her sons, Jake and Michael, came along. Being their mom was her dream job, but now that they are grown, her new dream is to write books. When she's not writing, Amy loves photography, baking, reading, and sweet tea. She spends her days in Goose Pimple Junction and her nights in Louisville, Kentucky. Online you can find her at her blog, A Blue Million Books, (http://abluemillionbooks. blogspot.com) and her website: http://amymetz.com. She can be reached at: amy@amymetz.com and would love to hear from you.

Visit Amy at:

Website: amymetz.com
Facebook: www.facebook.com/AuthorAmyMetz
Twitter: twitter.com/authoramymetz
Goodreads: www.goodreads.com/author/show/6436458.Amy_Metz

Made in the USA
San Bernardino, CA
26 February 2015